THE
ANGEL
CREEK
GIRLS

BOOKS BY LESLIE WOLFE

THE ANGEL CREEK GIRLS

LESLIE WOLFE

bookouture

Published by Bookouture in 2021

An imprint of Storyfire Ltd.
Carmelite House
50 Victoria Embankment
London EC4Y 0DZ

www.bookouture.com

ISBN: 978-1-80019-756-5
eBook ISBN: 978-1-80019-755-8

ACKNOWLEDGMENT

A special thank you to my New York City legal eagle and friend, Mark Freyberg, who expertly guided me through the intricacies of the judicial system.

ACKNOWLEDGMENT

CHAPTER ONE

The Guest

A quick rap against the dark window startled Cheryl.

The knife veered sideways in her trembling hand, stabbing the flesh of her finger, right where it held the carrot in place on the cutting board.

She whimpered quietly and put the throbbing finger in her mouth, easing the pain, while she stared into the pitch blackness outside the window.

Was Julie finally coming home? What in the world had possessed her to let her sixteen-year-old daughter go out when they should've been long gone by now? She'd told Julie she needed to come home early, but nothing stuck to that child, regardless of what had happened. Where could she be on a stormy night like this? Probably with that new boyfriend of hers, making out in his truck somewhere, completely forgetting everything they'd talked about. And still, she couldn't be too mad at her; the poor girl had been through hell over the past two days. She just hoped she wasn't sharing too much with that boyfriend of hers.

Another rap against the window, lifting hope in her chest only to send it plummeting a moment later. It was just rain, falling harder, heavier, large droplets smashing against the windowpanes under the strength of gale-force gusts of wind.

It would be senseless to leave now. The drive to San Francisco was long, a good four hours on the highway. She couldn't see herself pulling that off with three children in the car when she couldn't even see twenty yards in front of her. What if something went wrong? What if the car broke down? No... she'd have to live through one more night of terror, then leave first thing tomorrow.

She forced herself to breathe, containing the flood of worry-fueled tears that threatened to burst out in the open. Heather, her eight-year-old, lifted her eyes from her phone for a split second and gave her one of those penetrating stares that Cheryl had grown to expect from her daughter whenever she was upset. It was as if the child had an uncanny ability to read her mother's mind.

Cheryl took her finger out of her mouth and forced a smile. "Are you hungry, baby?"

"Uh-uh." Heather frowned, then returned to whatever she was doing on her phone, probably playing a game. She sat on the white sofa with her legs folded underneath her, dressed in oversized pajama pants and the sweatshirt she'd worn to school that day, her latest favorite she would've worn to bed if she had a chance. Her Mickey Mouse socks were scattered on the floor, discarded minutes after Cheryl had made her put them on.

"Mommy?" her youngest called from behind a spoonful of Cheerios dripping milk all over the table. The four-year-old girl had learned to use a spoon but still wielded it like a weapon, her tiny fist clutching it as if it were King Arthur's sword, sending food flying through the air. Her pigtails bounced around with every move she made, held in place by green hair ties that were starting to slide loose.

"Yes, Erin, what is it?" Cheryl asked, unable to take her eyes off the blackness lining the kitchen window, droplets of rainwater making it seem more menacing than any other night. In the distance, rolling thunder struck an ominous vibration through the air, sending a chill down Cheryl's spine.

"Heather is eating her hair again," Erin reported proudly, her high-pitched voice teeming with laughter as her older sister shot her an unforgiving glare.

"You weasel," Heather whispered under her breath after promptly removing a long strand of dark hair from her mouth. She liked twirling her hair into ropes and then chewing on them mindlessly while her fingers tapped her phone's screen, or Julie's tablet, or whatever device she could get her hands on. "Tattletale."

"No name-calling your sister, Heather," Cheryl intervened. The darkness outside suddenly vanished under a robust set of beams as a truck pulled up. Through the window, covered in a web of water drops creating shards of rainbow-edged light, she saw Julie throw the young driver a tear-filled smile, then rush out of the truck and toward the door, splashing carelessly through the puddles lining the driveway. The truck pulled away, and darkness regained its ownership of the land.

Cheryl's chest swelled with relief. Still angry at her eldest's recklessness, she returned to the pile of vegetables waiting on the cutting board. In the time it took Julie to unlock the door and step inside, she'd chopped the rest of the carrots into uneven pieces and dumped them in the pot, instantly bringing the boiling stew to a mild simmer.

"Hey, Mom," Julie greeted her from the doorway with a tiny, guilt-ridden smile, ready to bolt toward her bedroom. "Smells good in here." Her wet chestnut hair was pasted on her face, dripping onto her cheeks and her chest. Her clothes were soaked, small pools of water starting to form at her feet.

"Not so fast," Cheryl tempered her. "You're going straight into the shower, you hear me? You'll catch a cold. It's freezing out there." She shuddered as she remembered how, only two days ago, it had felt to be outside in that weather for hours, and wiped her hands against her apron nervously.

The girl's smile withered. "I don't need to. Brent's truck was warm enough."

Cheryl swallowed a long sigh. Youth. Fueling everything, from high hopes to the body's ability to endure the cold and humid

October weather on the slopes of Mount Chester. "And how old is this Brent, anyway? Should he be driving at night in this weather?"

Julie's eyebrows converged above the root of her nose. "He's almost eighteen, Mom. I told you that already." She shifted her weight from one leg to the other and removed a sticky strand of hair from her face with long, pale fingers, tucking it behind her ear. "Can I go now?"

As the darkness outside seemed to fade again, Cheryl's gaze veered to the window. Maybe it was a passing car or something. "Dinner will be ready in half an hour," she replied, fear traveling through her blood, tension grinding her teeth. "You know we should've left today. We talked about it. I can't believe you did this to me, Julie."

Julie raised her hands in the air, then let them drop against her jeans-clad thighs with a loud splat. "I know how you feel about this entire thing, but I'm not afraid. Call me crazy, but I'm not. I want to stay. Please… you can't be serious about it. We have nowhere to go."

The escalating pitch of her daughter's voice mirrored Cheryl's deepest fears. Where would they go? How would they live? Life on the run was no walk in the park for a widowed mother of three. But there was no other choice, not after what had happened on Saturday night.

"I'm dead serious, Jules," she replied sternly, her hands propped firmly on her thighs. "We're leaving tomorrow first thing. We should've left today, but you and your boyfriend decided otherwise, now didn't you?"

Julie shot the pile of suitcases lining the hallway a guilty, sideways look. "I'm sorry, Mom. I just can't believe this is real. Stuff like this doesn't happen to people these days. We would've heard about it on social media."

"Social media has nothing to do with it. Now go clean yourself, dry your hair, and come back down for dinner." The tension in her voice must've piqued Heather's attention, because her eight-year-old had abandoned the phone and was staring at her with her mouth slightly open, seeming frightened. *Damn.*

The sound of the doorbell startled Cheryl. A faint whimper left her lips before she covered her agape mouth with a wobbling hand. She looked out the window and thought she saw a truck in the driveway, its headlights off. The white paint of the vehicle reflected whatever light escaped through the kitchen window; its appearance spectral in the falling rain.

Julie rushed to her mother's side and grabbed her arm with both her hands. "Don't answer it, Mom," she whispered, her voice shaky. All her stated courage had vanished without a trace.

Cheryl gave the idea a moment's thought. Whoever was at the door had already seen them through the window. Had seen the lights were on, had heard their voices through the closed door. She threw a rushed glance at the clock on the wall, right above the fireplace. Nine twenty-seven. The unexpected guest surely was bad news, but bad news had to be dealt with.

"Who is it, Mom?" Heather called, peeling her eyes off the phone's screen for a brief moment.

Cheryl made her mind up. She was going to face whomever it was like she'd done before, with courage and a willingness to do whatever it took to protect her family, and she'd be fine. They'd all be fine, and come next morning, they'd be gone from this horrible place. Pushing Julie away, she approached the door. "Take your sisters upstairs, Jules."

"But, Mom—"

"Just a second," Cheryl spoke loudly for the benefit of the late-hour guest. "Now," she whispered, in response to Julie's disobedience, her eyes drilling into her daughter's. She waited a moment until Julie scooped Erin in her arms and grabbed Heather's hand, taking them upstairs. When she saw them reach the upper level, she unlocked the door.

She forced air into her lungs, then opened the door just a little, without removing the chain. In the dim, yellowish light coming from the porch bulb, she recognized the guest's face. Not who she'd thought it would be, but still bad news, nevertheless. Thankfully, he was alone. "Oh, it's you," she said, closing the door just enough to remove the chain.

Inviting the man inside, she avoided his scrutinizing eyes. Seeing him had sent her senses into a frenzy, her fear raw, threatening to emerge in unwanted words. As she showed him in and motioned for him to take a seat at the dining-room table, she could barely steady her hands, the pounding in her chest so strong it rattled her entire body.

From the top of the stairs, Julie watched the scene with eyes rounded in terror. She was leaning over the rail, evidently trying to catch every word spoken between the two adults.

"Glass of wine?" Cheryl asked, and the man nodded with a hint of a smile on his lips.

"I'll have some," he replied, then followed every move she made, setting the glasses, uncorking a bottle, and pouring the blood-red liquid. His piercing gaze curiously watched her as if she were an exotic species he was eager to dissect.

Cheryl sat at the table and took a sip of wine, almost choking on it, the knot in her throat unwilling to give way to the chilled, flavorful liquid. She set the glass back on the table, then rested her trembling hands in her lap, waiting. Whatever the man was there to do or discuss, it would soon happen. And then it would be over.

A loud, hissing sound made her jump. The stew had boiled over, the sauce sizzling where it touched the red, hot surface, sending whirls of smoke upward. She stirred the pot and cut the power to the burner, ignoring the splash that had reached the floor by the stove. Then she sat down again, playing nervously with the hem of her white-and-green checkered apron.

The man staring at her had cold gray eyes, direct and unyielding, and didn't seem to be bothered by the water dripping from his short hair down his neck. He looked at her as if he knew everything. As if he'd somehow found out what she'd done.

But there was no way.

"You know why I'm here," he eventually said, his voice steady, matter-of-fact. "It's time."

His words shot icicles through her blood. "No," she whispered, shaking her head and pushing herself away from the table. Her chair screeched against the tiles in protest. "No… leave us alone, please," she begged, her voice a trembling whimper. Standing, she faltered backward until she reached the wall. "You don't have to do this."

A quick smile twitched the corners of the man's lips. "It has to happen," he said, looking at her in that intense, merciless way. "You've known this all along."

"We were going to leave," she replied, gesturing to the suitcases in the hallway. "I was going to disappear. If you would've come tomorrow, you would've never found us."

The twitch had bloomed into a grin, the coldest one she'd ever seen. "But you're here," he argued. "One can never escape their fate. You know that, right?" He stood and took a few slow steps toward her. It took every ounce of self-control to not shriek in terror. "You know she must fulfill hers." He shoved his hands into his pockets. "Tonight."

"No," she shouted, bolting toward the front door. If she could escape the house, then maybe she'd make it to their next-door neighbor. Perhaps he could help her.

From the top of the stairs, she heard Julie shout, "Heather, call nine-one-one, just like Mom taught you. Do it now! And don't come down." Then she rushed downstairs, her feet pounding as they landed on the steps.

That girl never listened to her. Not even when her life depended on it.

Cheryl couldn't bring herself to run for help and leave her daughter alone with that man. She froze in place for a brief moment, then turned back and stepped between Julie and him, sheltering her daughter with her own body. "You won't take her, you hear me? I won't let you," she said, adrenaline fueling the courage that somehow filled her voice. "Let us go."

The man took two more steps toward her. "Not going to happen. She's coming with me. Tonight. Like it's meant to be."

A stifled sob swelled her chest. Not again. This madness wasn't happening again. She thought she'd dealt with it. She'd thought they were safe. "I wanted to leave. Please let us leave. No one has to know." She clasped her hands together in a pleading gesture while tears sprung from her eyes. "Please, I'm begging you, let us go."

He didn't budge. There wasn't a flicker of understanding in the man's cold eyes. "I can't," he replied with what seemed like an indifferent shrug. "You know I can't. This has to happen, and you know it." A lopsided grin stretched his lips for a brief moment. "That's why you're still here; that's why you haven't left. It's her... her power pulling you back, holding you here. It has to be done."

Cheryl looked around for something she could use, a weapon, anything. By her side, on the counter, the knife block was within her reach. She lunged for a knife, but she wasn't fast enough.

He was faster.

She felt the blade ripping through her abdomen like a steel fist. She gasped and tried to scream, but no sound came off her lips. As she fell, she heard the knife drop to the ground, clattering on the kitchen floor by her side.

As her world was starting to turn dark, she saw the man pounce and grab Julie. Her baby screamed and called for her, kicking and writhing with all her might. Then the sound of a blow, and Julie falling, quiet and inert in the man's strong grip.

Then there was silence, darkness descending over Cheryl's mind, thick, impenetrable, although she fought it with every drop of life still coursing through her veins.

From the top of the stairs, Heather called with a quivering voice. "Mommy?"

No one answered.

CHAPTER TWO

A Rainy Morning

Detective Kay Sharp rushed barefoot across the kitchen, too sleepy to feel the cold floor under her toes. Her long blonde hair hung in loose strands over her face, resisting her attempts to keep it in place with one hand. The chilly air seeded goosebumps on her skin, but she ignored them and filled the coffee pot with water. She poured it quickly, then added a new filter and a few scoops of freshly ground coffee before pressing the button.

The machine chimed to life.

Satisfied, she leaned against the counter and inhaled the aroma. It dissipated the fog engulfing her brain and injected some zest into her body, although a touch of migraine still threatened her morning. Squinting in the gloomy light coming through the window from the overcast sky that had been pouring rain all the week, she asked herself the question she'd been avoiding since her alarm had gone off, blaring louder than a siren.

Was she a little hungover?

A smile crept up on her as she recalled last night's dinner. Detective Elliot Young, her partner since she'd joined Mount Chester Sheriff's Office, had been seated across the table from her, barely saying a word over the excellent, medium-rare steak and too much beer that went with it. She remembered ordering another and another, but the truth was she'd drank all that brew because she didn't want to call it a night.

Not yet.

Not while his blue eyes were looking at her like that, saying more than he'd ever let himself be caught actually saying. Not while she hadn't made up her mind about him.

Or was all that in her imagination? Even if it wasn't, wouldn't it be better for her to ignore everything and avoid the ultimate professional mistake, getting involved with another cop?

Kay's eyes shifted to the badge and gun she'd left on the counter the night before when she'd been too tired to lock them up in the usual drawer. Her brother, Jacob, knew the rules and would've never touched her stuff.

Seeing that seven-point gold star made her chest swell, eagerly anticipating the start of her shift. But that had less to do with police work and more with her partner. Maybe. Although she loved the work and couldn't see herself doing anything else other than law enforcement.

She chuckled quietly. "Some shrink you are," she muttered to herself, still smiling. "Can't see what's staring you right in the face."

About a year ago, she had returned home to Mount Chester, leaving behind a career as an FBI profiler assigned to the San Francisco regional office. She'd traded all that for being a detective in the small town she had grown up in and living with her brother in a house loaded with grim memories.

Good thing the man slept like a log, because she'd rushed to start the coffee pot in the T-shirt and panties she'd worn to bed last night. She wanted to take one sip before hurrying into the shower, knowing she'd barely have time to wash her hair before Elliot was supposed to pick her up.

Elliot.

Him again, at the center of her thoughts, like most days. Driving her to and from work as if she didn't have her own vehicle. Did that mean—

A noise caught her attention, and she froze. The door to her brother's bedroom was ajar, slowly opening. She frowned and stepped behind the kitchen island, hiding her naked legs, getting ready to greet Jacob. Hopefully, he'd just wobble through on his way to the bathroom, and she could bolt out of the kitchen before he noticed her state of undress.

The door opened quietly, and a young woman emerged, her hair tousled, running in auburn, messy strands over the collar of Jacob's plaid shirt that barely covered her butt. Her back toward Kay, she squeezed the door handle gently, closing it without a sound, then turned and froze the moment she laid eyes on Kay.

"Oh," she whispered, her cheeks flushing with embarrassment. She gathered the shirt around her slender body and stepped in place, unsure what to do.

"Coffee?" Kay asked, holding the pot in the air.

She nodded a couple of times nervously, then replied in a soft-spoken, choked voice, "Yes, please." She kept the shirt tightly closed around her chest with one hand while the other tugged at the hem.

Kay bit her lip and hid her smile as she turned around to pull a mug from the cabinet. Her little brother had a girlfriend. Nice. He deserved to be happy. She filled the mug and handed it over. *Here you go, um——?* The unspoken question hung in the air, filled with the girl's embarrassment thick as San Francisco morning fog as she took the cup from Kay's hand.

"Lynn," she finally said, her hand stuck in midair holding the mug. She eventually decided to set it down on the island, her unburdened hand immediately tasked with tugging at the hem of Jacob's shirt. "You're his sister, right? The cop?" she added, shooting Kay's badge and weapon a side glance.

Instinctively, Kay took a step to come between the girl and her gun. She didn't reply immediately, her eyes riveted on the back of Lynn's hand. At the root of her thumb, she had a small tattoo, five little dots arranged as they normally show on the five side of a die. The girl had done some time in her life; that was a prison tat.

"I believe it's time for you to leave," Kay said coldly. "I'll wait."

Turning pale, Lynn rushed back into Jacob's bedroom, closing the door behind her with a loud thud. A few minutes later, she emerged fully dressed and bolted through the door, avoiding Kay's glance and Jacob's questions.

"What's got into you?" Jacob shouted after her from his bedroom, but Lynn had already left.

Oh, crap, Kay thought, warily anticipating the conversation that was about to begin.

Jacob came into the kitchen, scratching the roots of his thinning tufts of hair, squinting under the dim light as if he'd been the one drinking too many beers at the Hilltop the night before. He wore a sleeveless shirt and striped pajama pants, wrinkled and sweaty.

"Why'd you scare her off?" he asked. "What's she done to you?"

Kay breathed, decided to stay calm.

"She's got a record, Jacob. Where did you find her?"

He scratched his belly, his fingers pulling at the shirt, lifting it up until he could run his fingernails across his skin.

"How do you know she's got a record? You just met her!"

"That tattoo on her hand, the five dots? That's prison ink. Each dot represents one of the four walls of a prison cell, and the center dot represents the inmate."

He shrugged, halfway turned from her. "I've been in jail too, and I have done nothing to deserve the time I served. In case you forgot."

Kay raised her hands in a pacifying gesture, already missing the coffee cup she'd abandoned on the counter. "Yes, I know that, but this is different."

He shook his head and pursed his lips. Walking past her, he opened the fridge, not giving her attire a single moment's attention, then pulled out a sausage from a pack of franks she'd bought the other day. "Want some?" he asked, and she shook her head. He bit into it and chewed loudly, with his mouth open. When her brother was upset, he ate. Even if that meant eating uncooked franks straight from the deli pack.

"I've seen this kind of tat in—" she started to say, but he silenced her with a hand gesture.

Thrusting his chin forward, he turned to face her, then swallowed the remnants of sausage half-chewed. "Listen, sis, I'm not the catch of the century, if you get my drift. I work seasonal jobs when I can find them and live with my sister, for crying out loud. To make things worse, my sister's a cop, and the entire town knows she had to yank my ass out of the joint."

"But you were innocent—"

"How many people do you think actually believe that? Huh? I think most of them think you pulled some strings to make my record go away just because you're a cop and can get your way. So, pardon me if I don't give a shit if Lynn has done time." He wiped his mouth angrily with the back of his hand. "I don't think she did, though. She would've told me."

"Really?" Kay blurted, immediately regretting it. She didn't want to upset her brother. It was her job, the people she dealt with every day, that made her see the world a certain way, every person a possible felon, a liar, a cheater, a thief, maybe even a killer.

Jacob sighed, his eyes clouded by sadness and resignation. "Yeah, really. I'm not a complete moron, you know. I can tell when someone's truthful with me."

She lowered her eyes. Jacob was an adult who'd been living on his own until she'd returned to Mount Chester after having been gone for eleven years. He was more than capable of taking care of himself, and she was his sister, not his mother. Their history together, the rough times they'd shared growing up, had made her overprotective. He was the only family she had left. "I'm sorry, little brother," she said, touching his arm gently. "I'll get off your case, permanently."

"And that's a promise?" he asked, grinning like a cat who'd just opened the cream jar.

"It's a promise," she replied quickly. "I wish you both the best that romance has to offer," she added, still planning to run the girl's background as soon as she got to the office.

A car pulled into the driveway, crunching pebbles under its wheels. Kay looked out the window and recognized Elliot's unmarked Ford Interceptor. "Shit," she muttered, rushing into her bedroom.

"Speaking of bad decisions," Jacob laughed, "when are you going to make this Texan a happy man, sis?"

"Ugh, butt out, will you? We're just partners," she replied, putting on deodorant in a hurry, then sliding a turtleneck on while rummaging through her closet for a pair of clean, pressed slacks. "We work together, that's all."

"Sure, you are," Jacob said mockingly as the doorbell rang. He opened the door, inviting Elliot in.

As she emerged from the bedroom a few moments later, she looked neat and ready to start another day, her hair tied in a ponytail with a clip, her makeup simple, and only the faintest hint of perfume around her like morning ocean mist. There wasn't a shred of evidence to the drama that had transpired in their kitchen or to the absence of her planned shower.

When he saw her, Elliot bowed his head and lifted two fingers to the rim of his wide-brimmed hat, hiding the sparkle in his blue eyes for a moment, just as she tried to contain her smile.

Then her phone rang. She picked it up, and her smile vanished, leaving behind a deep frown that persisted after she ended the call. Taking another sip of coffee, she grabbed her weapon, tucking it in her belt.

"They found a body in Angel Creek."

CHAPTER THREE

Crime Scene

Not much was said between Kay and Elliot on the drive over to Angel Creek. Another murder in their small, peaceful community was a dark cloud adding to the ones shedding rain incessantly. The wipers whirred rhythmically, filling the silence, encouraging Kay's mind to wander.

Elliot veered a little to the right to pass the Angel Creek Pointe landmark, welcoming them into the neighborhood. It was one of the most recent ones, built only a few years before Kay's return to her hometown. The houses were brick bungalows, detached, on half-acre, wooded lots. Looking at the deserted streets, you couldn't tell that one of the community's residents had been found dead that very morning.

The loud clicking of the SUV's turn signal brought her back to reality. They approached the address, and Elliot was about to turn right on the small street already crowded with police cars, an ambulance, and the coroner's van.

A few people were gathered across the street, huddled tightly under touching umbrellas that could barely withstand the strong winds and pouring rain. Yet they didn't give up, closing ranks as if the proximity of one's neighbors increased their own chances of survival when a deadly predator lurked nearby.

"Go home, people, there's nothing to see here," she muttered, but only Elliot heard her words.

"They won't," he replied, pulling as close to the house cordoned with yellow do-not-cross tape as he could. "I never understood people's morbid curiosity, but it's the same in California just as it was in Texas."

"It's instinct." She grabbed her umbrella from the floor where it had dripped on the way there. "Back in the day, before news media and the internet, gossip used to be the primordial form of information as herd safety measure, and closing ranks with one's peers increases one's chances of survival regardless of species."

As he brought the SUV to a stop, his brief grin exposed two rows of perfectly white teeth. "Well, if you put it like that."

She'd already stepped into the pouring rain, where the wind took about two seconds to turn her umbrella inside out. Grunting, she lowered her head, and rushed toward the front door. Once she found herself under cover of the porch, she abandoned the damaged umbrella and stomped her feet to rid herself of the water dripping from her boots.

"That won't be enough this time," Dr. Whitmore said, rushing from his van and meeting her by the door. "I'll give you both coveralls and booties." He beckoned his assistant, who readily shared two sets of sealed plastic pouches and a third for the doctor himself.

Kay studied the man's face as he ripped through the wrapping and extracted a disposable coverall that he slipped over his clothing. He looked grim, the ridges on his forehead deeper than she'd seen at the crime scenes they'd worked together in the past. They went way back, their professional relationship dating from before he'd semiretired to Mount Chester, and she'd joined the local sheriff's office. They had shared seven years of crime scenes in San Francisco when she was still a special agent and a profiler with the FBI, fresh out of college, and he was the chief medical examiner for San Francisco County.

"What's it like in there?" she asked, leaning against the porch rail to lift her foot and slip the shoe protectors over her boot.

"I just got here," Dr. Whitmore replied. "Brace yourself; this one's a doozy from what I heard from first on the scene. The victim is Cheryl Coleman, former married name Montgomery, thirty-five, a dental hygienist and widowed mother of three. Two of the girls are missing, per the neighbor who discovered the body. That's him, over there." Doc Whitmore pointed at a middle-age man shivering under a blanket in the back of the ambulance. "County's bringing everyone in to help with the search." He pulled the coverall's hood up over his head and tightened the string snugly around his face.

Knotted muscles lined Elliot's clenched jaws. Kay sighed and swallowed an oath as she put on the coveralls. They were about to enter a crime scene in severe weather. The risk of forensic contamination increased dramatically with every drop of rainwater. Kay followed suit and tightened her hood, capturing her soaked hair underneath it. She already felt as if she'd entered a sauna, and it was going to be a while until she could take off the suit.

"Ready?" Dr. Whitmore asked, giving them both a good look over before he opened the door and stepped inside.

The first thing Kay noticed as she entered the house was the smell of stew. It was probably going to be a while before she could have a serving without thinking of that crime scene.

Doc led the way to the kitchen as if following the strong scent. Halfway through the hallway, her nostrils picked up another scent, heavier, metallic, the smell of blood.

She almost bumped against Dr. Whitmore's broad back. He'd stopped abruptly at the end of the hallway, muttering an oath. Then he stepped to the side, making room for her and Elliot to approach.

Her heart pounded as she took in the scene, her stomach twisted into a knot. A woman lay curled on her side in a congealed pool of blood, still holding her abdomen with one livid hand. Burgundy traces of dried blood rivulets wove patterns on her frozen fingers, where she'd kept pressure on her wound to no avail. Her chestnut hair, long and shiny, fanned around her head, moving gently when the breeze made it through the door. Her eyes, still open, stared at the back entrance, and her other hand stretched out in the same direction in a pleading gesture. Her lips, bluish pale under the rosy lip gloss, were parted as if to whisper one last word, to draw one last breath.

A little girl, not more than three or four years old, pale as a sheet, lay inert against her mother's body. Her head was resting on her mother's arm, her thumb wedged firmly in her mouth. One of her pigtails had come loose, and a green elastic tie was on the floor by her side. Loose strands of hair covered part of her tear-stained face, auburn curls entangled and caked in blood. Inches away from her head, a sizeable fileting knife was abandoned on the floor, probably dropped by the murderer right after he'd stabbed her mother.

Kay's heart froze. *Oh, no,* she thought, her eyes searching for a breath, an eye movement, anything.

When Doc touched the toddler's neck, searching for a heartbeat, the little girl shifted and whimpered quietly, without waking up from her death-like sleep.

"Oh, God," Kay whispered, covering her mouth with a gloved hand. "She's alive. Let me take her—"

"We need photos first," Doc replied, the sadness in his voice unmistakable. "Before this pool of blood gets trampled some more. I promise you we'll work fast."

His assistant started taking photos, moving swiftly through the crowded kitchen and shooting various angles after placing crime scene markers near all the relevant smudges and bloodstains.

"The neighbor found the body," Elliot announced. "Frank Livingston. He lives next door with his wife and his mother. They're outside if you'd like to speak with them."

"I will, yes," Kay replied, unable to take her eyes off the little girl. Every fiber of her was urging her to pick that child up and take her somewhere safe, somewhere where she could be cleaned of her mother's blood and cuddled in dry, warm clothes. Where she could start forgetting the horrors she'd witnessed.

But her blood-soaked clothes were evidence, and her tormented memories could hold the key to catching her mother's killer.

"There were three girls in the household," Elliot continued. "Julie, sixteen, and Heather, eight, are missing."

That poor little girl is essential to finding her sisters. "How much longer?" she asked Doc Whitmore's assistant in an impatient voice.

The young woman glanced at her, surprised. "About ten minutes, maybe?" she replied, immediately resuming her task.

"Make it five while I walk the scene," she replied, and immediately rushed away. She couldn't bear seeing that little girl lying in her mother's blood for another moment. She wanted to scream.

"I'll get formal statements from the neighbors," Elliot offered after shooting her a somber look. He didn't move though, as if waiting for something.

She went straight to the back entrance, the focal point of Cheryl Coleman's last seconds of life. Three suitcases were clustered next to the wall. The light was still on in the kitchen, fighting the gloomy daylight that came in through the windows, but Kay turned on her powerful flashlight to examine some scuff marks on the floor closely. A chair downed with one of its legs broken, a long, deep gash into the side of a cabinet, and scattered shards from a teapot spoke of the struggle that had taken place.

"Single stab wound to the lower abdomen," Doc Whitmore announced. "She bled to death in a matter of minutes. By the volume of blood loss, I'd be willing to bet a pretty penny the blade severed her abdominal aorta."

"Time of death?" Kay asked, staring at the back-door handle, smeared with blood. The unsub had stabbed Cheryl, and then what? Grabbed two girls and walked out? No... a fight had ensued. He'd dropped the knife on the floor, and that meant he didn't feel threatened by either girl. But he had to subdue them, to silence their screams somehow, because they must've screamed. Those scuff marks, that's where one of the girls must've kicked erratically, trying to free herself from his grip. Why not hold on to the knife, and threaten the girls into submission with it?

Ah, but you've never stabbed a woman before, have you? Kay thought, pacing the floor slowly, examining the scene from all angles. *You had no idea what it would feel like, how slippery gushing blood could be, and that's why you dropped the knife. Right... there.* She ended her thought with a finger pointed straight at where the knife was still on the floor, marked with a yellow tag bearing the number four in black font. "Then what happened? I believe the eldest attacked you, didn't she?" Kay whispered, unaware she was voicing her thoughts.

Kay crouched by Cheryl's body, now positioned faceup, ready for Doc Whitmore's liver probe to take a temperature reading. Although touched by death's fog, her eyes were still intense, as if she was about to come back to life and rush to find her missing daughters. Once again, Kay stared along the line-of-sight Cheryl had during the last moments of her life.

The back entrance door.

"Liver temp puts the time of death between nine and eleven p.m. last night," Doc Whitmore said, sighing heavily when he stood up, the probe still in his hand. "This door was found open, and it was nearly freezing last night. That will increase the margin of error in the time of death determination—"

"The door was still open when they found her, right?" Kay asked, not even acknowledging Doc's statement.

"Yes, that's how the neighbor knew something was wrong," Elliot said, approaching her slowly.

Kay shot him a quick glance, wondering why he'd delayed interviewing the neighbor's family. Then she looked out the back door's window. The driveway ran parallel to the house, and it had been kept empty by first responders in a desperate attempt to preserve the integrity of the crime scene despite the weather. Cheryl's car must've been parked in the garage. Maybe the assailant's vehicle was in the driveway the night before? Then, maybe the neighbor might've noticed something.

A few yards to the right, she could see the back of the ambulance. A couple of deputies had erected canopies that barely withstood the wind, weighed down with sandbags, improvised rain shelters for the deputies, and crime scene technicians swarming the place. Underneath one of them, stomping in place and wrapped in an EMS blanket, was the neighbor who'd found Cheryl's body. He was speaking with two women, probably his wife and his mother, huddled closely together.

They were out of earshot, the sound of the howling wind and hammering rain making it difficult to hear someone, even if they stood a couple of feet away. But their body language was a different story. The older woman kept saying something that made the man shake his head several times, then underline his statement with appeasing hand gestures. Whatever she was saying, he disagreed with her and wanted her to shut up. The younger woman, sporting a bad haircut with unevenly trimmed bangs, wearing a huge shawl wrapped around her neck, threw side glances all the time, her eyes round with fear.

"Let's talk to them," Kay said, then opened the door and rushed through the rain in her disposable coveralls. They were now ruined for their intended purpose, but at least they did a good job of keeping the weather from soaking her clothes some more. She slipped and nearly fell when her plastic bootie landed in a puddle of mud, but Elliot's hand grabbed her arm and stabilized her.

"Thanks," she shouted over her shoulder, just as they reached the canopy. "Detectives Sharp and Young," she said, patting her pocket out of the habit of showing her badge, but it was unreachable without removing her coveralls. "I understand you were the one who found the body?"

The neighbor was pale and visibly upset, the corners of his eyes drawing lower, brimming with tears. Tension drew two deep, vertical lines flanking his mouth. His hair, all white, showed a receding line that made his forehead appear tall, distinguished, composed. Yet, he seemed perplexed and far more affected by the neighbor's death than Kay had expected.

"Um, yes, it was me. I'm Frank Livingston, and this is my wife, Diane," he said, turning halfway toward the woman with the bad haircut. "My mother, Elizabeth," he added, touching the woman's forearm. "Go home, Mother, please. It's too cold for you."

The older woman ignored him, probably thrilled to have some excitement in her life, even if it were of the morbid kind. That's what her entire demeanor was telling Kay. She had a willful spark in her watery blue eyes and a stern smile on her lips, the mark of stubbornness. She was dressed too neatly for a casual walk across a driveway and about fifty feet of soaked lawn and had bothered to apply lipstick and put on jewelry. The old woman wasn't going anywhere.

"Call me Betty, my dear," she said, revealing age-stained teeth when her smile widened. "Everyone does."

"Thanks, I will," Kay replied, then turned her attention to Frank Livingston, whose squirrely gaze avoided his wife's but tried to stare his mother down. The man had secrets. "Mr. Livingston, please tell us how you found the body."

Frowning deeply, he clenched his fists for a brief moment, his eyes shooting daggers at Kay. "The body, the body. All you people can think of is the body. She was a human being! Cheryl was her name. Can't we at least pretend to show some civility?"

Oh, so it hurts on a personal level, Kay thought. *Interesting.* She raised an apologetic hand. "You're absolutely right, Mr. Livingston, and I apologize. Please tell me about Cheryl. How did you know something was wrong?"

He cleared his throat quietly before speaking, his eyes darting again, avoiding hers just as he'd been avoiding his wife's. "That door was open, and that never happens. I saw it as I was getting into my car to go to work."

"Where is work?" Elliot asked.

"Chester High," he replied quickly. "I'm the science teacher."

"Did you go inside the house?" Elliot asked.

"Y—yes. I called out, and when she didn't answer, I went inside." As if realizing he might've done something wrong, he rushed to explain. "I didn't step on anything, didn't touch anything either. When I saw them lying there like that, I rushed out and called nine-one-one."

Diane Livingston was watching her husband with an intense stare, her mouth slightly agape. If there had been more than a neighborly relationship between Frank and Cheryl, Diane didn't know anything about it. But she seemed afraid, as if Frank was about to say the wrong thing. She didn't seem hurt, or suspicious, or jealous. No, just genuinely sad about Cheryl's death and unexpectedly afraid.

"Had you noticed anything last night?" Elliot asked. "Unusual traffic, loud noises, maybe a car in the driveway?"

Frank locked eyes with his wife for a moment, then shook his head. "No, nothing. With this storm raging, I didn't hear anything either. Maybe she screamed, called for help or something, but I didn't hear her." His voice trailed off toward the end. He sounded choked. "I can't believe this happened, only a few yards away from where we're sleeping."

"Was Cheryl's daughter near her body when you found her?" Kay asked.

He managed eye contact with Kay for the briefest of moments. "Erin? Yes. I assumed she was dead too." Swallowing with difficulty, he took one step closer to her. "Two other girls are missing, you know, Julie and Heather. I told the other cops. Maybe they ran away, scared. But why didn't they come to us?"

"Ran away?" the older woman blurted, grabbing Frank's sleeve with knotted fingers. "How can you be so naïve? I told you… how many times did I tell you?" The more she spoke, the higher the pitch of her voice, as if the fire of her emotions was fanned by her words. "I told you, and you didn't do anything about it. And now she's gone. That sweet, innocent girl, gone."

"Never mind my mother," Frank intervened, physically inserting himself between Betty and Kay. "It's just her Alzheimer's talking. She was diagnosed last January."

"I'm not crazy!" Betty reacted, slapping her son with her frail hand. "Now that she's gone, you'll never find her again," she said to Kay, then shifted her attention to Elliot. She braced her hand on Elliot's forearm.

Uneasy, the detective took a step back. "Ma'am, please—"

"Will you listen to me?" Betty insisted. The gaze in her fixed eyes was intense, almost maniacal. "That girl's gone! And everyone knew it was coming."

CHAPTER FOUR

Sacrifice

The sky wept.

He stood in front of the tall windows and watched the heavy rain hit the ground, exploding in tiny droplets, then melding into rivulets of muddy water streaming down his driveway. Seen through the wisps of white sheers lit by yellow, dimmed chandeliers, the gray, loaded clouds didn't seem any less menacing. Every now and then, one of them flashed with bluish light, then thunder rolled, sending echoes of doom through his heart.

Mother was angry.

She must believe he'd forsaken her, and now she was demanding her due.

But he hadn't forsaken her; he would rather have his own life ripped out of his chest. He hadn't shut his eyes to sleep a single night without whispering a prayer to her, without thinking of her. She was in every dropped leaf touching the ground in fall and in every budding blade of grass pushing through molten snow in spring. She was in the call of the birds and the howling of the wolves on the slopes of Mount Chester. She was in the mesmerizing blue California skies just as much as she was in the forlorn gathering of clouds, hemmed with lightning and reminiscent of slate and charcoal and graphite.

She was in his blood. She'd always been.

Pushing aside the sheers with pale, thin fingers, he drew closer to the window and rested his heated forehead against the cold glass. From up close, the sound of rain hitting the pavement of the driveway seemed louder, as if the transparent pane was not able to keep her demons at bay.

Her message was clear. She demanded another sacrifice.

Water had pooled on his lawn, raising mud above the dormant, trim blades of grass and escaping between the edge boulders onto the asphalt. Right between the concrete slabs that formed the path to the entrance, rain had washed the earth away, leaving crevices between, tiny openings that were nothing if not reminders of the big ones.

He hadn't offered Mother a sacrifice in a long time.

Too long.

Under the threat of tears, he closed his eyes with heavy lids that welcomed the darkness. He steepled his hands in front of his chest and rested in silent darkness for a while, the only sound the drumming of rain against everything it touched.

"Mother Earth, hear me," he whispered, "I beg your mercy and forgiveness. Hear your child, as I stand before you today. The tears you cry for your children burn my skin and stab my chest. Show me the chosen path, and let me bring you a worthy sacrifice to heal your wounds and dry your tears." He paused for a moment, listening, and gentle, distant thunder answered his prayer. "Mother Earth, hear your child," he continued. "Be the bond between the worlds of Earth and those of Spirit. Let the sacred winds echo your voice and carry your wisdom across the land."

He listened again, but only rain rapped heavily against the windows. She was still angry, waiting for him to deliver on his promises, to heal her wounds. By the edge of a concrete slab, the crevice had deepened, ominous, reminding him of another, a hundred feet deep, where Mother's wounds were bleeding heavily.

"This time, the sacrifice will make you happy," he whispered, leaving the comfort of the cold glass panes and starting to pace the room slowly, his feet making the gleaming hardwood squeak quietly. Yet he couldn't take his eyes off the rain-soaked landscape outside. Those were Mother's tears, falling heavy, filled with anguish and pain, unforgiving.

He returned to the window and clutched his hands together, his grip tight, white-knuckled. "You'll be happy, Mother; I swear it on my life," he whispered in a low baritone. "The girl is young and pure, untouched. And her blood... her blood is the real sacrifice."

Maybe it was his imagination, but it seemed that the skies were starting to clear somewhere toward the west.

Mother had heard him. She was accepting the sacrifice.

CHAPTER FIVE

Heather

Elliot stayed behind to wrap up the Livingstons' interviews while Kay returned inside the house after swapping her coveralls and booties for dry ones. She didn't mind having to change and didn't say a word to Jodi, Dr. Whitmore's versatile assistant. The young brunette avoided Kay's glance, fearing reprimand for not wrapping up the photos faster, but Kay's mind was elsewhere, still under the spell of the old Mrs. Livingston's strange statements. Was she a senile woman, like her son had insisted? Or did she know something that her son and daughter-in-law Diane didn't want Kay to learn about? As soon as she got a moment, she'd go back to speak with Betty, ideally with no witnesses around, just for diligence's sake. Considering the woman was most likely pushing eighty, chances were the interview would end up proving to be a waste of time and reconfirming the Alzheimer's diagnosis.

For now, there were more pressing issues, a little girl in dire need of immediate care and finding her two older sisters alive. The first hours are always critical in child abductions. The two Montgomery sisters had been taken almost twelve hours ago, halving the time when the odds of recovering an abducted minor alive were highest. After the first twenty-four hours elapse, the chances of ever seeing the child returned alive drop with every hour to almost zero after two full days.

Forcing her lungs to fill with air and exhaling slowly, Kay took a brief moment to think of her priorities. First, she needed some DNA to attach to the missing persons case files. With DNA on record, law enforcement everywhere could have something to match against if either of the sisters were recovered. Realizing she hadn't yet walked the upstairs part of the scene, and knowing that she'd be more likely to find Julie's DNA on a hairbrush or in loose hair fibers with roots attached she could recover from the girl's bed, she climbed the stairs quickly, taking in every detail of the scene.

There wasn't a single drop of blood that she could see upstairs, and everything was in order, as much order as could be expected from a household with a working mother and three daughters. Each of the bedrooms had its own brand of clutter and mess. The largest room, where Cheryl had slept alone, showed only her side of the bed covers tangled and messy, while the other half was untouched. The clothes she must've worn the day before were still hanging on the back of a chair, a beige, button-up blouse, and black slacks. There was a vague smell of dental office in the room, probably brought with her clothes. The dressing table was littered with cosmetics and accessories, nothing fancy, just the typical drugstore brands. The room seemed peaceful, utterly untouched by the tragedy that had brought the demise of its resident.

Moving on, Kay entered the next bedroom. The moment she stepped over the threshold, she knew it was Julie's. Large posters with Justin Bieber and Taylor Swift covered some of the walls. The floor was littered with discarded clothing, socks, and shoes, as if a whirlwind had swept through the closet, leaving barren hangers, fallen soldiers in an unfair fight.

Julie had abandoned her hairbrush on the dresser, and Kay quickly sealed it in an evidence bag. Several long strands of chestnut hair were still attached to it, and Doc Whitmore would be able to extract DNA from the roots. Julie's DNA could be attached to both girls' missing persons reports, the close familial match being enough to offer positive identification in case Heather was found. From that perspective, Cheryl's DNA could've been used, but Julie's was ideal.

A pang of fear stabbed Kay in the chest. She kept collecting evidence as if the girls were never to be found alive, just like the old Mrs. Livingston had said, although it made no sense. Kidnappers could change a girl's appearance and name, even get her fake papers, and brainwash her into believing she was someone else, but DNA never lied. One day, hopefully soon, those girls would be found and returned to their remaining family.

Shaking off the sense of doom that chilled her blood, Kay moved on to the last bedroom. *We'll find them today, enough with this nonsense,* she admonished herself as she entered. A different kind of chaos ruled, with Lego pieces and comic books and glitter, and the smell of Barbie plastic. Lots and lots of glitter, stuck in the carpet's fibers, covering the desk and the blankets of the two unmade bunk beds. Just a normal, ordinary girls' bedroom, seemingly serene and sheltered from all of life's perils.

There was nothing else left for her to do on the second floor.

She walked over to the stairs and grabbed the railing, then started down the flight of stairs, holding on tight, her booties slippery on the carpet. She was about halfway there when she thought she heard a beep.

It sounded like a phone. Running out of battery.

Cheryl's phone had been found in her purse, downstairs. Was this one Julie's?

Climbing back up in a hurry, Kay followed the source of the sound into the largest bedroom and looked around. She opened drawers and entered the closet, listening intently, but was met only with silence. She searched the bathroom thoroughly, then went back into the bedroom, running her gloved hands over the sheets, under the pillow, in the folds of the comforter.

Nothing.

She listened intently, holding her breath, but all she could hear was the distant noise of the medical examiner's team downstairs, collecting evidence, chatting in low voices, wheeling equipment in and out of the house, all against a backdrop of heavy rain drumming against the roof and windows.

She was about to leave, writing the sound off as something she might've heard from downstairs, when she felt something tug at her ankle. She froze in place, her heart pumping fast. Standing perfectly still, she looked down and saw a girl's hand, fingernails covered in pink glitter nail polish, holding on tight to a fistful of coverall fabric.

"Oh," Kay whispered, kneeling slowly and looking under the bed.

The girl hiding under there was about eight years old. Her thin body fit loosely under the bed as she was lying on her stomach. She stared at Kay with eyes round, her mouth agape, not saying a single word. She held a phone in her left hand, clutched tightly.

"Hello, Heather," Kay whispered. "My name is Kay, and I'm with the police. You're safe now."

The girl stared at her, perfectly silent, not acknowledging in any way the words she'd just heard.

"Let's get you out of there, all right?" Kay held out her hands, inviting the girl to hold on and let herself be pulled out, but the child didn't budge. A shiver ran through the child's thin body, clattering her teeth for a moment.

The girl was in shock.

Kay reached under the bed and touched her hand gently. "We're going to play a game, you and I, something like thumb war, but you have to hold on to my hand and can't let go, or we both lose." She held out her hand and waited for Heather to grab it. After what seemed like forever, the girl's cold, shaky fingers clutched her own. "Ready?" Kay asked, but no reply came. Pulling gently, she got the child out from under the bed, then scooped her up in her arms and rushed toward the stairs.

She slipped and nearly fell with the girl in her arms, the plastic of her booties not gritty enough for carpet. Peeling them off, she climbed down the steps and headed for the living room, avoiding the kitchen stained in Cheryl's blood.

"Doc?" she called out with urgency in her voice.

The medical examiner rushed over.

"Ah," he reacted when he saw the girl. A smile of relief stretched the corners of his mouth, and Kay could've sworn she saw tears in the old man's eyes. "I am so happy to see you, my dear," he said, then disappeared for a brief moment and returned, slowly pushing a stretcher with one tiny passenger strapped on it.

Erin sat on the side of the stretcher, wrapped in a blanket, sucking her thumb, the straps running around her waist holding her in place. Kay set Heather by her sister's side, and Doc brought another blanket for her.

Kay took a rebel strand of hair off Heather's face, tucking it gently behind her ear. "Do you know who took your sister?" she asked, looking straight at the girl.

She remained silent, her eyes glassy and vacant.

"It's important that you tell me what happened here last night," Kay spoke gently. "We need to find your sister."

Heather didn't give any sign she'd heard Kay. She stared into thin air, her hand still clutching the phone. She hadn't acknowledged her little sister in any way, nor anyone else. Her eyes were dry, her mouth slack-jawed. She was dissociated.

"Monster," Erin said, taking her thumb out of her mouth.

Kay turned toward her. "What did you say?" she asked, her voice a soft whisper. "Do you know who took Julie?"

"Monster," she repeated. "A monster came."

Tell me something I don't know, she thought. With a long sigh, Kay propped her hands on her hips. It was going to be an uphill battle.

"I heard the good news," she heard a voice behind her. "You found one of the girls." Sheriff Logan had entered, wearing coveralls and booties like everyone else, the one size tight around his girth. He was a bulky man with puffy, dark circles under his eyes and lines woven around the corners of his mouth and across his brow. His strong voice made Heather startle, her eyes focused and fearful for a moment before drifting into nothingness again. "I'll put a call in to social services."

"Sir, if I may, let's delay that."

"You know we can't, Detective; we have procedures to follow. It's the law."

"We do, but this is a special situation," she pleaded, approaching him and lowering her voice. "These girls are witnesses, covered in evidence. They're in shock, and Heather won't speak a word."

"I understand all that, but—"

"I'm a psychologist. That's what these girls need, a trained professional who can help them cope with the trauma. At the same time, I can extract valuable information that could help us find Julie."

Sheriff Logan scratched the roots of his buzz-cut hair. "I don't know, Kay. Things could get ugly if the family comes calling. I've tasked Deputy Hobbs to dig into next of kin. We have no right to—"

"They're witnesses in a murder-kidnapping, Sheriff. And they're in shock. Social services will put them in a children's psychiatric hospital, where they'll pump them full of drugs. We'll never see Julie again."

"And what are you planning to do with them, Detective? Take them home with you like a couple of rescue puppies?"

The thought had crossed her mind, but she couldn't do it. She had to catch a killer and find Julie. She couldn't afford to take care of the girls all by herself.

"No. I was thinking of repurposing the nap room for a while." That was a room in the back of the sheriff's office building, where several bunk beds were set for cops pulling double shifts to catch some shuteye when needed.

"And you think that's appropriate for two young girls?"

"It beats the psych ward, Sheriff," she replied, looking at him with an unspoken plea. "Let me at least try to get to them. I'll need a few days, not more."

"You have twenty-four hours, Detective, then I make the call. And if the family comes calling, you handle it."

She frowned but decided against arguing for more time. For that, there was always tomorrow, when maybe she could show some progress. Instead, she pasted a grateful smile on her lips. "Thank you. I'll need a couple of deputies to help me take care of them. Farrell, for one, she's a mother; she'll do fine. She can get us some clothing—"

Logan scoffed, raising his arms in the air. "We have a missing child, and you want two deputies sidelined as babysitters?"

"Witness sitters, Sheriff," she replied. With the corner of her eye, she spotted Elliot approaching. Good. She needed reinforcements, all the help she could get. "Once the killer learns he left some loose ends last night, he might want to finish the job."

"You're saying he didn't know there were two other girls here last night?" Logan asked, his voice seeded with disbelief.

"I'm saying that I, for one, don't want to take the chance," she replied calmly, knowing the effect her words would have on her boss. "What if he didn't know? What if Heather and Erin were upstairs and hidden?"

The sheriff rubbed his chin with short, stubby fingers stained yellow from chain-smoking cigars. "How are you handling the ransom calls?"

"I don't really expect any," Kay replied. "Cheryl was a widow, and the killer knows she's gone. This house doesn't really speak of money." She thought for a second, then continued, "I'll forward the landline to my phone, just in case. Maybe we'll get that lucky. But until then, the girls—"

Logan had been gazing at her intently as if trying to read her mind. "Twenty-four hours, Sharp, not a moment more." His phone rang as he was voicing his ultimatum. He answered with a short, "Yes," listening for a moment, then ended the call without a word. "Detective Young, I'm assigning you to another case."

So much for reinforcements.

Elliot nodded and approached. "What's going on?"

"A man's been found dead on the side of the interstate. First on the scene said he's taken a bullet through his heart."

CHAPTER SIX

Julie

The only light came from a yellow bulb hanging by its wires from the ceiling, several feet above her head. The room was cold and musty, the air loaded with an odor of mildew and staleness that she stopped sensing a while ago. There was only one window, closer to the high ceiling and fully boarded, as if she'd be able to reach it, even if she tried her best. The floor was barren, hard concrete and cold as ice, but Julie sat on it, hugging her knees, rocking back and forth as bitter tears fell from her swollen eyes.

"Oh, Mom, I'm so sorry," she whimpered, as she'd done time and again since she'd come to in that dreadful place. "Please, forgive me… please, Mom, forgive me." How she wished she'd taken her mother seriously in the first place and left Mount Chester instead of what she'd done, and then going out on a date on top of it all. How she wished she would've listened to her… now she'd still be alive, giving her crap for the mess in her bedroom.

Instead, she was locked up in that forsaken place, her most vivid memory of her mother's body falling to the ground, blood gushing from her wound, while that dreadful man laughed. And her sisters… what happened to them? Were they still alive, upstairs, where she'd told them to stay put? Or were they—

She couldn't bring herself to finish the thought, afraid it would make it true. Shivering, she wrapped her arms tighter around her knees and prayed silently, just like her mother had taught her many years ago when she was little. After a while, the words of the repeated prayer melded into a simple request. "Please, let them be alive."

Then she sobbed again until she couldn't breathe anymore. The moment she closed her eyes, the image of her mother's body formed against her eyelids, deepening the hollow, burning chasm in her chest.

She shouted against the concrete walls at times, but no one ever responded. "Why did you kill her?" she asked, pounding against the large metallic door with her fists. "Why? Why not just take me, and let her live? It's me you wanted, you sick son of a bitch, so why kill her?"

Then the answer she already knew came to her weary mind, sucking the breath out of her lungs and chilling her blood.

Her mother had died defending her. Her mother had died because of her. Because of what she'd done. Because she wouldn't listen. Because she ran out of the house and went with Brent to the movies instead of staying home so they could escape to San Francisco. She'd made out with him, so taken with his kisses that she hadn't even noticed the movie had ended and another had started. Only on the drive back home had she remembered her mother's warning, the reality of her situation hitting her like a freight train, leaving her a whimpering, guilt-ridden mess on Brent's passenger seat, someone he couldn't get rid of fast enough.

She'd forgotten all her mother had asked of her, and now her blood was on her hands.

Would she ever forgive herself for what she'd done?

She buried her face between her knees, too weak to scream. She deserved to die, just like her mother had died, maybe her sisters too. Because she'd been such a careless, selfish idiot who didn't realize the danger they were in, although her mother had explained it over and over again, even if she knew what her daughter had done. Julie had seen it with her own eyes and still couldn't believe it.

Stupid, reckless… that's what she was.

Restless, she rose to her feet and started pacing the floor, back and forth, listening. Only the sound of rain came through the boarded window, the unmistakable patter against the metal gutters. At times, low thunder echoed strangely against the concrete walls, making them vibrate almost imperceptibly, as if the house itself feared the storm, shuddering from the foundation.

Someone had hung a mirror on one of the gray unfinished walls, a sick sense of humor or an even sicker sense of who knows what she didn't even understand. In the weathered glass surface, she caught glimpses of herself captive, desperate, hopeless, every time she paced by. She was still in the clothes she'd worn when she'd returned from the movies the night before, now almost completely dry from her body heat. Yet she didn't recognize herself whenever she passed by the mirror and saw herself out of the corner of her eye. That girl with hollow eyes and an unsteady gait couldn't be her. It was just a bad dream, and she'd soon wake up. But how could she, when she wasn't even sleeping?

In the far corner stood a bed with sheets, pillows, and a duvet she hadn't touched, preferring the coldness of the floor, the hardness of the locked door to the risk of falling asleep on soft pillows and being taken by surprise by whoever could walk in.

She wasn't planning on being surprised ever again. No, she wanted to ask the man who'd taken her what he'd done with her sisters. Then she'd let herself go limp in his hands, deserving to be punished for the harm she had caused and unwilling to live through yet another day.

Her head hanging low under the renewed threat of tears, she sat on the musty, hard concrete floor and wrapped her arms around her knees, sobbing quietly. If only she could know about her sisters. If only anyone would tell her.

CHAPTER SEVEN

Shelter

Mount Chester Sheriff's Office rarely had any use for the so-called nap room. On the rarest of days when all shifts were pulling double duty in search of a missing child or a lost tourist, the occasional deputy would grab one of the six bunks, placed along the walls in two rows of three. They weren't very comfortable; only male deputies used them, the women more likely to drive home to the comfort of their own beds. Narrow and some bent out of shape, the bunks each came with a knotty pillow and a coarse, drab blanket that smelled of stale air and dirty socks.

The room served many other purposes, doubling as a storage closet for janitorial and office supplies, an old printer covered in a layer of dust so thick it seemed alive, and several computer monitors, probably busted but still showing up somewhere on a fixed asset inventory. A shelf against the back wall housed the ammo supply for the entire precinct, right next to spare bulbs and several neatly folded uniforms.

Kay had pushed together two of the better bunks and had lined each with spare blankets. Deputy Farrell had rushed home and returned with clean, dry clothes that the girls could wear and a set of bed sheets with a colorful, Lion King animal print. Then the two women went through the heart-wrenching process of collecting evidence off the girls' bodies.

Heather resisted Kay's request to let go of the phone she'd been clutching the entire time; she had to gently pry her little fingers off the device. Having it taken from her brought tears to Heather's haunted eyes, the first Kay had seen, silent tears that rolled on a perfectly still face. With increasing concern for the girl's ability to cope with her trauma, Kay slid the phone into her pocket, then spent a few minutes holding the child's hands and speaking to Heather in a soothing voice about how she was going to get it right back after she collected evidence from it. How everything was going to be all right eventually, although it didn't seem like that right now. How she was a brave little girl, so brave Kay wished she had a daughter just like her. And as she spoke the words, she found herself believing them.

Then the girls' clothing was removed, piece by piece, and sealed in evidence pouches, Jodi helping them every step of the way, Heather not seeming to care. Dr. Whitmore's assistant guided them through the entire process with few words, spoken in a choked voice.

Once the girls were wrapped in clean sheets and stood on a large stretch of paper placed on the floor, Jodi slowly and gently combed their hair with a brush. Erin's blood-caked hair posed the most challenges, but eventually, Jodi cut a few strands and sealed them in a small evidence pouch to shorten the ordeal. Scraping under the fingernails came next, on the off chance they might've scratched their mother's killer.

Finally, the girls were given a shower, Farrell volunteering for the task and cordoning off the women's locker room for the duration. She was about twenty-five years old and a great cop, smart, energetic, and all heart. She sang to little Erin, trying to keep her attention away from the bloodstained water whirling around the little girl's feet, her voice occasionally breaking, toneless on shattered breaths, while the child sucked her thumb so forcefully her teeth left deep bite marks around her finger.

Heather stayed dissociated and silent throughout the entire ordeal, her mouth refusing to articulate a single word, her eyes out of focus, lost in a distance that made her trauma bearable. When she was finally done, she let herself be guided into the nap room and sat on the side of the double bunk Kay had improvised, and waited, silent and lost, probably not even aware of her surroundings or the passing of time.

Double servings of syrup-drenched pancakes that filled the sheriff's office with the smell of Sunday mornings got rushed over from the Waffle House, but the girls barely touched them, nor the chamomile tea someone had made using the microwave oven.

A little later, they were finally asleep, dressed in clean but ill-fitting clothes that Deputy Farrell had borrowed from her daughter's closet. Erin continued to suck her thumb but slept soundly, her breathing regular, silent. Heather breathed heavily, her sleep restless, agitated, probably invaded by unspeakable nightmares. Kay stood and looked at them for a moment, then left the room quietly, closing the door after her, while in her mind she saw herself shooting the man responsible, over and over again.

In the hallway, she ran into Sheriff Logan, who must have been watching over the girls for a while through the small window built into the nap room's door.

"Anything yet?" he asked, his brow tense, furrowed. He chewed his usual minty gum impatiently, muscles dancing in knots on his jawline, the rhythm of his chomping a loud and rapid one, far from casual.

"Nothing," she had to admit. "I didn't expect anything this early," she added quickly, knowing Logan could easily change his mind and put that dreaded call into social services. "They need some rest, then I'll talk to them. Anything on the search?"

He ran his hand quickly across his forehead, then through the bristles of his hair. "Nothing. The K9 unit came back empty, but we were expecting that. Dogs can't do much when vics are taken in vehicles. The AMBER Alert went out a couple of hours ago."

"Any calls?"

He scoffed. "Just the usual schmucks who don't know what they're doing. Wasted a bunch of hours chasing false reports." He looked at the girls for a brief moment, then back at Kay. "Do you think the missing sister is still local? Roadblocks didn't get us anything."

She wanted to tell him there wasn't enough data to formulate a profile, not nearly enough to grasp what the unsub's intentions might've been. "There's no way of knowing," she replied instead. "I'm hoping I'll be able to figure that out once the girls start talking. Have you noticed the glasses of wine on the table? That tells me the killer wasn't a stranger. There was no forced entry either. Cheryl knew the unsub."

"Maybe the girls knew him too," the sheriff said, his hand kneading his chin, something visibly bothering him. "Romance gone wrong?"

She shrugged. Out of all things that could jeopardize the outcome of an investigation, one stood out as the single, most significant reason for unsolved cases, and that was jumping to baseless conclusions too early, then sticking to them. "We don't know that."

"That's usually what happens," Logan insisted with a quick grin that briefly exposed the gum held between his left molars. "Someone cheats, or someone leaves someone. A woman scorned, her lover's wife, that kind of stuff. All my years in law enforcement, and I can tell you it's either women, drugs, or money—nothing else driving people to kill here, in our neck of the woods."

"Yes, it could be a woman," Kay admitted, although in her gut, it felt wrong. A woman would've probably left lipstick marks on the wine glass. And the kidnapping of a teenage girl made much more sense for a male assailant, for all the wrong, sickening reasons. "Doc Whitmore will clarify that as soon as he processes the wine glass. Chances are there's enough saliva on it to pull DNA."

The sheriff's lopsided grin fluttered on his lips again, then vanished. "But you're the profiler. What do you think?"

"I think it's too soon to tell," she replied cautiously. "The opportunistic murder weapon, a knife from Cheryl's block, speaks to a lack of premeditation, to a crime of passion. But the kidnapping speaks of something completely different, something that doesn't fit. I don't believe we have all the pieces of this puzzle yet." She checked the time, feeling a pang of angst rushing through her gut. "Julie's been gone for sixteen hours already, and we're nowhere. No ransom call, and I didn't expect one, for that matter. No idea what had happened. All we know is last night, what started as a casual visit ended up in a bloodbath and a girl being taken."

The sheriff looked through the window at the two sleeping children, watched closely by Deputy Farrell. Kay followed his gaze and repressed a sigh. She felt the urge to rush in there and wake them up; maybe they could give her something, anything she could use to find Julie. But they'd be more likely to communicate with her and remember critical details after they'd caught an hour of sleep. That's when the traumatized brain heals.

"The answers are with these two girls," she said, checking the time again, tension seeping in her voice. "Only they can give us the information we need to find Julie. And every moment counts."

CHAPTER EIGHT

Second Crime Scene

It was a toad strangler of a weather.

Remnants of a Pacific hurricane battered the West Coast with a vengeance, dumping more rain than the area had seen in a year.

Elliot lifted the collar of his jacket and pressed firmly on the top of his hat, making sure it remained where it belonged once he got out of the car. Angry gusts of wind sent rain swirling in circular patterns on the asphalt, drops so heavy they formed large bubbles when they hit the ground. Rainwater washed the interstate then drained toward the shoulder, passing each vehicle on the northbound lane sending splashes of it over the median, even as the drivers slowed down to gawk at the large number of law enforcement vehicles present at the scene. After clearing the narrow shoulder, water flowed onto the side of the road, where gravel met grass under a couple of inches of accumulation.

Where the victim lay.

Rain washing away any trace of evidence he might've had on his body.

Several deputies had already erected a few canopies. One had succumbed to the wind, one leg bent, the roof tilted sideways, threatening to collapse.

"You two," Elliot called, shouting at a couple of officers to be heard against the storm. "Grab a tarp and hold it over the body until the ME gets here. Run straighter than a fast trip to the outhouse."

The victim, a man in his fifties, had been rolled into the ditch. He lay face down, his body aligned with the side of the road, his legs crossed at the ankles from the spin, his pant legs twisted around his ankles in the same direction. What was visible of his face was bluish pale and blotchy, his salt-and-pepper, neatly trimmed beard studded with raindrops and mud.

He wore a navy blue, water-repelling jacket that must've been pricey, seeing how after all that time spent under the rage of the elements it had not crinkled one bit. Because the man had been dumped there a while ago, any visible trace of blood was long gone. Elliot thought he might've been shot by the side of the road or brought here from a primary crime scene. But who stops their car on the side of the interstate, where vehicles zoom by incredibly fast, and shoots someone?

He crouched by the body and examined the hole in the man's jacket, visible right between the shoulder blades. Touching the edges of the hole with the tip of his pen, he squinted in the dim light. The edges had been burned off, the polyester fabric hardened by the heat; the bullet had been fired close range, the muzzle of the gun in direct contact with the man's body or under six inches away.

The two deputies rushed over with a stretch of blue tarp and extended it over the man's body, holding on to its corners about four feet above the ground. "That okay, Detective?" one of the men asked, squinting under the rain slamming him straight in the face.

"Tilt it sideways, so it doesn't pool," Elliot instructed him. The wheel was turning with that cop, but the hamster was dead.

"And set it on the ground?"

"No. Hold it like that until the ME gets here." It was as if they'd never worked a crime scene in the rain before.

The man's lips tensed and moved soundlessly. He was probably mumbling a curse. Just as he was about to say something after all, the medical examiner's van pulled up by the guardrail, and Dr. Whitmore rushed to the body.

"You're keeping me busy these days," he said, instead of a greeting. "Looks less and less like retirement to me."

"Don't pin this on me, Doc," Elliot replied, holding his hat on top of his head as the wind turned worse. "If I had my way, you'd only come to see us when you were really bored with your wife's social schedule, and we'd shoot pool and down some brews instead of hanging out in this turd floater."

Dr. Whitmore crouched by the victim's side, under the tarp. "You have a way with words, I'll give you that," he said, frowning as he examined the body quickly, then he flipped it to a supine position. "Single gunshot wound to the upper body," he announced. "Point of entry through the back. I'll know more when I have him on my table." He lifted the man's arm and examined the skin closely, peeling his sleeve up a couple of inches. He flexed it at the wrist and the elbow, then he lifted the man's shirt and jacket a little, looking at a section of his abdomen.

"Time of death?" Elliot asked.

"He's been here a while," the doc replied. "Based on rigor and discoloration, I'd say a couple of days." Doc Whitmore stood, walking backward and emerging from the blue tarp. "Let's load him up," he told his assistant, a young woman who looked miserable under the pouring rain. "Body bag," he further instructed, seeing her grab the stretcher. "No point trying to roll that in this mess."

"Can I?" Elliot asked, gesturing vaguely toward the body.

"Have at it," Doc Whitmore replied.

Crouching by the man's side once more, Elliot scoured his pockets, looking for a wallet or something to help identify him. There was nothing, no wallet, no keys or phone. The killer had done a good, thorough job before dumping him there.

Doc Whitmore waited until the body bag was laid on the ground by the man's body and unzipped. Then he grabbed the victim's shoulders while his assistant grabbed his legs. In perfect sync forged by practice, they lifted the body then set it down in the body bag. A few moments later, zipped and secured with straps, it was loaded into the van, ready to be taken in for the autopsy.

Elliot started searching for the murder weapon, the two deputies joining him as soon as the blue tarp was no longer needed. The two were the only resources he had; the rest of the sheriff's team were deployed in the search for Julie Montgomery. They walked the area in a grid pattern, carefully looking behind every shrub and into every ditch. Doc Whitmore lent them a magnet roller that made their job easier, not having to bend down and sink their hands into water-filled trenches where the gun might've been discarded.

About two frustrating hours later, they gave up. There was no murder weapon to be found.

CHAPTER NINE

Window

The tall windows let all the gloom inside, barely lightened by its passing through white, ethereal voile sheers falling in perfectly aligned waves from the ceiling all the way down to the floor. He'd turned off the two chandeliers, inviting in all of Mother's dismay. He'd never avoided her anger; out of all her children, he was the one who understood her, who knew how to heal her wounds and dry her tears.

He'd been chosen a long time ago.

He ran his fingers through his slicked-back hair, down to the upward curls where it touched his shoulders with uneven ends, untrimmed in a while. Rubbing his hands to warm them, he stood a few feet away from the window, his beige cardigan unbuttoned over a white silk shirt and black slacks. A shiver ran down his spine, and he sunk his hands into the small pockets, tightening them into fists. He didn't draw closer to the fire burning lively in the fireplace. His eyes stayed riveted to the dreary landscape outside, where Mother wept.

Where she bled. Right by the concrete slabs of his pathway, a deepening crevice that was a mere reminder of the abyssal one opened in the side of Ash Brook Hill, at least a hundred feet deep. Oh, how that must hurt Mother!

He clenched his hands tightly together, his skin cold and damp to the touch even after the relative comfort of the knitted pockets, as if his own blood refused to nourish his body.

"Mother Earth, hear your child," he whispered. "I stand before you, begging your mercy and forgiveness. Show me the path to follow, and I will stop your bleeding and dry your tears." He breathed and lowered his eyelids, welcoming the darkness where Mother spoke to him. "I have found her, Mother, the one who will soothe your suffering. She's ready for you."

He breathed deeply, slowly, feeling Mother's hand touching him, easing his fears, filling him with peace. He opened his eyes and searched the sky, but clouds were packed thick in a dreaded layer of gloom, and rain was falling even harder than before.

Moving slowly, he ambled toward the bookcase and stopped in front of the third section. He touched a button hidden behind one of his most cherished books, *The Symbol of Glory* by George Oliver, and the bookcase slid to the right, opening up a section of bare wall with a window in the middle of it. He approached it slowly, tentatively, as if afraid of what he was going to see.

That window didn't lead outside. Through a number of paired mirrors installed at forty-five-degree angles in descending tunnels, it captured a glimpse of what was going on in the basement, two levels below him, where the girl was sleeping. At her end, she could only see a mirror, nothing else, while he could watch her endlessly, seeing her every move and hearing her every word in the tiny speakers mounted in the window frame.

He looked at her, mesmerized. He couldn't believe his eyes at how breathtakingly beautiful she was, the kind of beauty only the young and pure exude through every pore of their skin. His eyes fixed on the girl's image, he let his frozen fingers touch the glass where her lips were parted as she cried quietly, curled up on her side, where her hair reached the gray concrete, where her chest swelled with every shattered breath.

"I'm so sorry, Mom," the girl whimpered, startling him.

It wasn't the first time she'd disturbed his thoughts with this nonsense. Irritated, he turned off the speakers with one quick, angry twist of a knob. If she'd only stopped crying, maybe he could hold on to her a little longer. What beautiful things they could do together if they only had the time!

His imagination weaving endless plans and visions of blissful days with the girl in his arms, his dedication to Mother faltered for a quick moment before he shrugged the temptation off. And still, perhaps he'd keep her for a while.

Only if Mother would allow it.

CHAPTER TEN

Travel Plans

After tying her long blonde hair to capture the strands that had escaped, Kay muttered a curse and clenched her fist, wishing there was something she could break. There was no good option she could take, the choices she had equally bad. One was to force the girls to wake up, when it was obvious they needed to get some rest before they could be yanked back into the midst of a horrifying reality. The other was to let them sleep, while at the same time Julie, who'd already been gone for eighteen hours, desperately needed their help. Any information she could extract from the two girls would've been a treasure trove, the start of a breadcrumb trail they could follow to find their missing sister.

She'd tried to wake Heather up, but the girl was in no shape to have a conversation. Barely standing and pale as a sheet, she wobbled to the restroom then returned with the same vacant stare in her eyes. Then she sat on the side of her bed, motionless and silent until Kay gave up and eased the child onto her side, covering her with the blanket. Before Kay could reach the door, she was fast asleep yet restless, battling the demons that haunted her nightmares.

It just couldn't be done. Not now, not before they'd had a chance to start healing, the trauma too severe to allow them to function without sleep's healing repose. Spending a long moment weighing right versus wrong and asking Hippocrates for advice in her mind, she left, closing the door silently behind her. Only the father of medicine would know the answer to her dilemma. She'd already denied them the soothing help of sleep medication, concerned with the short-term memory loss they could incur as a side effect. Still, she walked away with a rushed gait and a scowl, torn inside, knowing Julie was still out there.

But she wasn't going to sit idle and do nothing, while hours flew by like minutes and Julie was missing. She could still do her job, look at evidence, examine the crime scene one more time, search through records for any indication of similar crimes happening in Northern California. But was that, really, a possibility? That morning, seeing the murder weapon abandoned at the scene, she'd inferred that Cheryl might've been the unsub's first kill.

Deciding that revisiting the crime scene was her best choice, she floored it all the way to Angel Creek, siren and flashers on despite the relatively clear traffic. Earlier that day, when she'd walked through the rooms of the house, she'd been rushed and distracted by finding Erin and Heather, by her need to take them to a place of safety, to protect them, a little unsettled by her unexpectedly strong feelings toward the two little girls. What was that all about? She'd never had any maternal instincts that she'd acknowledged, nor had she envisioned a life for herself where she'd have children, knowing she could never completely leave behind the horrors of her job before coming home to cradle her offspring.

Seeing the yellow police tape fluttering in the wind brought her mind back to the moment. She pulled over by the house and waved at the deputy charged with keeping an eye on the place, then she climbed the five porch steps after a short and vigorous sprint through the falling rain, ignoring the puddles she stepped in and the water hitting her face like frozen needles. There wasn't a need for coveralls and booties anymore, once the evidence collection had been completed, but she thoroughly wiped her feet before entering and brushed raindrops off her navy blue jacket.

The house was silent and almost dark; what little light came in already filtered by heavy clouds and the pervasive grays that seemed to be the keynote of such days. Sunset was more than an hour away, but it seemed much darker; even the streetlights had begun their duty, shedding layers of sodium yellow that sent sparks of golden light against the wet asphalt, reflected in every raindrop. She turned the light on and stopped, closing the door and taking in the entire setting.

A modest but clean living room, with a sofa and a large TV, and little other furniture. A toy box took the far corner, filled with Erin's toys by the looks of it, stuffed animals mixed together with Lego pieces and dolls. A bookcase on the wall, holding a few books, photo albums, and a vase, devoid of flowers. The off-white, fabric sofa was clean and looked new, cheered up by colorful pillows in a green-and-black floral pattern that matched the green accents Cheryl had creatively inserted in the décor: the color of the curtains, the shade of the vase, the green plaid pattern of the dining-room table runner.

Kay walked slowly toward the kitchen, where a dark burgundy stain told the story of what had happened. A forgotten crime scene marker bearing the number eleven in black font on yellow plastic still stood by the knife block on the counter. The metallic smell of oxidized blood was present, faint yet still there, mixed in with the smell of the stew that no one had bothered to remove from the stove and throw away.

A chill engulfed her body. She wrapped her arms around herself, rubbing her arms with her hands as she imagined how the crew sent by the sheriff's office would come in there in a few days and start cleaning up everything, from the blood on the floor to the contents of the fridge, then sealing the house and preparing it for what was to come. A bunch of strangers going through Cheryl's things, touching everything, violating her life, her home.

In a few days, that stew will be maggots, she thought, then emptied the pot in the kitchen sink and turned on the garbage disposal. It whirred loudly, but she welcomed the noise, any noise bringing life to the house touched by death. She rushed through rinsing the pot and left it upside down in the sink, feeling a little guilty for the time she'd wasted on such a menial task.

She went to the dining-room table, from where the chair that had been broken was now missing. She stood in its place, imagining herself as Cheryl, sitting across from her guest after she'd just poured wine for the both of them. How did they get from drinking wine together to the stabbing? What had happened?

Kay visualized the scene, Cheryl pouring the wine, the guest already seated at the table, waiting, chatting, smiling. Maybe smiling; she didn't know that for sure. A man? A woman? Had to be a man. A woman wasn't completely impossible but felt wrong for a number of reasons. The evening had started the right way, but then… what went so wrong? Where were the girls during this time? Did he know there were three daughters in the house? Why did he leave witnesses?

She walked the kitchen floor inch by inch, studying the surface where the scuff marks disappeared into the living-room carpet, where the smashed chair had fallen to the ground. Then she turned and went to the back door, studying it. The deputies who'd worked the scene said there were no signs of forced entry. The unsub had entered through there, through the side door, not the front; they had found a small puddle of water on the tiles, two feet from the door, now almost completely dry.

He had to have been someone familiar with the property, someone who'd visited before.

Opening the side door, Kay looked outside. The driveway ran parallel to the house up to the garage door, a few yards farther from the road than the side door. It made sense to knock on that door in the rain, being closer to the car he must've driven to get there. But still… he had to have been there before. No first-time caller would've used the side entrance, rain or not.

Then she noticed the three suitcases on the side of the hallway and frowned. Had the crime scene technicians examined them? A quick phone call later, she learned that no, no one had looked at them. Pulling on a pair of blue nitrile gloves, she unzipped the first one.

They were packed with clothing for all the family members. She counted the underwear in the large suitcase and found that Cheryl was planning to be away at least two weeks, with all the girls. Where were they going? And when were they supposed to leave? It must've been for a different purpose than just a weekend trip, but when's the last time a single mom of three could afford to take a two-week vacation?

One thing was almost certain: Cheryl wasn't supposed to travel with the unsub, nor was she supposed to leave the night before, or there wouldn't've been any wine served. Who drinks wine before driving in such miserable, treacherous weather, at night no less?

Kay had to start asking questions of the people who knew Cheryl. Her family might know something about her travel plans, or maybe the neighbor. He seemed a little too close to Cheryl to not know.

What if her planned travel had something to do with her murder? Was she running away from someone? From whom?

It didn't fit.

The little Kay knew about Cheryl Coleman didn't tell the story of someone on the run.

She recalled what she'd learned about her earlier, at the precinct, while digging through her life as it was captured in the police and government databases. The woman's life had been perfectly vanilla. If that notion ever existed, it applied to Cheryl Coleman.

She'd been married to Calvin Montgomery, a construction engineer who'd died at age twenty-nine when a section of scaffolding collapsed, taking him down with it. The accident had been thoroughly investigated, and the builder had been cleared of any wrongdoing. But Cheryl had been left with three little girls, the youngest, Erin, only a baby at that time. Yet she'd survived somehow, her dental hygienist job probably barely enough to pay the bills.

Why would someone like Cheryl Coleman decide to up and leave one day, and, as it happened, the day she got killed?

Light beams traveling on the driveway next door smeared the walls with bluish bands, catching Kay's attention. The neighbor was home.

Time to ask him some questions.

Patting her pockets out of force of habit for her keys, although she was only going to walk across the lawn to see the Livingstons next door, she felt something that didn't belong.

Heather's phone.

While deep ridges seeded across her brow, she removed it and looked at it for a moment as if she'd never seen it before. The wallpaper was a photo of fluffy white kittens in a pink basket, what a girl her age would have. She tried to access it, swiping up, and it opened without being asked for a passcode.

Standing in the doorway and feeling for the light switch, Kay checked the text messages and call records. Then her blood turned to ice.

Heather had called nine-one-one the night before at 9:39 p.m. and had been on the phone with them for almost six minutes.

CHAPTER ELEVEN

At the Precinct

He'd drawn the short straw with that case.

Elliot didn't care as much about his personal case closing numbers as he did about catching the villains responsible for the crimes and holding their feet to the fire, but this John Doe's case was as easy as bagging flies.

He had nothing.

The body had been dumped there, by the side of the interstate, so he had no primary crime scene to investigate. Doc Whitmore said he'd been rotting by that ditch for about two days, under a barrage of heavy rain washing away all evidence. There was no ID on the body, no wallet, no phone, no jewelry, not even a set of keys. While there wasn't a murder weapon he could trace, the size of the entry wound pointed to a nine-mil handgun, the most common weapon used in shootings all across the country.

Nope, there wasn't a darn thing to write home about, but his momma hadn't raised a quitter. And he'd be damned if he let whoever turned that John Doe into buzzard bait get away with it. *Not on my watch*, he thought, still chewing on a piece of straw he'd picked up by his car. It tasted of wet fields in the fall, of nights after thunderstorms wash off the dust on a freshly harvested grain field.

He started the engine, and the wipers kicked in, whirring rhythmically, almost hypnotically, unable to keep the windshield clear of water for more than a split second. He shifted into gear and peeled off, eager to get back to the precinct and pull some missing persons reports.

Everything started from the victim's identity—the key point in determining motive and opportunity, two of the three cornerstones of criminal investigations. Without establishing those, he couldn't build a case. But John Doe had been shot a couple of days ago; maybe someone had reported him missing.

Yet, there was no surprise that case clearance percentages were at historic lows, hovering below the sixty percent mark for California. An unknown man who could be anyone from anywhere, dumped at the side of the road, washed clean by days of rain, and found through nothing short of a miracle, where no one was supposed to find him. If it weren't for a pregnant driver with a bad case of morning sickness, no one would've discovered him until, perhaps, never.

That took skill, the mind of a cold-blooded killer, to pull off.

He pulled over as close to the precinct entrance as he could manage and rushed inside, thankful to be out of the weather. He made a quick stop by the coffee machine to get a fix and looked for Kay, hoping he'd see her, at least in passing. She was nowhere in sight, but then again, almost no one was, the bullpen empty, only the faint smell of coffee and sweat and dust and grime left behind. Everyone was out there, searching for Julie.

"Look what the cat dragged in," a man shouted, his words slurred, spit filled. "Woo-hoo," he mock-cheered, banging his boot against the bars of his cell.

Great. Last night's DUIs and disorderlies, Elliot thought, not bothering to respond. Instead, he walked quickly past, ignoring the man who, judging by the pervasive smell of urine that surrounded him like a cloud, might've had difficulties understanding how to use the stainless-steel toilet in his cell.

"Hey, I got rights, ya' know," the man hollered, rattling the bars with his hands. "Hey!"

"Yeah, the right to remain silent," Elliot threw over his shoulder, not turning his head and not slowing down. Somewhere in that precinct, two little girls were sleeping, and if that wino had woken them up, Elliot would be right in his cell with a roll of duct tape to explain his rights to him.

He stopped in front of the nap room and peeked inside through the window. Deputy Farrell sat on the side of a bunk, reading, while the two girls slept.

But Kay wasn't there.

Disappointed, he turned to leave when Farrell lifted her gaze, spotting him. She beckoned him inside.

"Come on in, Detective," she said in a whisper. "Looking for Dr. Sharp?"

"N—no," he replied, a little flustered, thinking that she must've read his mind. "Just checking up on the girls."

"Aah," Farrell replied, with a smile and a slow, conspirative nod. "Everyone is."

"Did they say anything?"

"Nothing yet. Kay didn't want to wake them up too soon, and she left. She'll be back later. I believe she went to the crime scene again."

Elliot looked at Erin, studying her features. She slept soundly, sucking her thumb, her curls scattered on the pillow around her face. Watching her sleep, something stirred in him, although he couldn't pinpoint what it was.

"She's, um…" he started to say, then finished his phrase with a gesture, raising his thumb in the air.

"I tried," Farrell replied. "I pull it out of her mouth, she puts it right back in. Dr. Sharp said we shouldn't worry for now. She called it *soothing behavior*. A few days won't hurt her that much."

"Okay," he said, touching the brim of his hat and turning to leave. "Thanks."

"She said something," Farrell said quickly, her voice still a whisper. "Erin, she did speak. Just the word *monster*, nothing else."

He stared at Erin's angelic features for a long moment. Her eyelids fluttered as her eyes moved rapidly underneath; she was dreaming. Was she dreaming of the monster she'd seen?

Without a word, he left the room and went straight for the conference room. There was a flipchart on the stand in there and a bunch of markers. He grabbed them and took them back to the nap room, ignoring the jeering wino both times he walked past his cell.

"Give her these when she wakes up," he said, laying everything down on an empty bunk. "Tell her to draw the monster."

Deputy Farrell scratched her temple with the tips of her fingernails, careful not to loosen any of her hair from the perfect bun holding it together regulation-style. "She's four, Detective," she said, the disbelief in her voice sprinkled with amusement.

Uncomfortable, Elliot plunged his hands in the pockets of his jeans. "What age do they start, you know, drawing stuff?"

"They can scribble as early as two years old and hold a crayon, but from there to drawing the perp, I'd say we're not going to see anything we can use."

"But it won't hurt, will it?" he asked, smiling.

Deputy Farrell seemed to melt under his smile like some women did. He wished he had the same effect on Kay; then he would be the one unable to stop smiling.

"It won't, that's for sure," she replied, smiling back. "I'll do it."

He left the room, closing the door silently, then looked at the sleeping girls one more time. He remembered what he'd seen earlier on that had tugged the strings of his heart in an unexpected way.

He'd seen Kay.

Holding little Erin in her arms at the crime scene and speaking to her softly, as if only the two of them were in the world. He'd felt uneasy then as if spying on them and had rushed out of there before she could spot him. Before she could see his flushed cheeks, like a teenager's, because, for the briefest of moments, he'd asked himself a question: *what if?*

He'd never thought of Kay as maternal; she wasn't, not really. She was driven, smart as a hooty owl, and faster than small-town gossip. She seemed tough as nails sometimes, and better not to be the perp sitting across from her in an interview room, but there was a soft core to her, something unexpectedly warm and loving under that steeled armor she wore all the time.

Where did that leave him?

"Hey," the wino hollered, his gruff voice echoing on the long hallway. "I want my phone call!"

Elliot rushed over and grabbed him by his vomit-stained shirt through the bars of his cell.

"How would you like to wear your shoe so deep down your throat you'll call it lunch?" he asked, and the man's blood drained from his face as he nodded vigorously. "Not another sound, you hear me? And you'll get your phone call."

For the duration of his search through local and state databases for missing persons reports matching his John Doe, the wino remained completely silent, a heap on the floor against the back wall of his cell.

There was nothing. Not a single report matched the man found dead on the side of the interstate. Although more than a thousand open cases were still active in California, matching the gender and age range of his vic, none had been filed in the past forty-eight hours.

His only hope was Doc Whitmore and whatever he could uncover about the man during his examination. Knowing ahead of time the ME would roll his eyes at seeing Elliot show up uninvited on his doorstep, and dreading the brief run through the endless toad floater, he downed what little coffee remained in his cup and rushed out.

CHAPTER TWELVE

The Neighbors

Standing in the doorway and indifferent to the rain that crashed against the asphalt, sending ricochet fragments that soaked her pant legs, Kay was livid as she called the nine-one-one dispatch and asked to speak with the supervisor. After a moment of silence, the operator transferred her to a monotone-voiced man who identified himself with a call code.

"This is Detective Sharp with Mount Chester Sheriff's Office, badge number 161552."

"What can I do for you, Detective?"

She didn't recognize the voice. She breathed, willing herself to control the rage she feared was about to seep through her choice of words and the tone of her voice. She visualized little Heather making that nine-one-one call from underneath her mother's bed, shaking, her teeth clattering, the phone clutched in her trembling fingers, while the unsub was downstairs, killing her mother and kidnapping her sister.

Only to not have anyone bother to respond.

"There was a call made last night at nine thirty-nine p.m., from this number," she said, then spent a few good seconds retrieving Heather's phone number from the settings menu. She wasn't familiar with the model. It was a cheaper phone that seemed to have been purchased from a 7-Eleven. "Here you go, 415-555-2259. I need that recording pulled and sent to me, and an official write-up as to why the call wasn't responded to, why we weren't notified. We have one DOA and one abduction of a minor at that address."

The silence felt heavy on the other side of the line. "Copy that, Detective," the man replied eventually. "You'll have it within the hour."

She wished she could've smashed the phone against the man's wall or something, but the center was all the way in Redding; otherwise, she would've paid them a visit and listened to the recording right away.

Pulling the door shut behind her, she crossed the soaked lawn quickly, almost running, her footsteps sending water droplets high in the air. In passing, she noticed a few details about the family she was about to visit.

Opaque curtains covered all windows on the Livingstons' home. Little light was coming from inside, only where the curtain panels met, forming a faint vertical line. There were contact sensors installed on all the windows she passed by and motion detection sensors that activated two pairs of powerful floodlights as she turned the corner of their garage, then again toward the front door. Was there a history of break-ins in the neighborhood that she didn't know about?

Taking a mental note to ask the Livingstons about it, she rang the bell. Rushed footfalls on hardwood resounded behind the red-painted door. The younger Mrs. Livingston opened it with the dawning of a smile on her lips, her face turning pale when she recognized Kay.

"Oh," she reacted, stepping back and clutching the lapels of her blouse with pudgy fingers. Her entire body silently willed the detective to stay away, to keep her distance. Kay wondered why yet pretended she didn't notice anything.

"I was wondering if I could ask you and your husband a few more questions," Kay said, flashing her most disarming smile to put Mrs. Livingston's reluctance at ease.

The woman nodded, swallowing hard, and licked her dry, chapped lips still bearing traces of the crimson lipstick she'd worn that day. "Come on in."

They'd already sat down to eat, the old Mrs. Livingston the only one happy to see Kay.

"Ah, come on in, my dear, join us for dinner," the elderly woman said, clapping her hands with excitement.

Frank Livingston nodded in Kay's direction with the shortest of smiles, then leaned over and whispered something in his mother's ear.

"Why not?" the old woman pushed back loudly. "She's a nice person. I can tell."

Flushed with embarrassment, Frank stood and pulled out a chair, inviting Kay to take a seat at the table. She hesitated, police procedure clear on the matter; she couldn't touch anything they would offer, and a certain distance had to be maintained. But since when were distance and rejection the ingredients of a good conversation?

Instead, she smiled shyly and said, "Well, I'm not supposed to, but I don't want your food to get cold while we talk. Please, don't let my presence interrupt your dinner," she invited them, but only Betty picked up her fork and eagerly stabbed a piece of potato.

The food smelled delicious, mouthwatering fried fish with roasted potatoes with lemon and herbs, from what she could tell. The scent of lemon butter filled her nostrils and made her wonder if the potatoes had been roasted with slices of citrus. One of the Livingstons surely knew how to cook. Judging by the stained apron she was still wearing, that must've been Diane.

Frank and his wife sat quietly, hands folded in their laps, avoiding her glance, until Frank finally glanced at her briefly and asked, "What can we do for you, Detective?" Then he reached for his glass and took a thirsty swig of ice water he nearly choked on.

"I was wondering if you knew anything about Cheryl's life, anything that would help us with our investigation." She reminded herself to look at Diane, although she had a good idea who knew the most about Cheryl among those gathered around the table.

Blotches of red stained Frank's face. "I'm one of Julie's teachers, so yes." He cleared his throat and patted his lips with a napkin, then scrunched it nervously in his hand, holding on to it instead of discarding it on the table. "Um, I guess I know a little about them."

Diane Livingston stared firmly ahead, expressionless, while Betty ate with a healthy appetite. Frank glanced quickly at both women as if asking permission to continue, then added, "Julie's your typical teenager. Hangs out with other girls her age. They giggle all day long whispering in one another's ears, glance at boys, then giggle and whisper some more." He shrugged and pushed his unfinished plate aside. "I guess it's nature taking its course."

Interesting, Kay thought, how she'd asked about Cheryl, and he chose to talk about Julie. Maybe she'd been wrong, and Frank only knew Cheryl as the mother of one of his students, nothing more. Then why the weirdness, weighing heavy and bothersome like stale cigar smoke?

"Was she involved with anyone?" Kay asked, continuing on the road Frank Livingston wanted to take her.

He frowned briefly. "At their age, it's not real involvement, not like with adults. It's more like having a boyfriend and hanging out, holding hands, that sort of thing."

"Ah," Betty reacted, and everyone immediately looked at her. Her voice expressed interest, as if Frank's words had confirmed her suspicion. But the old woman didn't add anything else, and no one asked what she meant by her reaction. Seeing how both Frank and Diane preferred Betty didn't speak in Kay's presence, she didn't ask either, planning to do that later, right before leaving. There was no point in antagonizing them.

"My apologies," Kay said, "that's what I meant. So, there's a boyfriend?"

He pressed his lips together for a brief moment, thinking. "I don't believe so," he eventually replied. "But I can't be sure. I've only seen her hanging out with other girls. She's a good kid; she doesn't mix with the wrong crowds or anything."

"How about Cheryl?" Kay asked and carefully watched the effect of her question as it rippled around the table.

Diane bit her lip and chose to look sideways and down. She didn't seem jealous or suspicious, only afraid. Again, the same unusual reaction.

"What about her?" Frank asked, a little too quickly.

Betty placed her fork noisily on the side of her plate as if to draw everyone's attention. "Give this fine young woman a plate and some food, Frank. She's just skin and bones, poor thing."

"No, thank you," Kay said, smiling uncomfortably and shuffling in her seat just as Frank leaned against the table with both hands, about to stand. "I'm fine, really. I just ate."

Frank didn't insist; settling back on his chair, he seemed relieved, probably eager to see her gone, and so was Diane. The tension in the air was thick and loaded with static electricity as if sparks were about to fly between the two spouses, with Kay as the catalyst. Only Betty was happy and seemed detached, intrigued, the murder-kidnapping next door most likely an opportunity to break the boredom of her days.

"Do you happen to know if Cheryl was planning to travel anywhere?" Kay asked in the most casual tone of voice, hoping to catch another glimpse of the conflict brewing just underneath the surface.

Feigned surprise appeared in various degrees on the Livingstons' faces. As they'd done before, they looked at one another before Frank replied, the old woman nodding slowly, as if she were thinking, *I knew it.*

"Uh, I, um, we had no idea of any travel. Where was she going?"

"That's what we're trying to find out," Kay replied. "How about her relationships?" she asked serenely, finally poking the presumed elephant in the room right in the rear, if there was an elephant of that nature after all. "Was she seeing someone?"

Diane stood rather abruptly and started clearing the table, taking a handful of dishes to the kitchen. She seemed a little flustered, annoyed even, but not more.

"Not that I know of," Frank replied. "We weren't that close. She led a very busy life, with a job and those girls, and we, um, like to keep to ourselves."

"Yes, we do because we're cowards," Betty intervened in a loud, scratchy voice, like fingernails on a chalkboard.

"Shush, Mother," Frank said, touching her forearm and glaring at her.

"It's all right," Kay said, with a dismissive hand gesture, knowing very well that would ignite the old woman's appetite to talk. "I've seen your security system and floodlights. Do you have concerns with breaking and entering?"

"No," Frank replied, seeming relieved. "Not really."

"It's the darkness he's trying to keep at bay," Betty said, standing with difficulty and leaning on the table with bony, knotted hands. She wore a dress in a blue-gray flower pattern that brought out her blue eyes, making them seem more intense against the million lines of her withered face, almost maniacal. "But darkness won't—"

Back from the kitchen, Diane promptly grabbed her elbow. "Come on, Betty, it's time to go to bed." The fear was clearly visible on Diane's face. Whatever it was they were trying to keep the old woman from sharing scared both of them.

"I'll say when it's time to go," Betty snapped, pulling her elbow forcefully from Diane's grip, with the anger most old people feel when they're not taken seriously or shown respect.

"It's the Alzheimer's," Diane mouthed for Kay's benefit, holding her hands up in an apologetic gesture. She seemed genuinely embarrassed by her mother-in-law's outburst, her face flushed, her chest heaving rapidly with short, panicky breaths.

"It's all right," Kay repeated. "My mother struggled with it too," she lied without batting an eyelash, forgetting she'd returned to live in a small town where everyone knew everyone. A pang of guilt zapped through her mind for using her mother like that, shamelessly lying to suit her purpose, the memory of her dying of cancer still raw and haunting and unsettling. "In my experience," she added, lowering her voice to a conspirative whisper for the benefit of Frank and Diane, "it's best to let them unload whatever they feel the urge to say, then they'll find peace, and everyone can enjoy a relaxing evening."

Frank looked at Diane for a moment. The woman shrugged almost imperceptibly and walked away from the table with the remaining plates she collected quickly and quietly; as if distancing herself, as if saying, "I don't want any part of this."

"Or I could leave," Kay offered, seeing Betty wasn't saying anything. The woman looked dismayed, as if taken aback by her family's attitude toward her. "Thank you very much for your help," Kay added. "As you can imagine, we're doing everything we can to find Julie—"

"You won't find her!" Betty shouted, pointing a shaky finger at her and standing so unexpectedly Kay took a step back. "She was a firstborn daughter," she added, pacing toward Kay in an unsteady gait. "The spirits of the valley took her, and once she's gone, she's gone forever."

Slack-jawed, Kay listened, trying to figure out if there was any bit of usable information in the woman's words. She definitely believed strongly in what she was saying, but... the spirits of the valley? Imagine searching ViCAP, the Violent Criminal Apprehension Program database, for that, she thought, containing a bitter scoff. Maybe Frank and Diane were right, and the woman's Alzheimer's was more serious than she'd thought. Disappointed, she zipped up her jacket, getting ready to leave and face the elements raging outside.

"Hush, Mother," Frank said, clutching her hand and trying to lead her gently away from the table, from Kay. But Betty held her ground, grabbing a fistful of Kay's sleeve and tugging hard.

"It was always destined to be so," she said, her eyes shooting darts left and right, as if afraid the spirits might overhear the conversation. Then she turned to Frank with an accusatory stare, not letting go of Kay's sleeve. "I always told you this would happen. And what did we do? Nothing." She crinkled her nose in disgust. "That sweet woman died protecting her daughter because the spirits can't be defeated." As her pitch climbed, a tremor in her voice told Kay she was under the spell of powerful emotion. Alzheimer's or not, the woman truly believed what she was saying. And, for some reason, she thought Frank could've helped Cheryl but had chosen not to do so, and that was well worth pursuing.

"Why do you think this tragedy could've been avoided?" Kay asked Betty, watching fear drain the blood from Frank's face. She'd hit a nerve.

"Aah," the old woman groaned, rattling her sleeve as if to shake Kay back to reality. "We knew about it, that's why! Everyone knew about it. If you have a firstborn daughter, you're doomed to cry the tears of a broken-hearted mother," she recited. "He knew about it too," she added bitterly, throwing Frank a side glance. "Three days ago, he knew the time had come to—"

"That's it, Mother, you're going to bed." He tugged at her arm, and with his other hand tried to wrestle the old woman's fingers away from Kay's sleeve. "The detective was just leaving," he added, throwing Kay a short but meaningful glance.

"No need for that," she said, giving Frank a clear warning about mistreating Betty in a stern voice. "I'm leaving. For now."

She turned to leave, ignoring Betty's flailing arm as she was trying to grab onto her again.

"Don't believe me," Betty shouted, her voice sounding strangled from the effort. "Look for yourself. It's always been firstborn daughters, for as long as I can remember living on this Earth."

"Mother!" Frank snapped, trying to lead her away toward the back of the house.

Stunned, Kay stood only two steps from the front door, held open by Diane. Her amenable smile was gone, a frown visible under her badly cut bangs to match the deep, vertical lines flanking her tense mouth.

"Never a son, never a secondborn daughter," Betty shouted, pushing Frank away and managing to take a few steps toward Kay.

Defeated, Frank let his arms fall alongside his body. "Detective," he urged her, "as you can see, my mother isn't well. If you'll excuse us, please."

"Sure, no problem," Kay said and stepped outside, but then turned and asked him, "Did you have any prior knowledge of anything or anyone threatening Cheryl or Julie?"

His eyes were suddenly those of an old, tired, and sad man. "Absolutely not, Detective. I would've said something."

She waved goodbye and grabbed the patio railing, ready to sprint through the heavy rain across the lawn to her car.

Before Diane had a chance to close the door behind her, she heard Betty's voice once again, shouting, "Are you a firstborn daughter?"

CHAPTER THIRTEEN

Dawn

He still stood in front of the tall windows, his eyes riveted to the pitch-black sky occasionally set ablaze with shades of metallic blue and silver by distant lightning. The chandeliers had been turned off, leaving him engulfed in the same darkness that lay thick across the land, a heavy blanket of ominous obscurity. He hadn't slept that night, not for a single moment, breathlessly waiting for a sign from Mother.

Despite his many prayers, she'd stayed silent, foreboding, unwilling to cede.

The first light of dawn came as a hint of deep, dreary gray, so faint it seemed more like an illusion. Then it grew stronger, light defeating darkness yet again like it had done without exception, day after day. There was no hint of blue sky anywhere, only heavy, lead-lined clouds headed inland from the ocean in rolling, menacing clumps, an endless deluge with a hint of Pacific salt in every drop. Rain fell hard, opening deep wounds in Mother's body, wounds that only he could heal.

Only he knew how to appease her.

As he'd done many times over the long night that was just ending, he approached the window behind the bookcase and looked at the girl.

She slept on the floor, refusing to come anywhere near the bed he'd so carefully prepared for her with rustling white sheets and a duvet to keep her warm. Instead, she'd curled up on her side, hands tucked between her knees. She'd cried herself to sleep, mumbling endless, senseless apologies to her mother. What did her mother have to do with anything? Stupid, stupid girl.

Yet so beautiful, her skin so pristine and soft, her hair falling on her shoulders in waves of finest silk. He stared at his own fingertips for a long moment, fantasizing, then rubbed them against one another, slowly, gently, as if to kindle the sensation of touching that perfect skin, running his fingers down her shoulders, brushing against her budding breast, descending lower and lower, following the shape of her body as he would a curvy mountain road moistened by early morning dew.

"Dear Mother, hear your sinful child," he whispered, touching the cold glass where the image of the girl's body came to life before his eyes. She shifted in her sleep and whimpered, sending a rush of sensual urges through his body. He licked his parched lips and swallowed hard, the intensity of his emotions choking him. "I stand before you, begging your mercy and forgiveness. Show me the path and I will follow. I will heal your wounds and dry your tears like I have always done." He closed his eyes to block the girl's image from view in an attempt to control his urges, but the image persisted against the backdrop of his eyelids as if he and the girl had already become one.

He squeezed his eyelids shut and breathed, and a few moments later, the image dissipated, only to stubbornly return with a surge in the heat coursing through his blood. Deciding to keep the vision at bay, he walked slowly toward the tall window overlooking the soaked lawn and gazed toward the sky where the light was brightest.

"Dear Mother, hear your child." He pressed his hands together and brought them closer to his chest. "I've been alone for so long." An unexpected tear rolled down his cheek. "Since the day you chose me, demanding your first sacrifice. And I have never wavered," he continued, shaking his head as if to underline his whispered words, his voice gravelly. "Maybe just this time, and for a little while, not long, you could have mercy on my weary soul and let me keep her a while longer."

The rain kept falling hard, heavy, a low rumbling of distant thunder incessantly reminding him of Mother's brewing anger. It was a sin to ask what he just did, to even think it, as if he could ever be worthy. Mother liked her sacrifices pristine, untouched, their flawless skin to never have known a man's caress. Untamed, she continued to demand her due because there wasn't a single crack of blue in the fearfully gray skies, no matter how tiny, no matter how much he searched the cloud-covered expanse, inch by inch.

"Dear Mother," he whispered again as he'd done throughout the night, shivering when he saw lightning strike the hills just a few miles north of his house. "Please show your lost child mercy and grace, and grant him one last wish before he perishes from the world of the living. If I could only—"

Thunder crashed so loudly it rattled the windows and shook the massive house, a low-pitched rumbling prevailing over the sound of falling rain for a long, terrifying moment. Saddened, he lowered his forehead, again defeated.

"Please forgive me, Mother, for having dared to ask. She is yours and yours only."

CHAPTER FOURTEEN

Morning

The first light of dawn found Kay sleeping on one of the cots in the precinct nap room, her hand extended over to the next one, holding Heather's. She'd tried waking up the little girl the night before when she'd finally wrapped up her visit with the Livingstons and returned to the sheriff's office, soaking wet, hungry, cold, and miserable. But Heather was in no state to be woken, seemingly about to faint, and Kay had caved again, playing the guilt-ridden game of choosing between the dire urgency to find Julie and the concern for her sister's health.

That was no easy choice to make. Heather was in shock; forcing her to relive her trauma too early could have lasting effects on her fragile psyche. On the other hand, her sister's life hung in the balance, every minute Julie spent with her captors diminishing the chances she'd ever be found alive.

Although she wished badly for a hot shower and a glass of wine, Kay had relieved Deputy Farrell instead, letting her go home for the night. She'd rummaged through the precinct's only fridge and ate some peanut butter from a jar labeled HOBBS, knowing the young deputy wouldn't mind, then was left with no other alternative than the vending machine's choice of empty calories. At least they tasted good and crunchy as she ate the onion-flavored chips from the rustling bag, enough to motivate her to lick the salty, spicy dust off her fingers.

By the time she lay down on that cot, it was almost two in the morning; until then, she'd refused to give up, searching for leads in all the databases she had access to, looking for murder-kidnappings with similar modus operandi in the recent past. She'd found none. There had been numerous child abductions, most of them by a family member, resulting from custody battles or spousal abuse contentions gone wrong. Several abductions of girls Julie's age were recorded closer to the Los Angeles area, where human trafficking flourished despite local law enforcement's efforts to curb the disheartening number of new cases.

Could Julie have been taken by a human trafficking ring? There was no evidence of one operating in their little town, population 3,824. Not even during the high tourist season when almost a hundred thousand people traveled to Mount Chester to ski, staying in the hotels scattered along the interstate or in the mountain lodges. Traffickers preferred abducting people from large cities like San Francisco or LA. Their chances of getting caught were slim to none when they could quickly become lost in the massive crowds traveling in and out of the two large tourist hubs.

As for Cheryl's murder, it was a simple, opportunistic stabbing. There was no clear evidence of premeditation, no forced entry, no particularly distinguishable MO. When she entered the few details into the National Crime Information Center, her search returned thousands of unsolved cases.

That's why she was dying to hear that nine-one-one call.

Every few minutes, she'd checked her inbox for the recording she'd requested from the Redding emergency communications center, but that email refused to show up. At about one in the morning, she stepped out of the nap room and made a low-voiced call to the dispatch, but the supervisor she'd talked to earlier wasn't available. Grinding her teeth, she reiterated the urgency of the request and hung up, not even having the satisfaction of having yelled at someone.

Then she'd returned to the girls' side. Loosening her belt a couple of notches, she lay on the clumpy cot and allowed herself a little rest, holding Heather's hand as she slept. After what seemed like only seconds, she was startled awake by piercing shrieks.

Heather sat on the bed screaming, rocking back and forth, and covering her eyes with her hands. It must've been one of her terrible nightmares, snatching her from slumber mercilessly, leaving her breathlessly heaving against Kay's chest.

Also startled, Erin sobbed quietly, still lying down on her side, shooting Kay terrified glances from the tear-stained pillow. Realizing it would probably take a long time until she could put the girls back to sleep again, she moved over to the next cot and held Heather against her chest, speaking softly to her while wrapping her other arm around Erin's tiny shoulders.

"I want my mommy," Erin eventually whimpered, sniffling, then plunged her thumb into her mouth. Kay's heart twinged.

Then Sheriff Logan showed up, most likely drawn in by the screaming.

It was 5:43—time to go to work.

She pasted a weary smile on her lips. "Good morning."

He took in the entire situation with a quick glance around the room. Clothes scattered on the floor, the cots pulled together, the two girls she held tightly in her arms. "This situation is untenable, Kay, and you know it." His five o'clock shadow had grown into a blotchy, salt-and-pepper stubble he scratched with a lot of determination in his short, chubby fingers.

"I agree," Kay replied, already feeling guilty for holding on to the girls in the interest of finding Julie, when they could've slept in a decent bed, maybe even with the aid of some medication, instead of battling the monsters in their dreams in that smelly, dreary corner of the world. But at least they were safe; no one would be able to find them and tie up whatever loose ends they'd want to deal with once the word got out that there were witnesses to Monday night's murder. "It won't be for long, I promise," she offered before Logan could ask. "Right after breakfast, I'll start working with them."

"Your twenty-four hours are almost done. Then I make the call." He cleared his throat and looked briefly at the two girls. "I'm surprised family hasn't shown up yet."

She shook her head slowly with a sad smile. "Cheryl was a widow," she whispered. "I don't know if there are grandparents—"

A deputy knocked twice, then entered, bringing a tray with breakfast served on paper plates and hot tea for the girls. He placed the tray on a nearby table that used to serve a different purpose before one leg got crooked and it found its way to the nap room to gather some dust. Then he went away, quick to disappear and close the door behind him.

"These girls could be loose ends, Sheriff," she said, still whispering, realizing how little she knew about the girls' extended family. But she'd had different priorities, like Julie or the killer, who could decide anytime to pay the girls a visit. "They'll need protective custody until we eliminate this scenario. And they're our only chance to find Julie. Other than them," she added, lowering her voice even more to a barely audible murmur, "we have nothing. No witnesses, no evidence that hasn't been washed away by rain, nothing."

She caressed Heather's hair. The girl was well awake now, her stare vacant, her face expressionless and inert, just like the day before.

"But you have to agree, Kay, this doesn't make any sense," Logan insisted, gesturing vaguely with both hands. "As a parent, I'm telling you, this is no place for children, especially in their situation."

The worst part was she agreed wholeheartedly, yet she had to change his mind somehow. "If we turn them over to social services, we lose access to them. Any delay could seal Julie's fate, and you know it."

Logan pressed his lips together, visibly annoyed. He was a kind man with a reputation for being fair and thoughtful, even if he sometimes rushed into bad decisions, and then refused to change his mind out of concern for how that would reflect on his leadership. He must've believed that it was better to be wrong on occasions than be perceived as indecisive or a pushover.

"Any news on the AMBER Alert or the roadblocks?" Kay asked, knowing his own answers would help her make her case.

He wasn't stupid; he seemed to have read right into her gimmick and shook his head once with a disapproving glance. "Nothing, as I'm sure you might've guessed by the fact that no one's come to inform you of any progress."

She lowered her gaze for a moment, feeling a little ashamed. He was right to expect more from her. "I still didn't get a ransom call," she said, her voice calmer. "I wasn't expecting one, though. If there were a ransom demand involved, they wouldn't've killed the one person who was the most inclined to pay." She stood slowly, gently disentangling herself from the girls, then she invited him to step outside. As soon as the door was closed and the children out of earshot, she continued, "The neighbors weren't much help. They haven't seen anything they wanted to share, but I believe there's more to it than what they're saying. I'll revisit."

He nodded, running his hand through his buzz cut with a long sigh. "Door-to-door canvass returned zero results; it's the damn weather. It's almost as if the perp waited for this crap." He gestured toward the window, where large raindrops crashed with a constant rapping. "But I have the nine-one-one call recording cued up for you if you want."

"You have it?" she blurted, feeling her blood rush to her head in anger. "I've been checking my email all night, waiting for it." That sneaky bastard. He went over her head, knowing darn well she was ready to rip him a new one if he didn't have a valid explanation for the way it had been handled.

"Well, they sent it to me instead, citing your heightened emotional state," he replied, making air quotes with his fingers and shooting her a quick, inquisitive glance. "Are you making friends in the local law enforcement already, Detective?"

"I wouldn't call them friends, Sheriff," she replied, eager to hear what happened. "What did my new friend say was the reason they didn't dispatch us in response to the call?"

"They said they thought it was a hoax."

CHAPTER FIFTEEN

Postmortem

There was something about the morgue that creeped Elliot out—it wasn't that surprising, considering it was the morgue, after all. Holding a straight face and acting professionally while standing between two shiny, stainless-steel autopsy tables, one with its occupant on display, took every bit of willpower he had. He would've easily settled for the written ME report in his inbox, had he not known the importance of a face-to-face conversation with the medical examiner and the opportunity to ask urgent questions and get timely answers.

That's why he breathed through the mouth, where the stink of formaldehyde and the other chemicals he'd grown used to associating with Dr. Whitmore's white beard and kind eyes was dampened by the strong flavor of several Altoids Arctic Mints Elliot held in his cheeks as if he were a chipmunk.

Faint piano music emerged from the computer running on the doctor's desk, the bright notes of Vivaldi's "Spring" in stark contrast with the body lying on the table, disturbingly naked under powerful fluorescent lights with the exception of a cloth covering his privates. Vulnerable. Unable to defend himself, his modesty, his dignity. The man's Y incision gaped wide open, his body devoid of all organs, now neatly labeled and preserved in medical jars lined in perfect order on a table nearby. Staring at the source of the music, Elliot inhaled through his mouth, as shallowly as he could, keeping his mind on the music and willing his empty stomach to stay put where it belonged.

"It helps me think clearly," Dr. Whitmore said, evidently noticing where his attention was focused. "And I'm sure my clients wouldn't hold that against me," he added, peeling off his blue gloves and discarding them in a trash can bearing the biohazard symbol right below the motion sensor that pulled the lid open with a whir. "You're early, but I have a few things."

"Good," Elliot replied, shifting his weight from one foot to the other, wishing he was done already and out of there in the pouring rain. He needed a lead like he needed air, or else his John Doe wasn't going to become much else but an unsolved cold case, just a number assigned by a system and placed on all tags and labels right after the infamous name placeholder Elliot had learned to hate. "Because I have nothing," he admitted, still trying to hold his breath. The air smelled badly of death and chemicals, but it was the stink of decaying human flesh that unnerved him the most, reminding him of how fleeting life was, of how it could unexpectedly end without a moment's notice.

The medical examiner flipped through some forms housed in a blue folder. There was a case number printed on the label affixed to the upper right corner of its cover. Every now and then, he mumbled, "Uh-huh," and occasionally tapped the tip of his pen against a section of the page, probably where something had captured his attention.

"Why do you still do this, Doc?" Elliot asked, a little surprised with himself. It wasn't any of his business, and he knew better than to pry. His momma would've smacked him silly. "You're retired, aren't you?"

Whitmore smiled, showing two rows of teeth that looked much younger than he was. "I am retired, yes. But I offered my services to the county for the odd murder case, and, as of late, they keep calling me in."

It must've shown how confused he was, arranging his wide-brimmed hat over a tentative frown and leaning against a white tile wall because the doctor's smile widened.

"They have no one else, you know," Dr. Whitmore added, gesturing toward the body. "I like to think I can be their voice and help you get justice for them. That makes everything worthwhile. The smells, the heartbreak, the horror stories—I've witnessed a few that are unforgettable. Not here; back in San Francisco County. There was one particular case your partner and I worked on when she was still a federal agent, and I was still, well, unretired," he chuckled lightly, "that still keeps me up at night." His eyes veered toward the wall, where a digital clock displayed the time in military format. "Not last night, though, because I was here, wrapping this up. That story's for another time." He picked up the folder from where he'd dropped it and sifted through its pages until he found the one he was looking for.

"Do you have an ID yet?" Elliot asked, eager to get started on the victim's background.

"No ID yet, but his DNA is already running. His fingerprints weren't in the system, so he's got no priors. Great dental work that tells you social status. Considering the teeth, the brand-new leather shoes, and the top-shelf clothing, this man was comfortably wealthy." He turned the page, then nodded, without taking his eyes off the compact paragraphs typed underneath hand-drawn sketches. "Yes, cause of death. This was a contact shot like you suspected, the weapon, a nine-mil handgun, held snugly against his body when it was fired. There was singeing and powder burn tattooing around the wound. We recovered the bullet. Find me a gun, and I can match it to the round that killed this poor fellow."

That'll be like putting socks on a rooster, Elliot thought. He'd searched the entire crime scene for that weapon, crawled through ditches and under bushes, smelled deer dung up close and personal, and found nothing. The shooter could've easily driven off and thrown that gun out the window in an entirely different section of the woods that flanked the interstate for miles and miles. Or it could very well be on the perp's nightstand, all cleaned up, waiting for his next victim.

"He's a tall man, your vic," the doctor continued, his words scattered on short, shallow breaths. He pushed the bridge of his black-rimmed glasses toward the root of his nose with one quick, habitual gesture. "He measures 193 centimeters, or six feet four inches." He approached the back wall of the autopsy room, where digital X-rays were displayed on a wide, wall-mounted screen. He pointed toward one of the images, showing a man's torso in shades of gray, with the bullet bright white, clearly standing out. "See here? The bullet entered his body at a slightly downward angle and pierced his right ventricle, then lodged in his sternum. Given his height, I believe it's safe to assume he was shot while sitting down." Moving toward his desk, he held his hand in a fist with the index finger extended, simulating a pistol, and positioned it downward as if to shoot the imaginary person sitting on his four-legged lab stool. "Like this."

"I'm going to go out on a limb and assume you're ruling this a homicide, Doc," Elliot quipped, touching his stomach briefly as if to appease the angry turmoil in there.

"I tend to do that when people are shot in the back, yes," Dr. Whitmore replied with a quick smile that immediately vanished from his lips. He read from his notes, flipping through a couple of pages, while Elliot approached the man and studied his features, trying to ignore his open chest cavity.

The first thing that stood out was the tan. The man had spent considerable amounts of time in direct sunlight. His arms were dark from the wrists down and bluish pale elsewhere, speaking of long sleeves worn outdoors, even in the summer. Elliot had seen similar suntan patterns in boaters and surfers, where the crisp Pacific winds enhance the sunburns, even in low temperatures. Surfers wore full-body wetsuits in the ocean water that rarely exceeded sixty-five degrees. Boaters wore wind jackets and bundled up underneath to withstand the chilly gusts at sea, the wind burning skin just as badly as the sun. The man's feet were pale, as expected from both a surfer and a boater.

The second one was his appearance. His hair was neatly trimmed, and his beard had been as well at the time of his death, two more days of growth rendering it a little bristly and uneven in spots. Yet he looked really put together, charismatic even for a man in his fifties, lying dead on an autopsy table. There was an air of power, of authority to his features that had transcended his passing, probably carved into his facial tone from daily use. The way a woodworker's hands widen and become shaped a certain way, with square and wide palms and a strong, oversized thumb, John Doe's jaw muscles, tight, tense lips, and the lines around his mouth and across his tall forehead spoke of the power he once seemed to have wielded.

"Doc, do you have a time of death yet?" Elliot asked.

"I'd say, forty-eight to seventy-two hours, not more."

"Sunday evening, then?"

"Just Sunday; not sure if evening or morning. He's been out in the rain the entire time, and the water was cold. It slowed the decay process and kept the carrion feasters at bay some." He turned the folder he was holding the other way around for Elliot's benefit. "See the discoloration here, and here?" he asked, pointing to a section of the man's abdomen, captured in the photos attached to his report. "He was dumped there immediately after death and hasn't been moved. But your primary crime scene—"

"Is anyone's guess where that might be," Elliot muttered, shifting the mints around in his mouth to resist a wave of smells that invaded his nostrils when the doctor drew near. Formaldehyde seemed to ooze from the man's pores together with the smell of stale flesh. He almost dry-heaved but concealed the spasms of his stomach as a cough he covered in the crook of his elbow. Taking a few steps back, he found the tin of mints in his pocket, and threw a few more in his mouth.

Dr. Whitmore watched him with a slight frown. "Why didn't you say so?" He reached on a shelf and offered him a small jar of Vicks VapoRub for children. "Put some under your nose."

Elliot felt his cheeks flush with embarrassment. The man must've thought him a sissy, a greenhorn fixin' to lose his lunch at his first rodeo. But he didn't argue, nor did he pretend he was double-backboned when it came to the doc's fiefdom. Whatever it was about dead people, he had an issue with it and had known it all his life. Probably was gonna die with it too, unable to change or grow accustomed to it like Kay had. She was a natural; whatever she set her mind to do, she did.

"Thanks," he muttered, applying a generous amount under his nostrils and finally breathing normally.

"You'll thank me some more in just a minute," the ME said, a hint of a smile fluttering on his lips. "I found some evidence on the body."

"After all that rain?" Elliot whistled his admiration. "You could find a whisper in a whirlwind, Doc," he added, smiling widely and touching the brim of his hat with two fingers in a gesture of respect.

Doc Whitmore laughed, a soft, quiet laugh that brought myriad lines around the corners of his tired eyes. "I don't think that's true, but I found a long hair fiber, and we got lucky. It had the follicle still attached, and that means DNA."

Elliot frowned. "A woman's hair? You said long, right?"

"Yes, very, sixty-eight centimeters to be exact. Not sure yet if it's a woman's, but that's a strong possibility."

Elliot frowned. What did sixty-eight centimeters mean when it came to describing a suspect?

"Mid-back length," Dr. Whitmore added, as if reading his mind, "brown and straight. I found some carpet fibers too, in the creases of his jacket and pants. It could be from a car, but I can't confirm yet. Gray blue in color and polyester, that's all I can tell you right now."

Elliot nodded once, impressed. He stood and thanked him, getting ready to leave, but the doc picked up a small evidence pouch from the tray and showed it to him. It held a business card from a local psychiatrist with an appointment time and date, bent and softened and blurred by water but still in one piece, albeit barely legible.

"The chest pocket on his jacket was double-pouched. Found this inside. John Doe had a shrink."

Slack-jawed, Elliot wondered how he could've missed it when he'd searched the body. In his defense, the rain had been coming down hard, the fabric of the vic's jacket was soaked and sticky. It was nothing short of a miracle the card was still legible.

Elliot felt invigorated, chomping at the bit to go out there and find who his John Doe really was. He took a photo of the card with his phone, then of the vic's face. "This might be faster than your DNA, Doc," he said, hoping the medical examiner wouldn't find his comment insulting.

But Dr. Whitmore was already putting on fresh gloves, getting ready to continue his exam.

CHAPTER SIXTEEN

Call

"Nine-one-one, what's your emergency?" The operator's voice was a woman's, sounding calm and experienced.

The staticky recording played on Kay's laptop. She sat at her desk, leaning into it, volume at maximum, nervously running her sweaty palms against her thighs, hanging on every word. The bullpen had fallen eerily silent, the two deputies and Logan huddled behind her, listening. Even the drunk and disorderly in lockup stood still, clutching the bars of his cage and finally shutting up.

"Hello?" Kay recognized Heather's voice on the call. She was whispering and whimpering at the same time, her voice strangled by fear and loaded with tears. "Are you the police? Can you come?" she asked, against a backdrop of distant, muffled dialog and someone's rushed footsteps fading away.

"What's going on?" the operator asked. Kay had learned from the email forwarded by her boss that the operator, by the name of Carrie Keifer, was a veteran of the emergency communications center, with fifteen years on the job.

"He's come to take my sister," Heather whispered between sniffles. "Please," she begged, "he's gonna take Julie."

"Who is going to take her?"

"I—I don't know," the girl said, sadness strangling her as if she'd felt guilty for not knowing. "Julie told me to call you."

"What's your name?"

"Heather." She gasped and whimpered right after a loud bang was heard in the distant background.

"How old are you?" Carrie asked, the inflections in her voice a hint kinder.

"I'm eight," Heather replied. "Will you come?"

There was a brief pause on the call, while Carrie might've put her on mute and called someone else or checked her systems.

Emergency communications operators had an array of systems at their fingertips. They could efficiently dispatch first responders, locate an address on a map, triangulate the position of a mobile phone, and interact with local law enforcement, all while the caller was on the line. The procedure was simple. Pinpoint the location, verify it, validate there is an actual emergency, then send responders. Somewhere in this simple procedure, things had taken a wrong turn that had cost Cheryl her life. Maybe Julie's too. They better have a darn good explanation for that.

"Yes, someone will come soon. Who's in the house with you?" Carrie had asked, her voice a little muffled. Her headset mic might've shifted, or something else was happening. In the background, Kay could hear the operator typing fast, while at the same time the dialog continued in Cheryl's house, voices raised, Cheryl's pitch one of fear and alarm. She couldn't make out what she said, though; the call recording was of poor quality, loaded with static, which made no sense in the digital era. It might've come from the call recording system itself, and it might need the help of a technician to eliminate the sound frequencies that kept her from discerning what was said by Cheryl and the unsub.

"Heather," Carrie said, "who's there with you?"

"My mommy and my sisters," Heather replied. Kay could hear her shallow, rapid breathing against the mouthpiece. She must've been terrified, scared out of her mind. "A bad man came."

"Who is that man? Do you know him?"

"Umm," she hesitated, then said something unintelligible. "Please come quick." Then, in a muted voice, "Erin, no. Don't go downstairs." The thump of something hitting the floor, then Erin crying for a brief moment, until the cries became muffled. "Be quiet," Heather whispered. But the phone seemed now remote, probably abandoned on the floor while she'd taken care of her sister. "You can't let him hear you."

Those words tugged at Kay's heartstrings.

"Monster," Erin's crying voice was heard, barely intelligible.

"Shhh," Heather's voice, wobbly and broken, still sounded distant.

"Hello? Are you still with me?" Carrie intervened. "If you can hear me, say something."

"Yes," Heather whispered after some distinctive noises told Kay she'd picked up her phone again. In the background, she could hear the clattering of falling objects crashing on the floor and a long screech as if a piece of furniture was being dragged over the tiles; maybe a chair, or perhaps the table was being pushed. Gasps, grunts, and shouted words she couldn't comprehend, the sounds of the fierce struggle between Cheryl and her attacker.

Cheryl was about to be murdered.

"What's your address? Where do you live?" Carrie asked. "What color is your house?"

"I live in Angel—"

At that moment, Julie screamed, her shriek blood-curdling. A heavy thump followed, probably the sound of Cheryl's body hitting the ground.

"Hello?" Carrie asked. "Are you still with me? I need your address." Her calm was wearing off, undertones of alarm coloring her voice.

For what seemed like forever, the muffled struggle sounds continued in the distance, the occasional yelps and wails from

Julie making it clearly across the crashes and grunts and the clunking of objects landing on the floor. Heather's breathing had accelerated, and her whimpers were louder, fearful, panicked. Julie must've fought her attacker fiercely; she'd been able to resist a good thirty-two seconds. She screamed once more, but her scream ended abruptly in a gasp as if she'd been hit in the stomach. She called for her mother in a weak, shaky voice. Then she called again, louder, but half a heartbeat later, a blow silenced her, followed by the unmistakable thud of an inert body hitting the ground.

Kay's blood froze in her veins. Was Julie still alive? Had she survived that blow? She had to assume yes, being she'd been taken from the scene. But she could be hurt or incapacitated in the hands of a stone-cold killer.

"Hello?" Carrie had called, but Heather didn't respond. Only her fast breathing and muffled sobs were heard, while in the background, the killer had opened the side door, its hinges making a recognizable, loud squeak that Kay had noticed during her visits to the crime scene. Then Kay heard the even more distant hum of an engine coming to life. Car doors opening and being slammed shut, before the engine sound faded away.

"Hello?" Carrie kept insisting, but Heather had fallen silent, only her shattered gasps for air telling Kay she still held the phone in her hand.

Footsteps, hesitant and shuffled, and quiet whimpers were all that was heard for a long moment, sprinkled here and there with the familiar squeaking of old hardwood being stepped on. Then Heather's voice, calling, "Mommy?"

Then the call ended, leaving the bullpen eerily silent for a beat.

"Well, that's a Ford F-150 diesel, if I've ever heard one," the wino said.

One of the deputies walked over to the lockup and pounded his fist against the bars. "When we want your opinion, we'll ask for it. Now shut the hell up."

"When's he due for arraignment?" Sheriff Logan asked Deputy Hobbs, tilting his head toward the prisoner.

"Not till three," Hobbs replied with a frustrated scoff. "Something to do with backlogs and a judge being out with a bad case of the flu. But I believe he's right. I drive a diesel Ford truck, and it sounds just like that."

Kay played the end of the call again.

"Yup, that's it," Hobbs said. "Ford truck, diesel."

"And new too, if you schmucks are willin' to listen. That baby that's purrin' on your recorded call is a V6 turbo diesel B20 with autostart-stop technology," he recited, pride filling his voice.

Kay stood and walked closer to the lockup, instantly regretting it when the smell of metabolized alcohol and stale urine hit her nostrils. The man grinned, showing some stained teeth, then wiped his palms against his shirt as if she was going to shake his hand through the bars.

"Now, how could you possibly know that?" Kay asked.

"'Cause that's exactly what I drive, and it set me back north of sixty grand," he replied. "That click you heard, right before the engine turns? That's the engine block heater kicking in. It comes with autostart, and that's only available in a 3.0 V6 diesel." He grunted, then cleared his throat, thankfully refraining from spitting on the floor. "Well, it comes in the 2.7 liter too, but it don't sound like that."

Kay stared at him from underneath a frown, wondering how much stock she could put in his statement.

"Wanna hear it for yourself, pretty lady? Go check out the truck you impounded last night after you pulled me over. I only had a couple of beers, and you locked me up like an animal when that murderer's out there. You should be ashamed of yourselves," he muttered, "and you call yourselves cops." This time, a ball of spit landed on the concrete floor with a splat, right by Kay's shoe.

She ignored it. "You're saying you have a truck just like the one you think you heard on that call?"

"More like had... now *you* have it." He sniffled and quickly ran the sleeve of his dirty jacket against his nose. "Hey, if I'm proven right, do I get a reward or something?"

She'd already left, returning to the desk, a gnawing question still bothering her.

"Why didn't they respond? I want to speak to that operator."

"They sent the call disposition report," Logan said. "They thought it was a hoax, someone eager to get a million hits on social media or something by putting their kid up to it. The phone was a burner, triangulation failed because only a single tower picked it up, and they thought that was done on purpose."

"How could they possibly believe it was a hoax? Based on what?"

"Because Heather said the perp was going to take her sister. What kind of perp advertises?"

She shook her head in disbelief. "You've got to be kidding me! Have you listened to the call? Does it sound staged to you? And I heard real concern in the operator's voice."

The sheriff grimaced in a failed attempt to smile, but she could see she'd overstepped. He straightened his back and thrust his chin forward while his eyes turned steely. When he spoke, his voice was low-pitched and loaded. "Detective, in how many cases have you heard of perps walking into a home and saying, 'I'll take one hostage,' and then naming the one they are planning to take? It never happens like that. The comms center isn't the enemy here." He breathed, a long and frustrated sigh. "Toward the end of the call, they decided to respond just to be on the safe side, but they couldn't get an address. Without triangulation, they had a twenty-mile radius area to cover, with over forty locations whose names start with Angel." He lowered his gaze for a moment, then looked straight at her. "They even notified us that we might have a nine-one-one call faker in our area. They worked it by the book, Kay."

She pushed herself away from the desk and stood, pacing angrily. She would've loved to teach that Carrie a thing or two about fear and pain, about being all alone in the dark, hiding under a bed, while the people you're counting on for help just shrug you off like a bad joke. But she wasn't going to waste another moment on that, not while Julie was still out there.

She had better things to do. One or both of Julie's sisters had seen the unsub.

CHAPTER SEVENTEEN

Scribbles

Julie felt weak and sore, the effort of getting up from the concrete floor taking every bit of energy she had left. She'd lost track of time, her days and nights spent in the equalizing pale light of a yellow lightbulb hanging up high from the ceiling. Not a single ray of sun made it through the cracks of the boarded window; maybe it wasn't light outside, not anywhere in the world. Not anymore.

She threw a side glance at the bed, made with clean sheets and a comforter that looked so tempting after she'd slept on the floor, but she couldn't bring herself to go near the bed, as if touching it would've unleashed some sort of evil that loomed near it. As if resting in it would've made her descend into a new level of darkness, one she could never hope to emerge from.

She told herself it was better to sleep on the cold floor with her back against the door. As such, no one could surprise her, no one could sneak up on her and—

And what?

What was she terrified of? She hadn't seen her captor since she'd fought him at her house. She'd woken up alone in that cellar, groggy, her mouth parchment dry, jolts of migraine bouncing around in her head. She'd been drugged. Her mother had taught her about date rape drugs, about how it felt, so she could easily recognize the signs and save herself. Now she knew, for the little good that did her.

The thought of her mom, of the evening she'd given her a pill and asked her to mindfully note how it felt and never forget it, brought tears to her swollen eyes. Julie had been reckless and selfish beyond belief. Just because she didn't want to believe something was true didn't make it less of a threat, less likely to happen to her. And now, the image of her mother's body, lifeless in a pool of blood on the kitchen floor, was forever burned into her memory, for as long or as short as her life was going to be.

It wasn't like she'd made a mistake, no. She'd willfully disobeyed her, disregarded her plea to get ready, so they could leave that evening. After she'd seen what had happened and knowing what she'd done, and after she'd witnessed the lengths her mother had gone to keep her safe, she preferred to ignore the danger, the consequences, just because none of it seemed real. What kind of person does that? What kind of stupid could she be?

Shaky and feeble, she paced the room with an unsteady gait, ignoring the stomach pain she was feeling. She hadn't touched any food since she'd been taken; there wasn't any. She'd survived on water from the small sink in the bathroom, using the scoop of her hand to drink it. It smelled funny, of mildew and deep, dark, moss-covered well walls. Exhausted and too weak to stand, she let herself slide to the ground.

Fear held her stomach in a tight grip. It was primal and intense like she'd never felt before. She'd always been safe, sheltered by her mother, her teachers, her family. She'd never been preyed on until now. She had no words for it in her vocabulary and no idea what would happen to her. But she'd watched enough TV for her imagination to run wild with horror scenarios woven one after another as she sat awake, leaning against the door, hugging her knees.

How would he kill her?

In her mind, there was no doubt she was going to die. Every waking moment she waited and listened, holding her breath at times, wondering when he would come. What he would do. How she would die. And somehow, she found those thoughts less painful than wondering about her sisters or remembering her mother's last moments. How she'd looked at her, not blaming but pleading, worry and regret woven together wordlessly in a gaze she would never forget. How she'd reached for her, her hand extended toward her just as that man was pouncing and striking, not allowing her a single moment to say goodbye.

Tears burned her eyes, seeding a knot in her throat.

Restless, she stood again, leaning against the wall for support. She banged against the walls, the door, even in that stupid mirror that didn't belong, but no one came, and no other sound but the distant rain kept her company.

She wished he would come already. She wanted to ask him why.

She wanted to scream at him and pummel him with her fists until her knuckles turned raw. Then she wanted him to suffer, to feel the hurt that squeezed her heart and weighed on her chest until she couldn't breathe. She didn't know what she'd do to make that happen; her imagination never went that far.

She wanted to be awake when he came, alerted by the moving door against her back. Not asleep between those sheets, no matter how cold it would get, how hard the cellar floor.

But what if he never came?

What if she died of hunger, alone, not knowing if her sisters were still alive?

Feeling suddenly weak at the knees, she let herself slide against the wall until she hit the floor. Hugging her knees, she rested her cheek on her folded arm, letting her eyes wander aimlessly on the stained wall.

Something caught her attention.

By the door, there was something scrawled in the masonry, about a foot above the ground. She crawled the short distance on her hands and knees and squinted, crouched closer to the scribbles, almost impossible to decipher in the dim light.

HELP ME

Written in scratchy caps dug into a section of the drywall, the two words brought a deep, lasting shiver down her spine.

Someone had been held captive in there before.

CHAPTER EIGHTEEN

Colors

The unsub must've been someone who knew the family; Kay had no doubt about that.

To Sheriff Logan's clearly made point, kidnappers don't usually advertise. Some sadistic serial killers do—as part of their psychological torture routine, to get their victims to comply out of fear for their loved ones. But the typical kidnappers don't. They grab their victims and run, usually from a lower-risk location than their own home, where they are surrounded by other family members gathered around the dinner table, sharing a glass of wine and waiting for the stew to be done.

It didn't make sense unless the unsub was someone who had been, at least initially, welcome in the Coleman residence.

Nothing was typical about this case. The killer didn't care about loose ends, apparently. He'd killed Cheryl and immobilized Julie, rendering her unconscious, if not dead. Yet, before leaving, he didn't bother to check the rest of the house. He'd just grabbed Julie and made for his vehicle, then immediately left the area, without even bothering to close the door. It seemed that Julie was the reason he'd visited, and Cheryl had been in the way.

But then, why not grab Julie from somewhere else? Why risk a standoff with the girl's mother? What kind of kidnapper doesn't spend a few minutes casing out the place, seeing through the windows how many people live there? Was it possible he knew about the other girls but didn't care?

And, most of all, why take Julie? On the nine-one-one call, she'd heard Cheryl and the unsub arguing, although she couldn't make out what they were saying. That didn't suggest a blitz attack; that spoke of an existing relationship, of explaining, of pleading and persuading. If Julie's father weren't deceased, Kay would've thought this was a family abduction gone wrong. More common than the average citizen assumes, estranged and disgruntled spouses grab their own children and take them away from the parent who has legal custody; from the law's standpoint, they're kidnappers. Many times, the abducting parent's concerns are legitimate, especially when drugs or violence are factors, while other times people just snap after having lost their family, their reason to be alive, and can't tolerate a single moment without their child.

But that didn't fit at all, not with all immediate family members accounted for and completely lacking motive.

Someone knew who that man was, and that was Heather. Maybe Erin too.

She closed her laptop and walked quickly toward the back, passing by the holding cells where the wino greeted her with a sleazy smile and a whiff of back alley that churned her stomach. She found the girls in the nap room with Deputy Farrell. She'd set up Erin with a flipchart pad and some markers, and the little girl was doodling away, sharp-angled lines in black and green.

Heather sat on the edge of her bed, absentminded, her stare still vacant, her cheeks drained of blood. Since she'd woken up screaming, she hadn't cried a tear yet; she was still in shock. She held her head straight, with her hands folded neatly in her lap. Her chest barely moved; her breathing was shallow and slow.

"I need to speak with her," Kay said, speaking softly to Farrell.

"Um, I'll take Erin to the interview room. She won't know the difference."

Farrell must've been a great mother. She was patient and kind, always smiling when she talked to the girls, her voice calm and reassuring, her round face pleasant and seeming relaxed. She collected the girl's paper and markers, then took her little hand and walked out of the room with Erin in tow. As she was leaving, the child turned her head and looked regretfully behind, toward Heather, but her sister didn't react.

Kay waited a moment, ready to intervene if Heather had a delayed response to her sister leaving the room, but nothing happened. Then she approached her slowly and sat on the cot by her side. Wrapping her arm around the girl's shoulders, she waited, anticipating the tension in her body would start to ease off. A few long minutes later, it still hadn't.

"You were very brave," Kay said, her voice a soothing whisper, "calling for help the way you did."

She didn't react. Not a change in her shallow breathing, in her posture, in the tension in her shoulders.

"You held your own really well. You make me proud, you know," Kay continued. "And I think you can help me." She leaned over to look at Heather's face, partially hidden by unruly curls of long brown hair. "You could tell me where to look for your sister."

She sat perfectly still, staring into thin air. Kay couldn't be sure that girl had heard what was being said, but she continued, just in case there was some part of Heather's brain that could still process her messages, that could emerge from the trauma with a will to survive, to move past what had happened. She was dissociated, as if the trauma was still continuing, as if she were still at her house, witnessing her mother being killed, her sister being abducted. Her young mind struggled to process all that had happened, overwhelmed by intense emotions, choosing to shut itself down on some level until it could cope with everything. Forcing Heather out of that state was not only dangerous but also irresponsible and had the potential to cause permanent damage to the child's frail psyche. She hoped there was still a way to reach her, to get the answers she was looking for, by gently grounding her back into reality, with the speed and level of detail her mind was able to handle. Julie's life depended on it.

"Do you know who took Julie?" Kay asked, and silence was the answer. "Who came to visit your mother on Monday night?" She caressed Heather's hair with soft motions, inviting her to lean in and rest her head against Kay's shoulder, but it was as if the little girl wasn't really there. She sat completely still, seemingly unaware of her surroundings, her brain effectively shut off, distancing itself from a reality that was too painful to endure.

This was going nowhere, Kay had to admit. The only alternative left was to interview Heather under hypnosis while helping her get grounded and process her trauma response a little better. She'd had success in the past with both cognitive interviewing and hypnosis. And for that, she needed a controlled environment, free of noises and interruptions.

The interrogation room was soundproof to some extent, but on second thought, she decided to stay put instead and conduct the session from the nap room, provided someone could make sure there were no disruptions.

She opened the door and called for Deputy Farrell to ask her to take care of Erin for a while longer while setting everything up. When Farrell came out of the interview room, she brought a sheet of flipchart paper, scribbled in black and green marker.

"Detective Young suggested I give paper and markers to Erin, so she could draw her monster," she said, with a hesitant, incredulous smile. "This little girl is four; it's not like she can come up with the perp's composite, right?"

Kay nodded, wondering where that was going.

"Well, the little girl drew this," she said, keeping the sheet against the wall for Kay to see. "That's the monster she keeps talking about."

The doodle resembled teeth and fangs shown in an open mouth depicted simply as an oval line, with what appeared to be blood dripping from them, only drawn in green, not red. It could've been something she saw during the attack, and it might've had some relevance, but… green blood?

"Did she have a red marker available?"

Farrell nodded. "First thing I checked."

"Interesting." Taking the drawing with her, she went to the interview room where Erin was working on another version of the same drawing, only bigger, still using green instead of red for the blood.

As if that case could get any stranger.

She crouched by Erin's chair and took her hand in hers, squeezing gently.

"You have real talent; did you know that?"

The child continued drawing sharp, elongated teeth with the black marker. "Yes. My mommy told me," she whispered, her voice fraught with tears. "Where's my mommy?"

Kay and Farrell exchanged a brief look. The deputy stood in the doorway, keeping an eye on Heather through the open door to the nap room.

Kay lowered her voice to a whisper and asked, "Could you please help me with something?"

Erin lifted her eyes from the paper and nodded.

"You see, I'm a monster slayer."

"You are?" Her voice caught a higher pitch, lifted from the depths of her sadness by traces of excitement.

"Yes, I am, and there's nothing I'd like more than to catch the monster that came to your house the other night."

Erin's mouth opened a little, but she didn't say a word, her eyes rounded in amazement.

Without drawing any attention to herself, Kay swiped the green marker off the table with a sleight of hand. "Could you please draw this monster for me once more?" Erin nodded and pulled toward her the new sheet of paper Kay had detached from the flipchart pad. "Draw it carefully, with all the details you remember, so when I see this monster, I will recognize him and slay him." Kay gestured with her hands as if she were wielding a heavy sword. "Will you do that for me, sweetie?"

Surprisingly, the girl shook her head, her shoulder-length hair bouncing in lively curls of auburn silk. "I can't," she replied, looking at Kay with confusion written all over her scrunched features. "You took my green."

Speechless, Kay placed the green marker back on the table. "There you go, sweetie," she said, "now you draw me that monster, just like you saw it." She ruffled her curls playfully to silence the sadness that gripped her heart, watching the little girl doodling on the scratched and dented metallic table in the interview room, oblivious of where she was or how her circumstances had changed.

She drew a long breath to instill courage in herself for what she was about to do and tugged a little at the collar of her turtleneck, wishing she'd chosen a button-up shirt for that day's attire. For some reason, her favorite pullover seemed to choke her.

Then Kay walked over to Logan's office, her gait stern and determined, rushed.

His office door was open, the sound from a TV newscast loud enough for her to catch. It was coming from Logan's wall-mounted TV, the one they all turned to whenever local news channels covered any of their cases. But this time, Logan was watching something else.

"Remnants of Hurricane Edward still battering the West Coast, Northern California has been at the center of the storm as it made landfall only a hundred miles north of San Francisco," the familiar news anchor said. "Four people have been reported dead, twenty-six were injured, and forty-two are still missing after heavy rainfall led to landslides along the I-5 corridor, sweeping away houses, bridges, and critical infrastructure, and blocking access to emergency vehicles for several remote areas near Mount Chester in Franklin County. Emergency crews are headed toward the site where the new hospital is being built, where the threat of new landslides—"

"We're getting hit pretty badly," Logan said, muting the sound of the TV. The newscast continued, showing swelled waters rushing over what was left of a bridge on State Route 3. Then the image switched to a house being swept downstream when the side of the hill it was built on gave way and collapsed. "I'm calling off the search," he added, clasping his hands together in a gesture of powerlessness.

Kay stared at him in disbelief, but he avoided her gaze. "You can't—" she started but then stopped herself. She'd already stepped on his toes not too long ago; there was no reason to repeat the offense. "Please, think of Julie."

He stood and paced the floor angrily, staring out the window where the dark, loaded clouds rushed and clumped together in angry whirlwinds of rain and thunder. "What do you think I've been thinking of?" he said, raising his voice to the loudest she'd ever heard the man speak. "Don't you think I know I might be signing her death sentence right now?"

She let the air she'd been holding in her lungs escape. It wasn't like he had much choice. The weather was not letting up, and everyone had been pulling double shifts since Cheryl's body was found. Since that morning, calls for support with everything from traffic accidents to missing persons and storm-related injuries had quadrupled. It was about to get worse.

"What do *you* have?" Logan asked, turning to face her with his hands propped on his hips. "Are you ready to let those girls go? They've been here for longer than we agreed to. We need all hands on deck with this damn storm."

She thought for a moment before opening her mouth. "I'm about to start a hypnosis session with Heather."

"Now?" he asked, his pitch elevated in disbelief. "You said we'd have all the information from her by now. And you have nothing?"

She shook her head slowly for a brief moment, staring at the run-down, stained carpet, gathering her thoughts. Then she lifted her gaze, looking straight at him. "People's minds aren't like drawers we pull open, get what we want, then slam shut on our way out. Traumatized minds, even less so. Children's traumatized minds are the frailest and most sensitive. Accessing them the wrong way, too soon or too abruptly, can cause permanent damage. But I believe she's ready now, and so am I; we have to be. We'll know within the hour." She paused for a beat, waiting for questions or pushback. There was nothing but silence and a look of deep-seated concern tinged with doubt on his weary face.

"And you've done this before?" His eyes were piercing and filled with doubt in her abilities.

"I'm not a clinical hypnotherapist, if that's your question; I had chosen a different career path when I joined the FBI as a behavioral analyst," she replied, holding back a frustrated sigh. "I do have the knowledge and the formal training to be these girls' psychologist and conduct the hypnotic interview."

"I'll take this long-winded answer as a yes." His gaze remained focused, inquisitive. "Then why are you here? What do you need?" he asked, while a frown ridged his brow.

"Perfect silence and someone to make sure the session isn't interrupted. It's very important—"

"Hobbs, get in here," he called, not letting her finish.

The deputy rushed over. "Yes, boss."

"Get that DUI out of holding and put him in the van, outside. Make sure he's cuffed." The deputy nodded and disappeared. Sheriff Logan clicked the TV remote, and the screen went dark. "I'll keep things quiet for you myself, Detective. Now get me those answers."

CHAPTER NINETEEN

Hypnosis

There were so many ways interviewing Heather under hypnosis could go wrong.

Unlike cognitive interviews, questions asked under hypnosis could yield answers that were only partly real or not at all. But cognitive interviewing required the witness to be able to sustain a conversation, to access memories directly, lucidly, in a waking state, and that wasn't going to happen in Heather's case.

But the increase in recall with hypnosis techniques was often associated with misleading information that was regarded as highly reliable by law enforcement, *because* it was obtained under hypnosis. The susceptibility of the witness to be influenced by the questions she was asked during the interview made Kay rehearse the line of questioning she was about to engage in, whispering to herself, making sure they came across just as perfectly neutral when spoken as they sounded in her mind.

Before pushing the door open and entering the nap room, she stopped one more time and sent a quick email, requesting a favor from an old friend and colleague—an FBI technical analyst who had both the knowledge and the equipment necessary to clean the nine-one-one call recording of all the static, breathing sounds, and background noises, and enhance the voices.

Then she looked at Heather through the small window. She still sat on the side of the bed, hands folded in her lap, seemingly unaware of the passing of time. Kay took a moment to consider whether to move her to a more comfortable position, where she could rest her back against something. She decided some pillows would do the trick, because moving her could agitate her and make the hypnotic induction more challenging.

She entered the room quietly, then closed the door behind her without a sound. Throwing the window a quick look over her shoulder, she found Sheriff Logan was looking in, keeping watch. Gathering all the clumpy, white-and-blue-striped pillows from the other bunks, she spoke softly, in a soothing voice. "It's me, Kay, and you're safe with me." She propped the pillows behind her back. "There, you can lean back a little now. Your back must be sore after all this time."

She waited, her eyes fixed on the girl's shoulders, waiting for the smallest hint of movement. A long moment later, her shoulders dropped just a little bit. The shirt she wore, a couple of sizes too large, made her seem smaller than she was, more vulnerable.

Kay covered the girl's legs with a blanket and continued the breathing exercise, noticing how her body continued to relax in the tiniest of increments.

"Good," Kay said, "that's a good girl. You deserve to rest and relax and feel safe. Breathe with me," she continued, speaking softly, slowly. "Breathe in, hold it for a moment, then breathe out. In, hold, and out. That's it."

At first, Heather's breathing was offbeat, but slowly she started following her guidance. That meant she could be reached, she was listening, and willing to connect.

"Feel the pillows under your body supporting you," Kay said. "Hear my voice, and know you're safe. No harm will come to you. Breathe in, hold it for a moment, breathe out. Yes."

She watched Heather breathe, her chest rising and falling rhythmically, following her instructions. When she felt the girl was ready, she continued. "We'll go on a journey together. It will be like watching a movie. Whatever happens on the screen cannot touch you. Follow my voice and know you're perfectly safe."

The child still stared ahead with that disheartening, empty look in her eyes, but her eyelids were growing heavy.

"As I count down from five to one, you will be more and more relaxed." Kay counted, "Five," her voice calm, melodious, soothing. "You feel yourself relaxing. Four. Going deeper and deeper, doing great. Three. You're drifting further and further from the world, deeply relaxed. Two. Deeper, excellent, follow my voice into feeling totally relaxed. One. You are now in a deep trance."

For a moment, Kay wondered if her choice of words had been adequate. Would an eight-year-old know what a deep trance was? Apparently, this one did, judging by the relaxed posture and calm breathing.

"Hear my voice and know you're completely safe," Kay said, starting with grounding techniques—Heather's trauma was the biggest challenge to overcome before learning anything about the events that had taken place the night her mother was killed. "Feel the support under your body, the warmth of the blanket sheltering you in a cocoon of safety." She paused for a long moment, then asked, "Can you talk?"

Kay held her breath for what seemed like forever.

"Yes," Heather finally answered, her voice a little strangled, coarse. She hadn't spoken a word in almost two days.

"Take me to your house, two nights ago, and show me what you see," Kay said. Heather's breathing picked up, racing toward panicky. "I'm right here, and you're perfectly safe. Nothing you will see can hurt you." Heather's breathing slowed a little. "Can you see who came to visit your mom?"

"The little weasel is telling on me again," Heather said, her speech slightly slurred. Her jaws were tense, clenched tightly. "But Mom doesn't care. Julie's late and Mom wants us to go."

"Go where?" Kay asked.

Heather shook her head a couple of times, her hair dancing loosely around her face. "*Away. We have to run, to leave this place, to save Julie,*" she said, in what sounded like an imitation of an adult woman's voice. "But Julie doesn't believe her, and she's late, and Mom is angry," she continued in her normal, high-pitched and rushed voice.

She stopped talking, reliving memories in her mind. Her eyes moved rapidly under closed eyelids; her head shook occasionally as if she rejected what she was seeing.

"What's happening now?"

"Julie's back, and Mom is mad. It's too late to leave, it's dark outside. Mom's afraid." Her voice trailed off, strangled by fear.

"Who is she afraid of?"

She wrestled with a memory, making spasmodic gestures with her arms. "Someone's at the door, but Julie's taking us upstairs. He can't see her."

Kay frowned, clutching her hands tightly together to pace herself. "Who can't he see?"

"Julie," Heather said, then gasped. "He will take her."

The eye movements continued, and her agitation increased.

"You're safe with me," Kay repeated. "Nothing you see or hear can hurt you. It's like watching a movie. What happens next?"

"*Glass of wine?*" Heather said, in that imitation of her mother's voice. "*I'll have some,*" she replied, now imitating a man's voice. "*You know why I'm here,*" she continued in the same low-pitched voice that must've been the killer's. "*No, leave us alone, please,*" she continued, now in her mother's voice. "*You don't have to do this.*"

She fell silent, while her breathing accelerated, and her agitation increased.

"I'm right here, and you're safe. Breathe in, hold it in with me, breathe out. There. What's happening now?"

A spasm shook the girl's entire body, as if she'd been electrocuted. "*It has to happen,*" she spoke between clenched jaws, in a low-pitched voice. "*You've known all along. You know she must. Tonight.*" She started shaking badly, as if she were caught in a winter blizzard, her teeth clattering. "*No,*" she shouted, in what seemed to be her mother's voice. "*Heather, call nine-one-one, just like Mom taught you.*" That must've been Julie telling her to call for help.

"You're safe, here with me," Kay said calmly, watching with deep concern how her little body writhed reliving the horrors. She had to pull her out. "I will count to five, and you'll wake up, feeling rested and strong and safe. One, you're starting to—"

Heather shrieked, then called, "Mommy?"

"You're safe, waking up rested and relaxed," Kay continued, rushing through the waking process. "Two. You're following my voice and know you're safe; you're starting to wake up. Three. You feel like you're waking from a deep sleep." Her agitation subsided and her breathing stabilized. Then a long, pained sigh left her chest. "Four. You're getting ready to wake up, rested and refreshed. Five. You're awake."

Heather opened her eyes and focused them on Kay.

"Hello," Kay said. "Did you sleep well?"

For a moment she seemed disoriented, but then, as she remembered her reality, a heart-wrenching wail ripped through her chest. She broke down in uncontrollable sobs, clinging to Kay's neck.

"He killed my mommy," she said, barely able to speak between gasps and wails.

Kay wrapped her arms around her and rocked her back and forth, soothing her with soft-spoken words, while struggling to keep her own tears in check. Heather's sobs quickly subsided, too quickly, and her body turned inert, distant. Pulling away gently, Kay looked at the child, searching her eyes. The same vacant stare had returned, and her tears had stopped falling, the last of them drying out in stains on the colorful fabric of her borrowed shirt.

Her mind had shut off again.

Kay wanted to scream. If she'd had the unsub in front of her, she wouldn't need a gun to end him; she'd rip his heart out with her bare hands.

Forcing herself to breathe away her rage, she stood and walked to the door, where the sheriff's frown promised nothing good.

"What the hell was that?" he asked, as soon as she'd closed the door. "With the *has-to-happen* story? How did these folks know Julie was about to be taken, and why didn't they tell anyone? Geez…" Frustrated, he took his hand to his forehead so forcefully it sounded like a slap.

Suddenly she felt immensely tired, as if the last hour had burned all her energy somehow, leaving her an empty husk. There were no answers to the sheriff's questions, nor hers. Nothing made any sense.

But there wasn't any time for tiredness, not with Julie still missing. She wished Elliot was there, by her side, her secret weapon. When he was around, things seemed more logical somehow, easier, as if his broad shoulders sustained the weight of the world that was crushing her.

"I don't know what to believe," she replied honestly, although omitting to mention the high rate of error documented with hypnotic interviewing of witnesses. "I was expecting, um, I don't know what I was expecting. Maybe a name? I'm thinking this unsub was someone Cheryl knew, and I thought—"

"So, you have nothing," Logan summarized coldly, sucking his teeth in disappointment. "Well, this story's about to end. The girls' family is here to claim them, and they're threatening legal action if they're not released into their custody immediately."

"But, Sheriff, we have to try again. Heather will remember—"

"You see them, over there, by my office? Marleen and Avery Montgomery, the girls' great-aunt and great-grandfather." The sheriff pointed out a man and a woman who were impatiently pacing the small hallway back and forth. The woman, elegantly dressed in a beige suit and matching scarf over a black, silk blouse, was in her early fifties. Her sleek, shoulder-length hair was perfectly colored and styled as if she'd just left the salon. She seemed relatively pleasant when she wasn't looking in Kay's direction. When she did, her eyes turned into daggers, and her pretentious, menacing smile promised no good. The man who was with her must've been well over seventy. The dark navy blue of his shirt contrasted with his white, neatly trimmed beard and brought color to his eyes. He was tall and walked straight, his head held high, towering over his companion. Their overall demeanor spoke of wealth and power, ingrained in their behavior the way it becomes with people who have had it for a very long time. "I have a hurricane landfall to deal with. Whatever it is you want to say, say it to them and see if it sticks," the sheriff added, lowering his voice. "That was our agreement."

CHAPTER TWENTY

Dr. Edgell

Dr. Vella Edgell's office was housed in the Mount Chester Medical Center building, on the second floor. The small plaza in front of the building—usually teeming with pedestrian traffic attracted by the smell of fresh donuts and coffee spread generously by the coffee shop near the entrance—was now deserted, washed by heavy raindrops carried by the strong winds and slammed against the asphalt in angry bursts.

Elliot liked dry weather. Back where he grew up, it was so dry he was spitting cotton. For the most part, California had been reasonable from that perspective, only a few of these massive storms battering the area since he'd moved there from Austin, Texas. He'd left the Lone Star State in his rearview mirror because he just couldn't keep his head screwed on straight when it came to the woman he'd worked with, and now he had to deal with the stupid rain and learn to like it.

Eyeing the entrance and going slowly, he drove onto the deserted sidewalk all the way to the entrance, leaving his flashers on. From there, in a few quick large strides, he'd made it inside, but even so, he'd taken enough rain to feel the legs of his jeans getting soaked. He stomped his feet a couple of times, shaking off water like a stray dog, still mumbling curses after he'd slipped and almost fell on the wet concrete that bore the logo of the medical center in pink and gold.

Taking the stairs to the second floor, he found Dr. Edgell's office immediately, the first one on the left. Tastefully decorated, the waiting room was empty, but he could hear a voice coming from the office. The receptionist's desk was bare and cleared of the objects that normally clutter such workspaces, explaining why his calls to the office had gone straight to voicemail. A faint scent of lavender floated through the air, emerging from an essential oil dispenser plugged into a wall socket by the bookcase.

He hesitated for a moment, knowing how Kay would've reacted if she learned he'd interrupted a patient's therapy session. He listened, taking off his hat and putting his ear close to the door, and heard a woman's voice talking about carpeting several rooms, installation costs, and other such matters in a one-sided conversation. He wasn't going to interrupt much.

He knocked twice, then tentatively opened the door and looked inside.

The woman, a tall and slender blonde with long, sleek hair, raised a frustrated glance at him. Then she seemed to notice the badge he was holding and invited him in with a rushed hand gesture. Her frustration melted and turned into a pleasant, almost flirty smile with every step he took on her thick, oriental carpet as she sized him up without the faintest attempt to hide her interest.

She wrapped up the call with a quick and unceremonious, "I'll have to ring you back," then extended her hand. "Vella Edgell," she introduced herself.

He shook her hand briefly, then took two steps back as he said his name. "Detective Young."

She leaned against the large oak desk and crossed her legs at the ankles, showing off tan skin and high heel, black patent shoes, while he stood awkwardly, still holding his hat in his hand.

"Please, take a seat," she motioned toward her couch. "What can I do for you, um, Detective?"

He set his hat on the couch but chose to remain standing. He pulled up the photo of the doctor's business card on his phone and showed her the screen. "We're investigating the death of a man who had your appointment card on him. Seems he was your patient."

"Oh?" she reacted, surprised, worry washing over her face. "Can you share his name?"

"Well, that's exactly what we're trying to figure out. For now, he's a John Doe. According to this, he was supposed to see you next Monday at ten." He flipped a few screens over, then showed her the man's photo.

She looked at the picture, then at him for a moment, before walking around her desk swaying her hips, her heels clacking loudly on the hardwood floor not covered by the rug. She sat in front of her computer and tapped a few keys, her fingernails clicking against the keyboard. A few moments later, she said, "I wanted to make sure, but yes, that's Mr. Smith."

He smiled incredulously. "That's it? That's all you're going to give me? Mr. Smith?"

She batted her eyelids a couple of times and lowered her gaze, then looked at him with an apologetic smile. "That's all I have, Detective, because that's all he would say. He only had one session, paid in cash, and was reluctant to come into the office; he requested we do the sessions by phone, but that's not how I work," she added, her voice soft and melodious, yet professional at the same time. She leaned over the desk, resting her elbows on the shiny surface and clasping her hands together. "I study the patients' body language to identify areas where therapy can best assist in achieving their goals."

The way she looked at him made him uncomfortable. He shifted his weight from one foot to the other, stepping in place. Maybe in another world, he would've been flattered by her interest. It was strange how women had stopped mattering since he'd met Kay.

"What was wrong with him?" he asked, his voice a little colder than he'd anticipated.

She pulled back, choosing to lean against the backrest of her leather chair, her smile gone, and her eyes loaded with unfiltered disappointment.

"You see, Detective, that's exactly why people choose to pay in cash and give fake names when they come into my office," she replied, anger seeping through the low notes of her voice. "It's easy to believe that people have to have something wrong with them to see a psychologist. But most of them have goals for their lives—want to better themselves, become someone more polished, more successful, someone happier. How this is wrong, I can't begin to understand."

"I apologize," Elliot started to say, taken aback by the passion in Dr. Edgell's voice.

"It's not your fault, Detective; it's the entire society's fault. As a society, people spread the stigma of mental health with the juvenile excitement of a pubescent boy reading foul messages on a restroom stall door. Because it feels so damn good to say that so-and-so is crazy, right?" She stared at him with firmness in her frown and a tense jawline. "You know what, Detective? My patients, dead or alive, have rights. Why don't you come back and see me after you've secured a warrant?" She stood, crossing her arms at her chest in a stance that was clear as day.

But he wasn't leaving without more information. Not too many options were left, except maybe his smile and sense of humor, both proven quite effective in two different states.

"On behalf of the entire human society, I apologize," he said, letting his smile touch his eyes. He knew a good apology disarmed a woman no matter how mad she was, even if she could start a fight in an empty house.

"And you think that makes it all right?" she asked, her voice a little tamer, although she still seemed to be in a horn-tossing mood.

"No, ma'am," he replied calmly. "But I don't believe Mr. Smith's killer should be given the time to flee the state and vanish, just because I used the wrong words to ask you a question." He held her gaze candidly, letting silence set in for a moment; heavy, meaningful.

"All right," she eventually said, ceding, her words almost whispered on the wings of a sigh. She circled the desk and sat on the couch, crossing her legs and showing her long, tan thighs from underneath a short skirt that rode up, so tight she must've slipped it on with a shoehorn. "What do you need to know?"

He smiled and tilted his head slightly. "Using my words?" She nodded while her smile widened. "I need to find out what brought him here, to see you," he said, still careful with his choice of language despite her invitation. "Please know that anything you choose to share with me will be kept in the strictest of confidence. All I want to do is catch his killer, nothing else."

She seemed to think for a moment while her eyes absently wandered toward the window. Outside, the gray skies poured water incessantly, as if the ocean had moved up there somewhere, the floodgates breaking open under the weight of it all. For a moment, the rapping of raindrops against the window was the only sound tearing through the silence.

"He seemed delusional," she eventually said, her words justifying her hesitation to speak. "He could've been schizophrenic even."

"You're not sure?" he blurted, surprised. In his opinion, she should've known.

"It's not that simple, cowboy," she said with a quick chuckle that immediately vanished off her lips. "He only showed some of the symptoms, not all of them." She must've noticed his frown because she continued to explain. "Yes, he seemed delusional, and that's a symptom of schizophrenia, but so are others that he didn't show. He wasn't an addict, and he wasn't looking for drugs. His speech wasn't disorganized, quite the opposite. He was articulate and calm."

"What was he looking for, if not drugs?"

"He wanted advice," she replied simply. "But the situations he wanted advice about seemed, well, delusional."

"Did he say he was in danger of being killed or hurt in any way? Was that the theme of his delusions?"

"No, not even close," she replied quickly. "And no, he didn't mention any concern for his well-being or immediate danger, any enemies or things like that."

"What was he delusional about?" He saw her reaction and quickly added, "Anything I could use to find his killer or establish motive?"

She shook her head with zeal. "No, Detective, nothing like that. He talked about conversations with imaginary beings about things that weren't real."

Great. A complete whack job, regardless of what Dr. Edgell wanted to call her patients. Whatever his name, it seemed the man had been crazier than a bullbat, a lot of cobwebs gathered in the corners of his attic.

"And you have no idea what his real name is?"

She shook her head, her layered hair sending a whiff of jasmine perfume in his direction that seemed to engulf him, a little dizzying. "I'm sorry, Detective." She stood with ease and walked to the door, opening it for him. "If I remember anything...?" she asked, her voice trailing off in a flirtatious smile.

He put on his hat and arranged it quickly, running his fingers along a section of the brim. "Just call the Franklin County Sheriff's Office, Dr. Edgell, and ask for me, Detective Young." He nodded quickly, rushing through the door, glad to be out of the office, away from the cloud of jasmine perfume and lavender and her smile.

Outside, he stood by the glass doors leading to the medical center where the rain didn't reach, happy to be breathing the fresh, moisture-filled air, chilled as it rolled off the slopes of Mount Chester—and thought of Dr. Vella Edgell. In any other scenario, she was quite a catch. Beautiful, sophisticated, intelligent, and, most of all, interested. In any other scenario, except the one in which he was hoping to see Kay later that day.

Carefully choosing where his footfalls landed to avoid the biggest puddles and glad he was wearing his boots, he rushed to the SUV and climbed behind the wheel. John Doe was still that, a John Doe, and the only thing he had learned about him was that he was delusional.

Did someone shoot him because he was a schizophrenic who'd turned violent? Or did his delusions drive him to do something he shouldn't have done? In any case, someone had stood behind him and pulled the trigger of a nine-mil handgun, ending his life. As to whether the killing had been justified or not, he had difficulties believing that it was, given he'd been shot cowardly in the back while he was sitting down. Either way, it wasn't his job to establish his own guilt or innocence, just to find the person who'd squeezed that trigger.

The only problem was that he had no idea how to do that.

CHAPTER TWENTY-ONE

Interview

"Hello, I'm Detective Kay Sharp," she greeted the two visitors. "If you could follow me, please." She didn't wait for an answer; instead, she started walking toward the second interview room, tucked in the back of the building, behind the holding cells. It was traditionally reserved for the loudest of perps, the filthiest of drunk and disorderlies, and the most violent offenders, but the front interview room, cleaner and in better shape, was taken by Erin and her monster doodles. Kay's priorities were clear; the highbrowed duo could rough it for a while. It might even do them some good.

She opened the door and invited them in. Marleen Montgomery froze in her tracks, taking in the view. The stains on the floor where perps had unloaded their stomachs or relieved themselves in protest, leaving behind enduring odors as evidence of their contributions, the dirty walls inscribed with the occasional profanity, the dented and bent metallic furniture, the scratched, stainless-steel table surface with loops for securing handcuffs during suspect interrogations. She turned to Kay, visibly upset.

"Really? You want to talk in here?"

"We're a small precinct," Kay said calmly, her voice stern, unapologetic.

"Come on, Marleen," the old man said, "let's get this circus over with."

Marleen held her ground. "Where are the girls?" she asked coldly, demanding, but Kay replied with a vague hand gesture, inviting her to take a seat.

She gave the bent and dirty piece of furniture an apprehensive look as if she'd been asked to take a seat on the electric chair. Avery Montgomery was less perturbed; he sat down without any regard for the state of cleanliness of the chair and dragged it closer to the table, its legs screeching against the concrete, sending echoes against the dirty walls, and making Kay grit her teeth.

Once seated, Marleen fidgeted in place, struggled a little to undo the knot of her scarf, then she finally settled, while Avery still bounced his foot rhythmically against the floor, the heel of his shoe tapping it occasionally with dull sounds.

"Are you bringing the girls to us?" Marleen asked.

"The girls are in protective custody," Kay replied, taking a seat across from Marleen and Avery.

"What the hell for?" Avery asked, his tall brow ruffled by a deep, angry frown. When he spoke, his white beard moved as if he were a mall Santa Claus with badly fitted makeup, thanks to his sagging jowls.

Kay shrugged, putting just enough feigned indifference in her gesture to sell what she was about to say. "Standard procedure. They are what we call loose ends. Their mother's killer could learn from the media that there were witnesses to the murder and could be inclined to take measures to correct his oversight."

Marleen's jaw dropped a little, but no words came out.

"They're witnesses?" Avery asked, his voice now lower, less bellicose.

"But, first of all, please allow me to express my condolences for your loss," Kay said. Both seemed somewhat surprised as if not expecting that, as if they'd forgotten all about Cheryl's death.

"Ah, yes, thank you," Avery replied, the fastest of the two to think on his feet.

"Are we being interrogated, Detective?" Marleen asked, her eyebrow raised, her mouth a tense, thin line. "This is unbelievable. I've never been so insulted in my entire life. And this place is... unspeakable."

Kay allowed the flicker of a smile to tug at the corner of her mouth, knowing how that would infuriate the woman. "We're only having a friendly conversation, Mrs. Montgomery. If you were being interrogated, you'd know it." She paused for a beat, then added coldly, "And your rights."

That hit hard, leaving silence in its wake like heavy fog, filling every corner of the room.

"When can we take the girls home?" Avery asked, his voice courteous, almost friendly. What a change from only moments ago.

Kay paused as if she was considering it, then asked, "How are you related to Cheryl and these girls?"

Marleen shook her head in disbelief and groaned.

"Hush, dear, they can't possibly know who everyone is," Avery whispered her way quickly as if trying to control the woman's reactions, as if afraid she'd make matters worse. "They only want what's best for the girls," he added, turning a smiling face broken into a million wrinkles toward Kay. "Am I correct, Detective?"

"Absolutely," Kay replied, then waited for him to answer her question.

He paused, seemingly confused as to why Kay was silent, then appeared to remember he owed an answer. "Ah, yes. Cheryl married my grandson, Calvin. He died, unfortunately, in a work accident."

"And Mrs. Montgomery? Is she your—"

"She's my daughter-in-law," Avery quickly replied before Kay could finish her question. "She's Dan's wife."

"Was Calvin Dan's son?"

"Oh, no, goodness gracious," Marleen blurted, and Avery immediately glared at her. "Thankfully, my son's still alive." For a moment, she seemed terrified that her son could've shared Calvin's fate somehow.

"I have three sons," Avery said proudly, thrusting his chin forward, his beard fluttering in the air, smelling faintly of cigars and cologne, the expensive kind. "Mitchell is my eldest; he's Calvin's father. He also has a daughter, Lynn. She's twenty-six, still a child barely out of college. Dan," he said, looking briefly at Marleen, who nodded, seemingly deferring to Avery without a word, "is my middle child. They gave me a wonderful grandson, Victor." His eyes sparkled with pride when he said his name.

For some reason, hearing him speak, Kay's mind wandered to Betty Livingston and her craziness about firstborn daughters. She waited, but Avery didn't continue, leaving out one son. "And the youngest?" she eventually asked.

"Ah, yes, that's Raymond." The pride brought by Victor's name on his face vanished quickly, leaving disappointment and shame, his voice faltering, trailing off as if he wanted his words and the man's name to go unnoticed. Whatever Raymond had done to fall from his father's graces, it wasn't forgiven yet, and it would probably never be.

"Thank you for clarifying that," Kay replied. "It's safe to assume you would become the girls' legal guardian, Mr. Montgomery, but we are still ascertaining if Cheryl indicated her guardianship preference in a will."

Marleen scoffed. "Cheryl? A will? Well, good luck with that. She never thought of anyone but herself, that one."

"Marleen, for the love of God, be quiet," Avery whispered, his voice strong. The woman clammed up and lowered her gaze.

"Would you mind sharing with me your whereabouts on Monday night? Say, from about eight p.m. to midnight?"

That blew a fuse on Marleen's remaining self-control. She pounded against the table angrily, raising her voice to a shrill. "Now we're suspects?"

"Standard procedure, ma'am. You do realize that before we consider entrusting you with the safety of these girls, we must first clear you of any suspicion."

"Of course," Avery replied in her place, his tone pacifying, while his blue eyes shot darts at his daughter-in-law. She seemed to have grown fed up with being silenced, no longer lowering her brow under his stare. "Well, I was having dinner with the mayor on Monday night. The folks at the ski lodge can confirm, and, of course, the mayor himself."

"Until what time?" Kay asked, smiling encouragingly.

"We played a game of cards after that with a couple of his friends and spent some time discussing the politics of the moment, state and nation." He scratched his beard with steady hands, his knuckles knotty, a telltale sign of arthritis. "Say, until about eleven-thirty or so? The club people might know better; my car was valeted; they might have records."

Kay thanked him with a nod, then turned to Marleen. "And you, Mrs. Montgomery?"

Keeping a stiff upper lip, the woman eventually replied, scowling at Kay. "I hosted my book club at the house. They didn't leave until late—after ten sometime." Her voice was choked with anger. "You mean to tell me you'll embarrass me in front of all those women by checking my alibi with them?"

"Well, is there anyone else who can vouch for your whereabouts? Your husband, maybe?"

She shook her head. "He left on a business trip last Thursday. And I let the help go home early that night."

Kay pulled a small notepad from her pocket and pushed it toward her. "I'll need their names and phone numbers, Mrs. Montgomery. They'll understand. If you're telling the truth, there's nothing to be ashamed of." She handed her a pen that she hesitated for a long moment before accepting and started to write reluctantly.

Kay remained silent while she scribbled, discreetly watching their reactions, their body language. Avery seemed calm, almost relaxed, while she was inexplicably angry. But both of their behavior was off in a big way: neither had asked about Julie or had demanded that the police do everything in their power to find the missing girl. It was as if she didn't exist to them.

One thing she was certain of: Heather and Erin weren't going anywhere with those people, not until the gnawing sensation in Kay's gut ceased stirring her senses up with all sorts of red flags.

When Marleen was done writing the names of her book club friends, she pushed the pad across the table to Kay. "There. Now can I get the girls, so we can leave?"

"The girls are in protective custody," Kay repeated calmly as if she was saying it for the first time. "They are witnesses in a murder-kidnapping and have been a tremendous help to get us started in solving this crime."

"Have they, now?" Avery asked, sounding a little irritated. "What on earth could an eight-year-old and a four-year-old have to say?"

"A lot more than you'd think," Kay replied.

"At least you should let us see them," Avery said, and Marleen nodded enthusiastically.

Kay considered it for a moment. She didn't want them to see the state Heather was in, but their reaction to the girls' presence might prove helpful. She texted Deputy Farrell, instructing her to put Erin in the nap room with her sister and close the door.

"Just a moment, until we set things up," she said, noticing how immediately they both seemed to relax a little. Then her phone chimed, with a one-word confirmation from Farrell via text message. *Done.*

Kay invited them to follow her, leading the way. "You'll be able to see the girls through a window. No direct contact for now, I'm afraid." She could sense their frustration in their silence as they followed her toward the nap room.

Heather sat on the side of her bed just as she had been since she got there, her back facing the door. Erin scribbled something on a piece of paper, then showed it to Heather, who didn't react. Deputy Farrell was on the next bunk, holding all the colored markers in her hands and smiling gently.

She watched the Montgomerys as they looked at the girls through the narrow window, their heads almost touching. Marleen seemed overcome by emotion; her eyes welled up, surprisingly. Avery was dark and quiet, seeming sad and distraught. She allowed them a couple of minutes, then she invited them to the front of the building.

"This is no place for little girls," Avery said coldly as they reached the main lobby. "I'm advising you, Detective, the moment I get home I will call my attorney and make sure these girls will be released into my custody immediately."

"That's your prerogative, sir," she replied. "If you bring a court order, then we'll see what we can do."

"You'll see what you can do?" he said, his words spoken in a menacing whisper. "Do not test me, Detective."

"Are you threatening me?" Kay asked calmly. He instantly took a step back. Behind him, Deputy Hobbs grinned.

"No," he replied cautiously. "I'm just curious to know what kind of information you could possibly be getting from these children to warrant such determination to keep them here, in these terrible conditions."

"Yes, I want to know that too," Marleen jumped into the middle of the tense exchange. She seemed fearful, restless. Her emotional moment was gone without a trace.

How interesting. Was she hiding something?

"Heather has been able to tell us a few things about what happened," Kay replied vaguely. "You do realize I can't share the details of an ongoing investigation with anyone? But we have strong leads, and we're estimating the girls will continue to have a critical role in catching their mother's killer."

As she spoke, she noticed Marleen's anxiety subsiding. Maybe she was hiding something, but not what Kay had initially suspected. Perhaps she was hiding her own fear of being targeted next. Why would she be?

"Were you aware of any problems in Cheryl's life? Anyone looking to harm her or the girls?"

They briefly looked at each other, then Avery replied, "No. Absolutely not."

Kay turned to Marleen, but she shook her head.

"Were you close?" Kay continued to probe. It seemed there was a notable difference in the standard of living between Cheryl, the single mom who improvised and saved and thrifted through life to make ends meet, and the two Montgomerys.

"Not as much as I would've wanted," Avery replied. "You see, after Calvin died, Cheryl blamed me, even if the investigation cleared the company of any wrongdoing."

"The company?"

"Montgomery Construction, my company," he said, his voice tinted by a mix of pride and amazement that she didn't know what should've been obvious. "My sons work at the company, and their children too. They will take my legacy further and build it into what will most likely be the largest general contractor in Northern California." He paused, looking at Kay intently, like he was measuring the impact his words had on the detective. Then, as if he remembered something, he added, veering his gaze sideways, "All my sons, except Raymond, of course. He couldn't be bothered to care about the family business. He's an artist." He spat the word as if it left a bad taste in his mouth.

That was the unforgivable offense, Kay thought. Rejection. The most hurtful of them all.

"I would've loved to have my great-granddaughters closer to me—to all of us—but Cheryl kept her distance and her pride, despite obvious financial difficulties. She wouldn't even accept the college funds that I set up when each of the girls was born. After Calvin passed, she returned everything to me."

Kay wondered if it was worthwhile looking into Calvin's death. Was there more to the work accident that had happened two years ago? Had it been covered up, Avery surely rich enough to afford it?

"Detective, I promise I'll take good care of these girls," Avery insisted. "You have my word. And you can speak with them however often you may choose to do so."

She nodded, acknowledging his statement but not budging. "As soon as they can be released, I'll be in touch."

"Fine." Without another word, he left, holding his head up high and followed closely by Marleen, not before the woman glared at Kay one more time.

The main entrance door was still coming to a close after their departure when her phone chimed. A text message from Dr. Whitmore said, *Need to see you ASAP.*

The entire time it took her to drive through the relentless downpour, a thought kept bugging her, whirling in her head over and over. Why no mention of Julie from either of the Montgomerys? Why no questions, threats, or promises? Why no curiosity as to who might've taken her and why?

It was as if they already knew and just didn't care.

CHAPTER TWENTY-TWO

Nightfall

Dusk was falling heavy, filling every corner with darkness that crawled inside the room as if it were alive, conquering all it touched, seeping from the windows as if it poured in through the glass, the white voile sheers unable to keep it at bay. On the other side of the massive windowpanes, the deluge continued, heavy rain lashing against glass in monotone obstinacy. The bulging dark clouds above rushing northeast like refugees fleeing the site of a disaster.

He'd watched the skies the entire day and not a single crack of blue had appeared in the immense cluster of gray wads endlessly shedding water. Not one, not for a single moment, as far as the eye could see.

Mother was still angry.

Her tears were flooding the fields, her wounds were opening wider than he'd ever seen them, bleeding profusely, leaving the stains all over the landscape in the deep brown of displaced earth carried away by rivulets of merciless rainwater.

"Oh, dear Mother, how it must hurt you," he whispered, holding on to the windowsill with pale, frozen fingers. He'd been awake for the past two days, unwilling to leave Mother's side for a night's rest, when he was all she had. "It will be tomorrow, I promise, not a day later."

Distant, fading rumblings reassured him Mother had heard him. Moving slowly as if in a trance, he unbuttoned the collar of his shirt and tugged at the thin, silver chain he wore around his neck, pulling the small locket outside. Then, gently holding it in his hand, he pressed it against his quivering lips.

Tomorrow morning's sky would tell him what Mother wants. Whatever she asks of him, he will deliver. Otherwise, her rage will be destructive, taking everything away from him like she'd done it before, back when he didn't know what she expected of him or how to soothe her pain.

"Dear Mother, hear your child." His breath warmed the locket he still held in his hand close to his lips, as if the words he was whispering were a continuation of the humble kiss he'd laid on the shiny metal surface moments ago. "Whatever your will, I shall deliver." He pressed his lips against the metal once more, then slid the locket back under his shirt, where its warmth touched his chest as it had done since the first day he'd worn it. No one had seen that locket or knew of its existence, its content his best-kept secret, one that no one deserved to know.

"I'm begging you still, please let me keep this one." His fingers grabbed a clump of white voile, crushing the fine fabric, feeling its delicate texture rub against his skin. "She could keep me company for a while, bring some warmth to my long days."

He looked at the sky again, almost completely engulfed by nightfall, only a trace of pewter coloring the horizon where the sun had set a while ago, disrobed of its glorious reds and oranges and purples, sentenced to vanish in an entourage of ashen gray. He listened for Mother's voice, only the sound of rain unsettling the silence.

"This beautiful girl could fill my heart, dear Mother," he pleaded, encouraged by her silence. "Oh, what I wouldn't give to touch her. To hold her in my arms."

Rain-filled silence continued, yet he felt shivers traveling down his spine, the absence of Mother's answer as ominous as her thunderous rage.

"Show me the way," he murmured against the soft fabric he'd pulled close to his lips. "I'll be here, waiting for a sign." His breath shuddered as it left his chest.

At dawn's first light, he'd be there, standing by the window, waiting, searching the skies for the faintest trace of azure, a sign that Mother's rage had waned, and he could keep the girl for a while longer.

Now that she had spoken to him once more in her punishing silence, he felt a chill in his blood, coursing through his veins as a harbinger of doom, the foreboding clear as if she'd thundered her will from above.

Tomorrow's sky at dawn would show him what Mother demanded of him. Then, by high noon the next day, her will shall be done.

CHAPTER TWENTY-THREE

DNA

The peak of Mount Chester hid its white in heavily leaded clouds that swirled around it angrily, stirred by descending cold air and gusts of stormy winds. The lower slopes had borrowed their color from the surrounding gray and mist-engulfed fir green, almost indiscernible from the nearby landscape, the forests of the preserve and the pines and firs that adorned the town.

Kay didn't notice much of that, although she loved the sight of Mount Chester in any season and any weather. Instead, she replayed her conversation with the Montgomerys in her mind, line by line, searching for a hint as to what they knew about Julie's disappearance and didn't tell. She'd put money down they knew more about the subject than they'd shared, but they didn't seem to be involved. There was no guilt in their behavior, no fear of getting caught. Marleen Montgomery seemed afraid of something, but she'd shown relief when told the police were getting valuable information from the girls. Nevertheless, Kay still had an uneasy feeling about them, something tugging at her gut, telling her she should talk with them again. Until then, Deputy Hobbs was tasked with checking their alibis, thoroughly, in person.

Could they have been involved? How?

Cheryl's killer was a man, and that eliminated Marleen, although not her knowledge of who the perp was; maybe she was hiding the killer's identity. But then, why would she be relieved the police were making progress?

As for Avery, at his eighty-three years of age, he would've been easily subdued by Cheryl, with or without Julie's help. Not to mention, people don't invent alibis involving numerous witnesses including the mayor. That one was probably going to check out just fine.

Finally, what motive could they possibly have? Nah… they probably weren't involved, Kay concluded.

Then, why didn't they ask a single question about Julie? About finding her, and the progress of the investigation? Was it because they'd assumed Kay would've led the conversation with any news about Julie? Or because she'd freely shared the progress they were making using the information gathered from the girls?

In the absence of motive and logic, she shrugged the thought of them off. People were all sorts of strange these days, more and more self-absorbed, narrowly focused on what they wanted, and those two just wanted to get the girls. That part, she could understand; knowing the two traumatized little girls were sleeping in a police precinct, anyone with half a heart would've been motivated to intervene, especially when they were family, the daughters of a dearly missed grandson who'd passed. That part made sense.

She turned the blinker on and pulled onto the small street where the single-story morgue awaited with its rain-soaked brown stone walls, almost empty parking lot, and a single tall palm tree in front. Pulling in, as close to the entrance as possible, she smiled without realizing it.

Elliot's SUV was there.

The taillights of his vehicle were on, the engine still running. Her partner was in the car, waiting with his foot on the brake.

She parked by his side, hiding her foolish smile. The proximity of her approaching car must've caught his attention, because he lifted his gaze from his phone and looked her way. The moment he recognized her, his face lit up and he smiled, a wide grin that had matched hers, all for a split second before he lowered his head and hid everything under the wide brim of his hat. When he looked at her again, only his eyes retained the spark of that initial moment that had lit an unexpected fire in her blood.

Rushing through the rain, she reached the morgue door at the same time as Elliot did. He opened the door for her, and she stepped in, somewhat hesitant to make eye contact with him again, the fleeting moment they had shared still resonating in her entire being. If there was one thing she didn't want, that was for her partner to learn about the effect he had on her.

"Did he text you too?" she asked instead, leading the way to Dr. Whitmore's autopsy room.

"He sure did." Elliot removed his hat and shook off the raindrops that had clung to the felt. Then he put it back on. "It's not my first visit here today either."

"Huh," she said, while a frown scrunched her brow. They were working two different cases; she wondered why the doc would've summoned them both. "We'll learn soon enough." As she walked through the morgue doors, the smell of death greeted her with a chill down her spine.

Dr. Whitmore was seated behind his wide desk, rolling from one piece of equipment to the next on his four-legged stool on smooth casters that didn't make a sound. Behind him, two of the six refrigerated body-storage shelves held the bodies of Cheryl Coleman and Elliot's John Doe, the compressor humming quietly, harmonizing with the fluorescent light above and the centrifuge still spinning on a lab table, in an orchestra of droning lab implements.

Even if the bodies were laid to rest on their temperature-controlled shelves, a faint smell of formaldehyde still lingered, mixed with disinfectants and some other odors that she couldn't identify. She didn't mind them as much as Elliot did though; since he'd entered the morgue her partner had resigned himself to breathing though his mouth.

After giving the doctor a side hug and a smooch on his cheek that caught him a little by surprise and made him blush, Kay pulled out another stool and sat by the desk. "What are you still doing here so late? I thought you'd gone home by now."

The medical examiner let out a soft, tired chuckle without veering his attention from the test tubes he was manipulating. He extracted serum from one of the two tubes, then put two drops into one small container and closed its cap. Then he wrote the initials "CC" on the tube and inserted it into the specimen holder of an automated testing machine, closing the lid. Another tone of quiet whirring started contributing to the symphony of sounds. "I thought I'd be home by now too, and so did my wife. But I knew once I was going to share with you the fruits of my labor, you'd ask me if I could test everything again." He shrugged with an amused grin. "So, preemptively, I'm doing exactly that. Only, you see, I've already tested these twice." He touched her arm after removing his blue glove with a quick, well-rehearsed gesture. "Not that I don't like your questions, my dear."

"Okay, you made me curious, Doc. What's going on?"

She threw Elliot a glance, wondering, again, why they'd both been summoned by the medical examiner when they were working on different cases. Elliot was keeping his distance, his aversion to everything morgue no secret to anyone who had eyes.

"It's about Cheryl Coleman." The doc stood and walked over to the large, wall-mounted screen, where several images were displayed. Clicking a small remote, he shifted through them until he found the image he was looking for—a close-up of the abdominal stab wound that had sealed her fate. "Single stab wound to the abdomen. The blade nicked her ribs and sliced through her abdominal aorta. She was dead within minutes." He cleared his throat and propped his hand on his hip, stretching his back with a groan. "The angle was downward and twisted, consistent with an unskilled killer, but your unsub is strong; the blow was forceful enough to cut through bone. You're looking for a well-built man with significant upper-body strength. I heard the nine-one-one call, so that clarified the gender at least."

She exchanged a quick glance with Elliot. "I was kind of expecting this," she replied. "Still waiting for the punch line that will have me ask you to repeat the tests."

"Yeah, about that," he said, rubbing his forehead with his fingers, as if trying to scare off a migraine, or maybe just his tiredness. "I had Cheryl's DNA run first thing, just in case we'd learn something interesting from it. Then I ran DNA samples from blood collected at the scene in various places in the kitchen, hoping I'd find the killer's mixed in there. Since I got my own sequencer, I go nuts with DNA testing."

Kay whistled. "You got your own sequencer, Doc? That machine must've been expensive."

"I know," he laughed, "some people buy golf clubs when they retire. I got tired of having our cases lining up forever behind San Francisco County, so I splurged." He raised his hands in the air in an apologetic gesture. "What can I say? I like collecting favors from other MEs across the state. It's my kind of fun."

She couldn't help laughing and shaking her head in amazement, as one would do when seeing a talented child invent a new, interesting game. "So, what about the DNA samples found at the scene?"

Elliot took a couple of steps, approaching them, his interest piqued.

"There were two different blood samples found. One was Cheryl's, of course, and there was a second sample mixed in there—male."

Kay rubbed her hands together. "I profiled the unsub that he might've killed for the first time. Please tell me he cut himself, and we have his DNA."

The long pause that followed was a bad omen and wiped Kay's excitement completely while the doctor seemed to collect his thoughts.

"The way I set up my system is simple. First, after a new sample is sequenced, the system will search for a match against the local samples here, already in the database, then go to county level, then state, then national. It makes sense to do it this way, because it saves time." He plunged his hands into his pockets, then his left hand emerged with a pack of gum. He didn't extract a piece; instead, he just played with it as he talked, twirling it between his nimble fingers. "I had just finished sequencing John Doe's DNA when I got a match." He paused for another beat. "A local match."

She tilted her head, not sure she understood correctly. "You mean to say—"

"Yes, John Doe's blood was found at the Angel Creek crime scene. On the Coleman residence floor."

The frown returned to Kay's forehead, as she tried to imagine scenarios in which that made sense. Okay, so John Doe couldn't've killed Cheryl and taken Julie, because he was already dead at the time. "Did you test it again?" As she asked the question, she remembered how their conversation started, and let a long breath of air deflate her lungs. She wasn't expecting an answer, but Doc Whitmore was pointing at the whirring machine.

"Twice," he replied. "This would be the third time I'm testing, with brand-new test tubes, never used, and freshly unsealed chemicals and cleaners."

"Walk me through the timeline of these deaths again," Kay asked, since she wasn't very familiar with the details of John Doe's case.

"We all know when Cheryl was killed, on Monday night at precisely nine forty-two p.m. I'm putting John Doe's time of death roughly one day, maybe thirty-six hours before that, so on Sunday, or, at the earliest, late Saturday night."

"Any other matches in your system?" Elliot asked. "Do we have his name?"

"He's still John Doe for now, I'm afraid. His shrink was the best lead I had to offer. I'm taking it didn't pan out?"

"Nope. He was using a fake name and paying cash. But if he visited with Cheryl Coleman, we have a place to start, I guess." Elliot hesitated for a brief moment, then added, "If you're sure he was there, Doc."

"You wouldn't be here if I wasn't sure," Dr. Whitmore replied. "I got more; maybe that will help." He turned over to the screen and clicked the remote a couple of times until it displayed the photo of a long, dark hair fiber. "This is the hair fiber we found on John Doe's body. It had the root follicle still attached, so I ran DNA. Again, it pinged locally. The hair fiber belonged to Cheryl Coleman."

CHAPTER TWENTY-FOUR

Questions

Julie hadn't moved in a while.

The stomachache had subsided, leaving in its wake a cold so unbearable it drained every last drop of her energy with shivers and shaking that were uncontrollable. Yet she remained determined to lay against the door, spending endless hours in a dazed state between sleep and wakefulness.

She'd taken the covers from the bed and set them on the floor, desperate to keep the cold at bay. Later, she'd given in and wrapped herself in the comforter she'd stripped off the bed, so white it reminded her of a shroud. She still kept her back against the door, ready, at least in her weary mind, to jump to her feet if someone came for her.

But she wasn't going to be able to do any of that. She'd be lucky if she could bring herself to stand.

Her mind wandered, searching for answers, for a reason why this was happening to her. Why it had happened to her mother, maybe to Heather and Erin too. She shuddered, her teeth clattering as if she were standing naked at the heart of a snow blizzard.

She'd read about girls missing, taken, found, held in dungeons and whatnot. Seen them on the news, featured in movies. But that was *them*, some other girls, just distant strangers no one really knew. Maybe they'd done something to provoke their captors, to tempt their fate. But her? She'd done nothing of the sort.

A suffocating sob erupted from her chest. Her mother... she was gone, and it was all her fault.

She'd told her they had to leave, to escape the danger she was in. She'd known ahead of time it was coming, and had made plans to save them, to save her, Julie, her oldest and most defiant of the three sisters. But Julie didn't obey, didn't take her seriously.

Because it was all surreal.

Maybe if her mother would've explained it to her, she would've understood why they had to run, leaving behind their lives, their house, all their friends. And Brent.

But maybe she couldn't explain, because it was inexplicable. What could possibly explain someone wanting to snatch a girl and keep her locked up in a basement?

Things like that didn't happen to people like them—to average, boring, small-town people. To a widow raising three girls by herself. To a dental hygienist and her kids. No... things like that happened to people in movies and TV shows, to stunningly beautiful girls who had stalkers and secret admirers, and who, for some reason, never had curtains hanging at their bedroom windows.

Why her?

What made her so special, enough for someone to kill her mother to get to her? Only to lock her in that cold and damp basement, without food, without a word?

It couldn't be explained.

No matter how hard she tried, her thoughts kept going back to the last image of her mother, fallen in a pool of gushing blood on the kitchen floor. Julie recalled ridiculous details, things she didn't think she'd noticed at the time. The small stain near the stove, right where the knife had dropped to the floor, by her mother's side. Was that tomato paste? And why was Heather wearing her pajama pants, dragging the pant legs throughout the kitchen, stepping on them, too long for her size? She used to do that a lot, steal her clothes and wear them around the house. And why had Mom fed Erin breakfast cereal for dinner?

Why didn't they all leave when they still could? Even if it was dark and raining, why stay, why wait another day if her mother knew this was going to happen? Had she known, really? How could she?

Another sob shook her entire body as it left her chest in a wail that resounded strangely weak against the gray concrete walls. The yellow light coming from the bulb hanging by its wires from the ceiling seemed to fade a little more, as cold engulfed her again, rattling her body in draining shivers that never ended.

Letting herself slip into oblivion a little deeper, she recalled his face, the man who'd killed her mother.

He seemed familiar, and still, she couldn't place him. She'd definitely seen him before, and her mother knew him too. Had she said his name at all? She tried to remember, but everything that had been said was a blur of senseless words that belonged to a surreal world.

Yet she remembered his face; he was a handsome young man with fascinating gray eyes, as gray as the concrete floor she lay on. A man she would've given a moment's attention if she'd met him at a party. A little too old for her, maybe, but not too much older. Twenty-fiveish was too old by law, but not by her law.

Then an unexpected thought dissipated the haze engulfing her mind. Had she met him somewhere else, under different circumstances, would she have been able to tell he was a murderer?

CHAPTER TWENTY-FIVE

Delusion

"She's been gone almost forty-eight hours," Kay said as they entered the precinct. "Her chances of being found alive have dropped to almost zero, but I'm not giving up on her."

They had driven their cars from the ME's office through pitch blackness lashed by unrelenting rain, the sky lighting up on occasion as a new line of thunderstorms crossed through their region. They had to make a three-mile detour to avoid a section of road that had been washed away by a landslide, giving Kay more time to think as she drove behind Elliot's SUV.

No matter how unlikely it seemed, her partner's case was closely related to Cheryl's murder and Julie's kidnapping. For some reason, John Doe had visited the Coleman residence and had left a small amount of his blood behind.

Before she could think of scenarios in which that could've happened, they had arrived, and Elliot was holding the door open for her, right after he'd asked, "Do you think she's still out there?"

It was more about the words he didn't say that had ignited the fire in her blood. Yes, her chances were slim to none, and Julie was entering her third night in captivity—if she was still alive—but the lead about John Doe visiting the Coleman house opened up a new array of questions.

Had Cheryl killed John Doe? Evidence pointed in that direction. If yes, why? What motive could the dental hygienist and single mom have to shoot a man in the back, in her house, especially if her children were there? And they probably were. Could it have been self-defense? If yes, what were the odds that two different men came to her house with the intention to cause harm, within a day or two of each other?

Zero.

Well, technically, the odds were more than zero, but so small Kay could easily say they didn't exist. And still, that was the only explanation for what they'd learned from Dr. Whitmore.

Reaching her desk, she took off her jacket and hung it on a nearby chair to dry, glad to be out of the soggy piece of clothing after a long day. She wished she'd driven by her house to get fresh clothes and get rid of the turtleneck that bothered her, but she couldn't bring herself to take time away from her work for such trivial matters.

"What do you think?" Elliot pulled his chair next to hers as she fired up her laptop. "Your vic killed my vic?"

"Seems that way," she replied, typing in her password with frozen fingers. Waiting for the screens to load, she rubbed her hands together to warm them up, then texted Jacob, asking if he could bring her dry clothes and some food. Hesitating for a moment before sending the message, she threw her partner a quick look, noticing the soaked pant legs and shirt collar, then added to the message, *For two*. She tapped send and slid the phone into her pocket, just as her laptop chimed. She had new email.

"Do you see your vic able to dispose of John Doe's body all by herself? She's five-foot-nothing, thin as a gnat's whisker," Elliot ended his comment with an incredulous chuckle.

"Maybe she had help or maybe she was that desperate." She must've been, if the girls had been in the house at the time, but there was no way of knowing.

A wave of excitement coursed through Kay's body when she saw the email she'd been waiting for. "The nine-one-one call is back." She double-clicked and the recording started to play.

It had been cleaned up digitally, and Heather's voice now sounded muffled, her breathing sounds almost gone. Carrie's voice had also been muffled, but somewhat less; her voice spanned too wide a frequency range to be completely removed without losing critical parts of the recording. The background had been amplified, now sounding closer, more real. Intelligible.

Holding her breath, Kay listened to the initial part of the recording, where the dialog between Heather and Carrie had taken most of the spectrum, and nothing much else could be understood. Then, she heard Cheryl's voice, her words intelligible, albeit only barely.

"You won't take her, you hear me? I won't let you," she had said, her voice coming across strong, determined. Brave. "Let us go."

Then a man's voice, stern and low and menacing. *"Not going to happen. She's coming with me. Tonight. Like it's meant to be."*

A small silence, during which Heather's muffled voice had replied to Carrie's question, then Cheryl, continuing to plead. She could hear tears in her voice, the tremor that usually accompanies intense pain and desperation. *"I wanted to leave. Please let us leave. No one has to know."* A beat. *"Please, I'm begging you, let us go."*

The man spoke again, the first part of what he said hard to discern, still buried under the dialog between Heather and Carrie. *"I can't,"* he replied with what sounded like a matter-of-fact, almost indifferent tone. *"You know I can't. This has to happen, and you—"* Words were unintelligible for a brief moment, drowned by Heather's voice. *"—why you haven't left. It's her... her power pulling you back, holding you here. It has to be done."*

A split second after the man's words, the sounds of struggle were all that was heard, the crashes and loud bangs of furniture, then the thump of Cheryl's body hitting the ground as Julie screamed. Then the teenager's heartbreaking voice, calling for her mother before she too was silenced.

Kay stopped the playback and took her head in her hands. "What the hell was that? Some shared delusion?"

"Who is *her*," Elliot asked, "the woman they're talking about? Cheryl didn't seem to doubt a word the man was saying, about *her power* and all that madness. That's crazier than a hare in a hat."

Kay let out a long breath of disappointment. She'd expected a lot more from the nine-one-one call; she'd expected answers. Solid leads. A name. Something she could use to find Julie before it was too late.

Instead, it was as if she'd glimpsed a world where nothing made any sense. It was, perhaps, the weirdest dialog she'd witnessed, and Cheryl had lost her life at the end of it.

For a moment, she kept thinking—if she were to label that conversation with one word, what would that word be? She liked that exercise, finding labels for situations or events, because it helped her crystallize her thinking and prioritize the many thoughts she had about what she'd just heard. That label was easy to find; only one word could characterize the conversation she'd witnessed.

Delusional.

"This unsub is a mission-driven killer-kidnapper," she said, pulling herself out of the myriad thoughts swirling in her mind. "We don't know what the mission was, but I believe we can agree Cheryl was aware of it, and, for some reason, didn't dispute it. As insane as that may sound, she wasn't challenging it."

"I know crazy when I see it," Elliot said, leaning back against his chair. He lifted his hat only long enough to run his fingers through his hair, then immediately set it back on his head. "Hear it, I should say. These folks sounded delusional to me."

The moment he spoke the word she'd been thinking, something tugged at her gut, but she couldn't put her finger on what it was.

"Are you thinking it's one of those weird cults?" he asked. "We had one of those in Waco, if you remember. Seventy-six people died in that one."

"I'm not so sure about that." Kay unscrewed the cap off a water bottle she took from a desk drawer and gulped half of it thirstily.

It helped wash away her hunger, for a while anyway. "You see, cult members aren't free to walk around unrestricted. From what we can tell, Cheryl was free. She held a job, visited with people. Cults don't normally let their members do that; they're afraid they'd lose their grip on their victims." She looked at him quickly. "Oops, I meant members."

He smiled, and, for a second, she forgot where she was, wishing they were sharing dinner and a bottle of wine. And whatever else the evening might bring for dessert.

Then Julie came back to her mind, front and center, and her daydream was ripped to shreds. Later, there'd be time for that dinner. Later, after Julie had been found safely and returned to her sisters. After her mother's killer had been locked up.

"Ta-da," she heard Jacob's voice behind her, a second after she'd picked up on the mouthwatering smell of hot pepperoni pizza and was about to wonder whom she could beg a slice from. She sprung from her chair and hugged him.

He was wearing his favorite plaid shirt, unbuttoned over a white T-shirt, and jeans. Water drops clung to his unruly mane of hair, but he didn't seem to mind. He seemed to be something he hadn't been in a while. Happy.

"Ugh, you're wet," Jacob said jokingly, pulling away, visibly embarrassed by her show of affection. "And you stink."

"Really?" she asked, her cheeks burning up. "Why don't you buy some ad space, put the news out there in the paper?" But she wasn't really mad; she'd already opened the box and grabbed the first slice. She bit into it, the juices filling her mouth with the urge to swallow it whole. She took her time chewing and savoring every bite, and beckoned Hobbs over, seeing how he was eyeing their small gathering from a distance.

"I got more for you two," Jacob said, handing her and Elliot shopping bags filled with clothes. "Lynn helped me choose yours," he added. Kay's jaw dropped.

"Dry socks, a shirt too," Elliot commented, then shook Jacob's hand. "And look at you, entering a precinct at your own will."

"Don't remind me—I still get the creeps when I see cops."

"Don't look at me," Hobbs replied, laughing and talking with his mouth full but keeping his hand in front of it. "I'm off the clock."

"So, you're not coming home any time soon, sis?" Jacob asked, lowering his voice just a tad. Her little brother must've had an agenda, and her name was Lynn. Good for him.

"No, little brother," she replied with a wide grin. "The house is all yours for the night."

He pecked her cheek and rushed out of there, shouting over his shoulder as he reached the main entrance. "You're the best."

No, he was the best brother a girl could wish for. He'd taken her in when she'd returned to live in Mount Chester. Despite all those years living apart, she'd been scarce to call. While away, she'd stayed a stranger, not sure he wanted to be reminded of her, of their challenging time growing up together, and, implicitly, of their abusive father. Yet, he'd welcomed her with open arms and showed her nothing but love and support. She was lucky. She should've remembered that before treating his girlfriend with that much suspicion.

Elliot pulled a napkin from the packet and wiped his mouth, then drank an entire bottle of water without drawing breath. "Now what?"

"Now I interview Heather again. She might know something about your John Doe."

CHAPTER TWENTY-SIX

Memories

Kay hadn't seen Heather since lunch, when she ended her first hypnosis session rather abruptly. She'd been worried about the little girl, but Deputy Farrell had kept her apprised with status reports via text throughout the day.

Erin was doing somewhat better—eating, sleeping, doodling monsters without seeming to ever get tired of it. Completely immersed into what she was doing, as if in a trance, she seemed unwilling to draw anything else, and she'd spoken very few words.

As for Heather, nothing much had changed. She didn't speak, barely touched food or water, and when she slept, she had terrible nightmares. The deputy had noticed tears rolling down her face a couple of times, the blank stare becoming slightly more focused, but only for moments at a time.

That was a good sign. She might be ready to start living again.

Kay checked her watch and swallowed a curse. It was almost nine-thirty. She hoped Heather was still awake. Before heading over to the nap room, she waited impatiently for Hobbs to finish his pizza.

"How did those alibis check out?" It was almost pointless for her to ask; if anything would've not checked out with the Montgomerys' alibis, she would've been notified right away. And still, there was something gnawing at her gut about those two; she wanted to make sure Hobbs did a thorough job.

Still chewing on the last mouthful of cheesy crust, the deputy lifted his greasy thumb up in the air. He swallowed with difficulty, rushed. "They both checked out just fine. The ski lodge has Avery Montgomery on premises until, um," he pulled his notepad and flipped through a few pages, "twelve forty-five a.m. That's the time stamp on his valet card."

"And you talked to people there?"

"Yes, I did. They showed me security footage placing him at the cards table. He was there. He didn't move; he barely got up once to use the restroom, but I don't blame him. He was on a winning streak; he was cleaning the mayor out, and the other two folks."

Ironclad. "How about Marleen Montgomery?"

"I spoke with three of her book club ladies," Hobbs replied, looking at his notepad again. "She was at the house with them until ten-thirtyish, talking Harlan Coben. Do you want me to do the rest?"

There was no point. "Nah, but thanks, Hobbs, I appreciate it."

"You bet."

She stopped by the kitchen to wash her hands, still a little greasy from the pizza, then quickly changed in the locker room, regretting she didn't have the time for a shower. Lynn was growing on her, but with mixed feelings; Jacob's new girlfriend had packed her deodorant in the bag, and clean underwear. Pushing the thought of a stranger going through her undies drawer out of her mind, she chose to be grateful for the clean and dry feel of her fresh clothes.

Emerging from the locker room with a smile on her lips, she found Elliot, wearing Jacob's red plaid shirt that looked unexpectedly good on him, waiting for her in front of the nap room, ready to keep watch while she conducted her session.

She opened the door slowly, seeing Erin asleep on the bed, but Heather still up, sitting as she usually did, on the side of her cot, her back straight, her shoulders tense, her entire body rigid. On the next cot, by her side, Farrell had fallen asleep. The deputy had taken her task seriously, not willing to go home for the night and leave the girls with someone else. As a mother, she had to know how important any trace of stability was for the girls, and rotating through caretakers wasn't cutting it.

Touching Farrell's shoulder, she woke her up. The deputy scooped Erin in her arms and walked out of the room, leaving Kay alone with Heather. A few moments later, propped against pillows and with her eyes closed, the little girl was ready for another session.

"Breathe with me, slowly, and follow my voice into deep relaxation. You are now in a profound trance."

Kay watched carefully to see if Heather was comfortable. Her shoulders had relaxed, the tension in her face was gone, her eyes were closed, still moving on occasions, but the thoughts that crossed her mind didn't seem to anguish her too much.

"What you will see cannot hurt you. You're safe, here with me. You're telling me the story of what happened on Monday night. It's like watching TV together. Tell me what you see."

Her jaws clenched slightly before she spoke. "Julie's late. Mom's mad. She wants us to go."

"Go where?"

"As far away from this place as possible," she replied, her voice altered, sounding more mature. Those must've been Cheryl's words.

"Someone's at the door. Do you know that man?"

The girl startled, her eyes moving rapidly. She writhed, as if her entire being was urging her to run, but she was stuck in place and time, on that terrible night.

"You're safe, and you're strong. Nothing can touch you." Kay spoke slowly, barely above a whisper. "Breathe in, hold it for a moment, and breathe out." She watched her relax, her eye movements slowing down. "Do you know that man?"

Heather shook her head a little, and a whimper came off her lips. "He's going to take Julie."

"Does your mom know him?"

"Yes."

She paused for a moment, thinking how to phrase the next question so that she wouldn't influence the answer. Heather didn't know the man's name; she'd asked her twice and got the same answer. "What does your mom say when she sees him?"

"*Oh, it's you,*" she replied, again in her imitation of her mother's voice.

How interesting. She must've been expecting someone else, but she definitely knew the man who later took her life.

"How about the day before? Was there another man visiting mom?"

"Uh-uh," she mumbled, a frown scrunching her forehead.

"Two days before, then?"

"Yes." She was becoming agitated again.

"Let's watch that story together," Kay whispered. "Tell me about that man."

Heather gritted her teeth and shifted in place, clasping her hands together in her lap. Whatever she was remembering was making her uncomfortable.

"Mom took us upstairs, in her bedroom." She paused between words, as if remembering with difficulty. "We're not allowed in there without her, but she says it's okay." She swallowed and licked her dry lips, then her jaws clenched again. "She does that every time he comes." A flicker of a smile touched her tense lips. "So we wouldn't hear what they talk about. But I don't mind, I like cartoons better."

"What did you watch that night?"

Another hint of a smile. "*Cars.* The weasel hates it, but Julie tells me the cars' names and I love Mater. He's funny. Julie likes *Cars* too." A shattered breath engulfed her last words, then a quick, reactive movement rippled through her body, as if something had startled her.

"What just happened?"

"*Bang.*" She clasped and unclasped her hands nervously. "Downstairs. But mom came up to us." Her voice changed pitch. "*You girls stay here, you hear me? Don't come down.*"

That must've been the moment when John Doe had been shot. Heather didn't speak of arguments or screaming or any violence. Just *bang*.

"Then what happened?"

"We watch Mommy through the window." Her voice had dropped to a conspiratorial whisper. "If she catches us, it's bad. She'll get mad."

"What did you see?"

"Lots of rain. She hates rain. Julie's afraid of the rain." A quiet, tense giggle. "Mommy carrying the man back to his truck. It's big, like Mater. Julie says he fell asleep, because he was tired, but I think she was lying. He got all wet in the puddles because Mommy dropped him." She chuckled lightly. "She carries me too when I'm sleepy. She says I'm too heavy now."

"Then what happened?"

"Julie didn't let me watch. She brought cookies and milk and we watched TV." She let a shuddering sigh leave her chest. "But Mommy left and didn't come back until, um, I don't know. Julie watched me brush my teeth, and she was mean. She pinched me and it hurt."

"Why was she mean?"

Another flutter of a smile. "I laughed at her at dinner. I told Mommy about Julie's boyfriend, told her she's in love with Brent. She kicked me under the table. Then she pulled my hair when Mommy wasn't looking."

Kay looked toward the door and saw Elliot's face in the window, watching, listening. There was a boyfriend in the picture too, someone they had no idea existed. Someone who could have answers.

"Tell me about the truck. Did you see it well?"

"Yes, but I wasn't supposed to," she whispered, her voice tinged with fear.

"It's all right. What color was it?"

She hesitated for a moment. "White."

"Was anything written on it?"

The answer didn't come immediately. Her eyes moved a little slower, frowns appearing and disappearing in rapid sequence on her brow. She was trying to see into her memory—into the images she'd captured a few nights ago without paying attention, through thick falling rain. "It wasn't written, but the letters were there anyway."

Kay wondered what that meant. "Can you read the letters?" She held her breath.

"Um, F, minus, one, five, zero."

Was she talking about the tag?

Frowning, Kay looked at Elliot. He was scribbling something on his notepad, then he tore the page and placed it against the window. Just as she read Elliot's note, she realized she already knew the answer.

She was describing a Ford F-150.

The F-150 branding wasn't written on the back of the truck; it was embossed into the truck gate. That's what she meant when she'd said, "It wasn't written, but the letters were there anyway." Smart little girl.

Then a thought chilled Kay's blood. The odds that two different men came by the Coleman residence seeking to do harm had just dropped even further. By all appearances, they also seemed to drive similar trucks. And *those* odds were infinitesimal.

Was Heather confused between the two days?

Or, could it have been the same truck? Where did Cheryl leave John Doe's truck, after dumping his body by the side of the interstate? This looked less and less like self-defense.

But she didn't learn from Heather that John Doe had threatened Cheryl in any way. On the contrary, she'd learned John Doe had visited before, more than once. Only last Saturday, for some reason,

Cheryl had shot him dead in her own kitchen, while her little girls watched cartoons in the upstairs bedroom.

As she visualized the scene, another question emerged, just as unsettling.

Why didn't Julie react in any way? Heather may have been too young to understand what was going on, although kids her age have watched enough TV and played enough video games to know more than their share about shootings and death and crime in general. But Julie should've screamed, should've shouted something like, "Mom, what have you done?" or "What happened?" Or something. Anything but bringing cookies and milk for her sisters and watching cartoons while she knew her mother was loading a corpse into a truck right outside their window.

Everything about this case was insane, as if she'd crossed into a parallel universe somehow, where things and people and events had a different way of unraveling.

She had one more question for Heather, although she didn't much expect an answer that made any sense.

"What did your mom call the man who fell asleep at your house on Saturday?"

The same flicker of a smile touched her tense lips. "Mom made us call him uncle, but she called him baby, like she calls us. But he wasn't my brother," she chuckled lightly. "He's way too old to be my brother."

"How old?"

"He's got white hair," she replied with the definitive stance children have about old age, a hint of distaste coloring her voice. "He's old."

She exchanged a quick glance with Elliot. John Doe had salt-and-pepper hair, but to a child, that could've seemed like white, and the middle-age man could've seemed like old.

Everything they'd learned so far seemed to point to Cheryl Coleman killing John Doe, the man she was probably having an affair with, in cold blood.

CHAPTER TWENTY-SEVEN

A New Day

The dawn of a new day found him dozing off in an armchair he'd pulled over by the tall window, the white voile sheers touching his face gently as he breathed through his mouth. His head rested on his bent arm, positioned so that the first light would reach his eyes.

Rain had fallen all night, an ominous concert of sounds he knew so well. Mother was still raging, her pain raw, her blood still being spilled.

At first, a somber shade of gray lent its light to the sheers, the first barrier between the new day dawning and the thick darkness still filling the room. Then light, wounded and drab and weak, crept inside the room, touching his eyes in passing.

He woke with a start, then left the comfort of his armchair for the close proximity of the window, from where he could see the sky, his hands propped against the sill, his head bent backward. Ashen and almost dark toward the west, it was shrouded in cotton-like clumps of dirty clouds, shaded and leaden and powdered with traces of electric silver, endlessly restless, fretful and spasmodic while heading north, pressed to make room for others just like them.

Not a patch of azure anywhere to be seen.

As soon as the light had started contouring cloud shapes in deep slate grays, he rushed from one window to the next, staring at the sky, looking for a sign as the sun was about to rise.

Instead, the skies opened, sending rain down angrily, Mother's fist slammed against his door in reverberating, menacing thunder.

She had spoken; she expected her atonement in young blood.

Tomorrow, when the sun would be at its highest, he would deliver.

Defeated, he walked over to the window behind the bookcase, dimly lit by the pale lightbulb hanging from the basement ceiling, and looked at the girl. She hadn't moved in a while, her tear-streaked face pale, seeming whiter against the dark strands of her hair. Sometimes, her lips moved, but he couldn't hear any sounds.

His heart yearning, he touched the glass with his hand, the coolness of the surface a reminder of death, of the frailty of life, of the ephemeral dream living people all shared, when it was Mother who decided who lived and who died.

A tear started for the corner of his eye and rolled down slowly on his face. He was still looking at the girl, but his mind had wandered in the past, recalling the first sacrifice he'd laid at Mother's feet, and how the agony of that offering had nearly killed him.

Would this time be the same?

Leaning his forehead against the cold glass, he pulled out his locket and inhaled the scent of warm earth, of life and death that came from it. Pressing his lips gently against it, he murmured words with no end, imploring, defending, appealing to Mother's warm heart to let the girl live, to spill his blood instead.

Nearby, lightning hit the ground. He heard the crack of electricity exploding in the moisture-filled air just before thunder rolled loudly, rattling the house on its foundation.

She had spoken, her patience worn thin by his indecisiveness, his constant pleading, his weakness.

Come tomorrow at noon, he would prove his allegiance to her, and she'd forgive him, as she'd done many times, lending him her infinite strength.

On the basement floor two stories below, the girl shifted and whimpered softly. He touched the glass with the tips of his fingers, as if caressing her face.

"Soon, my sweet, dear girl, soon. I promise."

CHAPTER TWENTY-EIGHT

Dentist

Sore from another night spent on a cot in the nap room by Heather's side, Kay rubbed the nape of her neck with frozen fingers, thankful she'd only caught three hours of shuteye. Any more, and she'd be completely stiff, unable to turn her head at all and enduring more pain than a whole bottle of Motrin could tackle. Shifting into the passenger seat of Elliot's SUV, she finally settled in a position where her back didn't hurt.

The last thought before she fell into a deep yet agitated sleep the night before had been what she should do about Heather and Erin. She couldn't hold on to them forever, not with the Montgomerys cleared of any suspicion, not when they firmly demanded to have the girls released into their guardianship, which any judge in his or her right mind would order. It was their right as immediate family, in the absence of a will. But there was something that didn't let her pick up the phone and make that call, something she couldn't put her finger on.

It was obvious the unsub was not worried about leaving any witnesses behind; based on the nine-one-one call, he'd been aware of their presence in the house and didn't care. This indifference to leaving witnesses behind was one of the many strange things about that case.

As for Heather's ability to provide any useful information that could lead to finding Julie, that was likely tapped out. Not to mention, everything she'd already obtained from Heather had been strange, puzzling, and leading to more questions than answers, as if Heather had shared the group delusion that seemed common to all the events and actors of the case.

Swallowing a frustrated sigh, she opened her laptop and checked the APB she'd put out late the night before on John Doe's truck, with the only descriptive detail being, "late-model Ford F-150 truck, white." She didn't hold much hope; the state's highways teemed with them. It was the single, most popular truck sold and driven on the roads of California, white being the color of preference in the state where the sun almost always shone.

Nothing. No news on the APB, and nothing useful on the AMBER Alert either.

"This has to be the slowest-moving hurricane I've ever seen," Elliot said, shooting her a quick glance like he'd done a few times since they'd left the precinct.

"It's technically not a hurricane anymore." She took a sip of bitter coffee, brewed double strength by a deputy who'd been pulling double duty just like everyone else, but had somehow found the strength to take care of everyone's needs at the start of a new shift. "It's a tropical cyclone or something, whatever it is they call a hurricane after it makes landfall and starts disintegrating."

The wipers whirred rhythmically, alert, accelerated, and were still barely able to keep the windshield clear enough for short-range visibility. Taking the exit ramp, the SUV skidded a little when it hit an area where mud had washed onto the road, carried by flash-flooding waters. Elliot controlled the vehicle with a swift movement and a muttered oath. There was a firm frown above his blue eyes, and his lips, firmly pressed together, revealed his tension.

"Whatever you wanna call it, I'm getting bone-tired of it. This storm's as welcome as an outhouse breeze," he muttered, swerving to a stop at the intersection, then turning on his flashers as he took the regional road due west. He was approaching an area where landslides had been reported, minor ones, not something disruptive, but another could happen at any time, and there was no telling how damaging and life-threatening it would be, after so many days of endless downpour.

It was dark, although it was past nine, and the sun had been up for a while, somewhere behind menacing clouds, laced with dark gray and silver, heavy with water.

"It will be a couple of days," she said, intending to encourage him, but the tone of her voice was beat, depressing. She willed herself more optimistic and added casually, "These are called storm bands, I believe. We have a few more of these and we're in the clear. Then it's sunshine again, until snow season starts." She gave Mount Chester a long look, as it appeared in the landscape from behind majestic firs with a turn of the highway. It was shrouded in thick clouds, its peak invisible, its base hazy and seeming farther away than the twenty-something miles as the crow flies.

"Not a moment too soon," Elliot replied, pulling over in the gravel-lined parking lot of a small dental office, the wheels throwing pebbles against the undercarriage as he slammed the brakes to a halt.

The sign above the building said, PERFECT SMILES DENTAL, in white font on blue background, alongside the traditional image of a perfectly white tooth. Cheryl Coleman's place of employment.

She remembered that place from when she was a kid, scared out of her mind of the dentist, hating the smell of disinfectant and mouthwash, and the grating sound of the drill. Her dentist, an older man with trembling fingers and a permanent expression of suffering on his face, had long since sold the practice to a younger dentist, Dr. Labarre.

The dental office didn't smell like she recalled—modern materials dealing away with the dreaded odors and replacing them with scents she had to admit were almost pleasing, although the same annoying high-frequency whirring could be heard from one of the exam rooms. Soon, she'd have to get herself on Dr. Labarre's patient list; her teeth deserved a cleaning every now and then.

Elliot had shown the smiling receptionist his badge, and she'd quickly disappeared with swaying hips to get the doctor. Kay threw him a quick glance, to check his reaction to the return of the smiling beauty who couldn't've been more than twenty-three, but he didn't seem to care, absorbed in reviewing his email.

"Dr. Labarre will see you now," she chirped, making eye contact with only one of the detectives, her preference in the matter as crystal clear as her melodious voice. Before entering the dentist's back office, Kay had to refrain herself from scowling at the young woman who deliberately ignored her.

"Detectives, what can I do for you?" Dr. Labarre was tall and a little hunched, probably from leaning over all those open mouths. He looked more like an accountant than a dentist, although Kay couldn't immediately visualize what a dentist was supposed to look like. This one had thin-rimmed glasses lending class to a round face that warned of a tendency to become overweight, and a nice smile that touched his rather small eyes. "I'm guessing this has to do with Cheryl."

"Yes," Kay replied, refusing to take a seat, her back still feeling sore after two Motrin washed down with half a cup of black coffee. "Do you know if she was seeing someone?"

"Romantically, you mean?" the doctor asked, scratching his forehead. "Yes, she was seeing a man." He frowned slightly, parallel lines running across his tall brow. "I don't believe she'd dated much since the death of her husband. She was devastated when that happened. I remember when she got the call here, at the office." He paused for a moment, looking absentmindedly out the window, seemingly lost in thought. "I was actually concerned for her, for a few months after Calvin, her husband, passed. It was just her and three girls, all alone, struggling to make ends meet."

"Aren't the Montgomerys well off?" Elliot asked. "Were they at odds, or something?"

Dr. Labarre pressed his lips together for a moment, probably wondering how much he should share. "She kept her distance from the family. One time—when she was still grieving, and I used to find her crying in the supply closet every time she had a free moment—she told me she wanted nothing to do with that viper pit; her words, not mine." He cleared his throat as his frown deepened. "I don't believe she meant that literally, Detective. She suspected there was some foul play involved in her husband's death. She even made some calls to the Occupational Safety and Health Administration, asking them to investigate."

"And?" Elliot leaned against the door and plunged his hands into his pockets.

"They cleared the company of any wrongdoing. She was frantic for a while, saying the family must've paid OSHA off, but she had no evidence, nothing. It was just her grief talking."

"What did you think at the time?" Kay asked, taking a step forward. "I bet people talk in your office just like they do everywhere else they go. Do you recall hearing anything?"

"Less, Detective." He smiled, probably noticing how confused she seemed. "People talk less here because I work in their mouths. But no, no one said anything nor mentioned foul play in any way. Like I said, I knew Cheryl really well as my employee; it was just her grief talking."

"How long had she been working for you?" Elliot probed.

"She was my first employee after I bought the practice, so that's, um, eleven years now."

"Tell me about the man she was seeing," Kay asked. "Do you know his name?"

"No, I'm afraid I don't."

Elliot brought up John Doe's photo on his phone and showed it to the doctor. "Is this him?"

"No," the answer came immediately, tinged with an unspoken question, probably because he'd seen the man in the photo was also dead. "But I believe I recall she told me once her boyfriend was, or used to be, a teacher at her daughters' school."

Elliot sifted through images until he brought up the neighbor's, Frank Livingston. "Him?"

"Yes, that's him," the doctor confirmed.

"And you're sure they were involved?" Kay asked.

"As far as I can tell, yes. He brought her flowers one night. Then they sat out there in the waiting room after closing, their heads together, holding hands, whispering, you know, like they were close."

The lying son of a bitch, Kay thought. *I knew it.* "When was that?"

"About six months ago."

"One more question, Doctor."

"Sure."

"Do you know if she was planning to leave, and, if so, where was she going?"

He sighed, hesitating for a beat. "She requested an extended leave of absence. She said she was going to take the girls away for a while." He leaned forward and steepled his hands together in front of him, on a patient's chart lying open on his desk. "My gut is telling me she was running away from something. I even called her on it and offered my help, but she didn't share what it was that was driving her to run." His eyes blinked away sadness. "In retrospect, I wish I'd said something, done something." He lowered his gaze.

"Thank you, Dr. Labarre, you've been very helpful."

She turned to leave, but he caught up with her and touched her arm briefly. An expression of concern was written on his face. "Tell me, Detective, do you think you're going to find Julie?"

"We're doing everything we can," she replied, then left the building with one thought at the center of her mind.

Finally, someone had asked about Julie.

CHAPTER TWENTY-NINE

Points on a Map

Elliot drove in silence, every now and then glancing at Kay, wondering where her mind was at. She seemed tense, upset about something. She also looked tired, which was no surprise, but he knew better than to tell her that, or ask her why she popped Motrin like breath mints. This entire case had gone completely cuckoo on them, and it must've been driving her up the wall. And Julie had been missing for almost three days; he didn't have to ask to know that's what his partner was thinking about almost all the time. Would they still find her alive, and when? How, when they hadn't uncovered a single viable lead in all that time?

She'd been staring out the window, thinking intensely. He knew her tell; a deep ridge across her brow and slight movement in her lips occasionally, as if words wanted to gush out of her mouth but she kept them locked inside.

And the stupid rain that would not let go already. The entire precinct, soaked and miserable, was tied up with traffic collisions and safety assignments, dispatch calls rolling in faster than anyone could handle them, especially since the landslides had started popping left and right. Through the blurriness of the windshield wipers set in high gear, he gave Ash Brook Hill a concerned look, seeing how the ground had started splitting on the side, threatening to take a section of the interstate down with it. And if that went, they'd be screwed, left isolated without access to Redding's hospitals and emergency services.

But Kay didn't seem to notice.

"At least, we know who offed my vic," he spoke, his own voice sounding tense, almost strangled despite his lame attempt at sounding lighthearted.

"Uh-huh."

"We don't know why, or who he was, but I'd call that a decent outcome for a John Doe."

Silence, heavy and taut except for the sound of the engine and the whirring of the wiper blades against wet glass. Every now and then, lightning hit the ground in the distance, the accompanying thunder distant and rumbling, barely discernible.

"What do you think of Cheryl's killer?" he asked. She always saw more in witness statements and evidence than anyone he'd ever worked with.

After a long moment, she replied, turning forward and looking at the deserted road ahead. "There's something off about this entire case, Elliot. It's as if we all went down the rabbit hole, and landed in a parallel universe. People act normally, totally unfazed, about things that are miles and miles from normal." She lowered her gaze for a moment, that frown deepening still. "I've never felt so helpless about a case." Her voice trailed off. "Did Cheryl shoot your vic in cold blood? Or self-defense? Truth is, we might never know."

"Talk me through everything," he offered. "I wasn't here for the best parts or so it seems."

"First, the nine-one-one call. The weirdest things were said, you heard it yourself. As if Cheryl and the unsub were sharing a common delusion. Then—what's the likelihood of such a call to not get units dispatched? Zilch. I searched the databases, looking to draw blood." She glanced at him quickly, as if apologizing for her statement. "It's never happened for as long as the Redding emergency communications center has been operational."

"I'm reading something in the statements Heather made on the call. She said something like, 'He will take Julie,' right? Because that's why the operator thought it was a prank."

"Keep going."

"Seems that was true, and that Cheryl and the girls somehow knew that Julie was in danger of being abducted. Then why not call for help? Why not run?"

"She was going to, remember? There were packed suitcases in the hallway, and you heard Dr. Labarre."

"But then, why was she still there?" He cranked up the air conditioning; the windshield was starting to fog up. "If I knew someone was coming for one of my kids, I'd run outta there faster than a scalded cat, guns blazing."

"Well, that's exactly it," she replied, rubbing her hands in excitement. He loved seeing that spark in her eyes, when that fantastic and terrifying mind of hers started to put things together. "Her gun did blaze, right? She killed your John Doe."

"You're saying—"

"I'm saying, it might be she was still there because she thought she'd taken care of the threat against Julie. Maybe she'd already packed her bags when John Doe happened by and stopped her from leaving. Then she shot him and got rid of the body. Why run?" She crinkled her nose. "Nah… still sounds a little delusional to me. I'd still run; I'd just killed a man, and for some reason, I can't claim self-defense, can't call for help. I'm killing myself hauling two-hundred-and-sixty pounds of John Doe to the interstate instead of calling the cops." She bit her lip in another one of her tells; now she was building scenarios and playing with them in her mind. "Then it's the weirdness of the Montgomerys, and how they didn't bother to ask about Julie. Do they know something, or are they part of the same craziness that's making people delusional around here?"

"Good point." All that talk about delusions had reminded him of Dr. Edgell. "John Doe's shrink said he was being delusional, by the way. Makes me wonder if—"

"And so was Frank Livingston's mother."

"Was she? I wasn't there for that part."

"For when Frank Livingston lied to my face?"

He smiled. "Can't blame the man for not admitting his affair in front of his wife, Kay. Maybe he wants to live to see tomorrow's daylight."

"Yeah, okay," she conceded, seeming a little entertained by his comment. "In any case, the old Mrs. Livingston kept saying stuff that didn't make sense, and her son said she was delusional because of her Alzheimer's. Now I wonder..."

"What?"

"You see, a person can appear to be delusional herself if she describes the actions or words of delusional people. The one thing that threw me off badly and sold me on the Alzheimer's explanation was her mentioning the spirits of the valley."

"The what?"

"She claimed the spirits of the valley had visited Cheryl and were responsible for Julie's abduction, and that Frank had known of their intention ahead of time and had done nothing."

He laughed. "Now, see, I would've bought the Alzheimer's theory too, at that point. What—"

She had fired up the laptop and was running a database search. "It was something she said. What if—spirits or no spirits—she was on to something?"

"What did she say?"

"That only the firstborn daughters had been taken from the area, ever since she can remember, and none of the girls have ever been found." She typed quickly, her nimble fingers dancing on top of the keyboard. "I find that hard to believe, though; I grew up in this area and I've never heard of any spirits of the valley taking firstborn daughters—" She fell silent for a beat. "I'll be damned," she muttered.

"Seriously?" This case was getting crazier by the minute. "You found others?"

"Thirty-seven others, Elliot." Her excitement had waned, replaced by a somber tension he knew well from other cases they'd worked together. His partner had smelled blood. "Says here, in the past fifty years, there were thirty-seven girls reported missing or abducted in the area, and all cases are still open. Five of these cases were murder-kidnappings, just like ours."

He braked forcefully and muttered a curse under his breath. Engulfed in the conversation, he'd almost missed the exit. The SUV swerved, skidding onto the accumulated layer of water, then regained its traction the moment Elliot stepped on the gas. "Any closed cases with the same parameters?"

"First thing I checked, and there are none. I would've expected at least some, at least coincidentally, but there are none." She clicked a few keys, then turned the screen sideways. "Elliot, look at the map. All these cases, they're centered here, in Mount Chester, within a twenty-five-mile radius or so." She stopped talking for a loaded beat. "Girls taken like Julie were never heard from again, not in fifty years."

He took his eyes off the road for a split second, enough to catch a glimpse of the cluster of red dots surrounding the area. The odd red dot appeared in other areas of the state, several in LA, a couple in San Francisco, both cities known hubs of kidnappings and open missing persons cases. Out of the many open missing persons cases, only some had been first daughters. "Why fifty years?"

"Good point. Let's go back a hundred." The map caught a few more colored pins. "There are forty-three now, here, in this area." She switched screens and squinted a little to read the fine print in the dates report. "The oldest one goes back to fifty-seven years ago."

Elliot turned into Angel Creek Pointe, sending a wave of puddled water up in the air, splashing the empty sidewalk.

"This is no longer a murder-kidnapping," she said, typing an email at the same time. "We'll treat this as a serial killer case. I'm bringing Logan up to speed." She stopped typing for a moment, as if gathering her thoughts. "It could, potentially, be cult-related after all. Otherwise, who keeps on kidnapping and killing for fifty-seven years?"

CHAPTER THIRTY

Whispers

Julie hadn't slept in a while, not deeply. She hadn't been awake either; she'd been slipping in and out of consciousness, lying on the floor with her back against the door, wrapped in the comforter she'd stripped from the bed but still not feeling warm. Not feeling cold either; just numb and faint and sleepy.

She'd stopped drinking water, too weak to get up and walk to the bathroom, where the small sink could quench her thirst. She wasn't feeling thirsty either; just floating away, distanced from her own agonizing body while her mother was right there, by her side.

She wasn't bleeding anymore. Her mother's face was serene and kind, smiling gently as she caressed her hair the way she always did, running her fingers through it while her thumb swiped across her eyebrow, straightening its rebellious strands.

"Are you angry with me, Mom?" she whispered, words only she could hear as they left her parched lips.

She wasn't. She smiled and told her she loved her. Julie couldn't hear her voice, but could read the words in the movement of her pale lips. Was she really there? She didn't know… she couldn't be sure.

Her consciousness slipped again into nothingness, then came back, and her mother was still there. The memory of her body lying on the kitchen floor in a pool of blood had faded away, as if millennia had passed, as if it never really happened.

She must've fallen asleep for a while, because she startled awake, but then wondered if she was really awake or not. She'd felt her mother's warm hand caressing her frozen face, but now she was gone.

"Mom?" she called, but no one answered. "Are you here?"

She wasn't, but her words, fainter than a sigh, couldn't've reached too far. Maybe she would return. She'd just wait there for her, grateful she felt sleepy instead of cold, and falling asleep seemed easy, easier than it had ever been.

Startling awake again, she listened for sounds, any proof she was still alive, any promise she could survive her ordeal. Only rain drumming against metal gutters, and distant thunder ominous, as if the earth itself was looking back in anger.

The future no longer scared her. She wished her fate would meet her already, while she still had an ounce of energy rushing through her veins. She wanted to have a chance and fight her captor, the man who'd taken her, while she could still stand. But could she, really?

As if to test herself, she propped herself against the floor, lifting her weak body slowly, painfully, as her arms trembled with the effort. Dizzy and nauseated, she had to stop, leaning onto her right arm, her legs folded underneath her trembling body. Yet she'd rather die fighting, trying to free herself, than to die a slow death in that basement, where probably other girls had before her.

HELP ME

Those two words she'd found scratched into the masonry right by the door came into her mind vividly, spreading terror and angst, but she still couldn't raise herself up to her feet, not even if she reached for the door handle and grabbed onto that.

"Shhh, baby," her mother said, caressing her cheek.

She let herself fall back onto the concrete floor and managed a weak smile, her dry lips cracking open. "Mom." She was there, and she wasn't angry. "I'm so sorry," she whispered, "for everything

I've done." She wanted to shift a little, to remove her numb arm from underneath her, but couldn't find the strength. As darkness fell around her, she wasn't afraid anymore, only sad. "Oh, Mom, you were right to cry the day I was born."

CHAPTER THIRTY-ONE

Spirits

Frank Livingston was just pulling out of his driveway as they approached, and Elliot turned on his flashers for a second to get his attention. With frustration clearly visible on his face, he put his white Toyota Tacoma in reverse and stopped short of entering the garage. Then the garage door came down, as he left the comfort of his truck and rushed under the shelter of his covered porch.

That was an interesting choice, considering the heavy downpour. In his place, Kay would've reversed all the way into the garage, opting for dry clothes; maybe he had something to hide in his garage, or was just embarrassed by the cluttered space, common for California garages turned storage space.

Livingston waited for them with a stern expression on his face, arms crossed at his chest despite the raincoat he was wearing, its sides flapping in the wind with a rustling sound.

"You're making me late for work, Detectives. What now?"

Kay rushed to the porch, but by the time she got there, her shoes were squelching, and her jacket was soaked. She swallowed a long curse; this rainy season might've been a record or something; it should've been over already.

"No worries, Mr. Livingston, they know we were coming to see you. We called the school first."

That shut him up promptly and brought a shade of ash to his face. "What's this about?"

"Lying," she replied coldly. He instinctively took a small step back. "Like when you omitted to tell us about the true nature of your relationship with Cheryl Coleman."

Panic drained the blood from his face. His dilated pupils locked on Kay, pleading, scared. "Please, Detective, I didn't mean anything by it. It's just that my wife," he added, lowering his voice, "doesn't know. And it's not like Cheryl and I were seeing each other anymore. That's over, for almost six months now." He clasped his hands together, tightly, his knuckles white. "Please, Detectives, can we keep this between us?"

He glanced briefly at Elliot, then back at her. Her partner didn't react in any way. He seemed more interested in studying the man, in hearing what he had to say.

"That depends, Mr. Livingston. If we have your cooperation, you'll have ours."

"Thank you," he replied quickly, letting out a long, relieved breath of air. "Anything you want to know, just ask." He looked around quickly. "It's better if we stay out here. I hope you understand."

There wasn't any other car in the garage, and his was the only vehicle in the driveway. His wife must've left for work already.

"Is your wife at home?" Kay asked, regardless.

"No, but my mother... um, she can't keep secrets that well, you know. It's her Alzheimer's."

"All right, we'll stay put and we'll keep our voices down," Kay reassured him. "Tell me about your affair with Cheryl."

He shrugged ever so slightly. "It didn't last long, only a few months. She'd been alone after Calvin died, grieving, struggling. Then, one day she asked for my help to change the fluorescent light on her kitchen ceiling. One thing led to another, and..." He veered his gaze sideways, his cheeks flushed. "I really don't know how it happened or who started it. I do remember telling her my marriage was over though."

Kay listened, unwilling to interrupt, eager to hear what he'd be willing to share.

"Cheryl was a beautiful woman, Detective. Charming, funny, and vulnerable. Strong too and hardheaded sometimes, stubborn as they come."

"How did your relationship end? Who broke it off?"

"She did," he replied, lowering his gaze for a brief moment. His voice was tinted with sadness that was reflected in the lines around his mouth and the drooping corners of his eyes. "She said she'd met someone else, and soon thereafter, there was another man coming by to see her." He sighed, pained. "My guess is she was uncomfortable living next door to me, to my wife. And I was, um… too much of a coward to tell Diane I wanted a divorce." He drew breath and looked at his shoes for a long moment of silence. He seemed defeated, empty inside. "Because I loved Cheryl with all my heart, Detective. She was my second chance at feeling young again, at being alive. She was only thirty-five and I—I'm pushing fifty." He swallowed with difficulty, still avoiding Kay's eyes. "She was right to leave me behind."

"Were you upset when she dumped you?" Elliot asked. "I bet that made you feel like crap."

"I was heartbroken," he answered candidly. "But if you're asking if I held a grudge or anything, the answer is no. I loved Cheryl and wanted her to be happy. That's why—" he stopped mid-phrase and bit his lip. "Anyway, do you have any other questions? I need to run."

"That's why what, Mr. Livingston?" Kay asked.

"Nothing, really, just feeling guilty for having slept through her ordeal, that's all," he replied a little too quickly for Kay's liking. He was definitely hiding something, and he'd almost spilled it. He shifted his eyes as if following the trail of a fly through the air, but couldn't escape Kay's intense, demanding gaze. "Something she said, that's all, but I don't think—"

"What was it?"

"When she was asking me to not be upset when we were parting ways, she said there was someone else and that she had to find the truth."

"That's what she said? She had to find the truth? About what?"

He shook his head. "That was all of it, I swear. I asked her a few times, but she pulled away, as if regretting saying even that much." He clenched his jaws for a moment. "I remember asking her because she was cold about it, factual, sad even. She didn't sound like a woman who had found a new love, but I chose to think she refrained from saying more, from showing emotion, because she didn't want to hurt me."

Kay changed direction. "Do you know the name of Cheryl's new boyfriend?"

He shook his head firmly. "No. I never met him, just saw him from the driveway a couple of times, and both times it was almost dark."

Elliot showed him John Doe's photo on his phone. "Could this be him?"

He looked at the photo, seemingly puzzled and worried at the same time, while a frown landed on his brow. "Yes, this could've been him; I recognize his hair. But this man's also dead. What's going on, Detective?"

"That's what we're trying to figure out," Kay replied. "One more thing, Mr. Livingston. Could we speak with your mother?"

"My mother? Why?" He plunged his hands in the deep pockets of his raincoat. Kay could tell he'd clenched his fists.

"She might know more than she's saying. Does she look out the window often?"

He seemed uneasy, hesitant, as if what he was about to say would be self-incriminating. "She spends her entire day by her window, daydreaming. Her mind's not what it used to be."

"Where does her window face?"

A short sigh left his lips. "That way," he pointed toward Cheryl's driveway, then slid his hand back into his pocket, as if trying to hide the slight tremor Kay had already caught.

"Then she might know something, Mr. Livingston. Please, we won't take long."

Reluctantly, he unlocked the front door and invited them in. Kay gave the familiar living room a quick look, noticing what had changed. The dining-room table was clean and set for dinner, with a table runner holding spices and a vase with fresh-cut wildflowers. Everything was in perfect order—the sofa pillows symmetrically laid out and fluffed, all surfaces shiny and clear of dust. Diane Livingston might've stopped being her husband's lover, but she was definitely trying to be a good wife.

The old Mrs. Livingston came eagerly to meet them, and, to Kay's surprise, approached her with an unsteady but energetic gait and placed two hearty smooches on her cheeks. "Dear girl, come, sit down with me." She grabbed Kay's hand with bony fingers and dragged her to the table. She took a seat, while Frank helped his mother take hers. "No one comes to visit me, you know. What a pleasure!"

"Same here," Kay replied. "I wanted to ask you about Cheryl, and what happened the night Julie disappeared."

"Aah, that," she replied, then extended a trembling hand and pinched Kay's chin with a loving gesture normally reserved for young children. "Are you a first daughter, my dear?"

Kay locked eyes with Elliot for a brief moment. There was amusement in his eyes, mixed with incredulity. "Yes, I am," she replied, feeling an unexpected chill travel down her spine as she said the words.

"How old are you?" she asked, and Elliot stifled a smile. Then Betty touched her arm in a reassuring gesture. "Never mind, my dear, and forgive me for asking. I remember you're a police officer, and that means you're too old."

Kay frowned. "Too old for what?"

"For the spirits to take you," she replied, and Elliot turned away to hide a smile. But the woman seemed to firmly believe what she was saying. What if she wasn't delusional after all? If Kay were to admit for a weird, twisted moment that Betty was sane, what questions would she ask of her?

"How old would you have to be, to be taken?"

"Under twenty, I presume," she replied calmly, as if she were the sanest person to ever walk the earth. "I never really kept track. The spirits want them young—fifteen or sixteen, rarely older than that. I was happy I had a son, not a daughter, and he had sons too."

Kay bit her lip, angry she hadn't paid more attention to the report, where the victims' ages were clearly mentioned. Finding out that there were so many had been unsettling. In her entire career, she'd never heard of a serial killer to keep on killing for fifty-seven years, without stopping, without getting caught. And what did that mean for Julie? Being taken by someone with so much experience in abducting and probably killing women? She didn't have a chance... she was probably dead already. Without realizing, she gritted her teeth and thrust her chin forward. Until she found Julie's remains, she wasn't going to stop looking for her.

"Tell me more about these spirits."

"Ever since I can remember, they have taken girls to never be seen again. They are merciless, you know, the spirits of the valley; they can't be defeated. Cheryl tried, twice, and she still died. They took that sweet little girl anyway." She turned to Frank and asked, "Where are your manners? Give us a glass of lemonade, or something." Then she turned back to Kay. "They live forever."

"Have you seen any men visiting Cheryl?"

She shot her son a quick, inquisitive glance. The old woman knew a lot more than her son was giving her credit for. "No," she replied calmly. "Just the spirits came calling. Twice," she added, raising her frail voice a little and holding two knotty fingers in the air.

Frank Livingston brought a pitcher of cold lemonade from the fridge and filled three glasses with slightly trembling hands. Whatever his mother knew, it scared him—the same uneasiness she'd witnessed before when speaking with the Livingstons still present, although his affair had been exposed. It had to be about something else.

She didn't touch her glass, and neither did Elliot, but Betty brought hers to her lips with both hands and took a few sips.

"What do the spirits look like? Can you describe them?"

"I don't see all that well," she said, a touch of sadness in her voice, "but I'll try."

Kay kept a straight face, although she felt like swearing out loud. Was she wasting precious time on a woman who made absolutely no sense?

"First, darkness swirls around the houses where firstborn daughters live. Then, when the spirits come calling, darkness engulfs the house, and only wisps of white can be seen streaking through as they approach." She lowered her voice to a whisper, just as Kay was getting ready to leave. Reluctantly, she had to admit her time was more valuable than that.

She rose from her seat with an apologetic smile, and Frank followed suit, seemingly relieved.

"Then they take human form," she whispered. Kay let herself slide back into her chair. "But I never saw their faces."

"Then what happens?"

"Trails of their blood, bright, living red streaking through the darkness as they leave, taking those poor girls with them."

"Have you seen them before, these spirits?"

"No." Betty shook her head. "Not until a few nights ago, I don't remember exactly when. But I've heard stories about them all my life."

Kay stood, ready to leave. There was nothing there. And still, before leaving, she wanted to see one more thing. "Could you please show me your window, where you saw the spirits from?"

She rose, leaning against the table for support as Frank pulled out her chair and offered his arm, then led the way to a small bedroom decorated with old books, macrame, and several china ballerinas on bookcase shelves. The room smelled of antiquities, of yellowed paper and stale fabric gathering dust. Of old age.

In front of the window, there was a large armchair, covered with a faded blanket. She sat in it, putting her legs up on a small ottoman, then turned to Kay and smiled, her withered lips stretched thin across two rows of aging teeth, still hers. "This is where I spend my days, my dear."

The window overlooked the Coleman property driveway and the side entrance that the unsub had used. At the street end of the driveway, a lamppost stood tall. At night, it would've flushed the property in bright yellow light. So, where was that darkness-whirling-around-the-house notion coming from? What had she seen?

She turned to look at Betty to ask, but froze with her mouth agape. Now in full daylight, she could see the old woman more clearly.

She had cataracts on both eyes.

Everything she might've seen would've been through a thick blur.

She thanked Frank Livingston and left the house, happy to breathe the fresh, moist air outside. Then, without any words spoken where the Livingstons might still hear them, she grabbed Elliot's sleeve and tugged gently. "Follow me."

"Sure will," he replied, as she was already rushing through the thick rain across the lawn, to the Coleman property. Once there, they stopped under the porch roof.

"I wonder about this darkness whirling nonsense," she said, eyeing the lamppost. "This thing would've lit the place up really well. But we've only seen this crime scene during daytime, so I wonder—"

"She's got cataracts, Kay, she's legally blind."

"Yeah, I know. She can't drive or read, but she can still tell between darkness and light."

"And she's got Alzheimer's, you know better than I do how that screws with people's minds."

"Yeah, I know all that, but I still think there's something to all this madness. The way Frank Livingston seems scared we'll learn something he's trying to hide, his mother's convictions about these spirits, whatever the heck they are—and don't forget it was the legally blind, Alzheimer's woman who led us to find there's a serial killer at large, Elliot. As far as I'm concerned, Betty's earned some solid credit, and I'm willing to buy everything she's saying, no matter how delusional it sounds."

"Fair enough," he replied, frowning as he saw her taking off her shoes and socks, and rolling up the hems of her pants. "What are you doing?"

"Oh, wipe that smirk off your face, cowboy. Don't get any crazy ideas in your head." He hid his widening grin under the brim of his hat for a brief moment, then he lifted it from his head and put it on hers, still smiling as she sprinted through heavy rain toward the lamppost.

She circled it, feeling the pounding of icy razor blades in each heavy raindrop that hit her skin. At the root of the lamppost, the housing had been put on crookedly, making it easy to remove with her bare hands.

Inside, all the wires had been cut.

CHAPTER THIRTY-TWO

In the Rain

He wore a yellow Helly Hansen waterproof jacket and jeans that were already soaked below the knee. He didn't feel much of that; he'd pulled the pant legs over his calf-high boots, and carelessly stepped in puddles and mud, only thinking of her.

He turned his face up high, squinting between raindrops to see the sky, to restlessly search for that elusive patch of blue that would mean life, for the two of them, together. Instead, the gloom seemed lower and heavier than ever, the wind gusts carried rain-frozen blades stabbing his skin.

He welcomed the cold, refreshing needles against his face. It reinvigorated him, reminding him of Mother's wrath and her unquenched thirst for blood.

His blood.

"Dear Mother, forgive me, forgive your weak, wavering child," he whispered, tasting the water on his lips as he spoke. Raindrops seemed to rush toward him, accelerating, driven by a force like he'd never seen before—like white, shiny blades cutting through air, hitting the ground mercilessly one after another by the millions every second, their strength in their infinite number and just as infinite cruelty.

The water tasted a bit salty, as if the immense ocean had been swept by the storm and lifted to the depths of the skies, only to be slammed against the ground later.

He stood on the edge of such a wound, almost at the top of the hill. The gentle slope had opened under the forces of falling water, a slice of the hill sliding downward, carried forward by gravity and its lubricant, water. Where once greenery covered the banks, now the dark brown of the earth was exposed, rivulets of mud rushing to the bottom of the valley like blood leaving the body of a dying wounded.

His dear Mother was bleeding, unable to heal until he did the right thing.

It was decided; despite the burning ache in his heart at the thought of the sacrifice awaiting him tomorrow, this time he wouldn't implore Mother's mercy to spare the girl, nor would he waver again. He'd seen with his own eyes the size of her wounds, the depth, the hurt.

He opened his arms wide and took in the force of the rain, welcoming it, wishing his body was large enough to shield Mother from it. Cleansing and at the same time murderous, rain didn't care… just kept coming down, accompanied by roars and rumbles of thunder, some near, some distant, far away, where the woods met the sky on the horizon.

His mind drifted, his heart clasped in the iron fist of worry.

This time, two little girls were left behind. Two little girls who were now with the police, telling them everything they'd seen, putting him and his work at risk. Was it fated for him to die in shame, locked in a cage like an animal? Or would his work outlive him, glorifying his existence and the many sacrifices he'd endured for Mother's sake, his name forever remembered and spoken in awe?

"Dear Mother, hear your child," he shouted as loudly as he could, because only she could hear him now. Rain washed over him in bursts, pasting his hair across his face, filling his mouth when he spoke. "Protect me as I will protect you. Defend me and hold me in your arms, as I deliver the ultimate sacrifice to you, my own blood." He laughed and danced, spinning with his arms raised high in the air like a dervish, carried into near hysteria by frenzied elation.

When he stood like that—feeling her support under his feet, receiving her protection in the wind wrapping around his body—he knew she and her earthly child were one, joined as it was forever intended to be, and no sacrifice would be unworthy.

No matter how agonizing.

CHAPTER THIRTY-THREE

Monster

When Kay rushed in through the precinct door, she was still barefoot, carrying her shoes in one hand and her laptop in the other tightly shielded at her chest, her wet feet stamping footprints on the carpet. She'd given Elliot his hat back, putting it on his head herself, and still recalled the loaded smile he'd accepted it with and the spark between them when their eyes met under the wide brim.

The precinct smelled musty and acrid, as if the rain outside had seeped through the walls or the floor somehow. Deputies had come and gone all day long wearing soaked jackets and boots that dripped water on the carpet, the air too humid to let it evaporate. The place would probably stink for a while, maybe until the air would dry again, after the first snowfall.

There was an unexpected welcoming committee waiting for them. Sheriff Logan, seemingly fuming, had emerged from his office the moment Elliot had pulled up in front of the building. Rushing from the back, Deputy Farrell carried several flipchart sheets filled with Erin's doodles. Without a real choice in the matter, she turned to the sheriff, but didn't get the opportunity to open her mouth.

"Glad you have email, Detective, so you can drop a bomb on me without the courtesy of looking me in the eye." He stood with his hands propped on his hips, a stance he favored since he'd packed a few pounds around his waistline. His bulging abdomen threatened the integrity of several of his shirt buttons, one barely hanging by a couple of threads. "Do you have any idea how forty-three unsolved serial kidnappings, possibly homicides, are going to reflect on this unit? How do we contain this?"

Of course, he was taking it personally, mostly because he cared deeply about the people he was sworn to protect. He was a good man, almost always making solid decisions, but in an election year he had every right to be concerned with voters' perceptions.

"I'd say it will reflect positively," she replied calmly. "After all, this has been going on for fifty-seven years, and only under your leadership was it discovered."

"Damn right it was," he replied quickly, grabbing the lifesaver and running with it. "Now, what are we doing about it?"

"I'll review these cases, even the old ones, and work them by the book. Discover patterns, study victimology, interview the families of recent victims. We'll generate a profile, and we'll catch him," she promised, hoping she'd be able to deliver. It was the unsub's longevity that worried her. It was unprecedented.

Doubt flashed in his eyes, quickly replaced by the same defensive indignation she'd managed to defeat only for a brief moment. "What, you're saying we didn't do our jobs? That's what everyone will think. Forty-three victims, my goodness…" He cupped his mouth in the palm of his hand, visibly distraught. "The people will freak out, and they have every right."

"Investigating a kidnapping is entirely different from catching a serial killer." Her voice was reassuring, instilled with a confidence she was only partly feeling. Yes, she'd hunted serial killers for eight years after she joined the FBI and had a perfect case record to show for it, but this one was different. This unsub had managed not to get caught all those years, but there was something else about him just as unlikely: he'd never escalated. The vast majority of serial killers escalated, accelerating the time between victims, once hooked on the thrill of the kill always seeking more, blood junkies looking for their next fix.

Except this one.

She fired up her laptop and set it on a nearby desk, so eager to dig through the data she didn't take the time to slip on her socks and shoes. Pulling up the missing persons reports, she sorted them by date, from the most recent.

"I worked that one," Elliot said, his voice somber. "I still talk with the parents; they never gave up hope. Lauren Costin, she was fifteen when she vanished on her way back from school." He paused for a beat, staring at her name on the screen, listed second, just under Julie's. "I had nothing to go on. One moment she was there, the next one she was gone, and no one had seen a thing. It was as if the earth had swallowed her whole. It was two years ago."

"I worked *her* case," Logan tapped on the screen next to the third name on the list, Stephanie Guerrero. He shook his head, his earlier anguish replaced with frustrated powerlessness. "Catch this son of a bitch, Kay. We have a lot of families waiting for closure, and one girl who might still be alive."

She raised her eyes from the screen and looked at the sheriff sternly. "We'll get the bastard."

"Detective—" Farrell pushed through between Logan and Elliot, still holding her sheets of paper. "Take a look at this." She laid a piece of paper on the desk, keeping it flat with her hands where the corners rolled up.

The drawing had improved a little in terms of detail, but it still depicted the same thing. An open mouth, drawn in black, simplistically represented by a rounded, down-pointing triangular shape with zig-zagging lines that looked like teeth. From the center of the teeth-flanked triangle, blood dripped green.

"I tried everything I could think of," Farrell, said. "I took her green pen, I only let her have the blue and the red, she didn't draw anything. I gave her the black, she only drew the mouth with the teeth. Whatever she's drawing, it must've been green." She sighed. "Not sure how much good this will—"

"Let me see this," Elliot said, stepping closer to the desk. He frowned as he studied the drawing, then muttered, "I wonder if that's not—" He took out his phone and started typing quickly in his browser window. Moments later, he showed Kay the screen of his phone, where a stylized snake head was displayed.

Her blood turned to icicles.

"It's green because it's not blood, it's a snake's tongue," he said. "It's an Austin, Texas, sports team logo, Vipers Lacrosse."

"What are the chances that it's for real?" Logan asked in disbelief. "She's four years old, for goodness' sake. Last thing we need is another wild goose chase."

Head slightly tilted, Kay compared the two images. The resemblance was clear, if she took the artist's age into account. She turned to ask Farrell to bring Erin, but the deputy was already returning from the interview room with the girl in tow. She seemed a little scared, her round eyes darting from person to person as she trailed behind her a soft blanket, which must have been another item on loan from Deputy Farrell.

Elliot crouched in front of her and took his hat off. "Hello, young lady," he said with a smile Erin found hard to resist. She reached for his tousled blond hair, dropping the blanket. "Mind if you looked at something for me?"

Erin smiled with her mouth open, the most relaxed Kay had seen her since she was found sleeping by her mother's cold body. The man had skills that seriously competed with Farrell's when it came to making children feel at ease, quite an unexpected feature for a young cop from Austin, Texas.

He took the phone from Kay but held it face down for a moment. "I'm going to show you a picture. Can you tell me if you recognize the animal in the picture? It won't hurt you; I swear. Cross my heart and hope to die."

The little girl nodded, the tip of her thumb finding its way into her mouth while her eyes were fixed on Elliot's hand as he positioned the phone screen for her to see.

Her face transformed as she studied the image, the smile replaced by a grimace of fear and agony. Her finger pointing at the screen, in a brittle voice she said, "Monster."

CHAPTER THIRTY-FOUR

Plan

"Who kidnaps girls and potentially kills them, for more than fifty years in a row?" Kay asked, without really expecting an answer. The question was addressed mostly to herself, although Elliot's input was always welcome.

They'd returned to her desk, where he'd pulled out a chair and was looking at the screen, offering bits and pieces of information about recent cases that sounded familiar. He'd moved to Mount Chester six years ago, long after Kay had relocated to San Francisco, but had only worked one of the kidnappings himself.

There was one thing bugging her, annoying her like a mosquito buzzing in the dark. She'd grown up in that town, and she was a first daughter. Yet she'd never heard about these kidnappings, nor did her mother ever warn her to watch her back—not any more than what a typical mother would. She'd never mentioned the spirits of the valley or any related folklore. Was any of it real?

Kay had grown up in her own brand of hell; before her mother would've had the time to worry about surreal beings and the local folklore, she'd had to deal with an abusive, chronically intoxicated husband, and two children she routinely had to shield from his rages. The folklore—even if her mother had heard it—had been too remote, while Kay's father's rage had been close, raw, undiluted.

"Denise, got a moment?" she called, seeing Deputy Farrell walk by with the girls' oatmeal in two small microwaveable bowls. Like

Kay, she'd grown up locally, in a large family with ancient roots in the region.

Farrell stopped by Kay's desk, still holding the bowls in her hands. "What's up?" A hint of worry tainted her voice.

"I was wondering if you'd heard about this first-daughter-folklore bit. You grew up here, right?"

"Yeah," Farrell smiled nostalgically. Her eyes softened. She must've had a pleasant childhood filled with fond memories. "My mother used to say that the fairies cried by the birthing mother's bed if the firstborn child was a daughter. I was one, but no one ever snatched me. But I remember feeling sad every time my mother used to say that. I thought maybe she didn't want me or something." She chuckled lightly. "That's until I grew older and knew better. She was awesome, my mom." She waited patiently for a moment, but Kay didn't reply. "Anything else? I left the girls alone."

"No, that's it, thank you," Kay replied, and Farrell rushed to the kitchen to warm up the oatmeal.

It wasn't just Betty Livingston's Alzheimer's mind populated with such incredible stories; the legend was rooted somewhere in the past of Mount Chester's small-town community. It had probably emerged when devastated parents had tried to make sense of their tragedy after their daughters had gone missing without a trace. Fifty years ago—without the constant distractions brought by the internet and television and social media—people had more time to think, to talk, to put things together and notice patterns such as the first-daughter commonality in the victimology.

"He'd have to be, what, eighty years old now?" Elliot asked, staring intently at the screen. While she'd been chatting with Deputy Farrell, he reviewed the victim list, reading the details of the most recent few cases.

"Or more," she replied dryly. "He'd be eighty if he started taking these girls at twenty-three, which is relatively young. But

that's not even the biggest problem I'm seeing with this profile."
She took a sip of hot, bitter coffee from the paper cup by her side,
after holding it for a while between her frozen hands to warm
them up. For a moment, she thought of Avery Montgomery, his
distinguished poise and white hair and club dinners with the mayor.
But no… he didn't fit, even if he didn't have the ironclad alibi. He
was too calm, too composed, and Julie was his great-grandchild.
She'd looked straight into his watery eyes and had not seen a trace
of guilt or fear, or the tiniest flicker of worry. Other than being
eighty-three years old, she had no reason to think of him as the
unsub. Even so, he was weak and frail, unable to load someone
like Julie in his truck. "What bugs me is he didn't devolve," she
said. "From what I could tell, his MO stayed the same for decades.
He didn't accelerate the timeline either."

"Why is that an issue?" Elliot asked.

"The majority of serial killers are sexually motivated, although
lust isn't the only driver behind the urge to kill. But we could safely
eliminate that motivation from the profile. Sexually motivated
sadists accelerate the timeline, as their search for the ultimate
thrill always leaves them wanting more, and they almost always
unravel. They also lose interest in killing once they age and their
sex drive diminishes." She stared at the screen filled with names,
seeing how it was always a year or more between abductions. "Well,
not this unsub. We have no choice but to consider this unsub a
mission-driven killer."

"If we haven't found any bodies, how can you be sure there
was no sexual component in the killings?"

"I can't be sure, but I'm willing to bet there isn't," she replied,
while her thoughts probed into her reasoning. As always, Elliot's
question, spot on, triggered another round of analysis. Was she
taking a leap here, assuming the unsub didn't rape his victims? But,
for a lust killer, how does a steady cooling-off period of over a year
make sense? "Not unless this killer has always had the libido of

an eighty-year-old." She took another sip of coffee, still thinking. "Nah, I guess we have to consider he's mission-driven."

She paused for a while, weighing the theory in her mind. Did it fit? Not entirely. Most mission-oriented serial killers wanted to eliminate some perceived evil from the world, or at least their corner of it. Some wanted their cities rid of homeless people, prostitutes, or drug users. Any social group that the killer's twisted mind would perceive as undesirable could potentially become a target. But what could possibly make young girls from low-risk, suburban families become undesirable? That was the part that didn't fit. She had to look into the victimology before she could be sure. The only alternative left was power- and control-seeking sadists, but most of them used sex as the means to control the victims, and sex just didn't jibe well with the unsub's longevity and meticulousness in executing perfectly organized kidnappings for almost six decades.

With a tinge of regret, she abandoned the warm coffee cup on the desk and flipped through some screens, landing on the map view of the cases.

"See how they're all centered here, in Mount Chester?" The red dots were scattered on the map all the way to the Pacific Coast, and inland a good twenty-five miles away from the town. Yet the pattern was clear. "He's local; he has to be."

"What about these other cases, in LA and San Francisco, and the one in Bakersfield?"

"They might be related, just as some of the forty-three here might be unrelated. It just makes more sense to focus here, and find out what these cases have in common. We should divide and conquer."

Elliot stood and pushed the chair away from the desk. "How do you explain his longevity?"

For a moment, she let her mind wander freely, while she looked out the window at the falling rain bashed against the glass by angry gusts of wind. "I don't," she eventually answered. "The most prolific serial killer on record is Samuel Little, with ninety-three victims over thirty-five years in twelve states. The FBI investigation is ongoing, and will probably not end very soon." She rubbed her hands together slowly, the gesture helping her think. "Thirty-five years, Elliot, the most prolific ever. Fifty-seven is unheard of. We're in record-breaking territory." She stood, closed the lid on her laptop and put on her jacket. It still felt moist and cold against her heated skin, enough to make her shiver. "It's not impossible, I guess. Or it could be more than one unsub."

"Like what, partners? A team?"

She nodded. "They are extremely rare and always devolve. They're never as neat, as precise as this one, nor as enduring." She grabbed two sheets of paper from the printer. "It makes sense, if you stop and think about it. Whatever motivates the first killer—whatever trauma, genetics, hormonal imbalance, or psychosis is at the root of his urges—will be genetically and environmentally different in his partner. The urges to kill and torture aren't identical. Before long, the fabric that holds the serial-killing team together starts tearing at the seams."

"Sheesh," he muttered. "Can you imagine, going out there and finding another killer just like you, and forging a partnership? How does one do that?" His face showed so much revulsion she decided not to tell him what she knew about some of those cases. "But if the girls were killed, like you seem to believe, where are they now? How come no one found their bodies in almost six decades?"

"All great questions," Kay replied, unable to shake the feeling that she was missing something.

"Why do you think he kills them, anyway?"

His question saddened her. "Statistically, it's what happens, with very few exceptions. Holding people captive is a treacherous and expensive business. As disheartening as this might sound, those exceptions are not the desirable outcome, not even close, not for the

girls held in endless captivity with no hope of ever being found."
She felt a chill down her spine at the thought of forty-three girls
held in captivity for so long. Were they killed? Did they wish they
would die, to escape who knows what horrible fate? "I have faith
we'll find Julie alive. Let's hope this unsub doesn't rush to kill her."

She pushed the disturbing thoughts out of her mind and
focused on the history of the abductions. Maybe his evolution over
time would tell her more about his location, his comfort zone.
She fired up her laptop again, still standing and leaning over her
desk instead of sitting, then displayed the map with the red dots
marking the missing persons cases in the area. She then set the
range of the report in increments of ten years, seeing where dots
appeared on the map.

There was no discernible pattern in the timing of the kidnappings. The cases had been local, yes, but the order in which they
appeared on the map offered no new insight.

With a loud groan, she flipped through some more screens and
loaded the DMV database. There, she entered the parameters for
the white Ford F-150, newer than five years, shooting from the
hip. She had no idea how old the truck was, but she had to start
somewhere.

"Put Texas in their past DMV history," Elliot suggested. "Maybe
we can narrow it down to people who might've gone to college in
Austin and played lacrosse for the Vipers."

The list of white Ford trucks registered to owners in the state
of California was even longer than she'd expected, returning
thousands of names. Adding Texas as a filter narrowed the search
dramatically, leaving only seventy-eight names across the entire
state, with one big problem.

None of them were local.

The closest registered owner of a white Ford F-150 that had
a DMV history with the state of Texas added lived two hundred

miles away, in Marin County. He was a forty-three-year-old, Beijing-born architect.

They had nothing.

She sighed and slammed the lid of her laptop shut. "All right, I'll take the family interviews, you go see Brent, Julie's boyfriend."

"Who will you see first?" he asked, walking briskly by her side down the hallway, heading for the exit.

She briefly checked the printouts. "The Costin family. Your old case."

CHAPTER THIRTY-FIVE

Lies

Julie never wanted to believe that was true.

When an old neighbor had told her the old superstition and the story of her birth—after having downed an unknown number of glasses of wine at her maternal grandmother's funeral—she thought the old harpy was making fun of her. She'd managed not to cry, at seven years of age, although she'd cried all morning after seeing her grandmother's body still and thin and surreal in the open casket. She'd dried her eyes and had walked away from the woman, shrugging off the harpy's words until later, when she could ask her mother.

But the weight of those words had turned into an obsession, consuming her young mind. On the drive back from the cemetery, she couldn't keep quiet about it anymore.

"Is it true you cried the day I was born, Mom?" she'd asked, interrupting the spirited conversation between her parents. She still recalled the bone-chilling silence that had followed. "Is it because I'm a girl?"

"Who told you that?" her dad had asked, his furrowed brow promising nothing good. He'd turned his head for a split second to look at her, then kept his eyes on the road, but she could still see his glances in the rearview mirror every now and then.

"Is it true?" she asked, her whimpering voice betraying the tears she'd been struggling to keep hidden.

Her mother had reached over the back of her seat and grabbed her hand in hers. "Oh, honey, that's just a stupid superstition, nothing else." She smiled at her through fresh tears. "I cried for joy, my dear girl. The day you were born was the best day of my life."

Those words played back in her memory, over and over, like a broken record playing a song she loved to hear, one she couldn't bring herself to turn off. How she wanted to believe that was true… so much, in fact, she'd convinced herself that it was the reality. She'd never spoken to that old neighbor again, simply turning her back to the woman on the street, at reunions, funerals, and other such events. The lady had to be a liar, one with no good intentions in mind. Her dad had told her to keep her distance, and she wanted nothing else.

Only nine years later, she was told that her mother had been keeping that secret from her. Julie didn't want to believe that could be true. Not then, when she was a little girl, not when she heard her mother explain why she'd lied about that old superstition through a veil of tears, and not now, when she was lying almost lifeless on the frozen floor, and ghosts of her past were gathered around her, talking, arguing, maybe still lying.

They weren't real. It must've been her imagination bringing them to life, because she was delusional from hunger and thirst, she told herself in a rare bout of rational thinking. But they felt real—as real as her mother's warm fingers caressing her cheek, her quiet voice promising her everything was going to be all right, because she wasn't alone.

"We're here, sweetie," her mom said, playing with a strand of her hair. "Your dad and I are here."

"Is it real?" she asked, or at least she thought she did. "Was this my fate since I was born, like Betty said?"

No one answered, but her mother kept on smiling, her eyes filled with a light Julie had never noticed before, when she'd been busy disobeying her.

That next-door neighbor… She wished she could ask her now what she should have asked her all those years ago. Who were the spirits taking the firstborn daughters? Because she could tell the old woman that a man—a flesh-and-blood man—had taken her, not a spirit. Maybe she knew why.

"Oh, Mom, why didn't you run?" she asked, but no one answered. "If you knew they were coming for me, why did you stay?"

Then she remembered, through a thick fog, as her mother's image faded away.

She didn't run because she waited for her to come home.

A fresh, warm tear rolled down her cheek.

In her fading mind where darkness had taken abode, she thought it was her mother's warm fingers caressing her skin.

CHAPTER THIRTY-SIX

The Costins

Sherman and Virginia Costin lived on a small ranch at the north end of the town. The property bore the signs of tragedy visible in the neglect of the front lawn and whatever part of the back yard Kay was able to see while pulling in at the curb. Weeds had overtaken the lawn, their stamina threatened by the cold weather. An old tire was abandoned by the driveway, a tall thistle bush growing unperturbed at the center of it. The state of the property strangely reminded her of her own family home when she'd returned from San Francisco, only the reasons were vastly different. The home she'd returned to after being away for many years still bore the mark of tragedy, just like the Costins' home, but her family had found closure. The Costins hadn't.

It was starting to get dark by the time she cut the engine and the windshield wipers finally stopped their rhythmic glide across glass. She couldn't tell without looking at the time if the sun had set already, its rays powerless against the thick cloud layer relentlessly gushing water in large, heavy drops that splashed loudly against the roof of her car.

She rushed to the front door and took a moment to brush off the raindrops clinging to her jacket before she rang the bell. A tired-looking, gaunt man opened the door seconds after she'd pressed the button. The hope that lit his eyes when she showed her badge tugged at her heart.

"May I come in for a moment? I have some questions for you."

The glimmer of hope faded, giving way to anguish. "Yes, of course." Shuffling his feet, he stepped aside and invited her in.

The living room was small and dim, lit poorly by a ceiling lamp with underpowered bulbs, as if the two Costins couldn't fight the darkness that engulfed their home. Mrs. Costin sat on the sofa, pale as a specter, her long, thinning blonde hair unwashed in days, clumped together in unsightly strands. She wore a housecoat, stained generously by old and new blotches of what appeared to be cooking mishaps. A faint smell of stale food and rotting garbage filled the air, but neither seemed to notice or care. On the living-room table, a pile of unopened mail gathered dust next to a cheap pair of thick-rimmed reading glasses. A side glance, and Kay was able to notice the kitchen sink was filled with dirty dishes, and the counters too.

"Thank you for seeing me," she said, looking around for a place to sit, then choosing to remain standing.

Mr. Costin sat on the sofa next to his wife. Their hands immediately found each other and intertwined like vines reaching for support. "Do you have any news of Lauren?"

"No, I'm afraid we don't," she replied, shuddering as she ripped off the Band-Aid. "But we're still investigating, and we have some new questions."

The man invited her to proceed with a hand gesture, then clasped his wife's fingers immediately.

"I know you probably told the story of that terrible day many times, but can you do it one more time? Walk me through everything that happened."

They looked at each other, as if agreeing who was going to speak.

"But why—" Mrs. Costin started to ask, her voice trailing off as if she'd run out of breath.

She opted for the truth, at least in part. "Before moving back here last year, where I was born and raised, I worked as a profiler with the FBI in San Francisco. I'm hoping I might be able to see something or uncover something my colleague, Detective Young, might've missed."

"You really don't have any news of Lauren," Mrs. Costin said, a tear rolling down her pale cheek. It was as if she'd hoped Kay had been lying to her. It was amazing to see the power of hope and how fiercely people clung to it, tooth and nail, against all reason and all evidence.

"I'm afraid we don't," Kay replied, her voice unexpectedly choked.

Mrs. Costin squeezed her husband's hand. "Lauren vanished on her way back from school," she said, her voice trembling and weak, forewarning of tears to come. "In September, two years ago." She pulled her fingers from her husband's grasp and took her hand to her chest, then clutched the lapel of her housecoat. "When she didn't show up for dinner that evening, I knew something was wrong. Even before I called her girlfriends, her teachers, the police, I knew. It was as if someone had ripped the heart out of my chest and left a hollow in there instead."

"Did she take the school bus home that day?"

Mrs. Costin shook her head, staring at the worn-out oriental rug under her feet.

"No, although it was raining," Mr. Costin said. "She sometimes did that, walked home. She said she loved the mountain air in the fall. She was active, an athlete." He paused for a moment, seeming lost. "Detective Young was here every day, telling us what he'd found out. He pounded on every door, all the way from school to here, on her normal route. Then we did the same." Mr. Costin stared at Kay with an unspoken question in his eyes. "She'd just vanished. No one saw anything. How could someone just—"

"Most people were at work, their kids in school," Mrs. Costin interrupted, speaking weakly. "Detective Young told us bad weather must've been why no one saw my baby getting…" she searched for the word, "taken. No one was outside, not even to roll their garbage bins to the curb. It was trash pickup the next morning."

"We pleaded with the authorities to keep looking, but I think they gave up too soon. We even went to see the mayor, but I don't know if he did anything." Mr. Costin reluctantly let go of his wife's other hand, then stood and started pacing the floor, looking out the window every few seconds. "We ran TV ads until we drained our retirement money. Now we wait. Virginia doesn't work anymore."

"I can't," she sobbed, putting her hand in front of her mouth. "What if she comes home and I'm not here? What if someone is looking for us, to tell us about Lauren?"

Kay bit her lip. Extreme duress had caused the Costins to act irrationally, although she could understand how Lauren's mother would find it impossible to leave the house where her daughter might, one day, return. The lack of closure was taking a terrible toll on the Costin family. Their pain resonated with her, although she couldn't begin to understand what that felt like.

"Tell me about Lauren," she asked. "What kind of girl was she?"

Mrs. Costin stood slowly, then walked over to the mantel of a dusty fireplace, which had probably never been used, and retrieved a photo framed in silver. With a trembling hand, she showed it to Kay. "She's so beautiful, my little girl. She's smart too. She has good grades, only As." She smiled, slightly embarrassed, averting her eyes for a brief moment. "A few Bs too, but mostly As. She wants to be a veterinarian." She held the photo to her chest tightly with both hands, as if hugging her daughter. "I've been sending college applications for her. When she comes back, it won't be too much of a problem."

Kay's vision blurred a little as she watched the Costins huddled together, falling apart together, waiting, hoping together against all reason. She wished there was something she could say to ease their burden, but there wasn't anything, not in the statistics of kidnappings and missing teenage girls in the archives of the FBI, not in the local folklore, nothing. Her simple presence in their home had offered them hope that was founded solely on their belief that a miracle could still happen and that one day their daughter would be found and returned to them.

"One more question," Kay said, hesitant to broach the subject. "Have you ever heard about a local superstition that mentions firstborn daughters disappearing?"

They drew closer, as if scared by her words. "What? Is there such a thing here?" Mrs. Costin's eyes were rounded, as if she'd become afraid of something, an unknown threat. Then she looked at her husband for a brief, loaded beat. "It was his job... We're not from here, originally. Sherman was offered the branch director position when the new California Star Credit Union opened in Mount Chester two years ago." Her breath shattered and she leaned against his arm for support. "Maybe if we would've not moved here, she'd still be with us."

"You moved right before she vanished?" That was an unexpected, new angle.

"No," Mr. Costin led his wife to the couch and sat next to her. "They had me come here from the start, before they even broke ground for the new building. I chose the location, hired the contractors, bought the furniture, did everything. Hired every single employee. When Lauren went missing, the building wasn't even finished yet."

"When exactly did you move, and where from?"

"Almost three years ago, this August." He paused for a moment, frowning, as if trying to recall something. "From San Francisco. I've been with this credit union since I graduated from college. That's where the main office is." He looked at Kay with renewed worry in his eyes. "Do you think this has something to do with my job?"

She considered her answer for a brief moment. Forty-three girls had been taken over almost sixty years. Chances were he was the only father that had relocated there for a new job. Victimology was going to confirm it. "No, I don't believe so, but I'm looking at every angle."

"Thank you, with all my heart," Mrs. Costin said, extending her hand. Kay squeezed it gently. It felt dry and warm and frail. "We're counting on you to bring our baby home."

She left the house burdened by their words, with some distant, unclear thought tugging at her gut. What was she missing?

She stopped for a moment under their porch roof before bolting to her SUV parked on the street. Closing her eyes, she recapped the highlights of the conversation, but she still couldn't put her finger on whatever was gnawing at her mind, like a tip-of-the-tongue word that was playing hide and seek in her brain. Then she checked the time and realized that she could still visit with the Guerrero family if she stepped on it.

Whatever that elusive thought was, it would come to her.

CHAPTER THIRTY-SEVEN

Brent

Brent Barcenas could strut sitting down. He represented everything that was wrong with the younger generation. A few days shy of his eighteenth birthday, per his DMV records, the young man leaned casually against the back of an expensive truck chock-full of options and custom features, putting his bare foot on the bumper and leaning into the elbow resting against his knee. Broad-shouldered and muscular, the young man must've been headed toward playing college ball in some form or another. But this hairstyle almost made Elliot laugh, bleached and spiky and loaded with gel, while the sides had been buzzed, one trend short of a modern mohawk.

The house he'd just emerged from was one of the most expensive on that side of town, his parents doing visibly well for themselves. A little research into the Barcenas family told Elliot they owned an interest in a large Napa Valley vineyard, and their accounting business in Mount Chester thrived, Mrs. Barcenas being ranked the best CPA in the region. Alongside, Mr. Barcenas had a strategic financial advisory practice that was probably responsible for paying the lease on the BMW X7 Elliot could see through the lit windows of the family garage.

"This baby yours?" Elliot asked, pointing at the brand-new Ram pickup truck.

"Yup," Brent replied with an amused, smug smile, shooting a side glance toward Elliot's SUV. It didn't bear any sheriff's office markings; only two flashers hidden behind the grille told it was a cop's car. "I bet that's your work ride, huh?"

The kid was unbelievable. His girlfriend had been kidnapped, and he talked cars, chilled and barefoot on the rain-soaked driveway, his parents not in the least interested why the police had come banging on their door looking to speak with their son at seven-thirty in the evening.

Elliot grinned. He could play the game the kid wanted, as long as he wasn't whistling up the wind. "Sure is. Not half bad either." His jacket and hat kept the rain away, but his jeans were getting soaked.

"Yeah, but Ford?" He obviously wasn't a fan.

"Specially built for the cops. It's called the Interceptor."

Brent ambled around Elliot's vehicle, not minding the rain, studying it, seemingly unimpressed. "Isn't this just like the Explorer?" The hair gel he was applying so generously must've been waterproof.

"On crack," Elliot laughed. He picked up a wet piece of straw from the side of the perfectly manicured Barcenas lawn and chewed on it. He was getting sodden in that miserable toad floater, and he could bet the spoiled brat was doing it on purpose, just to have a good laugh with his friends afterward. He withdrew under the porch roof. "I have a few questions for you."

"Can I look inside?" Brent asked, sticking his face against the driver-side window.

"Knock yourself out," Elliot replied, swallowing a curse as Brent opened the door. "Uh-uh, can't climb behind the wheel, sorry."

Frustrated, the kid slammed the door shut a little harder than was necessary and approached Elliot on the porch. Probably no one had told him no that entire month. "What do you need? I'm busy."

"Tell me about Julie Montgomery. She's your girlfriend, right?"

The smug grin returned. "One of them, anyway. What do you want to know?"

"Anything you can tell me to help us figure out who took her and killed her mother."

He shrugged, then pulled out an electronic cigarette and took a quick drag that lit its tip in electric blue, without the slightest concern his parents might see him. A sickly sweet scent of cinnamon and vanilla filled the air before a gust of wind thankfully blew it away. "She was quiet and withdrawn; didn't say much. She didn't put out either. To me it wasn't much of a loss if she moved away."

"Moved where?"

"San Francisco." He pursed his lips, visibly angered by something. Elliot waited. Brent had the self-control capability of a geyser; he was bound to blow up sooner or later. "That night, Monday, her mother was going to take them all to San Fran, to start a new life or something. And Julie, she wasn't very bright. She was, ooh, all heartbroken about it, like someone actually *wants* to live in this shitty hole of a town."

"Why the past tense?"

"Huh?"

"You spoke of Julie in past tense." Elliot's patience was wearing thin. Why anyone would want to date him was beyond comprehension. "Why is that?"

"What, you actually think she's coming back? Seriously? Don't you watch *Criminal Minds*, or something, to learn about these things?" He scoffed and turned his back to Elliot for a long moment. Another cloud of sweet vapor engulfed them briefly. "That girl's toast, man. Some dude is having a ball with her, giving it to her all she can take." A lopsided, lustful grin blooming on his face made Elliot want to slap him unconscious.

"Do you know why she didn't want to move to San Francisco?"

"I asked, but she didn't make any sense, something about here being her home and some other crazy shit like that." Another drag from his vaping device. "One crazy bitch, I'll give you that. Took after her mother. That one was the craziest yet."

"Cheryl?"

"She was changing boyfriends like a bitch in heat. I would've tapped that one myself," he'd lowered his voice to a conspirative whisper, "if you know what I mean. The bitches were hot as hell, both of them."

"Tell me about the men she was dating," he asked between clenched teeth.

"Julie and I were happy when she was screwing the science teacher. We'd stare at the guy in class until he'd feel guilty and give us straight As. Easy as pie. He must've been scared we'd tell his wife or something." He gazed into the distance, now engulfed by darkness, streaks of rain reflecting the porch light falling under an angle like their own personal meteor shower. "Honestly, if he would've as much as given me a B plus, just once, I would've told her." He laughed, seemingly thrilled with his own deviousness. "But no, dear old Cheryl had to dump that guy, and started fu—" Elliot glared at him. "Um, dating someone else."

"Do you know whom?"

"Julie said something about him possibly being a distant relative or something. I wondered if that was even legal, but they weren't really relatives. Not by blood anyway." He puffed again, churning Elliot's empty stomach. "Of course, this dude was married too, from what I'd heard. Not very smart, the late Mrs. Coleman." He laughed quietly, a cold, heartless laugh that chilled Elliot's blood. "Or maybe she wanted them like that, to get the action, but not the day-by-day shit."

"Was Cheryl running away from this man or his wife?"

He shoved his hands into his jean's pockets, and put one bare foot up on a yellow Adirondack. "Dunno. All I knew was that Julie didn't want to get out of this hole and move someplace cool, like San Fran, which makes her a complete idiot. This is Mount Chester, middle of nowhere. Hello?" He gestured dramatically, spreading his arms out as if calling on an invisible crowd. "What am I missing?"

"When's the last time you saw Julie?"

"Monday night, when I drove her home after the movies. It was raining worse than now, if that's even possible." Not a trace of hesitation before he'd replied. "She was crying the whole damn time, as if I'm out to hear her whimpers. I wanna have a good time, man. That's why I'm springing for the movie and the dinner and all that shit. You know what that's all about," he elbowed Elliot in his ribs with a low, loaded laugh. "I wanted to get to third base that night. Instead, what do I get? The damn crying, and all sorts of bullshit about feeling guilty, about what she'd done. Maybe she ran away, who the hell knows."

Brent Barcenas was giving him the creeps, but maybe he was on to something. Had Julie done something that brought terrible consequences?

"Did she say what she'd done, exactly? What was she feeling guilty about?"

The boy shrugged, his broad shoulders stretching the fabric of his T-shirt. Black with a brown-and-white imprint, it read, MY PEOPLE SKILLS ARE JUST FINE. IT'S MY TOLERANCE TO IDIOTS THAT NEEDS WORK.

"No idea." He scoffed again, then plunged his hands back into his pockets. Barefoot in that cold rain, he must've been freezing, but was too proud to admit it. His toes had turned bluish white. "What, you think I cared? Screw that, man," he walked away from Elliot, as if his proximity infuriated him. "I ain't got time to waste." He pulled out his phone and gestured with it. "Plenty more where Julie came from, and some are willing to make this little man happy." He patted his crotch then winked at Elliot. "Anything else? I'm missing my show."

"No, we're good, thanks." He handed him a card. "In case you remember anything else."

He slid it in the back pocket of his jeans and went inside, slamming the door behind him without as much as an acknowledg-

ment. By his attitude, at almost eighteen, Elliot didn't give him
more than five years before he'd end up wearing his handcuffs,
or some other cop's. The question that remained was, for what
crime? Was Brent Barcenas a killer? That was highly improbable;
he seemed all hat and no cattle. But he was a no-account person,
born sorry and raised even sorrier. In the future, could he become
a rapist, a stalker, or a wife beater? Perhaps. He seemed to have
the right combination of genes and education for it, unless his
parents suddenly awakened and put some horse sense and some
core values into the young man.

Rushing through the rain toward his SUV, Elliot wondered
what Kay would've said about Brent. The thought of her brought
a smile that lingered on his lips for a while, even as he started his
engine and tapped through the list of names displayed on the
media center until he found the one he was looking for, an old
colleague of his from the sheriff's department in Austin, Texas.

The man didn't pick up, but Elliot left him a voice message.

"Hey, bud, I need a favor from you, and I need it faster than
small-town gossip. Can you track down any college kids from
California who might've been on the Austin Vipers Lacrosse team?"

CHAPTER THIRTY-EIGHT

The Guerreros

It was still raining when Kay reached the Guerrero residence. After a few hours of relative silence, thunder rolled though the valley renewed, sending muffled echoes against the hills, while lightning illuminated the dark skies in blinding flashes of light.

The Guerreros lived far from the highway, their old ranch tucked against the hillside, the only one north of the winding road. Kay had driven across several smaller bridges on her way from the interstate—a couple of them barely a few inches above the swollen river, the first ones to give if flash floods continued. Hurricane Edward must've been the slowest-moving storm in history, its bands endlessly renewing their load of water over the Pacific as the four-hundred-mile-wide storm spun and whirled, slowly, menacingly.

She checked the time before ringing the doorbell. It was getting late, but the lights were still on in the living room, and she could hear the TV, loudly playing the Spanish commentary of a soccer game.

A woman in her forties opened the door, quickly running her hand over her hair and clothes, as if to check if she was present-able enough to receive guests. She had kind eyes with dark circles underneath and long, straight, black hair held back by a hoop band that gave the illusion of braiding.

"Yes?" she said, seeming ready to rush back indoors to safety, as if startled by Kay's presence.

She showed her badge. "Detective Kay Sharp with the sheriff's office. Mrs. Guerrero?" The woman nodded. "I wonder if I could ask you a couple of questions."

She stepped aside, letting her in.

Unlike the Costins, the Guerreros were a large family, three generations sharing the home. The dining table was large, with eight chairs around it, one with an untouched plate set in front of it, while the rest had been used. A preteen girl was clearing the mess, carrying only a few dirty plates at a time, careful not to drop them, then scraping the leftovers and rinsing them in the sink before loading them into the dishwasher. The air was thick with the smell of guacamole and fajitas and mouthwatering spices.

"Isela, *quien es ella?*" an older man asked. He was seated on a recliner in front of the TV, the upholstered arms worn out to the weave.

"*Es policía, papa,*" she replied, then smiled apologetically. "My father doesn't speak English very well."

The man sprung from his chair as if he were still twenty and approached Kay with a determined gait. "Did you find our Stephania?" He seemed to struggle to articulate even the simplest words.

"No, I'm afraid we haven't, but we're looking into new evidence." Déjà vu. It felt as if she were talking with the Costins all over again, shattering the same hopes, kindling the same fears, fueling the same tears. Only there were more of them to disappoint.

"We always set the table for her," Isela said, seeing where Kay's eyes were wandering. "Maybe one day our prayers will be answered, and she will join us for dinner again." She wiped the corner of her eye with her apron.

"What new evidence?" another man asked, most likely Stephanie's father, Mauricio. He'd been standing in the hallway, as if frozen by Kay's appearance. Now he approached slowly, nervously, his gaze elusive like a fearful deer's in the hunter's sights, ready to bolt at the tiniest rustling of leaves. He grabbed Kay's hand between both of his. "Do you think I'll ever see my little girl again?" Kay realized he wasn't afraid of her; he was anxious at the thought of bad news, of having to endure the worst pain a father could ever live through.

The water in the kitchen sink was turned off, and a heavy silence filled the room. The girl had fallen still, holding a plate midair between sink and dishwasher, listening with her mouth agape.

Kay lowered her eyes for a brief moment. "We have no way of knowing, Mr. Guerrero, but we're doing the best we can."

He let go of her hand and seemed to have aged ten years in the span of a second. His back hunched and his arms fell limp alongside his thin body. His eyes wandered into nothingness, as his chin trembled ever so slightly. "What do you need to know?" His voice was filled with unspeakable sadness.

"Tell me everything you can remember about that day."

"What I can remember?" he scoffed bitterly. "I'll never forget a single moment of that cursed day." He clasped his hands together, wringing them hard. "We were waiting for Stephanie to come back from work. She'd just finished school that year. Martinez, a friend of ours, gave her a job waiting tables at his diner. She was happy, saving her money for college, proud to be a grownup and work her first real job." He sniffled and turned his face away from Kay for a brief moment. "Then she didn't come home one day. *That* day." He pressed his forearm to his mouth, as if to stifle a sob. Isela had drawn closer, touching his shoulder while hiding behind him, as if Kay was menacing, dangerous. "*El día en que dios nos abandonó*. The day our Lord forsook us."

"*Sí, sí,*" the old man said, then crossed himself quickly.

"She just vanished, on her way back from the diner, three years ago this past Saturday," Mauricio continued. "She was nineteen, my little girl. She's twenty-two now," he added, his eyes lit by fierce belief fueling his hope for her return. "Three years," he sobbed, covering his mouth with trembling hands. "*Ay, Dios mío.*"

Kay had read the case notes, but she was looking for something more, the things that don't normally get documented in records and reports. Emotions, perceptions, gossip, the hindsight vision that is rarely wrong.

"What were your thoughts at the time? Was there anyone you suspected? Any idea who would've wanted to harm your daughter?"

Mauricio stared at the scuffs on the floor for a beat. "We asked everyone, we banged on every door. I printed flyers at my office and put them on all the trees between here and the diner. Martinez still has the flyer up on his wall."

"Did anyone see anything?"

He shook his head, defeated. "It was as if we angered God somehow. It rained so badly that day, I—"

Kay stopped listening, icicles running through her blood. Rain again? She didn't think much when the Costins had mentioned rain; in the fall, rain was quite common for Mount Chester before it turned to snow and lined the versants with perfectly white powder glimmering in myriad diamonds, the kind of snow skiers from around the world traveled to enjoy. What were the odds of yet another abduction in the rain? The Northern California coast is famously dry, rarely adding up to more than ten wet days each year, but those always happen in the fall, fueled by hurricane remnants, during what the locals call the rainy season.

"So sorry, Mr. Guerrero, please run this by me again. You were saying, it was raining hard that day?"

"Just like now, or even worse," he said.

"Worse," Isela intervened. "I remember we were afraid our house would be taken by the floods coming down from the mountain."

Was rain a forensic countermeasure for the unsub? Did he purposefully wait for rain to prey on the victims, knowing witnesses would see very little from underneath umbrellas, focused on the difficult traffic, or just staying inside behind closed curtains? Could it be a part of his MO? She frowned, considering the implications and her next steps. She had to verify and make sure it wasn't just a fluke, but if other abductions had also happened during heavy rainfall, she had to consider rain as a critical element of the profile. Somehow, weather seemed to play an important role in his very precise execution. Not only did he patiently wait for the right weather—if that was the case—but had the self-control over his killing urges to wait for the right circumstances—out of his control—and seize the opportunities the moment they presented themselves. The unsub's apparent lack of control over the circumstances of each abduction didn't support the power or control sadist scenario; the power sadist is, by definition, an extreme control freak. All facts, while some still needing verification, pointed toward the mission-driven profile, regardless of how much she believed it didn't quite fit.

Kay handed Isela and Mr. Guerrero each a business card. "In case you remember anything else, I'd appreciate a call." She thanked the Guerreros and left, quickly climbing behind the wheel of her car. Engine running and blowing warm, dry air against the fogged-up windows, she typed a text to Elliot. *Meet me for dinner at Hilltop.* Then she shifted into gear, eager to get there and do some more research—this time into weather patterns.

Before she could peel off from the curb, a chime got her attention, barely noticeable over the hypnotic cadence of the wipers. A message from Elliot said simply, *On my way.*

CHAPTER THIRTY-NINE

Ritual

He recalled his first sacrifice, the one that had torn his heart out of his chest, the one Mother had chosen for herself, despite his commitment to lay at her feet a pure and innocent life, worthy of her with every fiber in her pristine body.

He still remembered how he feared her wrath then just as he did today, afraid of her as much as he was in awe of her, knowing her pain; her gaping wounds could ruin everything, swallow everything, burying him alive.

Just like today, rain had carved deep into Mother's flesh, entire versants falling, carried downhill by flash floods, taking lives with them—people, *children*—swallowed by the restless, swollen waters never to be seen again, as nature screamed around them in thunder and the roar of maddened winds.

He'd struggled to understand Mother's will, to read her thoughts, but had failed, speeding day and night trying, but never succeeding. He'd begged her to make it simple for him to deliver, to obey her, to give her what she needed to be healed, but his prayers had been left unheard.

Until she came, and Mother took her, pointing her finger at the love of his life and choosing her as her due sacrifice, above all others, just as he'd chosen the same woman above all others to have and to hold.

He recalled how he couldn't believe what was happening, his willpower subdued by Mother effortlessly. She was so beautiful, so happy… the pride of his life. Then she was gone. In taking her, Mother ensured that she would never be forgotten, that her life would have meaning, a worthy meaning most people only dream of.

She'd become immortal, laid forever to rest at Mother's bosom, in atonement for human's sins against nature.

Now, only a few hours before the new sacrifice, he felt energized, eager to experience Mother's gratitude. Once the offering would be accepted, her wounds would heal, and the sun would shine again. She would smile on her child once more, the only one who really understood her, like she'd done so many times in the past. And that smile made everything worthwhile.

His mind wandered to the many who'd been sacrificed over the eons, each time a painful and fear-filled sacrifice, but none as agonizing as this one. So much was riding on what was going to happen at high noon tomorrow. This time, the ritual had to be executed to perfection.

He was ready.

CHAPTER FORTY

Dinner

Kay couldn't believe she'd grown to have a favorite table at the Hilltop Bar and Grill. In the year since she'd returned to Mount Chester, she'd built many fond memories in that place, most of them work-related, or so she liked to think when she avoided acknowledging that they'd all been centered around her partner.

Elliot. The reason why she smiled while she entered the old bar and made for her favorite table, glad to see it was empty. No other deputies were there that night; everyone was pulling nonstop duty keeping the treacherous roads safe and helping people flee their homes, threatened by landslides during what had to be one of the worst storms of the decade.

She also felt a sense of anticipation, of excitement, eager to confirm her theory that the unsub's crimes had some correlation with the weather. It would be the first real insight into who this man was, the first discernible feature on his profile. And it almost always started like that, with a single, uniquely defining feature that penciled in who the unsub was, why he killed or kidnapped, what fueled his impulses.

Kay set her laptop on the tacky table, pushing aside the menu holder, the napkin dispenser, and the saltshaker. She fired it up, tapping her heel against the floor impatiently, while her eyes wandered over the smoke-stained walls, covered in old photos hanging in cheap frames or just pasted up without frames, close to one another. It was as if she was reviewing an illustrated history of Mount Chester. Weddings, birthdays, smiling happy faces, but also a picture of the mayor, several of the sheriffs, current and past. Hunters and their dogs, skiers and their trophies, even a dogsled racing team. Almost like a family album, because, ultimately, that's what the town of Mount Chester was: a family.

And someone was taking its children.

Typing quickly, she ran an internet search for historical weather data, and immediately found that Weather Underground had kept impeccable records of their weather stations' readings. She accessed the service, and chose the Redding weather station. There wasn't one for Mount Chester, but Redding was close enough; only two hundred miles.

Flipping quickly between the report and the weather data screens, she started checking the abduction dates, one by one, going down the forty-three names on the list. And one by one, the data confirmed her theory—with each name her blood chilling a little more, raising goosebumps on her skin.

"What can I get you, hon?"

She managed to smile at the server who knew her by name but still used that endearing term with all her female customers.

"Just some pretzels and club soda. I'm waiting for—"

"That gorgeous cowboy of yours?" She laughed with girlish familiarity and winked at her, patting her on the shoulder. "I, for one, don't know what you're waiting for."

Kay smiled, a little uneasy, her eyes riveted to the computer screen. The server took the hint and left. Moments later, a bowl of salt-encrusted pretzels and a chilled glass of club soda were set on the table. "There you go, hon. Enjoy."

"Thanks." Munching absentmindedly, she worked her way through the entire list, checking weather, comparing inches of rainfall with what the region had seen in the past week, and, specifically, on the day Julie had been taken.

Every single time a first daughter had been kidnapped, it had rained hard, heavy downpours bringing down several inches over twenty-four-hour intervals. Even if that meant the unsub had to wait three years for his next opportunity, back in 1984.

Her excitement withered when the online weather data archive returned, *No data recorded*, for all years prior to 1973. There weren't many abductions older than that; just a few. After finding a phone number for the head office, she called and explained what she was looking for.

"That's because those archives haven't been digitized yet, Detective," the meteorologist on duty explained in a pleasant baritone. "Or maybe the Redding weather station wasn't built until 1973; we can find out if you wish. But if you give me the dates you're looking for, I can pull the data from the paper archives and call you back."

"That's perfect, thank you." Scrolling through the last few names, she read the dates one by one, while a nagging question bugged her. What if the weather records weren't the only ones that hadn't been digitized prior to certain dates? What if the kidnappings of firstborn daughters were going back further than fifty-seven years?

She read the date by the last name on the list and froze. "I'll have to call you back." She hung up, staring at the name on the screen. How could she have missed that?

The oldest name on the open cases report was Anna Montgomery, twenty-three years old.

The unsub had taken Montgomery girls before.

"Hello," she heard Elliot's voice and her frozen blood started rushing through her veins again.

She looked up, smiling without even realizing it. Then she frowned a little, painfully self-conscious. He'd managed to go by his place and take a shower, get fresh clothes, and now smelled of shower gel and aftershave and dryer sheets, while she stank of acrid, rained-over clothing that had repeatedly dried from body heat. Even his hat was new, a dark brown one she'd never seen before. The whitewashed jeans and blue plaid shirt went with it perfectly, bringing out the blue in his eyes.

The server popped by the table before he'd had a chance to sit down, notepad in hands and a wide, inviting smile on her lips. He took his hat off and set it on a chair, then pulled the one across from Kay for himself.

"We'll need a moment," Elliot said, and she vanished. "I see you're buried in work. Found anything interesting?"

She took half a second before replying, clinging to the image of her smiling partner before diving into the abyss of serial killer minds. "Yeah," she replied, aware her voice was tinged with under-tones of regret. She wished she could take the time and enjoy their dinner, forgetting all about the unsub as she'd already forgotten about her smelly clothes and her ruined hair. But Julie was still out there somewhere in that wet darkness, and every second mattered. "Every time he's taken a girl, it rained. Seriously rained—like now, like the world is ending with Noah's ark and the Great Flood."

"What?" he reacted. "I didn't see this one coming."

"There's more. His first vic—well, the first one we have on file anyway—was also a Montgomery, Anna Montgomery." She threw a pretzel in her mouth and chewed it quickly, the salty crunch deeply satisfying, addictive. "Turns out she was Avery's wife. He was the one who reported her missing, fifty-seven years ago."

"What do you mean, the first one we have on file anyway?"

"What if there were more, dating back before records were digitized?"

"I got it." With a deep frown cutting across his brow, he picked up the laminated menu they both knew by heart. "Avery's wife? What are the odds of that?"

"Zilch. We need to put that family under a microscope." She beckoned the server and she trotted over, beaming.

"I'll have a Hilltop burger, with everything on it except onions, and double fries." She needed the artery-popping goodness to fuel her body. The next few hours were critical.

"Same for me," Elliot said, abandoning the menu in its usual place, the wrought-iron holder Kay had pushed to the side to make room for her laptop.

"How did it go with Brent?" Kay asked, as soon as the server disappeared from earshot.

"Oh, we have a budding fine citizen in that young man," he replied.

She laughed. "That bad, huh?"

"Worse. I wondered what you'd make of him." Fire coursed through her blood hearing that he'd been thinking of her. "But he's not our perp. He's got a ten-gallon mouth and no solid values whatsoever. One day he'll cross our paths again, you'll see."

"Did he give you anything useful? Or just an inkling of his charming personality?"

Elliot shook his head. "Nothing we didn't already know." He took a pretzel from the bowl, but his hand stopped midair. "Maybe this. Julie was deeply upset about something, feeling guilty and all that, and definitely not thrilled about leaving town. They were going to San Francisco, moving there by Brent's account. Nothing the little creep said pointed to Julie and her mom running away *from* something."

"Strange," Kay said, lost in thought.

The server set their food in front of them, filling the air with mouthwatering smells of sizzling bacon, molten Swiss cheese, and salty fries.

"Enjoy," she said, then walked away quickly, swaying her hips.

"You think?" he asked humorously. "I can't think of anything that's not strange about this case."

"No, I meant, at the time of Julie's date with Brent, Cheryl had already shot your John Doe. Yet she didn't say anything about that; instead, she seemed to have blamed herself. For what, we don't know." She took one fry and chewed it hungrily. She would've taken more, but they were still too hot. "Imagine this, a teenage girl who witnesses—at least indirectly—her mother shooting a man in their house. Yet, two days later, she goes out on a date, albeit crying, but still. What the heck are we missing?"

He took a big bite out of his burger, his half-closed eyes lighting up with satisfaction when his perfectly white teeth bit into it. "From what Brent said, she was crying because she didn't want to move away from here."

That made absolutely no sense. Her mother shot someone, yet her biggest concern was moving?

The charm of the shared dinner faded, as if the darkness of the case engulfed them. Always heavy rains. A superstition, decades old or maybe more, proven right by statistical case history. And a victim whose family seemed to be involved in more than one way. A family who didn't bother to ask about Julie, as if she were a foregone conclusion. And the first girl taken fifty-seven years ago, Anna Montgomery, a first daughter herself, was also a member of the family.

She took a bite from her burger, her appetite now gone, only to find it had lost its taste. The fries seemed dull too; she washed down the few she'd put in her mouth with a hearty gulp of sparkling water and pushed her plate aside.

"This family holds all the answers, Elliot," she said, glancing at him for the first time since he'd arrived, afraid to see the fire in his eyes, afraid of what it did to her. "That's where we have to look." She checked the time; it was almost half past ten, a few long hours until she could question the Montgomerys again. Another night for Heather and Erin to sleep in improvised conditions. Another long night for Julie in captivity, if she was still alive.

Elliot called for the check with a hand gesture, just as both their phones chimed. She took out hers and found a message from Dr. Whitmore, which read:

John Doe has 12.5 cMs in common with the missing girl, Julie, but none with the mother. That means he's a paternal great-uncle. Based on that, I pulled DMV records. John Doe's name is Dan Montgomery.

The message ended with the fingers crossed emoji.

"Ah, Montgomery again," Kay said, intrigued. "What do you know? Marleen's husband." She wondered how that piece of the puzzle fit into the bigger picture, what new angles it presented.

"What the heck is a cMs?" Elliot asked with a shy smile, scratching the roots of his hair.

She smiled widely. He seemed embarrassed like a schoolboy caught without his homework done, when he shouldn't've been. The term belonged to the medical examiner's specialty glossary. "Centimorgans. It's a unit to measure genetic linkage. It's defined as the distance between chromosome markers—"

He held his hand in the air to stop her, then waved it above his head with a quiet whistling sound, as if to convey the information was way over his head. "Okay, I think I'm good, thank you." His grin widened, while the corners of his eyes softened, touched by it. The spark she'd noticed earlier in their endless blue had reappeared as he looked at her. Her gaze veered sideways as her face flushed.

Still avoiding his eyes, she stood. "Now that John Doe has a name, we need to find out more about this family and how they're involved."

CHAPTER FORTY-ONE

Court Order

The first light of dawn woke Kay up to find Heather sleeping cuddled with her back against her body. During the three hours she'd slept, the little girl must've crawled toward her, finding warmth and comfort near her even if that meant sleeping on the hard edges of the joined cots. For some reason, feeling the child shifting in her restless sleep against her body stirred up feelings inside her, yearnings she never knew she had.

As gently as she could, she rose, pulling slowly away to not wake her, then covering her body with the soft, Lion King blanket on loan from the Farrell household. Heather woke anyway. She opened her eyes and looked at Kay through a haze of sleep. "Hello," she whispered, the first word she'd spoken out of hypnosis since her mother was killed. Kay's heart swelled. She set her comfortably on her pillow, and caressed her hair. "Sleep some more, all right? I'll get us something to eat, and I'll be back soon," she whispered, but the girl was already asleep.

She checked on Erin, who slept tightly with her thumb in her mouth, then tiptoed out of the room, only to run into Sheriff Logan in the dark hallway.

She gasped. "Oh, good morning," she muttered, wishing she'd had time to brush her hair and rinse her mouth.

"Maybe for you, Detective," he replied somberly. He smelled of aftershave, but didn't look as if he'd caught more than a couple of hours of rest. Judging by the wrinkles on his shirt, those hours might've been in his service car, and the shave electrical, using a buzz shaver powered by the lighter plug in the same vehicle.

She didn't need to ask why; it was the fifth day since Julie had been taken, the sixth since the storm had started, the third since the first landslide that had caused losses of lives. All she heard on the radio when she drove was about weather-related death tolls and Julie's disappearance, sprinkled with the occasional tongue-in-cheek comment from announcers who wondered what the police were doing and why there were no answers yet.

"What's up?" she asked instead, warily.

"The aunt is here again, this time with a court order. I'm letting her take the girls." He took one more step toward the nap-room door, but she cut firmly in his path.

"I don't care about that court order, Sheriff," she said, but immediately sweetened her tone, seeing her boss's eyebrows ruffle. "All evidence leads to the family being involved, and no judge, knowing what I know now, would've signed that order."

He propped his hands on his hips with a groan of frustration. "And why don't I know what you know now?" His tone was menacing, impatient. He must've perceived her delay in informing him as intentional, maybe even malicious.

"Because I only learned of these facts late last night, when you'd already gone."

"And?"

"At the risk of sounding defensive, you told me to never drop bombs on you by email. I was planning to speak to you today, in person."

He folded his arms at his chest, still frowning. "I'm listening."

She drew a long breath of air, steadying herself. This was no place for emotions and raw nerves. "First off, John Doe is Marleen's husband," she said gesturing with her head toward the entrance, where she could see the familiar silhouette in the distance, pacing relentlessly. "I didn't have time to deliver next of kin. By the time we learned his ID, it was almost midnight." His frown eased up a little. "But that's not all."

"What else? I'm not seeing that bomb yet, Detective."

"Think about it. He was having an affair with Cheryl, who ends up shooting him. I'm telling you, this family is somehow involved."

"I'm not seeing any evidence of that, only circumstance." He stopped talking for a beat, pressing his lips together. "We can't ignore the court order, Kay. She's taking them with her; nothing we can do."

"They're involved in the kidnapping, boss. We can't let them take these girls."

"You said this was a serial killer case, right?"

She nodded.

"You mean to tell me the Montgomerys are involved in forty-three kidnapping cases?"

She stifled a sigh. "I don't know about forty-three right now, but I know they're involved in this one."

"But didn't you say—"

"Yes, I said it's a serial, and I have further evidence that points this way, but—"

"What evidence?" His hands found his hips again, and he took another step, closer to her, as if ready to force his way through.

"All kidnappings happened during bouts of weather like this."

That final argument must've hit home, because his shoulders dropped a little, and he stepped sideways, making room for her to pass by through the narrow corridor. "All right, grill her some more. I'm guessing that's what you want to do?"

"And then some," she replied, unable to contain a smile.

With Erin sleeping in the nap room with her sister, and the early hour of day with no suspects in custody, the front interview room was open, and that's where she took Marleen Montgomery. The woman looked pissed, walking with her chin thrust out and her back straight, waving the court order in her gloved hand like a fan.

She wore another scarf, this time one with a flowery oriental pattern in shades of burgundy, gold, and dark blue, wrapped tightly around her neck and knotted as if it became loose something terrible could happen. The colors of the scarf went harmoniously with the elegant, dark blue business suit and her fine burgundy kid gloves with purse and pumps to match.

Kay invited her inside the interview room, then closed the door.

"I don't see why the delay, Detective," she said, raising her voice. "I have a court order—"

"Please, take a seat," Kay said, sitting down across from her.

Hesitantly, the woman pulled the metallic chair away from the table and examined it with a critical glare. "Mind if I stand? I won't be here that long."

We'll see about that, Kay almost said out loud. *I might want to keep you for twenty-five-to-life.* "Suit yourself," she replied instead.

She stood in front of Kay, not pacing, not flexing one knee, simply standing straight. "What's this about?"

"Where is your husband, Mrs. Montgomery?"

She frowned ever so slightly, a brief look of confusion clouding her steeled eyes. "Traveling for business. Why?"

"What kind of business is that?"

"You might've heard our family has a construction company," she replied, the sarcasm in her voice heavy. "He's visiting vendors for next year's supply."

"Tell me more, please. What vendors, specifically? And where?"

She sighed, rolling her eyes. "My husband and I manage the supply chain for the business. I manage shipments, paperwork, and payments, but he goes out there and chooses granite, drywall, flooring, and so on. Again, why do you ask?"

Again, Kay ignored her question. Marleen was starting to become unnerved, just like she wanted her to be. "Which specific vendors is he visiting with this time?"

From annoyed, the woman's look turned wary. She spoke slowly, carefully choosing her words. "Last week, he visited with a vendor in New Mexico, for granite countertops. Then he was off to Texas, for appliances and light fixtures, a wholesale dealer. Finally, he was going to look at a piece of land just north of Marin County; Avery sent him. He wants to bid on that land and build acre-lot houses." She paused for a moment, carefully watching Kay, as if to tell her she was on to her game. "If you want their names, I can provide that."

"When's the last time you spoke with your husband?"

That simple question threw her off. A cloud of concern darkened her glare. She veered her eyes quickly, but not fast enough for Kay to miss the panic written in them. "Um, the weekend, I suppose."

"You don't normally speak on the phone when he's away?"

No longer caring about the state of the furniture, she slammed her leather purse on the bent, stained table, right by the handcuff ring.

"How is that your concern, Detective?" The words came out in a menacing whisper.

"I'm really sorry to inform you, Mrs. Montgomery, that your husband was shot and killed last Saturday." She'd softened her voice; after all, she was still a wife who was receiving the worst news of her life. Despite her suspicions, Kay empathized.

Speechless and turning pale under her carefully applied makeup, Marleen pulled the chair away from the table, its legs screeching loudly against the concrete floor. Then she let herself fall in it. Her eyes found Kay's as she whispered, "How?"

"We're still investigating," Kay replied cautiously. She wasn't just a victim's wife; she was also a suspect.

Tears started to pool in the woman's eyes, but her lips were pressed into a firm, angry line. "Why tell me now? If I hadn't come here with this," she slammed her palm down on the court order, "what, you would've never told me?"

"I'm sorry, ma'am, but we only identified him late last night. We were going to come see you this morning, but you beat us to it." Kay studied her for a moment. Grief and shock and anger collided on the woman's face, taking turns at winning, but anger still held the upper hand. "I'm afraid there's more bad news."

Her mouth opened slightly, but no sound came out. She was bracing herself.

"We have reason to believe your husband was having an affair with Cheryl Coleman."

"What? No, I can't believe that!" she reacted, seemingly shocked at the idea.

"Tell me, Mrs. Montgomery, how did you kill Cheryl? Because now we know why."

The woman stood abruptly, sending the chair toppling backward, ready to run out of there like a bat out of hell. She took a few steps toward the door, then froze in place. "What are you asking me? Are you deranged or something? You already checked my alibi. Maybe you're just lazy, looking to pin this on the easiest opportunity."

Kay remained calm, studying her reactions. She was still hiding something, although she couldn't figure out why. But she didn't seem to show guilt or fear when Cheryl's death was brought up, only surprise. "There are ways people can kill without getting any blood directly on their hands," Kay replied, testing another theory. Maybe she'd learned about her husband's affair, and had contracted the kill, although Kay didn't really believe it was a viable scenario, given Julie's disappearance and the witnesses left behind. No contract killer worth his salt would leave witnesses.

Marleen shook her head so forcefully the knot of her silk scarf came undone. "I don't know what you're talking about. I had no idea," her voice shattered, "that Dan was having an affair with… her." A hint of resentment, of preexisting contempt toward the young mother. Unwanted tears flooded her eyes and started trailing down her face. She covered her open mouth with her gloved hand. "Oh, dear God, no."

Kay allowed her a few moments to regain her composure. That came quicker than expected. Within less than a minute, her eyes were dry, her lips pressed tightly together, and her head held high.

"I believe we're done here, yes?"

"What have you done with Julie?" Kay asked, leaning back in her chair and crossing her legs.

"Excuse me?" Her reaction seemed genuine.

"You never asked about her, so you must already know. Where is she?"

Marleen shook her head again, just once. "I don't know what you're talking about. I believe it's time—"

"Walk me through the last twenty-four hours with your husband," Kay interrupted. "What happened? Step by step, every little detail, no matter how small."

The woman sighed and weighed her options. She was probably considering calling her attorney, but that would've taken some time, and she seemed in a rush to leave. "It was Friday," she eventually said. "We woke up at five-thirty, as always. Had our showers, made breakfast, he packed his bag and left."

"Driving or flying?"

"Driving," she replied immediately. "He was going to see the roof tile vendor first, then drive to Marin."

"You didn't mention a roof tile vendor when I asked earlier."

She tilted her head at Kay, mockingly. "I forgot, so sue me. Better even, throw me in jail."

"Then what happened?"

"He left, and I went to the office, where I stayed all day long, with witnesses present."

"And you weren't worried to not hear from your husband for a week?"

Her chest heaved in a forced breath. She looked away briefly. "We were having some difficulties. I didn't know about the affair with, um, Cheryl, but I suspected he was seeing someone." She lowered her gaze, embarrassed. "It doesn't take much to figure it out, when business trips start on Fridays and the first vendor appointment is the following Monday." Her voice had turned bitter, venomous. When she raised her eyes, she looked at Kay with renewed anger, as if her husband's indiscretions were somehow her fault. "If you're not arresting me, this interview is over."

She swiped her precious court order from the table and walked out of the door. Kay escorted her to the entrance.

Then she stopped in her tracks, staring Kay straight in the eye. "You're wasting your time, Detective, and what little time poor Julie might still have, by chasing me and my family over this. You should be out there instead, finding who killed my husband."

Kay felt something touch her leg. Looking down, she saw Heather, dragging her Lion King blanket on the floor and clasping her hand with trembling fingers. She must've snuck out. Instinctively, she pushed the girl behind her back, shielding her.

"I believe this is still valid," Mrs. Montgomery said, waving the court order. "I'm taking the girls with me."

Heather whimpered. At her feet, a puddle of liquid was growing, as the little girl stared at her great-aunt with eyes rounded in fear.

Behind her, Deputy Farrell was rushing over from the nap room, with an apologetic look on her face. Kay put Heather's hand in Farrell's. "Take her back, please. I'll be right there." Then she turned to Marleen Montgomery and said, "If court is what you want, then let's see this judge."

CHAPTER FORTY-TWO

White

Julie felt she was floating through air, lifted by strong arms that whisked her away.

"Mom?" she called, her words merely a faint whisper that no one caught.

She was being laid down on a soft surface, seemingly gently, but she couldn't feel much anymore. She willed herself to wake up, to stand and fight, to claw her way out of there just like she'd promised herself she would. Through a blur, she saw a man working on something by her side. She knew that man; she'd seen him before a couple of times, but couldn't remember his name.

Weeping, she tried to grab his hand, to get him to look at her. Maybe if she saw his face, she'd remember his name. But he didn't seem to care when her weak fingers swiped through the air, missing his arm, and fell limp by her body.

The man's hands moved quickly, removing her clothing with deft gestures. He supported her head as he took off her blouse, and tugged gently as he pulled off her jeans. Scared, she fidgeted and squirmed, but she was no match for the man's strong arms. One by one, the legs of her jeans were peeled off, then her underwear was next.

She wanted to scream, but all that came off her lips was a weak whimper. Desperate, she turned her blurry gaze to all the corners of the room, trying to see if there was anyone else there who could help her.

If her mother was still there.

Or had she imagined it all? Had she been alone all along?

That thought rushed a suffocating wave of panic over her. She tried to get up, but her weak arms wouldn't support her. Without a word, the man slid his arm under her back and set her down again.

With the jolt of strength and awareness thanks to the adrenaline coursing through her body, she realized she was lying on the bed she'd been avoiding since she'd been brought there. The man must've pushed her body as he'd entered her prison cell, and she hadn't even woken up to fight him. Everything had been in vain.

"Why…" she whispered, but he didn't hear, or didn't care to answer. His back was turned to her. She drew breath and tried to speak louder. "Why are you doing this?"

He turned and came closer, carrying something white in his arms, a dress that rustled like silk and shone in brilliant sparks.

"It's the way it has to be, my dear," he replied calmly, his voice somber and eerily soothing.

He set the dress on the bed by her side, and started adorning her. Everything he clad her with was white, and his hands were gentle and quick. At the edge of her consciousness a thought emerged. He'd done that before… more than once.

"Water… please," she whispered when he was close enough to hear her.

He shook his head slowly, his eyes sad. "It doesn't matter now. Soon it will be over." He touched her hand in a soft caress. "I'm sorry it took so long."

Then he propped her body up to slide the dress over her head. He lifted her hair over the collar and arranged the sleeves until they fell into place, then he helped her lie back against the pillows. He arranged the skirt, pulling it down and straightening it until it reached her ankles.

He combed her hair and put on a soft, creamy ChapStick, running it against his finger first, then tapping that finger against her lips.

Leaning over her, he adjusted a strand of her hair, tucking it over her ear, and whispered, "You're ready. And you're the most beautiful one yet."

That moment, before everything went dark, she finally recognized him. Just as he picked her up from the bed and walked out of the basement carrying her in his arms, she asked him one more time, "Why?"

There was no answer.

CHAPTER FORTY-THREE

In Court

The early morning drive to Redding had been a tense one. Marleen Montgomery had insisted on driving herself to Redding and back, but Kay didn't agree. If she drove, she could shave a good chunk of time using her flashers and flooring it all the way down on the interstate despite the heavy downpour—but she wasn't going to endanger the safety of a civilian by having to keep up, or waste any precious time by driving the speed limit. Instead, she insisted that the defiant Mrs. Montgomery take a seat in the back of her unmarked SUV.

Once they were finally on their way, Marleen did not stop bickering about the conditions she was forced to put up with and how she was treated, being hauled against her will onto the back seat of a police car, where all the thugs and the scum of the earth had sat before her.

"This is a brand-new detective's vehicle," Kay explained, at the end of her wits, yet still feeling sympathetic for the woman who'd just been notified her husband had been killed. "No scum of the earth has sat there yet."

"But what if someone sees me?" she'd continued to argue, her voice an irritating high pitch reminding Kay of fingernails dragged against the blackboard.

"It's an unmarked vehicle, Mrs. Montgomery. No one would know, unless you tell them. I'm not even using the flashers."

"I still believe you somehow violated my rights, and I'll ask my attorney how to hold you accountable for this, make you pay for it. It wouldn't be fair if you got away with it, just wouldn't."

Kay repressed a frustrated groan. "It's the fastest way both of us can deal with this issue and be done with it."

"No," she snapped. "The fastest way would've been for you to comply with this court order and release the girls to me. My attorney will—"

That was it; the woman's obnoxiousness had eroded whatever sympathy Kay was feeling for the new widow, despite believing she withheld critical information that could've helped the detective find Julie. "At this point, I'll have to strongly suggest that you remain silent." Kay's words fell heavily loaded with the meaning she knew the woman would find in them—the unspoken threat. Finally, there was some silence. Intimidated yet fuming, Mrs. Montgomery lay back against her seat scowling, arms crossed at her chest, and did, in fact, remain silent for the rest of the trip.

They discovered Judge Drysdale was still in chambers, his caseload full for the day, but Kay wasn't willing to wait. She found her way to his chambers and knocked on the scratched door.

His Honor was sliding on his robe and was positively infuriated by the intrusion. A well-built man with at least fifty pounds extra on his frame, his face showed signs of habitual alcohol use. Red, almost purple blotches on his face and throat, right above the tight collar of his white shirt, were a clear indication he should have had his blood pressure checked. That skin discoloration so early in the morning could only mean he had drunk his share the night before, and managed to stay awake that morning with the help of stiff coffee, downed one Starbucks venti paper cup after another, as testified by the one already empty discarded in the trash basket by the door, and the other one on his desk. A fine dandruff dust covered the shoulders of his robe, and more flew off his head when he ran his hands through his short white hair, exasperated.

"When I'm woken up at five in the morning to issue a court order because cops, none other than the people who are paid to enforce the law, violate it and refuse to turn over custody to the rightful family members, I don't really expect that order to be ignored."

"Your Honor, I'm Detective Kay Sharp with the Mount Chester Sheriff's Office. If you'd allow me to explain—"

"I've heard a lot about you, Detective." He was almost shouting, while pointing at the two chairs in front of his desk. "You're the one who's been keeping two children hostage, locked up in the back of a police precinct, are you not?"

"Well, I—"

"Let me tell you something, Detective. I *chose* family law because there's nothing in this world I care more about than the welfare of children," he bellowed, standing behind his desk, leaning forward, towering over Kay menacingly. "Yet you jeopardize the welfare of these children, when there's a respectable family, their grandparent and their aunt, willing to take them in and give them a good life." He looked at her as if she were despicable beyond words. "How can you live with yourself?" He loosened his collar, the red blotches on his face turning more and more purple. "Make no mistake, I *will* hold you in contempt. What do you have to say for yourself?"

She swallowed hard, her throat suddenly constricted and dry. "Your Honor, we have reasons to believe Mrs. Montgomery, and potentially other members of the Montgomery family, are directly involved in the death of Cheryl Coleman and the abduction of Julie Montgomery."

His white, untrimmed brows furrowed. "Involved, how?"

"The investigation is still undergoing," she said, painfully aware just how lame that sounded, but with Marleen Montgomery present, there was only so much she could disclose without jeopardizing her case. "We have established that Mrs. Montgomery's late husband visited the Coleman residence before Cheryl Coleman's death. We have also established that Mrs. Montgomery's husband was having an affair with Cheryl Coleman, and that speaks to potential motive."

"Your Honor, I provided law enforcement with an alibi that checked out for the time of Cheryl Coleman's death and Julie's abduction. They have no evidence against me, or I would be wearing handcuffs," Marleen explained, holding her hands out as if to demonstrate she wasn't wearing any restraints.

Judge Drysdale turned the focus of his dark brown eyes to Kay. "Is that true, Detective?"

She nodded reluctantly. "We did check her alibi, yes, but there are other ways in which—"

"From where I'm standing, you've got nothing, and I have work to do. The court order stands."

Marleen grinned widely and shot Kay a triumphant look. "Thank you, Your Honor."

"Your Honor, we have established that Julie's kidnapping is part of a series of kidnappings that spans over fifty years," she blurted out quickly, afraid he was going to cut her off again. But he was taken aback by her words, silent and slack jawed. "We're looking at a serial offender. We just need a little more time. And these girls are essential to our investigation. Their safety is a big concern to us, being they witnessed the killing of their mother and the abduction of their sister." He stared at her without interrupting, his attention piqued to the point where it had dissolved his earlier frustration. "I swear to you, they're well taken care of."

Marleen stared at the judge, visibly appalled, slack-jawed and stiff with indignation.

Kay stopped talking, holding her breath, waiting for him to decide. She'd already said more than she should have, and was painfully aware how Sheriff Logan would feel about it if he ever found out. Only facts backed by solid evidence were to be presented in court, regardless of circumstances. Speculation and unproven theories only hurt people and careers.

Judge Drysdale reached out across his desk and swiftly grabbed the court order from Mrs. Montgomery's hand. Her jaw dropped.

"You have forty-eight hours, Detective." His voice was back to normal, and the purplish blotches on his skin were waning toward their normal shade of wino red. "In forty-eight hours, you either charge Mrs. Montgomery with a crime, or she takes full custody of these children. So ordered."

A wave of relief washed over her, while Mrs. Montgomery protested, her voice weak and humble, with undertones of desperation. "But, Your Honor—"

"Mrs. Montgomery, don't get me started," the judge replied, walking toward the door with large steps that made his robe flutter behind him like a cape. "You conveniently left out several critical facts, like these girls being, in fact, in protective custody as witnesses to a crime. Don't waste my time anymore." He opened the door and held it for them with an impatient scowl on his face. "What are you waiting for? My clerk will draw up the new order and this time, Detective, you'd better comply." He spoke those words sternly, right as Kay was leaving his chambers. He slammed the door behind her unceremoniously, and walked briskly toward the courtrooms.

The drive back started in silence, interrupted only by Kay's passenger's sniffles. At some point, she broke down, sobbing uncontrollably, the emotional toll of the situation finally catching up with her. By the time they reached Mount Chester, she'd recomposed herself, at least on the surface.

Kay pulled in right by her car and waited. The rain was still falling heavily, but the lightning had subsided some, only rarely a flicker illuminating distant clouds. The sheriff's office parking lot was one big puddle endlessly rippled by falling raindrops, but there was nothing Kay could do about it. Her reluctant passenger was about to get her pumps soaked.

"This isn't over," Mrs. Montgomery said before stepping out of the SUV. "My attorney will be in touch." She slammed the door behind her, and Kay waited until she climbed into her S-Class Mercedes, unwilling to soak her in sprayed puddle water if she drove off too soon.

Then she pulled away slowly, watching Marleen in the rearview mirror. The woman was sobbing hard, her arms hugging the steering wheel, her head buried between them, her shoulders heaving spasmodically.

Losing a husband was never easy. Finding out that he'd been cheating must've been unbearable, heart-wrenching. Yet, Kay had to look at this family closer, their involvement a safe bet in her mind. She was still missing a few critical pieces of the puzzle and couldn't yet grasp the whole picture, but asking the right questions of the right people would probably fix that.

She pulled around the building, looking for a peaceful place where she could spend a few minutes. She wanted to do some homework on the Montgomerys before starting to knock on doors; it always paid to be prepared. As she shifted into park, a chime warned her of a new text message.

Dr. Whitmore was inviting her and Elliot to the morgue; he had new evidence.

Torn between priorities, she hesitated for a moment, but then decided to ask Elliot to visit with the ME alone, while she got an early start interviewing the family.

Time was running out. For Julie, it might've already expired.

CHAPTER FORTY-FOUR

History

Rain rapped loudly against the roof of her SUV, prompting her to move it under a tree, where the noise subsided some, only the heaviest of drops making it through the thick, turning foliage. Occasionally, a torn branch or an acorn fell with a louder thud, but Kay barely noticed.

She'd pulled up the profile of Montgomery Construction. Founded soon after the end of World War II, the corporation had been held privately in the Montgomery family ever since. Its founder, William Montgomery, a decorated war veteran, had returned home and found that the nation was rebuilding faster than contractors could be found. So, he became one.

The company had struggled at first, battling the 1945 recession, not many people able to afford new housing so soon after the war, but William had used his veteran status to get some contracts from the government. He'd built several local state and federal buildings, some of which had since been replaced by newer ones, but most still endured.

Avery was his only son.

The first time that official records showed Avery's name was relatively soon after the corporation had been founded, when Avery was barely twenty-two years old. A subsequent filing three months later showed Avery taking over the company from his father, who, per a newspaper article buried deep inside the local

City Hall archives, had been battling pancreatic cancer. A small note a few months later accompanied his obituary; he'd lost the battle. Another few months later, his wife, Avery's mother, followed him to the Valley Rose Cemetery.

Then there was nothing, no articles and no notable filings, other than the one announcing the birth of Avery's youngest son, Raymond. Probably the earlier announcements for his two older sons and for his marriage had become lost, such old records never digitized properly by a library that struggled to keep the lights on.

Then, about a year after Raymond's birth, Avery's wife was reported missing.

Anna Montgomery, twenty-three at the time, was a stunning blonde, her body untouched by her three pregnancies, if the faded photo Kay was looking at had been taken right before she disappeared. Black and white with a tinge of sepia, the picture was a scan of the original missing persons report, probably the one Avery carried in his wallet. The corners had been rounded by wear, and it had numerous lines running through it, a web of them speaking to the many times that photo had been handled. Anna smiled joyfully in the portrait, sporting a white summer dress, almost transparent against the sun. She seemed happy, serene, full of life.

Kay's gaze lingered on the woman's face—her beautiful features—and wished she could find out more about who she'd been as a person. It was always the first victim of a serial offender that held the most meaning. She hadn't fully validated yet that no other first-daughter kidnappings had taken place prior to fifty-seven years ago and were somehow left out of the archives. Until proof to the contrary, she looked at Anna as the first victim in the unsub's daunting list, and she was different from the rest in at least one aspect.

She was a wife.

Unlike the other forty-two victims, who'd all been girls still living with their parents, Anna had been someone's wife, someone's mother.

All the victims had been White, Native, or Hispanic, but Anna and only a handful of others had been blondes. For the unsub, race and physiognomy didn't seem to matter much, his choice of victims matching, in almost perfect proportions, the population makeup of the region. Whatever it was they had in common, it wasn't their physical aspects, and that seemed to support her theory about mission-driven killings.

She closed the municipal archives and opened Anna's missing persons report. Avery had filed it himself, less than a day after she'd disappeared. Per his statement, he'd been gone all day working at the construction site and he'd returned after sunset, only to find the door open and his wife gone. His children, all under the age of four at the time, were found inside the house, unharmed.

Huh, Kay thought, *another instance of leaving witnesses alive. Seems he only cares about these firstborn daughters and no one else.* Because yes, per the city's records, Anna had also been a firstborn daughter, a single child.

There had been no signs of forced entry, and no fingerprints that didn't belong. The detective who'd investigated the case had found it necessary to put it in his report that Mrs. Anna Montgomery seemed to have left of her own volition, although no luggage, passport, or money were missing from the house. All her jewelry was still there, evidence against a breaking and entering gone bad. Reading between the lines of his report, Kay deduced he'd felt less than motivated to investigate, assuming the young mother had just deserted her husband and young boys and left for San Francisco, by herself or with an unknown lover, in the search of a better life in the city by the bay.

One critical detail was missing from the case file, and that was the weather, never really required to be included. Scrolling through her recent calls, Kay called Weather Underground at the same number she'd dialed the night before. She recognized the pleasant baritone the moment the man picked up.

"It's Detective Kay Sharp, we spoke yesterday."

"Ah, yes, Detective, I have your list almost ready," the man replied jovially. "It took me a while to dig them up, you know."

Kay suspected her list of dates was the reason why he was picking up the phone long after his shift might've ended. "Which one did you start with?"

"The oldest one. I figured they'd be the most difficult to dig up."

"Perfect. Could you please tell me, what was the weather like on the oldest of dates, the, um, August 29—"

"Yeah, I have it right here. Four inches of rain, wind gusting up to forty-five miles per hour, temperature dropping twenty degrees. The typical cyclone remnants, courtesy of Hurricane Elba." The meteorologist stopped talking for a moment, only the rustling of paper coming across the open line. "Actually, I just realized, but all the dates you had me pull up were major tropical storms generated by Pacific hurricanes."

"How come we get so many of them? We're not exactly in the Bahamas here."

"They're not that many," he replied, the smile in his voice obvious. Her ignorance must've been entertaining for him. "Typically, we see about sixteen named storms in the Pacific each year. Ten of them on average develop into hurricanes, and tend to drift west-northwest, like all the Northern Hemisphere hurricanes do. Most of them die at sea; a few make landfall in Mexico. We rarely see a hurricane landfall in Northern California; it almost never happens. We get the occasional cyclone—hurricane leftovers if you'd like, usually just a tropical storm. It could be two, three years before we see one, and it's always in the fall."

The man loved talking about weather. She could tell he was passionate about his chosen profession. "And how bad are they, normally?"

"By the time they reach us, these storm systems are far less dangerous than a hurricane, although sometimes the name of the storm that has generated the post-tropical cyclone or remnants still lingers."

That was unexpected. "Then, what's this?" she gestured at the rain outside her car, as if the meteorologist could see her.

"This weather, right now? Just a storm system fueled by Hurricane Edward. You see, a hurricane is a huge storm, its center pressure so low it pulls moisture from hundreds of miles away." He paused, but she could hear him laughing quietly. "I take it you've never experienced a hurricane, Detective?"

"No, I haven't had the pleasure," she replied, staring at the gusty rainfall battering her car viciously and wondering how much worse a hurricane could be.

She thanked him and hung up. The only thing that mattered was the weather on the day Anna Montgomery had gone missing, and it had been just as bad, if not worse. And that fact brought more questions than answers.

What did the storm mean for the unsub? Nature's forensic countermeasure? Or did it hold some secret meaning only he understood? Was he repeating an earlier trauma that might've happened during a storm? Either way, everything pointed at Montgomery Construction, and that's where she was headed for answers.

She turned on the radio and peeled off, sending four-foot-high waves of puddle water in the air. She was headed for the company headquarters, a building she knew well, passing by it every morning on her way to work.

She turned on the radio, barely paying any attention to the music that was playing. After Imagine Dragons finished their song about liars and how they failed to make their partners happy, the announcer mentioned something about rainfall causing more landslides along the coastal highways and threatening the interstate at two of the bridges over Blackwater River.

She stepped on the gas pedal and turned her wipers to the max, squinting hard to see where she was going. A distant thunder echoed strangely in her heart, sending shivers down her spine.

CHAPTER FORTY-FIVE

Murder Weapon

Good thing that Kay's text message reached Elliot before he took a bite from his sandwich. Just seeing the medical examiner's name on the phone screen made the mouthwatering smell of honey-baked ham seem tainted with formaldehyde. Feeling his stomach churn, he wrapped up the sandwich and abandoned it on his desk, choosing black coffee instead.

He'd been running solely on coffee for the past twelve hours, since Kay and he shared a dinner he couldn't get out of his mind. He'd been up all night, tossing and turning, questions about John Doe aka Dan Montgomery spinning in his mind, intertwined with other questions, about Kay. About the image of her with the two young girls that was seared forever in his memory, seeding unspoken scenarios in his mind.

He was in awe of her, and that made everything more complicated. She was as smart as a whip; just being next to her made him think he didn't know which end was up, about pretty much everything. To make things worse, she was his partner, and he knew better than to think of a partner like that, ever again. Last time, it made him leave Texas behind, when his personal relationship with his former partner was used in court to let a perp walk free. That was one heck of a lesson he'd never forget.

Yet the thought of Kay Sharp kept him up at night, wondering. What if she was the one? What if he'd never be the same if he somehow managed to walk away from her? And why on earth would he have the fortune, big as Dallas, to have this fine woman look at him that way, even for a second?

He pushed those questions out of his mind as he drove to the morgue, bracing himself for yet another session of torture.

When he walked through the front door at the medical examiner's office, his nose was slathered thick in VapoRub, and he couldn't smell a rotting wild hog if the thing were laid dead at his feet.

Thankfully, the two stainless-steel exam tables were empty, their surfaces clean and shiny, the entire morgue spotless. As for the smells, he couldn't tell with all that Vicks on his nostrils.

"Ah, there you are," Dr. Whitmore greeted him. His lab coat was freshly cleaned and pressed, but he didn't seem to have just arrived at work. He was wearing yesterday's shirt and slacks, a little more wrinkled than Elliot recalled, as if he'd caught some shuteye on the vinyl couch in the corner, by the door.

He shook the doctor's hand, somewhat confused by his amused grin.

"No need for all that menthol today," he commented with a quick laugh. "All my tenants are tucked neatly in their refrigerated storage units." He turned to the side and pointed to a gallon coffee can on a lab table. "This is what I wanted to show you." He frowned slightly, then glanced toward the door. "Where's Kay?"

"She's interviewing a suspect. I'm all you get today, Doc."

"Okay." Dr. Whitmore tapped his fingernails against the metallic coffee can. "Two rounds of crime scene searches missed it." He smiled, bringing up lines in the corners of his eyes. "It was well worth sending them back to do another search." A glint of excitement lit his eyes as his smile widened. "We found the murder weapon." He walked over to another lab table on wheels and brought it closer. It held a nine-mil Glock on a sheet of paper. "It was completely dismantled and soaked in chlorine, so fingerprints and any DNA are out of the question, but I was able to match it to the bullet we recovered from Dan Montgomery's body."

"That means, beyond any reasonable doubt, my vic was shot in the Coleman residence, huh?"

"Yup, precisely."

"How the heck did they miss it?"

"This," he pointed at the can, "was tucked under the kitchen sink, open and full of dirty fluid, as if set there to catch sewage from a leaky drain." He tilted his head and ran his hand through his white hair. "Gotta give it to Cheryl, that's smart."

"Right." Elliot shifted his weight from one leg to the other, wondering if that was all. Smells or no smells, he still wanted to get out of there as soon as possible.

"Then the fibers on Dan Montgomery's body—they're confirmed to have come from a Ford truck." He sat in front of his computer and brought up his DMV profile. "Once I identified him, we had the year and model of his F-150, and it's a match with the fibers we found." He paused for a moment, looking at the screen but seemingly thinking of something else. "It's a *generic* match, meaning the fibers match all Fords from that model year and that color scheme. I'd need to see the actual truck to see if I can further match any of the other particulates I found on the victim's clothes. Then I could upgrade this to a *specific* match instead of generic."

"I added the tags to the APB this morning," Elliot replied. "If it's out there, we'll find it."

Doc Whitmore's smile reappeared, timid, hesitant. "It's a pretty weird coincidence, isn't it?"

"What?"

"The trucks. Dan drove a white Ford F-150 diesel, and the unsub's vehicle is believed to have been the same make and model, based on the nine-one-one call analysis."

"Yeah," Elliot replied. It was a weird coincidence. Like with everything else in that case, what were the odds?

"Do you think it could be the same truck?"

"You're saying the unsub found Dan's truck, then drove it to Cheryl's—to do what? Finish the job Dan might've started? Get some revenge for his death? But if he knew about Dan's death and cared, would he have left him to rot in a ditch by the interstate?" Elliot shook his head. "We'll find out soon enough, Doc, and these things will start making sense. Kay won't rest until everything lines up to perfection."

"Kay and yourself, you mean?"

He felt a wave of heat rushing to his face. "Yeah, that's what I meant. Although she's by far better equipped to deal with this kind of case than I'll ever be." Words poured out of his mouth like a torrent once the floodgates were open. "I've caught burglars and drug dealers, collared a few kidnappers and more than my share of disorderlies, rapists, and wife-beaters, but the scum she's put away, I can't even begin to comprehend how someone decides they want to do that for a living. And there's no slack in her rope either, not a single inch."

Doc Whitmore's smile widened as he studied Elliot until he had to lower his gaze, afraid the doctor would see right through him. "She's awesome, our Kay, isn't she?"

Elliot nodded, keeping his eyes shielded under the brim of his hat. "Damn right she is. How does one partner with someone like that?" he asked, instantly regretting he'd said the words out loud.

"You learn from her, that's all there is to it," the doctor replied, his voice thoughtful and warm, almost father-like. "From what I've seen, she's more than happy to show you the ropes."

"Yeah, she is," Elliot replied quickly, uneasy, eager to change the subject. "Got anything else for me, Doc? I gotta run."

"For you, not so much as for her, but I guess that's the same, now that you're working both cases together, right?"

"What's up?"

The doc clicked and typed for a moment, then several images were displayed on the wall screen. "It's about Cheryl. I have formally finished my postmortem, and there was something I missed during the preliminary." He stood and walked over to the screen, then pointed at two photos of Cheryl's face and neck. "These were not immediately visible due to blood pooling and lividity, and they are a little older. See here, and here?" He pointed at her lips, then at her throat, where the skin discoloration was only slightly darker. "This tells me someone tried to strangle her, even covered her mouth with his fingers, like this." He demonstrated without touching, using a skeleton on a stand in the corner of his lab. "From behind. He covered her mouth, then tried to strangle her with his arm, military style, but there were no petechiae. For some reason, he stopped and didn't use the full force he could have used. It wasn't forceful enough to show without the fluoroscope, leaving only subdermal hematomas."

"How old are these, um—"

"Bruises? They were inflicted about forty-eight hours before her death."

"That's around the time Dan Montgomery was there, right?"

"Exactly." He turned off the wall-mounted screen and sat at his desk with a loud, pained groan. "That's all I have for you."

Elliot touched the brim of his hat in a gesture of thanks. "When are you going home, Doc? You look like chewed twine."

He burst into a hearty laughter that echoed eerily in the morgue. "I've never been called *that* before, son. I'll go grab some shuteye right away if that's the case." He took off his lab coat and started to turn off his computer. "You have both reports in your inbox—you and your fine partner."

Unlike before, when he could barely wait to get out of there, Elliot found himself lingering, waiting for the doctor to shut down everything he needed to before he could lock up.

"It's this family, Doc, it has to be," he said, wondering what he was missing.

Doc cancelled the shutdown on his computer and pulled Dan Montgomery's profile up on the screen.

"What about the family?" he said, sitting down on his four-legged stool on wheels, an expression of excitement on his face. "It's been a while since I tried my sleuthing skills."

"It's something Kay said." Elliot looked at Dan Montgomery's DMV photo over the doc's shoulder. He'd been a handsome man, with a certain harshness in his features, in his eyes. He seemed cold, determined, and that tan he'd noticed the day he found him was there four years ago when he'd renewed his license. Now that he knew the man worked construction, it made sense. He was out in the California sun and coastal winds all day long, probably wearing a hard hat, one that didn't shield his face from all that UV.

Dr. Whitmore held his hands above the keyboard, seeming ready to type. He was waiting for him to finish his thoughts.

"She said no serial killer in history has killed for fifty-seven years, and that we could have a generational serial killer on our hands." He stopped talking, worried he didn't remember it right. "Or that's what I believe she said."

"Ah, interesting." Doc typed quickly, bringing up on the small screen, one by one, the profiles of the male Montgomery family members. "Turn on the big screen for me, will you?"

He obliged, even if that meant having to walk past a shelf holding specimens in jars, way closer than he would've wanted to ever find himself to someone's liver.

"Dan was Avery's son," Dr. Whitmore said. "But we can scratch him off the list; he was dead at the time. And Avery? I heard you cleared him already."

"Yeah, we did. Rock-solid alibi."

"There's Mitchell, he's sixty-one years old. He's the father of Calvin, Cheryl's late husband." He sighed from the bottom of his lungs. "Somehow, I find the scenario beyond sickening—that the girl's grandfather was involved in any way. It's against everything I've seen in my entire life behind the autopsy table, and I've given the job forty-five years."

But Elliot had stopped listening a while ago, his eyes riveted on Raymond's photo. The youngest of Avery's sons, he was the one who'd left town and moved to San Francisco years ago, per his DMV records. Maybe, if he'd chosen to leave behind the family business and become something else, someplace else, he was worth talking with.

Perhaps it wasn't his passion for fashion photography that drove him away... maybe it was family secrets. Or something terrible to hide.

CHAPTER FORTY-SIX

Lynn

The Montgomery Construction headquarters was a three-story building shaped as a cube and built at the top of a gentle hill, with sufficient elevation to give the building an imposing look, towering over the interstate. The logo—also a cube set in perspective, with four of its lines bolder to form the letter "M" in California sky blue—was tastefully set on the vertical edge of the building, visible from four directions on the highway.

Slightly sloped, the parking lot didn't hold water; instead of pooling in puddles like everywhere else, rainwater flowed toward grille-covered intakes, maintained free of debris and in perfect working order. The building entrance was under a wide covered area like usually seen in luxury hotels, allowing Kay to stop her SUV and enter the building without a single drop of rain touching her clothes.

She minded the threshold as she stepped onto the white marble floor, the doors sliding open and immediately closing behind with a subdued whoosh. She'd taken two steps toward the large reception desk when the girl behind it stood up abruptly, seeming flustered, as if ready to run.

Lynn.

Jacob's new girlfriend, the woman who'd sunk her prison-tattooed hand into Kay's underwear drawer and packed a clean change of clothes for which she was still grateful. The woman whose record she never got a chance to run.

Kay forced the nascent frown off her forehead and smiled. "It's you." Her smile bloomed wider. "That's a surprise. I didn't know you worked for the Montgomerys."

Lynn blushed and looked to the side, hiding her eyes for a brief moment before facing Kay. "I *am* a Montgomery." Her words were accompanied with an apologetic shrug, as if to say she had no choice in the matter.

"I had no idea. I actually thought—"

She put her tattooed hand on the desk counter. She had long, elegant fingers and a perfect manicure. "Oh, this? Jacob told me. I've never been arrested," she said, looking away again, her cheeks turning a darker shade of embarrassed. "But you might know that already. Jacob was willing to bet you were going to check the moment you got to the office."

Her brother knew her well, but she'd been called to the Angel Creek Pointe crime scene before she'd had the chance. "Then, why the prison tat?"

"I was dating this oh-so-very-wrong guy in college—biker, leather, hard rock, the works—and he had one. He somehow talked me into getting a matching one, and I didn't think there was a hidden meaning to it. By the time I found out, everyone who knew what it meant was shunning me and I had no idea why." She shrugged, still staring down. "What can I say? I was an idiot. At least Jacob was open about it."

"He's direct, if anything, isn't he?"

Her smile lit up her eyes as she looked at Kay. "He's great. Honesty is so rare in men these days." She took her seat behind the reception desk and Kay leaned casually against the counter. The girl purposefully ignored a call that lit up her complex phone, chiming softly.

"Do you need to take that?" Finding someone Kay knew personally, seated comfortably at the heart of the Montgomery family business, was an unexpected advantage, and she wanted to be very careful about it. She owed it to Julie, but also to her brother, to not screw up his relationship.

Lynn waved her concern off. "It can go to voicemail. I'll call them back later. What can I do for you, Detective?"

Kay laughed. "I guess we're past that. You've seen all my underwear. Please call me Kay."

She blushed some more and joined Kay with shy laughter, veering her gaze.

"Thanks for that, by the way. You saved my life."

"I asked Jacob not to tell you," she admitted simply. "I thought you'd be mad. He said the alternative was worse. He told me of a time when you caught him going through your drawers."

She'd almost forgot. "We were kids, he was just a little boy, not knowing what he was doing. He ran away with my panties, played with them in the yard, hung them up in his favorite tree. Can you imagine?" Kay laughed fondly at the memory. "I told him if he ever came close to my stuff, I'd wring his neck."

"He believed you," Lynn said, turning serious. "He wouldn't touch that drawer or anything else in your room. He respects you a whole deal, you know."

Kay knew that well. It was Lynn, the stranger in their lives that was a bit troublesome, a third person joining the two siblings on their journey through life. Then a surprising thought surfaced in her mind. What if the situation were reversed, and she was bringing Elliot into their lives? Would Jacob choose to be a total ass? Or would he choose to remain the same loving and supportive brother she'd always relied on? The answer was obvious.

"Well, I'm happy he found someone like you," she said, realizing she really felt that way. Lynn was kind, pleasant, and could think on her feet. She had gumption and liked to stand up for her beliefs and speak her mind, even to someone as intimidating as a cop with Kay's reputation could be. Jacob was lucky. But he had to date a Montgomery? Really? Out of all the boring names in the local *White Pages*, he had to pick that one.

She smiled in lieu of thanks and nodded.

"Tell me, did you know Cheryl?"

Lynn's eyes darkened, and her smile waned. "She was my sister-in-law. Calvin, her husband, was my brother."

"What did you think of her?"

She looked out the window in the distance for a brief moment, thinking. "She loved my brother very much. She was a good wife to him; they shared the perfect romance," she added with a sad smile. "They'd been dating since high school. Even with Calvin gone to college, their relationship endured, got even stronger with the distance."

"She changed her name after Calvin passed, didn't she?"

"Yeah, she went back to her maiden name, Coleman."

"Why did she do that, do you know?"

She hesitated, visibly uncomfortable. "This is my family. I don't—well, please take this with a grain of salt." Another pause. "They're good people."

"Sure," Kay replied, her eyebrows twitching into a slight frown.

"Um, right before his accident, Calvin got into an argument with Avery and Mitchell, our father. It was routine, something they argued over a lot."

"What were they arguing about?"

Another hesitation, then her face shifted as if she'd decided to lie about it, or hold things closer to her chest than Kay would've liked. "Some concrete-pouring procedure or foundations or something like that. Just, um, construction stuff, but it could get loud. Calvin was hot-blooded, young, and Avery, well, he's old and can be quite obstinate. He wants things done his way or else." She sighed and her eyes welled up. "Then Calvin fell with the scaffolding and died on the spot." Lynn clasped her hands, nervously wringing them. "Cheryl never wanted to believe it was by accident. She was frantic, telling everyone who wanted to listen that Avery got rid of the grandson who didn't toe the line. But the company was cleared."

Kay leaned closer, her elbows propped on the glossy counter. "What do you think?" she asked, lowering her voice to a conspiratorial whisper.

Lynn veered her eyes away for a brief moment. "I loved Calvin very much; he was my only brother. I don't believe there was any foul play in his death, just bad luck. All safeties were in place, the scaffolding was new, installed correctly, that's what OSHA put in their report."

"Then what happened?"

"Bad luck," she repeated, looking out the window. "Weather, even nastier than this. I remember the rain that day. Sheesh… unbelievable. Avery should've stopped operations, but he can be obstinate." She sighed, a shuddered breath leaving her chest. "It wasn't really his fault, but it can be easy to think that. Calvin shouldn't've climbed on the scaffolding that day. It just gave," she sniffled and wiped a tear from the corner of her eye with a quick swipe of her finger. "Not the scaffolding, the earth."

"A landslide, you mean?"

"A small one," she added quietly. "But it had to be right under that scaffolding, right when my brother was up there, in that rain."

Weather, again. Kay made a mental note to cross-reference the date Calvin died with any open missing persons report. She didn't really know why or what the two events could have in common, but it was worth a shot.

"Yeah, I can see how this was entirely bad luck," she said, to put Lynn's fears at ease. She looked around for a moment, at the three-story-high lobby and the huge, modern chandelier hanging from the ceiling, at the large windows against which rain rapped incessantly, at the ominous clouds she could see in the distance, bulging restlessly, occasionally lit by lightning. "A lot of the family works for the company. Is it a good work life?"

"*Everyone* in the family works for the company," Lynn laughed awkwardly. "Well, except Ray. It's how Avery wants it. But it's a good life; he pays me more than anyone else would pay a receptionist. When Marleen retires, I'll take over vendor management. It's a big opportunity for me."

"So, the company is managed strictly by the family?" It wasn't unheard of; a limiting and strange choice for someone with Avery's ambition. To make the company the largest contractor in California he'd have to scale the business, and that meant bringing in a few strangers in key leadership positions.

"Yes," she replied. "It's always been like that."

"How about Dan and Marleen? Are they happy to be in the business?" Kay wondered if Lynn had learned about Dan's passing.

She gave half a shrug. "They seem to be, at least content if not happy. Sometimes Marleen is, um, can be a bitch," she added, lowering her voice. "When things don't go her way."

"How about Raymond? He's Avery's son too, isn't he?"

"Yeah, but he left, a long time ago. I was still in school." She took a sip from a paper cup without markings, something she might've picked up from the building cafeteria Kay could see in the distance, through the hallway. "I still remember how bad it was. Avery took it personally, wanted to disown him, ugh, what a mess."

"Why did he leave?" Kay smiled encouragingly. "If the life is good…"

"He wanted to do something else, more artistic. He wasn't into construction. He hated it, and hated Avery for forcing him to go to school for it, get a useless degree, and all that. What a shouting match that was," she snickered with a guilty look on her face. "Can you imagine these windows rattling?"

"Do you still see him? Raymond?"

"No, Uncle Ray never came back. Not for Thanksgiving dinners or Christmas, not since he went away. I heard he's doing well for himself in San Francisco, but we're not supposed to mention his name, not when Avery is around."

"Speaking of the devil," she quipped, "can you announce me, please? I'd like to speak with Avery."

"Oh, he's not here," Lynn replied immediately. "And I don't think he's coming back today." She gave the weather outside a look filled with disappointment.

"How about Mitchell, your dad? Is he in? I just have a few questions." She decided to share a little more, in the hope it would open some doors. "I'm not sure if you knew, but Dan Montgomery has been killed."

Lynn gasped, her hands covering her open mouth. "Oh, my goodness… When did that happen?" She seemed wholeheartedly upset by the news, rattled even, a flicker of fear coloring her eyes.

"Last Saturday, it seems. We're still investigating."

"He was my uncle, Dad's younger brother." Her voice trailed off, loaded with tears. "They were really tight. Does Marleen know?"

"Yes. Have you seen her today?"

"No, she hasn't been in. I was wondering—" she paused, but then she must've remembered Kay's initial request. "No, Dad isn't here either. They're all at the site."

"In this weather?"

Lynn shrugged again and threw her long, silky hair over her shoulder with a swift move. "It's not like they're pouring concrete today, but work still goes on at the site. They have trailers over there, mobile offices." She stopped for a moment, frowning. "Avery might be over there too. I know Victor is." She saw Kay's confused look. "He's my cousin, Dan's son. Although, with Dan gone… I don't know, I really don't, I'm sorry." A long, shuddering breath of air left her lungs and ended in a stifled sob. She pulled a Kleenex from the box on her desk and patted her eyes dry with it.

"Where is this site you're talking about?"

She livened up just a little, but her eyes were still brimming with tears. "Oh, it's on Ash Brook Hill. You can't miss it. We're building the largest hospital ever constructed in this area," she added, pride coloring her voice.

"Oh, I know where it is," Kay replied. "It is big." Huge would've been a better term for it. They'd sliced off the top of the hill to pour the foundation.

"When you get there, ask Dad to show you the rendering. It's going to be amazing. I heard Avery say it's our biggest project yet, with three hundred beds."

"Oh, wow," Kay reacted, in passing wondering why anyone would invest and build a hospital with hundreds of beds in a town of barely thirty-eight hundred, the last time she'd checked the green road sign at the town limits. It probably had something to do with the projected influx of retirees and cottage owners that would bring the population up to almost ten thousand over the next few years. And still, it was huge. Perhaps it was going to be another posh rehab unit for Silicon Valley's overworked cocaine addicts, or something like that.

"Thank you," Kay smiled warmly. "You've been a tremendous help. My brother is a lucky man." Lynn blushed. Kay held her arms open wide in an inviting gesture, and Lynn quickly rushed from behind the desk and into her arms with youthful enthusiasm, the hug warm and ending with a kiss on Kay's cheek. She thanked her and left, feeling grateful again for the ability to walk on dry asphalt to her car.

Driving off, Kay kept her speed as high as the heavy rainfall allowed. She reached the Ash Brook Hill site in only five minutes, and took the unpaved access road to the site, her all-wheel-drive barely able to climb the slope in the foot-deep ruts filled with reddish, chunky mud. The side of the hill facing the interstate had started to slide, threatening the foundation that was still being poured, the limit of the exposed ground barely a few yards away from the edge of the concrete.

As she followed the winding road to the trailer, she turned and gasped as it came into view. Parked side by side and facing the trailer, three identical white Ford F-150 trucks were lined up. The one closest to her had the Power Stroke emblem on the side. Per her truck-savvy colleagues, that meant they were diesel trucks.

She stopped her vehicle by the three trucks and stepped out in the heavy rain, looking around.

The hospital was positioned atop Ash Brook Hill and would dominate the area in a majestic way when finished. But not much work had been completed; it was far from being done. They had leveled off the top of the hill and had only recently started to pour the foundation, but, as she could figure out by a maze of temporary posts and yellow DANGER—KEEP OUT tape, they had an issue with one side of the hill, where the terrain had turned unstable, shifting downhill—the landslide she'd spotted earlier driving up.

Except for the three Ford F-150 trucks, no other personal vehicles could be seen, only construction equipment. A couple of bulldozers, a front loader, several heavy-duty dirt haulers. It seemed all workers had been sent home due to the inclement weather that had soaked her to the bone, making her teeth clatter.

She was about to head to the trailer, eager to have a conversation with the Montgomerys, and wondered if they knew about Dan, if Marleen had already told them. Maybe that's why they were huddled up on Ash Brook Hill on such a terrible weather day.

A wind gust brought a shiver down her spine that coiled inside her gut, her hair on end, as if she'd felt someone's breath on her nape. As she turned to look behind her, the blow came hard, bringing pitch blackness into her head. Stars burst in an explosion of searing, unbearable pain. By the time her face reached the mud, they were gone, only darkness remaining.

CHAPTER FORTY-SEVEN

Family

He stared for a moment at the woman slumped on the metallic chair, her wrists and ankles secured with cable ties so tightly they cut into her flesh. Her head hung forward, her blonde hair almost entirely covering her face. He could still see the blood smear on her cheek, mixed with mud that was beginning to dry. At the back of her head, her hair was parted where the blow had split her scalp and blood had congealed, clumping strands together in an unsightly mess.

Mitchell and his heavy hand. He'd raised such a brute... Mother would not be pleased.

He lifted his searing glance and stared at his son. Mitchell still wore his hard hat, and had a blood smear across his forehead where he must've run the soiled back of his hand to wipe away the raindrops. He'd plunged his hands deep into the pockets of his jeans and held his gaze straight, defiantly, standing a few feet in front of him. The tiniest hint of a smile tugged at the right corner of his lips.

"You wanted this," Mitchell said, "and I was dumb enough to listen to you. She's that fed, or cop, or whatever, for Pete's sake, and you knew who she was when you sent me after her." He paced the room with an anxious spring in his gait. "We should've let her go. She would've asked a few questions, then she would've been gone. Why the hell do we all bother to get alibis, if we're going to do stupid shit like this?" His words were filled with fear and anger, spilled quickly.

"Yeah, Gramps, why the hell did we take a cop?" Victor asked derisively. He was half-seated on the scratched desk surface, normally covered in blueprints, rolled-up plans, and technical drawings. "Do you feel like the electric chair? 'Cause I'm way too young for that."

His arrogant, insolent voice reminded him of Dan. Just thinking of his dead son twisted a blade through his heart and he choked, for a while unable to breathe, suffocated by a grief he'd never felt possible. His son, his own flesh and blood, shot in the back and dumped over by the asphalt like worthless roadkill... How did he not feel it when it happened? How did Mother let his son be murdered like that?

It must've been that scrawny little bitch, Cheryl—that ungrateful, good-for-nothing piece of trailer trash that Calvin had dragged through their door one cursed day. Mitchell, his firstborn son, had given him his first grandson in Calvin, and he'd been immensely proud of the boy until the day he brought her into the family. Still, like a good grandfather, he'd welcomed her into the family, but she'd turned on him and accused him of his grandson's murder. She gave up *his name,* and cut him off from seeing those girls, his own granddaughters. She told everyone who would listen that Avery Montgomery had killed his grandson for some made-up reason that only she understood. Only Cheryl could've done something as despicable as shooting a man in the back and leaving him to rot by the interstate; it was probably how her people did things in the trailer park. But she had to have had help, and he would not rest until he found out who that was.

"It was Cheryl," he whispered, staring out the window at the gloomy skies unloading their bounty. "It had to be her."

"You can't be sure, Dad," Mitchell pushed back.

"Yes, I can. I can feel it inside," he replied, his voice brittle, pounding his fist against his chest. It sounded hollow, just as it felt. "Dan was supposed to bring Julie that night. He went there to get her and never came back. That tramp, th—that snake," he stammered, "I could snap her neck like a twig with my own hands." He held his hands in front of him, squeezing Cheryl's imaginary neck while a hate-filled grimace stretched his lips, exposing his teeth.

"She already got what she deserved, Gramps," Victor interrupted matter-of-factly. "Now, what the hell do we do about *her*?" he gestured toward Kay with disdain. He turned to Mitchell and smirked. "Mitchell, what the heck were you thinking?"

"She came to us!" Avery bellowed, so loudly Mitchell took a step back. "Just like my sweet Anna came to my first building and tore my heart open when she did. Mother Earth had spoken! It's her decision, and she wants this woman. Otherwise, she wouldn't be here. She wouldn't've come." He sighed, not in relief but in frustration. "Have you seen how hard it was to get here this morning? The road is nearly washed out, the muddy ruts are axle deep, and you drive powerful four-by-four trucks. She would've never made it up here without Mother's help, just like Anna."

"This is ridiculous," Victor replied. "She's driving a—"

Before he could finish speaking, a hard slap fell across his cheek. Avery's hand smarted after delivering the blow, and his arthritic wrist hurt, but he didn't care. "I won't tolerate any more disrespect in this family! One more time, and I'll put you into the ground myself."

Victor finally lowered his eyes, still glinting with rage and humiliation. "I'm sorry, Grandpa, I didn't mean to offend you."

"Then what *did* you mean, talking back at me?" Victor would someday soon take over the business. With Dan and Calvin now both gone, there wasn't that much time until that would happen, and by then, he better know how things had to be done. He'd better learn to show Mother the respect she was due, or her vengeance would be swift and the fruits of an entire life of hard work would wash away, taken by the floods of her rage.

Silence was the only reply he got. Satisfied he'd finally got Victor to come to his senses, he walked over to where Kay was seated and grabbed a fistful of her blood-soaked hair. He pulled backward, to expose her face, and grunted.

"You sure she's still alive?" he asked Mitchell.

"Yeah, she's just unconscious, but won't stay that way for long. And it's almost noon."

"Damn it," Avery muttered, pacing toward the design table, where Julie was lying on her back, her hands folded at her chest. "We're running out of time. Let's get it done."

Mitchell looked outside, worried. "Have you seen how badly it rains? We can't pour concrete in this; it would never set, and come Monday morning when the workers come back, she'll just lay there, exposed, for them to find." He paced angrily toward Avery, but stopped a few feet away from him, his clenched fist held up in a gesture of revolt. "You'll doom us all with your insanity."

"They," Avery said calmly, looking out the window. It was raining hard, but it was what Mother wanted. When he laid the sacrifice at her feet, the skies would close, even if for a few moments, enough for the concrete to start setting. She'd gladly accept the sacrifice.

"Huh?" Mitchell reacted. "What do you mean?"

"They, not she," Avery explained, his tone casual and calm as if he were teaching his son how to simply pour concrete without the human sacrifice. That part didn't matter to Avery; it was what needed to get done.

"So, you want to bury the cop, *and* Julie?" Victor reacted, approaching the two men after glancing at the still body of the girl dressed in the perfectly white dress. "Mother never demanded two sacrifices at the same time. And she's family, your own flesh and blood."

Avery clenched his fist then took it to his mouth, where he sank his teeth into his finger, the pain he felt easing the intensity of the grief that tore his heart apart. Tears threatened to break, unwanted, nothing but a sign of weakness in the face of delivering Mother's demands. "It happened before," he eventually said, speaking against his clenched fist, barely intelligible. "The year she took my grandson, Calvin, right after we'd given her that redheaded girl, Lauren." He sighed, the long, pain-filled breath of air shattered, as if he was about to break down and cry. Yet he fought the knot in his throat, the burning sensation in his tear-filled eyes, and managed to stifle the sobs. There would be a time for grieving later, in the privacy of his own study, looking at the blue sky and begging Mother to not forsake her lost and heartbroken child.

Victor smirked. "How convenient that was," he muttered. Mitchell turned and glared at him, as if urging him to shut up.

"No, let him speak," Avery hissed, feeling just about ready to slap Victor again. His attitude could bring the company down faster than Mother's rage. If hatred festered in that boy, or contempt, he wanted it exposed and cut out of his soul, the way a surgeon exposes a tumor before excising it.

Victor veered his eyes sideways and zipped up his rain jacket as if getting ready to leave, then plunged his hands into its pockets. "I'm just saying, Calvin was starting to ask the wrong questions around that time, wasn't he?"

Avery stared at him without a word inviting him to say more, his chin thrust forward and quivering in anger.

"Let's face it," Victor added with an arrogant chuckle, "he never really had the balls for what we're doing. You wanted him induced, but he was too soft for it. Him, his nightmares, and his bloody conscience were going to get us all locked up." He shrugged indifferently. "I'm just saying *Mother* took him at a convenient time." He'd accented the word in a sarcastic way.

Avery took a step forward, his eyes piercing Victor's. The young man didn't lower his gray, steeled gaze. "Do you have anything else to add, my dear boy?" he whispered.

Mitchell took a step back and cursed under his breath.

Victor remained still, unwavering. "I'm just saying Julie is family, and unlike Calvin, she's done nothing wrong. There's no need—"

"She is blood from my blood, and flesh from my flesh! Don't you think I know it? That's what Mother demands. She always chooses the first daughters we sacrifice. That's what building this house of healing will take!" Avery bellowed, his voice echoing strangely in the small trailer. As if to underline his words, thunder roared outside, rattling the trailer and bringing a glint of fear to Victor's rebellious eyes.

Avery rushed to the door and opened it. A gust of wind swirled inside like an invisible hand, shifting the fabric of Julie's skirt, grabbing papers and lifting them up in the air, and bringing rain inside. Yet he stood in the doorway, indifferent to the water soaking his hair and slapping his face. His fanatical gaze lifted toward the dark skies as he shouted, "I heard you, Mother! Your will is my law."

CHAPTER FORTY-EIGHT

Awake

The first thing Kay felt was an excruciating, throbbing pain in the back of her head. She quickly realized she was restrained, cable ties cutting into her flesh around her wrists and ankles. Her head hung low, and she wished she could lift it to ease the pain in her split scalp, but she heard voices around her, too close for comfort.

Without moving, enduring through the pain and breathing shallow, she listened.

She recognized Avery's baritone, and opened her eyes slowly, to take in the scene. She couldn't see his face, and could distinguish very little from the setting. Her hair fell like a curtain in front of her face, shielding her, but at the same time, limiting her view.

Two other men were present, and argued with Avery over what was to be done with her, and over concrete setting properly. Yet something else had grabbed her attention, something Avery had said about his sweet Anna coming to his first building much like Kay had come to visit, unwanted, but instantly condemned to death.

Her eyesight was blurry, maybe because of the blow to her head, the strands of hair in front of her face not helping her much. Through the window by her side, the sky was a dark, threatening gray, clouds rolling, racing across the sky as they dropped their load of rain. Through the window, she recognized the Ford F-150 trucks that the men drove, which must have been the brand and model of choice for their construction company. That specific truck was one of the most popular with contractors.

But then, as Avery went on and on about the youngest man being disrespectful, she realized she didn't really recognize the trucks; she knew they were there because she'd seen them earlier, the loud, metallic rapping of raindrops against the roof confirming she was in the trailer office. No, through her fuzzy vision and with her hair making things worse, she could barely see the trucks.

Only wisps of white can be seen streaking through as they approach. Betty's crumbling voice resonated in her memory. With her cataracts, that's what a white truck would look like, a wisp of white streaking in front of her window. The lamppost being out of commission, the driveway must've been engulfed in darkness, and all she would've seen was the white of the truck's body, maybe its headlights if the unsub didn't turn them off.

And what was it she'd said a little later about the spirits of the valley? Something about trails of their blood, bright, living red through the darkness as they leave. What if those were their brake lights as they departed? After the unsub had pulled out of Cheryl's driveway, Betty could've caught a blurry glimpse of something red leaving into the night, and her Alzheimer's-fueled imagination had created the rest.

The old woman wasn't crazy after all.

Kay almost smiled, when something caught her attention in what the men were arguing about. Based on what the youngest of them was saying, Calvin had opposed Avery and somehow had ended up dead. That brought a new perspective to Cheryl's actions, one that had completely eluded Kay.

Whatever Calvin's gripe had been, he must've shared it with his wife. That's why Cheryl was adamant he'd been killed. That's why she'd changed her name, further deepening the rift between her and the old man.

But then, if she despised the Montgomery family so much, why had she been dating Dan?

Kay instantly remembered what Frank had said, that had made little sense at the time. He'd said something about Cheryl having or wanting to find the truth.

Her heart cried for the widow who'd been willing to sleep with a Montgomery only in the hope she'd expose her husband's killer. She must've known about the legend, or maybe even more than that, from Calvin. She must've felt safe, thinking she was family and Julie would never be taken, safe enough to stay in the town where she'd been born. Until one day, Dan had come to visit with a different agenda in mind.

The last piece of the puzzle fell into place and the entire image became clear, even if some questions still remained. Calvin had died when the scaffolding had collapsed due to a landslide in bad weather. But who was to say what he was doing on that scaffolding? Maybe Avery had sent him up, or someone else who wanted him silenced for good. A few hours with either of these men in her interrogation room and she'd know.

Avery approached her and grabbed her hair, pulling her head backward, wondering if she was still alive. She nearly shrieked, but managed to keep her eyes closed. Soon enough, he let go of her head, sending a renewed throb of pain through her skull, so strong she nearly fainted. She struggled to stay conscious, while the three men argued about pouring concrete in the rain and burying both her and Julie.

Julie… she had to be there somewhere, close.

She opened her eyes slowly, careful not to be seen. Thankfully, her hair still covered her face, and she could peek between the strands.

Laid on a large design table, the teenager was perfectly still, arms crossed at her chest as if she'd died, wearing a white dress. Her vision still blurry—she couldn't make out the details—but she thought she saw the girl's chest heaving, ever so slowly.

Julie was still alive.

Avery said something about Anna again, and the pain in his voice made Kay wonder. Had Anna's death been the trigger of his urge to kidnap and kill women, and, if what she'd heard was true, bury them in concrete? Or had he killed Anna himself, driven by a bout of psychosis, triggered by who knows what factor?

Weather.

That had been the factor. That's why he'd never accelerated, never devolved. His urges weren't sexual. His psychosis reminded Kay of a religious fanatic who hears voices driving him to kill. Only Avery's demons demanded the girls be buried in concrete or walled in, to appease the weather his psychotic mind saw as supernatural.

The answer had been in front of her the entire time. His propensity for buildings set proudly atop hills, like his own headquarters and this hospital, and several others she'd recognized from the company's portfolio of achievements. The landslide threatening the foundation of the building he was erecting. Landslides appearing everywhere in the region, driven by reckless deforestation done in the past century, leaving earth exposed to the elements without tree roots to stabilize the soil. That was what his words about Mother Earth had to be about.

She remembered Anna's missing persons report as if the pages were still in front of her. She'd burned every word in her memory. The children left behind unharmed. The side door left open. And Anna, vanished without a trace, never to be found again, because she'd been buried under who knows what building he was erecting at the time, a building that weather had threatened just like it did this one.

It was time for her to "wake up."

Lifting her head slowly, she grit her teeth as pain shot a throbbing blade through her skull. Right after Avery had closed the door to the trailer, the men argued fiercely about pouring concrete in the storm. From their DMV photos she'd reviewed earlier, she recognized Mitchell, Lynn's father, and Victor, Dan's son.

Three generations of killers.

She cleared her dry throat silently, then asked, "Your wife was your first sacrifice, wasn't she?"

CHAPTER FORTY-NINE

Anna

Fifty-seven years ago

The past couple of years had been a challenging time for young Avery Montgomery. Intense happiness mixed with heartbreak and grief, over and over, until his heart had grown numb. He'd lost his father, a man he'd loved dearly, after a sickening and hollowing battle with cancer he'd witnessed powerlessly and increasingly angry. Then, a few months later, his beautiful wife, Anna, had given birth to his first son, Mitchell. But joy was short-lived in the Montgomery family.

Avery's mother, Hope, had been wasting away; within months of her husband's death only a shadow of what she used to be. Until his passing, Avery rarely remembered he'd had an older sister, Grace, who'd died very young, before he was born. Hope's devastating grief after the loss of her husband had brought with it memories of Grace, the two loved ones she'd lost forever connected in her mind just as she believed they'd become connected in heaven.

Avery wasn't sure how Grace had died; it had something to do with a landslide or perhaps an earthquake, because Hope talked about "the day the earth opened and took my baby girl," always touching the locket she wore around her neck every time she spoke of her daughter. Or maybe the little girl's funeral had been so devastating for Hope she only remembered that moment when the earth was open to receive her body, and not the actual moment of her daughter's death. Even so, she rarely mentioned her; she barely said a few words anymore.

She'd stopped eating, and soon couldn't keep anything down if she tried. The only times she emerged from her room and stopped grieving were when she fixed the family meals.

Wearing black clothing that no longer fit but adamantly refusing to give up her mourning habit, she wandered aimlessly through the house like a ghost, as if searching for her absent spouse. The locket she always wore was a mystery to Avery; she never shared what she kept inside. Sometimes, when she didn't think anyone was hearing, she talked to her husband and to Grace as if they were still there. The only times she seemed to be better, even if in the slightest, was when she was making dinner. She never tasted her own cooking, nor did she eat, although Avery had insisted she at least sat at the table with them, thinking maybe she'd grow a little bit of an appetite seeing them wolf down her delicious meals. Reluctantly, she'd obliged a couple of times, then turned angry and shouted at Avery to leave her alone.

He had done just that, too tired to fight her after sleepless nights with a screaming, colic-ridden infant and a difficult and demanding job in charge of his father's legacy, the construction company. Sometimes he stopped by his mother's bedroom and stuck his head in after knocking and pointlessly waiting to be invited in. He always found her in the same spot, in her chair, looking at her bedroom door as if waiting for her husband to return, absentmindedly touching the locket on her chest. She never had a smile for him, nor a good word, only harsh ones if he tried to pull her out of her all-consuming grief.

Then, one day, while cooking dinner, she just dropped to the floor, lifeless, without showing a sign of distress or making a sound. Nothing Avery did could bring her back. Doctors had told him she died of a broken heart; Avery said she just wanted to be with her husband so badly, she left her son behind without hesitation.

He was heartbroken by her passing, but also enraged, blaming Hope for dying as if she'd done it on purpose, because Avery strongly believed she had. Otherwise, she would've at least tried to enjoy life a little bit, get to know her new grandson, or grab a bite every now and then with her son and his family. By embracing her grief instead of the life he offered, by starving herself, she'd effectively killed herself, and he resented her for that, for abandoning and rejecting him.

He attended Hope's funeral with dry eyes and a stiff upper lip, watching her frail, emaciated body in the open casket without anything but resentment tugging at his heart. She seemed almost lifelike, wearing a black dress and the same locket he'd seen around her neck ever since he could remember. In a mindless impulse, he approached the open casket and snatched the locket from her body. Later, by the graveside, he opened it when no one was paying attention, and found inside the weathered, black-and-white photo of a beautiful little girl dressed in white. Seeing that girl twisted and broke something inside him as if he suddenly understood Hope's grief—as if he was starting to feel it also, for the sister he'd never met. Kneeling by the graveside, he took out the picture and placed it on the casket, then he picked up a few grains of earth and sprinkled them over the girl's photo, laying her memory to rest. A few of those grains of earth, smelling of raindrops in the spring, of grass blades and wildflowers, found their way into the locket he closed and slid under his shirt.

That's when his dreams of her started, about a week or so after her death, soon after the funeral had taken place and the flurry of activities had finally ceased to occupy his mind. He'd dream of her walking toward him in her black mourning attire, sometimes menacing, other times warm and kind, but always giving him some advice. What to say to an upset client, to make things better. How to deal with a problem employee. How to help Anna with her postpartum depression after the birth of their second son, Dan.

The mother in his dreams was entirely different from the one she'd been in reality. A young woman prematurely embittered with raising Avery by herself while her husband was away at war, she'd never been too soft with the little boy, and the thought of offering him a joy-filled childhood had never crossed her mind. Favoring dark, somber clothing and keeping her voice low and stern, she'd filled Avery's young mind with her opinions of life's perpetual miseries and how hard it all was. Rarely had she offered advice on anything while she was alive, having known little else than the adversities of raising a child by herself during an economy ravaged by war and crying herself to sleep every night, wondering if her husband was still alive.

But whatever advice she offered in his dreams he followed, and it worked. One by one, his most annoying problems went away, and he'd grown to rely on his mother's nocturnal calls so much he would nap in the middle of the day if he had an urgent problem to solve, inviting her to visit. Missing her dearly, yet still angry with her. Sometimes, that anger crossed the subconscious barrier and he dreamed of himself shouting at his mother in anger, asking her why she'd quit on him when he needed her most, with young children to raise and a business he knew little about running. But the specter of his dreams didn't reply; just told him what to do, her advice always proving correct, even if the solutions she offered were sometimes unusual.

By the time his third son was born, his business had started to pick up—the Montgomery name recognized in the area often enough to give him the occasional contract he didn't have to bust his back selling. The contracts were mostly for residential homes, few and far apart, the main source of income remained the deals with the local and federal government his father had initiated. William Montgomery's old contacts had frowned somewhat before signing deals with the twenty-six-year-old, but he had an entire business behind him, with knowledgeable workers, and he'd graduated from college cum laude in his field.

That's how he landed the contract for the new City Hall, without even trying, the client an old friend of his father, a tall and bony man by the name of Nestor Carson. With the voice of a town crier and blowing cigar-smelling breath in his face, he'd patted young Avery on the shoulder, then awarded him the contract for the construction of a new location for the town's leaders.

Carson had already secured the plans for the new building. The rendering showed the proud, 26,000-square-foot building atop a gentle sloping hill, the land bought from local owners.

When Avery visited the site, still covered in greenery and shrubs growing wildly, he fell in love with the future building. The setting gave it such majestic appeal, from up close and from the nearby highway, promising it would become a renowned landmark people would soon love.

Too proud and too ambitious to tell the client he didn't have the money to start working on the new building, Avery mortgaged the family house without saying a word to Anna. There was no reason to worry his beautiful wife. Then, knowing the loan barely covered the cost of the materials and equipment, he offered his workers a ten percent increase in pay if they agreed to accept deferred compensation, payable after the building had been eighty percent completed. The laws governing construction contracting and advance payments were strict, allowing for only a ten percent advance before work started. The standardized, nonnegotiable contract called for incremental payments as the work progressed, but the largest chunk of money, forty-five percent, was due only after the building had passed its final inspection.

The advance barely covered the cost of surveying the land, clearing it, and preparing the foundation pour. The concrete mixer trucks were expensive rentals, begrudgingly leased by the hour from a competitor outbid for the same project. But, one by one, the mixers paraded up that hill, their loads spinning slowly, then lined up to pour the foundation of what was going to become the city's most valued edifice.

Then the rain started.

At first, he wasn't worried, only annoyed. Anna was going through a particularly rough time with a new bout of postpartum depression, crying at night, face buried in the pillow, and there was nothing he could do to soothe her. He'd been gone from home a lot, working sixteen hours a day every day, leaving her to raise three young boys by herself. After he finished pouring the foundation and cashed the second installment, he was planning to bring in some help for his sweet Anna, even if he was a little worried the workers would get wind of that and frown that the boss had money for a new housekeeper or nanny, but didn't pay their salaries.

Every time thunder rolled, or lightning illuminated the room, he'd wake to find Anna's tear-streaked face on the pillow, her eyes watching him, loaded with love and yearning and infinite sadness. He held her tight, whispering promises and apologies in her ear, and falling asleep mid-word.

The first day the rain turned heavy, threatening the uncured concrete, the workers covered it with tarp and stopped pouring, paying a fortune for the concrete mixers to be parked down the road. With a satisfied grin, his competitor had warned Avery that if he returned the trucks for the duration of the storm, he couldn't lease them out again when the weather turned. Out of options, he resigned himself to incur the extra cost, his eyes on the final prize: a building to make him and everyone else proud, enough money to double the size of his business, and buy everything Anna wished for, to put a smile on those loving, quivering lips.

Three days later, the land started to slide, and took with it the northeast corner of the foundation. Within minutes, under his petrified stare, the concrete had crumbled into pieces as if it were a cookie, and had been washed by the rain to the base of the hill, in a cascade of mud, dirt, and shattered dreams.

Taking a second mortgage on the house took a lot of convincing, but he managed it somehow, showing the contract he'd signed for the City Hall and invoking his father's good name several times. He stated he needed the money not because of any hardship, but because of inclement weather delays, but bad weather doesn't last long, does it? Especially in California.

The second loan barely covered the land stabilization and the cost of new concrete, once the rains waned. He was just about done pouring the entire section, when long, ominous thunder told him his dues weren't paid yet. Within minutes, a deluge started, and he rushed, with his team, to lay sheeting all over the uncured foundation and the sides of the hill. By the time he was done, the entire top of the hill was covered in blue plastic, while rain fell heavily.

Workers now gone, he fell to his knees in the mud, looking at what he'd built, and realizing it was about to fall apart again if the soil shifted even a tiny fraction of an inch. Mr. Carson and his daughter were scheduled to visit the following day, expecting to find the entire foundation poured and cured. Instead, blue plastic covering everything would tell the man who'd taken a risk on Avery Montgomery that the soil under his new building wasn't stable enough to support a building, something Avery should've known.

His life was over.

Unable to deliver the building and cover the huge costs he'd incurred, he'd be going to jail, leaving his poor wife homeless, with three hungry boys clasping at her skirt.

He had raised his eyes toward the sky, squinting to keep the water out, and bellowed. "What do you want from me? What do I need to do to get this building done? Just tell me what you want, please!" Then, tired of pleading without an answer, he raised his fist and made threats he knew he couldn't deliver, shouting and sobbing until he couldn't draw breath anymore. Exhausted and broken, he fell on his side in the mud, his hands clasped together at his chest, shivering under the rain's forceful drumming against his weary body.

Maybe he'd fainted first, then shifted into sleep, because he couldn't believe one could fall asleep under those circumstances, but he had, and he had dreamed of his mother. In his dream, she was angry and scolded him for the risks he'd taken, but she seemed to forgive him and had said that some buildings are worth any sacrifice to erect.

"I'm going to jail, Mother," he cried in his dream. "Anna and the kids will be alone, broke, hungry, all because of me."

"A firstborn daughter needs to be sacrificed," his mother had replied, eerily calm about it. "Alive. Only then the foundation will hold strong, and the building will be finished. Her life will instill life into this building, and it will live, my son. It will live proudly for years to come."

His dream rendered him restless, as it had turned into a nightmare. Still in his dream, he thought of the client's only daughter, who was about to visit the site the next day. He made plans—how to grab her and sink her body into freshly poured concrete.

"*I* will choose your sacrifice," Mother spoke, reading his mind. The image he knew so well shifted ever so slightly, becoming someone else, with drops of rain as her tears, lush green vines as hair, and the dark color of the bare ground after a deluge as her body. She smelled of wet soil, of stormy meadows, and freshly split ground, where water had driven a blade into the body of the earth. When she spoke again, her voice still resembled the one he'd known since he was born. "I will choose your sacrifice, and once I have spoken, you must deliver. The first woman who comes up this hill will be a first daughter and shall be the sacrifice I demand."

In his dream, he breathed with ease. Carson's daughter was the only woman who was supposed to visit the next day. Mother's choice made sense; the sacrifice should be shared with the owner of the building, and in doing so, she would get to remain close to her loved ones even in death. A Sunday, when workers were off, and only he was going to be there.

"Now, go back and live, my son," the woman in his dreams ordered, touching his face briefly with wet, cold, muddy fingers.

He jolted awake. Later that night, after he'd barely said a word to Anna, he went to bed eager to dream of his mother again or this new spirit she'd shifted into, to ask again if she really demanded of him to take a life. All he got was thunder, menacing and haunting.

The next day, the rain had eased somewhat, and he took that as a sign. Mother Earth, as he'd since named her, was idling her rage until he could deliver the sacrifice she demanded. Still fighting the thought of taking a life, he lifted the blue sheeting and inspected the new concrete poured on the northeast corner of the building. After all, it was just a dream; maybe the foundation was fine, and he'd be fine.

A large crack was beginning to advance, starting four yards from the corner on the north side, and spidering toward the east side. He put his foot on the edge, and it gave effortlessly under half his weight.

Right there, right then, in that split second as the corner piece fell crumbling off, he'd made up his mind. He'd give Mother what she was asking for. He had no other choice.

In a frenzy, he drove three of the concrete mixer trucks to get fresh loads and parked them nearby. He removed the blue sheeting and prepared the surface for another pour, forming the shape, getting everything ready for when Miss Carson would come to visit.

By the time he finished, two hours remained until their arrival. Exhausted and out of breath, he sat on the edge of the foundation, resting his head in his hands, staring at his feet and contemplating what he was about to do… the unthinkable.

When he finally looked up, he saw a woman climbing the hill on foot, bracing the wind and the rain in a white dress, her blonde hair soaked, sticking in long, clumped strands to her face. She waved at him and called his name.

Anna.

"No, no," he shouted, looking at the sky, holding his fist up. "Don't do this to me. Don't!" he screamed, but only thunder replied. Then he tried to tell Anna to walk away, to turn around and leave. After all, she hadn't reached the top of the hill yet, had she?

When Mr. Carson and his daughter arrived later that day, fresh concrete had been poured on the northeast corner of the foundation. The rain had stopped, and a patch of blue sky was visible toward the west, just a crack in the clouds, the foretelling of fine weather to come.

As for Avery, he stood in front of the building, soaked and muddy, listening to Nestor Carson's praising words with an empty, haunted stare in his eyes.

CHAPTER FIFTY

Ray

Raymond Montgomery's studio was in the Sunset District of San Francisco, and the afternoon rush hour took its toll despite the flashers and occasional bursts of siren. Some streets were so densely packed with vehicles there was no alternative but to wait, stuck, with the rest of the drivers.

The studio was set up tastefully in a townhouse, the colors of its frontage bright and unusual, pink and crimson and marble gray. It stood out somewhat, although most of the houses on that street competed for the best original exterior. The fog was already dense, rolling onto the streets like solid clumps of clouds with zero altitude, but the cheerful houses counteracted the gloominess of that persistent, salty-tasting ocean fog.

Elliot climbed the flight of stairs that led to the entrance and was about to ring the bell when the door opened. A young woman, dressed in a transparent top and what had to be the tiniest skirt he'd ever seen, flashed a dazzling smile his way and wrapped her scrawny arms around his neck, thrusting her pelvis forward.

"Well, hello, Texas," she whispered, so close to his face he felt her breath on his lips and smelled the fruity scent of her lip gloss.

He pushed her away firmly then held his badge in front of her eyes. "I should charge you with assault of an officer," he said, not a trace of humor in his voice. Somehow, instead of feeling flattered or perhaps even excited, the interaction had made him feel used, worthless.

He shook it off and grinned as he watched the young woman clack her heels in a rush to get away from him, climbing down those stairs faster than a scalded cat.

"You know, some people would pay some serious dough to trade places with you," a man said, amusement sparkling in his voice. "That was Janessa, next month's *Vogue* cover girl."

Elliot shrugged. "Not what I came here to do. You're Raymond Montgomery, right?" he asked, recognizing the man from his DMV photo. "I'm Detective Young with the Mount Chester Sheriff's Office."

"Ah," the man reacted. A cloud of worry and sadness washed over his face as he stepped aside, inviting Elliot in.

Tall and well-built like his brothers, Ray had the aura of success, that self-confidence that accompanies people when they have reached their goals and are enjoying their lives, doing what has meaning to them and brings happiness to their existence. Head held up high, an expression of calm, a warm smile on his lips. Expensive clothes but not flashy, just a knit button-down causal shirt in navy blue, and gray slacks that looked new, as did his plain, white sneakers.

That entire aura of enjoyment and self-confidence waned the moment Elliot mentioned Mount Chester.

"What can I do for you, Detective?" He closed the door behind Elliot and locked it with one smooth move, grabbing the deadbolt to push the door closed. The neighborhood must've dictated his behavior. "Here, take a seat, please." He led Elliot to a group of tastefully arranged armchairs around a small coffee table. The smell of new leather and expensive air fresheners filled the room.

The studio was large, set up in what had to be the living room. The walls were white, the occasional framed photograph tastefully hung.

"What can I do for you, Detective?" he asked with a hint of a smile that seemed forced, quivering, as if an unspoken fear was hiding behind it.

"There's a girl missing from Mount Chester. Your niece, Julie Montgomery."

A frown creased his forehead. "Cheryl's daughter?"

Elliot nodded.

Ray lowered his gaze for a moment, as if considering what he was about to say. Then he looked at Elliot with a neutral expression on his face. "I haven't heard from her, I'm afraid. You might've learned already, I'm no longer in contact with my family." He briefly looked down again, shifting in his seat. "I'm afraid you wasted a trip coming down here, Detective." He crossed his legs, bringing his left ankle over his right knee, his relaxed posture seeming artificial, well-rehearsed.

"I believe you know more than you're saying, Mr. Montgomery," said Elliot, his voice a somber warning. "A young girl's life is at stake. Anything you can tell us could help save her life." He paused for a beat. "Anything you choose to withhold could land you in jail. Before you decide what happens next, weigh the implications carefully."

Ray's shoulders tightened and his relaxed demeanor turned into a wary, tense one. "How did she vanish?" he asked with the slightest tremble in his voice.

Jackpot. "That's precisely the right question to ask, Mr. Montgomery," Elliot replied. "She was taken from her home, after Cheryl was killed, fending off the attacker."

"Oh," he reacted, taken aback. "I had no idea Cheryl was—um, when did it happen?"

"This past Monday night." Elliot watched the man's reactions carefully. For some reason, when he'd mentioned Monday, Ray shot a quick glance to the window, where fog was sliced and diced by a cold drizzle, nowhere near as fierce or wind driven as the torrential rains battering Mount Chester. "I'm afraid the bad news doesn't stop here. Your brother, Dan Montgomery, was shot last Saturday."

"What?" He stood and started to pace the room, as if the answer lay somewhere with those walls. "Dan too?" There wasn't much grief written on his face, only shock, and a lot more of the fear Elliot had spotted earlier, dilating his pupils and drawing ridges across his forehead.

"I take it no one called you, Mr. Montgomery?"

"Please," he snapped, "call me Ray. Mr. Montgomery is my *father.*" He spat the word out, as if saying it burned his lips.

"Ray," Elliot acknowledged. "What aren't you telling me?" He leaned forward, his hands resting on his knees. But Ray continued to pace the room, a storm going on inside, scrunching his features at times, as if he were arguing with someone in his mind, maybe with himself. "Why does someone leave the family business behind and never look back? Not to mention brothers, nieces, and nephews?"

He froze in place and shoved his hands deep in his pants pockets, looking at Elliot as if he were weighing the detective, figuring out if he could be trusted. Then he sighed, the deep breath making his chest heave as if crushed under unspoken burdens. "All right, I'll tell you. Maybe the time has come." He bit his lip, still hesitating, but Elliot didn't press him in any way, although he was painfully aware of every minute that passed by. "I chose to steer clear of what I would call shared delusions."

That word again. "What do you mean?"

He scoffed bitterly. "Julie... you're never going to see her again." He shrugged then crossed his arms at his chest. "If you got so far as to ask *me* questions about her, then you know. None of them ever came back."

Elliot shook his head. "I *don't* know. That's precisely why I'm here. I'm hoping you can tell me what others won't or can't." He held Ray's gaze honestly.

As if he'd just aged by twenty years, Ray walked over to the armchair and sat, his posture tense, his shoulders hunched forward. "By the time I finished college, a few girls had gone missing from the area. People talked about a curse, about the spirits of the valley, but I never believed that kind of crap." He chuckled with sadness and shame in his voice, his eyes riveted on the gleaming hardwood floor. "I just chose to walk away."

"What were you suspecting?" Elliot asked, but Ray didn't reply, seeming lost in difficult memories. "What did you walk away from?" he added after a long silence.

Ray shot him a glance brimming with sadness. "My father had something to do with it… maybe." He clasped and unclasped his hands, nervous, unsettled. "I never dared to face this, to confront him, to expose him, afraid I'd be pointing my finger at a man who'd done his best to raise me well, at least by his standards and beliefs." He pressed his lips together into a tight line. "How can nothing more than a suspicion justify setting the cops on a good parent, the only one you have left?" He clasped his hands again. "I just walked away and never looked back, praying that my suspicions were wrong, and that I was doing the right thing by keeping my mouth shut." A sad smile tugged at the corners of his lips. "He never forgave me for leaving. For deserting him."

"That's it?" Elliot's tone carried clear undertones of incredulousness. "You never had more than a hunch that something was off with your family? No hard evidence?"

He covered his mouth with his hand and shook his head. "No, I had nothing, but I was too much of a coward to find out."

Elliot waited a moment, waiting for him to continue, but he didn't. "How's that?"

"My father is a very stubborn man, who thrives on controlling everyone's destinies." He looked at Elliot, seeming embarrassed of what he was about to say. "He never cared I hated construction, and I wanted to do something else with my life. He still had me go to college and study civil engineering, under the dire threat of cutting me off from everything: family, money, even the house."

"He would've kicked you out of the house if you chose another career?"

Ray nodded, the look of embarrassment still lingering on his face. "No one disobeys my father. I was young and had no means. It took me four years of utter misery to understand I'd be better off waiting on tables in San Francisco than living with my father and doing what he wanted."

"When did you leave Mount Chester?"

Ray's jaw clenched, as if anger had stirred up inside him. "Soon after I finished college, my father and my brothers started talking about my initiation into the family business—some sort of ritual I never understood, and they never bothered to explain. It just seemed to come from the same shared delusion I was talking about. I never wanted to participate in that, although both my brothers had." He veered his eyes sideways for a while, as if trying to remember. "You see, it made no sense, that ritual, because I was already working for the family business. My father said he was adamant about me going through initiation, but he kept pushing it off."

"Why?"

Ray made a quick, waving gesture with his hand near his temple. "Some kind of craziness, that much I know. He said, because of weather." Ray scoffed again. "If you can imagine, it had to take place during a severe thunderstorm."

Silence filled the air between them, loaded with unspoken words. Crazy or delusional, it was starting to add up somehow, and all leads pointed toward Avery. Even with his rock-solid alibi, he seemed to be at the center of this case.

Ray stood and folded his arms at his chest. The interview was over, but the sadness and shame in his eyes remained. "I hope you'll find Julie unharmed, and when you do, I hope you'll find that my worst fears were nothing but my share of the mass delusions haunting Mount Chester. Otherwise, I'm just as much to blame as he is, for not speaking up sooner." He looked one more time at Elliot with a strange force in his gaze, as if he'd reached a decision. "For that, there's no forgiveness."

But Elliot was already at the door, eager to warn Kay. Last they spoke, she was on her way to pay Avery a visit at the company headquarters, but that had been in the morning. Since then, not a peep from her.

Once behind the wheel, he stepped on the gas pedal and made for the nearest highway ramp, flashers on and siren blasting.

No matter how many times he kept redialing Kay's number, she wasn't picking up.

CHAPTER FIFTY-ONE

Victor

Kay's phone rang again, buried in her pocket. Elliot's cheerful ringtone enraged Avery, who ran his hands through his hair nervously, as if he were about to pull it from his head. "Enough with this shit already! I need to think."

Unflinching, she held Avery's fiery gaze and smiled. "They'll never stop looking for me."

Victor cursed, slapping his hand against his thigh in a gesture of frustration, as if to say, "Didn't I tell you so?"

Mitchell shot his nephew a disgusted look and approached Kay quickly. Plunging his hand into her pocket, he retrieved the offending piece of technology and threw it on the stained, wooden floor, then stomped on it with the heel of his steel toe boot.

The sound of rain was the only thing she heard for a moment, louder than the painful throbbing in her head and the constant ringing in her left ear. Still smiling, she continued to stare at Avery, not paying any attention to the other two men.

"You know I'm a cop, right?"

Avery didn't reply. His only reaction was to run his arthritic fingers through his hair again and groan. "If you'd only shut up already." He raised his hand as if he were about to slap her across the face, but she continued to look straight at him, unyielding.

"She was your first sacrifice, wasn't she?" she stated, almost whispering. "She broke your heart when she died, but you had to do it, didn't you?" His pupils dilated and tears shone in his bloodshot eyes. She was on the right track. "It's what *she* wants, isn't it?" His mouth ajar, he stared at her, his hand slowly descending, as if he were in a trance. "She wants me too, doesn't she? Otherwise, I wouldn't be here, would I?" she added, using everything she'd overheard earlier to get his focus on her.

"You understand," he whispered, the same hand now gently caressing her hair, triggering daggers of pain in her skull and nausea in the pit of her stomach.

"I do, but no one else will." She chilled the warmth she'd put in her voice and her eyes. "They won't leave one stone unturned until they find me."

"She's right, Dad," Mitchell intervened. "They're already looking for her. How long do you think—"

Avery turned toward his son and grabbed his lapels with unexpected force. "Get the mixers rolling. Prepare the loads and line them up. We pour in ten minutes," he added, hissing the words between clenched teeth. "It's already late."

"But—"

"I don't want to hear it!" Avery suddenly bellowed. "There's no room in my life, in my business, for a coward. If you don't have the guts to do what needs to be done, get ready to join them in the concrete."

Father and son locked eyes for a long, loaded moment, then Mitchell lowered his gaze. "As you wish. I was just concerned with pouring in this weather. Just look outside, is all I'm asking."

Avery approached the window quietly, his lips a tight, disapproving line. Rain was coming down persistently, rapping against the roof of the mobile office in an incessant, monotone drumming. The sky, now a solid leaded gray, was barely visible, hidden in the haze of raindrops falling endlessly. His lips moved, but Kay couldn't hear what he was saying. He seemed to mumble to himself. Then he turned to Mitchell, anger joining his bushy eyebrows at the root of his nose.

"We've done this before, haven't we?" he asked, disappointment heavy in his tone. "You know what you have to do, so quit playing dumb."

Mitchell and Victor—who'd sat silently on a chair by the window the entire time watching them as he would have an entertaining show—exchanged a quick, somber glance.

"I've set the sheeting already," Victor said. "We're ready to pour. The wind might still pick up overnight and rip the sheeting, and expose the concrete, wash it all away before it cures."

"That won't happen," Avery announced sternly. "She will accept the sacrifice and the storm will end. It always happens this way." A crooked smile twisted his white beard. "Feel free to spend the night watching over things if you're concerned."

For a dizzying moment, Kay wondered if what she heard was real. Accepting the sacrifice will end the storm? All storms ended, eventually. Avery's psychosis ran deeper than she'd estimated. He had done an amazing job hiding it from everyone.

Victor rolled his eyes but decided to stop talking. Maybe he hadn't done such a good job brainwashing Victor.

Satisfied with the defiant silence he probably interpreted as agreement, Avery turned to Mitchell and said, "Get that concrete ready. Now."

Mitchell nodded quickly and lifted his collar before stepping outside in the storm. As he closed the door behind him, thunder rolled loudly, and a gust of wind rattled the building.

Two was easier than three. Kay almost smiled, but it wasn't over yet. Far from it. She shot another glance toward Julie. The girl seemed to be sleeping or maybe she was unconscious, because she hadn't moved an inch since she'd first seen her, but her chest was still heaving, slowly, her breaths shallow and far apart. She was still alive.

Kay focused her attention on Victor, the youngest of the three and most likely the least driven to kill. The psychosis and urges behind the initial murders were Avery's. Based on what she'd witnessed already, his son and grandson had inherited some psychopathic traits, but lacked the determination to kill, the bloodlust. Maybe, like it happened in all documented cases of generational serial killers she'd read, they'd started questioning the motives, or the thrill of taking lives wasn't that great with them. Most likely they'd been led into a life of killing by Avery, then found themselves bound by the mere fact that they knew about the blood he'd spilled, and had spilled some themselves.

"You know, after a certain age, life in prison doesn't mean much." The statement, spoken in a neutral voice, earned her an angry scowl from Avery she was quick to ignore. "Although, killing a cop gets you the chair." She shrugged, instantly regretting the dramatic gesture when pain shot through the back of her skull. "Well, only for you it would matter. Him, he'd probably die on death row, waiting for someone to throw that switch."

She feigned a chuckle, observing the dynamics of the duo. Avery was increasingly angry, and she risked a silencing blow any moment now. But Victor was interested in what she had to say, his pupils enlarged with fear, his hands restless, fidgeting, his left foot tapping in a quick rhythm against the floor. A deep frown ruffled his brow, and tension twisted his mouth in a grimace. He was ready for some more.

"Oh, but let me tell you what happens to cop killers in jail," she added with a wicked smile she didn't have to fake, her voice brimming with excited amusement. "You'd think you'd be the hero of the general population, but in fact, you're spending your days on death row, isolated, at the whim of—you guessed it—other cops." She laughed quietly, wincing from the throb in her head. "You have no idea what those guys can do with a baton. Whew."

Victor sprung from his chair and approached her angrily, but Avery stopped him with a firm hand against the man's chest.

"She wants them pristine," murmured Avery. "Control yourself."

Victor growled, his eyes drilling into Kay's, loaded with homicidal rage. "I'll make you pay for this, you—"

Two short honks alerted them to the arrival of the concrete mixer. It passed by the mobile office and disappeared to the left, probably pulling over by the foundation, where the new concrete was about to be poured. Transformed, both Avery and Victor seemed to have forgotten all about her and focused on the job at hand.

"How do you want to do this?" Victor asked matter-of-factly.

"I'll take the girl, you bring her," Avery said, gesturing in Kay's direction. His eyes were shining with the glint of madness, as if his visions were present in flesh and blood, haunting him right there, under Kay's eyes. He seemed transfigured, possessed, touched by something beyond her comprehension.

Demonstrating unusual stamina for his age, Avery lifted Julie's inert body in his arms and headed for the door. Victor opened it, struggling to hold it in place as a forceful wind gust threatened to rip it off its hinges. A blast of cold air loaded with icy raindrops swirled through the space, then died when Victor closed the door.

And then there was just one.

"So far, you haven't really broken any laws yet," said Kay, without wasting any time.

Victor shot her a doubtful look, then crouched at her feet and cut through the cable ties around her ankles. "Shut the fuck up, bitch."

"Don't let yourself land in the electric chair, 'cause that's the punishment for killing a fed, and Mother Earth will not defend you in court," she added in one breath, seeing how quickly she was running out of time. "My partner was calling me, and he knows where I went this morning. He's already on to you and your entire family. They know how to track phones these days."

"Get up," he snarled, grabbing her by the shoulder and forcing her to stand. It felt good to be on her feet, but she didn't feel well enough to fight the man. He was young and strong, with the type of upper-body strength one develops when pumping iron or working in construction.

"Don't you want to walk away from this?" she asked, undertones of surprise in her voice. Had she been wrong about him? Maybe there was an urge to kill behind those gray, cold eyes, so demanding it annihilated his self-preservation instinct. Perhaps it had been there the entire time, and she'd missed it somehow.

He pushed her toward the door. A few more steps and she'd be outside, in the storm, where Avery and Mitchell were waiting to bury Julie and her under a layer of concrete.

"I'm sure you have some cash stashed away somewhere that could buy you a pretty decent life somewhere south of the border," she added, starting to oppose resistance as they approached the door. "Think margaritas and underage girls, as opposed to cops and their batons." Doubt was seeded deeply in his mind. "How did you end up mixed in this madness, anyway?"

Victor grunted, still pushing her, but not as convinced. "The damn initiation," he muttered, as if words were leaving his lips against his will. "I thought it was supposed to be some party, welcoming me to the company business in an official role. By the time I realized what they were doing, I'd already witnessed a crime—a kidnapping at first, then a murder. I could've turned them in, but—"

"The company would've been finished," Kay rushed to say, eager to finish the conversation before Avery could return.

"Screw the company!" he bellowed. "They're family! My father, my grandfather, my uncle." He swallowed hard, tension making his muscles dance under the skin of his jaws. "And once I'd witnessed the first sacrifice, I'd become an accomplice. But I've never killed anyone myself. Never."

She didn't see a flicker of deception on his face. "Then, why not make a run for it?"

"You'd really let me go?" he asked, although his hands tightly gripped her arms.

"You'd have to let me go first," she quipped, "and make it quick. My partner and the rest of the cavalry are minutes away, at best."

Hesitantly, he let go of her arms. She took a step sideways, putting some distance between them. Her hand reached instinctively for her holster. It was empty.

He laughed. "You didn't think we'd leave your gun, did you?" A thought wiped his smirk off his face and replaced it with worry and anger. "You were going to shoot me, weren't you? So much for trusting a cop."

"Nah, I'm good on my word. It was just reflex." He didn't seem convinced. "Do you know the amount of bullshit a cop's got to go through to justify the loss of a service weapon? Paperwork up the wazoo. It would be nice if I could avoid that."

The smirk returned. "Sorry, can't do. Avery snatched that off you the moment Mitchell dragged you in." He put his hand on the doorknob, and the other reached for her arm, but the grip was softer, tentative. "How come you'd let me go?"

She shrugged, immediately wincing from the pain. "One hand washes the other," she winked. "And you never killed anyone, as far as I know. The rest of the stuff is nothing. I'll get Avery and Mitchell to pay for my cracked head and bruised ego."

"No, I never killed anyone," he replied calmly. There was a glint of something indiscernible in his eyes. "And no love lost if Avery fries. I'm beyond tired of him ordering me around." His lips stretched into a satisfied grin. "His money will be well spent, I promise." He opened the door, and a draft of wind splashed rain against their faces.

"Then make for that truck of yours and don't stop until you reach the border," she said. "All I can give you is a few hours."

As she stepped out, her foot slid on the mud and she flailed, instinctively reaching for balance, grabbing Victor's jacket. The zipper gave and exposed the sweatshirt he was wearing. Staring her in the face, were the narrow eyes of a snake, the open mouth of a viper with sharp teeth and a green, slit tongue.

Monster.

She'd been wrong.

When she looked at him, he sensed immediately something was off. He raised his hand to strike her, but she was quick to avoid the blow and returned a direct hit to the side of his neck. Pain, shooting mercilessly through her skull, had her seeing stars again, but she didn't stop. She slid behind him and wrapped her arms around his throat then let her entire weight hang, in a lame attempt to suffocate him.

He was quick to free himself, throwing her to the ground where she landed hard, her breath knocked out of her lungs. She kicked him in the groin but not hard enough. Muttering a curse, he then straddled her and wrapped his hands around her neck, choking her. She writhed and pulled at his hands, but he was too strong. Resisting the urge to fight the constriction around her airway and knowing she had mere seconds left to live, she reached and felt around in the mud for something to strike him with.

The boulder wasn't large, but it had sharp edges. It was covered in slippery mud, and she struggled getting a good grip on it, but eventually she did. The blow to Victor's temple was hard, his hands letting go of her throat enough for a lifesaving breath of air to enter her lungs. He groaned and his fingers started squeezing again. Then she delivered a second blow, and felt the salty, metallic taste of blood on her lips as his body fell heavy and still over hers.

Heaving and gasping, she pulled herself from underneath his body and stood shakily on weak legs, then looked around to see where Avery had taken Julie's body. From where she stood, only a part of the foundation was visible. She turned the corner around the mobile office and stopped, stunned, when the full picture came into view.

CHAPTER FIFTY-TWO

Site

Crouched behind a pile of cement bags covered with a tarp weighed down with two-by-fours, Kay watched in horror at how Avery paced around Julie's thin body, his arms raised in the air, chanting and shouting unintelligible words covered by the rage of the storm. Under the blue plastic sheeting, elevated on posts, he'd set her down on the rebar grid in a section of foundation that had been formed and prepared for pouring, dangerously close to the crown of a fresh landslide. The side of the hill had drifted down, leaving the raw scarp exposed. Vengeful raindrops ate away at it, washing off the earth bit by bit and carrying it downhill in muddy streams.

Rebars were laid one foot apart, the inch-thick reinforcement steel bars, touched by the orange brown of rust, ready to reinforce the concrete soon to be poured, like a hidden skeleton under the gray, concrete surface. Only now, it served as support for the girl's weak body, not letting it touch the ground, keeping it elevated two inches above the muddy surface. Her white dress fluttered in the wind, already soaked and stained with mud, a shroud in the making.

Julie didn't move. From where she was, Kay couldn't tell if she was drawing breath anymore. In the cold and angry gusts of rain she should've woken up, she should've turned her head to shield her eyes and nose from the falling rain. She should've given a sign—any sign—that she was still alive.

Kay stared at Avery, thinking of a plan to take down both men with bare hands, seeing her gun bulging at Avery's belt. She always carried her service weapon in condition one, with a bullet on the spout, ready to be fired. No way she could approach him, not with his son nearby.

Mitchell was behind the wheel of a concrete mixer truck, maneuvering it close enough to pour. He reversed slowly, his rear wheels inches away from the edge of the landslide's crown, where fissures were already starting to appear under the massive weight of the loaded mixer. He stopped when the discharge chute was close enough to the form, and the rhythmic beeping that had accompanied the truck's movement ceased.

Then the concrete mix started to come down the chute, landing near Julie's legs. A tremendous roar of thunder seemed to shake the ground, and Kay crouched closer to the ground. Terrified, she watched the concrete coming down with speed, gushing down the chute faster than she'd expected. Within seconds, it reached Julie's feet and started to engulf them.

Julie shifted her leg slightly, nothing more than a twitch, pulling away from the cold concrete. She was still alive, but seemingly so weak or perhaps drugged that she couldn't fight back.

Frantic, Kay focused her attention on Mitchell. He'd turned off the truck's engine, but the drum was still spinning, and the concrete was still pouring down the chute. Soon it would reach Julie's head, suffocating her.

Mitchell jumped out of the truck and joined Avery under the tarp, and appeared to engage in a heated conversation. At some point, they both looked her way, most likely wondering where Victor was and why it was taking him so long to bring Kay. Then they continued their conversation, their voices raised, probably to hear each other over the storm's fury.

That was her opportunity.

Running in short sprints between the various piles of materials she could use for cover, Kay made for the truck's driver side door. She opened it slowly and climbed in, cautious to not be seen by the two men. She reached for the ignition, but the keys weren't there. A few yards away, Mitchell played with them casually, throwing them in the air then catching them, again and again.

Desperate, she started pushing buttons on the large dashboard, but nothing seemed to stop the flow of concrete. Even if she succeeded, they'd immediately be on to her and start it back again. She willed herself to breathe slowly and steady herself to the point where she could find real solutions to her current bind.

A lopsided smile stretched her lips. Carefully, she slowly released the parking brake, knowing the truck would immediately start sliding downhill. With a little bit of luck, it might end up at the foot of the landslide, smashed to bits.

The truck set in motion sooner than she'd expected, before she had the opportunity to get out. Alarmed shouting came from Avery and Mitchell, then the younger man rushed to the truck. She barely had the time to slide over to the passenger side, crawling across the seats with her head held down, and climbed out of the passenger door, expecting an immediate bullet through her aching skull from her own gun held by Avery's hand.

But he hadn't noticed her, and neither had Mitchell, who fought desperately to stop the truck's careening on the wet grass mixed with mud. Revving the engine, he had the wheels spinning in place and skidding over the damp grass, dislodging chunks of it and uncovering stretches of slippery mud underneath. Engine roaring, the truck still slid backward, almost to the edge of the landslide.

Good. Mitchell was going to be busy for a while.

Seizing the opportunity, she pounced and attacked Avery from behind, reaching for the gun at the same time. She managed to pull it from Avery's belt, but it slipped from her wet and muddy hands.

The old man was stronger than she would've given him credit for at eighty-three years of age. With the dilated, psychotic pupils of a maniac and his long white soaked hair whipping in the gusty wind, he bellowed and attacked her frontally, delivering blow after blow with his fists. One hit her in the jaw, and she screamed, the rapid twisting of her head rekindling the intense pain at the back of her skull. She felt the metallic taste of her own blood in her mouth as bursts of green stars exploded in front of her eyes. Forcing a few rushed breaths of cold air into her lungs, she managed to remain on her feet. She dodged Avery's next blow, then threw herself to the ground on her side, kicking Avery in the ankle forcefully with both her feet as she landed. He dropped to the ground like a log and remained immobile, his eyes wide open, appearing tear-filled under the relentless rain.

She picked herself up—groaning, dizzy and shaky, pain throbbing in her skull—and rushed to Julie's side. Kneeling between two rebars, she felt for a pulse. It was there, thready and weak. The girl was fading away, unable to withstand the coldness of the concrete, her heart at risk of stopping from the shock.

Kay slid her hands under Julie's armpits and tried to lift her up, but couldn't. The girl's lower body was already immersed in concrete, the dense material clinging to the many folds of her long white dress, and Kay wasn't able to budge her a single inch.

She threw a side glance toward the concrete truck and saw it reversing to the side of the hill, following the edge of the landslide. Mitchell had probably given up on trying to approach the form directly, and was about to turn and climb back up using the main road instead. Within seconds, he'd drive by Victor's body, lying in the mud in front of the mobile office. She had less than a minute, at best.

Propping herself against the rebars, she pulled hard at Julie's body, but to no avail. As the truck approached quickly from the other side and turned, she lifted the girl's head and slid her legs underneath for support.

Then the concrete started pouring again, gushing toward Julie's head. With a look of steeled determination in his eyes, Mitchell came at her with a crowbar.

As she willed herself back on her weary feet, she thought of Elliot and called his name in her thoughts. If he'd only find her. Soon.

She bent quickly to avoid the crowbar wielded by Mitchell and eyed her gun, several feet away. It was out of reach. Her hands, covered in dripping concrete, weren't much use for anything she wanted to grab to defend herself. Staring Mitchell straight in the eye to see where and when he was going to strike again, she scraped some of the concrete off her hands and built it into a small ball of mushy stone. Then, without warning, she threw it in his eyes, blinding him for a few precious seconds.

Desperate to clean his eyes, he dropped the crowbar, screaming and cursing. "I'll kill you, bitch, if it's the last thing I do." With trembling fingers, he wiped the sticky material from his eyes, blinking rapidly and swaying like a blind man who'd lost his footing. In a second, he'd be able to see again just enough to kill her.

She eyed her gun again, but it seemed too far for the time she had left, while the abandoned crowbar was right there, at her feet. She grabbed it with both hands, then said, "Mitchell Montgomery, you have the right to remain silent—"

He shouted as he leaped, holding out his hands, getting ready to grab her by the throat and choke her. With a swift move that took all the life she still had coursing through her veins, she wielded the crowbar up and sideways, aiming for his head.

The sound of his skull cracking was loud enough to briefly cover the thunder rolling in the distance, then was followed by the thud of his body falling to the muddy ground. Blood started to color the rainwater gushing away under the tarp.

Heaving from the effort, she fell to her knees by Mitchell's side and felt for a pulse. He was gone. Then she looked toward Julie. "Oh, no, please, God, no," she cried. The concrete had reached her face and almost completely engulfed it, only a portion of her lips and her nostrils were still above the gray mass.

Kay looked at the truck, remembering how long it had taken her to climb inside and remove the parking brake to make it slide backward, and decided there wasn't enough time for that. Instead, she crawled over by Julie's side and elevated her head on her legs, like she'd done before.

Holding Julie's head in her lap, she started gently cleaning the concrete away from her face. She couldn't stop the flow of concrete, but she could still reach for an edge of the plastic sheeting. She grabbed it with frozen fingers and yanked it as hard as she could, again and again, until it gave. A wave of accumulated rainwater washed over them, and Kay gasped, chilled to the bone, teeth clattering uncontrollably. But rain washed away some of the concrete, diluting the mix and sending it downhill, where it stained the brown of the exposed earth with shades of cement gray.

Somehow, seeing that made it all worthwhile.

Between wind gusts and the flapping of the torn plastic sheeting above her head, Kay almost missed Avery's rageful bellow. She turned her head to look, pain shooting up her nape, and saw the old man approaching, his hair whipping in the wind and his mouth open, spouting curses and shouting senseless words.

She realized she didn't have it in her to fight again. Desperate, she looked toward the highway, hoping she'd see Elliot's vehicle approaching, but there was nothing. Only rain. She'd always loved rain… until now.

"Mother Earth has spoken to me," she shouted, hoping her manipulative strategy would work.

Avery stopped shouting and listened, transfigured. "You can hear her?" he asked, grabbing the locket he carried on a chain around his neck and holding it in the palm of his hand, then taking it to his lips.

"She says you are forgiven, and you can rest now. Your sons will continue your work."

The moment she'd said it, she realized her mistake. He had no sons left... Dan had been killed the week before, Mitchell lay bloodied at Avery's feet, and Raymond had turned his back on him decades ago.

Enraged, he screamed so loudly Kay thought she heard an echo of his voice against the hillside, despite the rain. Lightning struck nearby, the flash of light blinding her, and the ensuing thunder shook the ground.

"Did you hear her?" he shouted. "She demands her chosen sacrifice!"

He charged, but Kay didn't move, still holding Julie's head in her lap. At the right moment, she lifted her foot and kicked forward, hitting Avery in the knee as he was leaping over rebar to pound on her. He yelped and fell to the ground, where his skull met the edge of the concrete form with one loud crack.

As he fell, his locket opened and a few grains of earth scattered on his chest, quickly turned to mud by the falling rain.

Kay's breath shuddered. With the adrenaline leaving her body, falling water drops felt like ice daggers piercing her skin. Shielding Julie's face and lifting her closer as rain washed off the concrete, she built up the strength to move. Then, willing herself to move sideways and touch Avery's dead body, she reached for his pockets, hoping to find a working phone.

In the distance, a police siren grew loud enough to cover the sound of rain, just as a ray of sun shone through a distant crack in the clouds.

CHAPTER FIFTY-THREE

Curtain Fall

Kay sat on the rear bumper of an ambulance, wearing the EMT's spare scrubs, and a blanket wrapped tightly around her shoulders. The site was crawling with people, seemingly going in all directions without any rhyme or reason, when in fact everyone did exactly what they were supposed to do. She didn't pay much attention to them; not to her boss, who barked orders a few yards away, keeping a safe distance from the edge of the landslide. Not to the mayor, who had put one hand on his head when he got out of his vehicle about an hour earlier, and seemed he hadn't taken it down since, apparently battling the mother of all headaches. He appeared to be in a total state of shocked dismay, staring at an utter disaster in an election year. It was understandable; after all, he'd come close to cutting the ribbon for a brand-new edifice and be among the first to walk only inches above the corpses of two women in what was supposed to be the region's largest healthcare facility. His name would forever be associated with Ash Brook Hill.

No, she only cared about the cop standing a few feet away from her, wearing a black, wide-rimmed cowboy hat that still retained a few droplets of rain sending diamond-like sparks in the piercing rays of the setting sun. He threw daggers with his eyes at anyone who wanted to approach her, and seemed ready to wring the neck of the EMT who'd made her whimper when he patched up her scalp wound.

"You'll need to ride with us to the hospital, Detective," said the EMT, a solid man by the name of Deshawn as per the embroidered tag he was wearing, and she was wearing also on the chest of her borrowed blue cotton top. He'd been kind enough to lend her his spare uniform, and she was grateful to be warm and dry for a change, even if the starched fabric smelled of disinfectants more than it did of fabric softener.

"Don't wanna do that, D," she replied, looking at him with pleading eyes. "I kind of need some time away from everything right now."

"You have to, D," he replied, laughing at his own joke and showing off two rows of incredibly white teeth. "You might have a concussion."

She rolled her eyes, but even that tiny movement of her eyeballs triggered a sharp bout of pain. "No, I don't. My vision is clear, I'm not sleepy, I don't feel dizzy, nauseated, or faint. I'm fine."

"But—"

"I'd rather wash off this damn cement from my hair, before it turns to stone and I have to shave my head."

He pressed his lips in a straight line and crossed his thick arms at his chest, the look of disapproval on his face needing no other words. She smiled as sweetly as she could manage and patted his elbow. "Thanks, D, I appreciate it."

She stood carefully, taking a thoughtful inventory of all her aches and pains. They were too many to count, but a couple of days of rest would fix most of them.

The rain had stopped, and the sun's shy rays warmed her face. She closed her eyes for a moment, noticing the birds were chirping, a sound she hadn't heard in a while.

"You'll never guess where they found Dan's truck," Elliot said.

Smiling, she opened her eyes and looked at him. There was a flicker in his gaze when their eyes met, a heat that she sensed for the most fleeting of moments before he looked away. It warmed her heart and seeded her mind with lots of maybes.

"Where?"

"The company was finalizing a government building—the new sorting facility for the postal service on the other side of the mountain. Cheryl must've known about it, because she parked Dan's truck behind that building. No one would've ever reported it."

"How did we find it?"

"*We* didn't." He laughed a quick, humble laugh that touched his eyes. "The man who lives up the road from there has insomnia and sometimes takes walks at night. He noticed it parked there for several nights in a row, and called it in an hour ago."

"Gotta give it to Cheryl, that's smart," Kay replied.

Elliot clapped his hands once, as if to show his excitement. "That's exactly what the doc said, when he was showing me where they found the murder weapon." She nodded, encouraging him to continue. "Under the sink, in plain sight, in a container that looked like it was there to catch leaky drainage."

Kay's smile widened. After the horrors she'd been through, just seeing sunshine and his smile gave her wings. "Makes me wonder, though, about Cheryl—what she'd been through, by herself, with no one she could trust. Living here, where her husband was killed, possibly by a grandfather she suspected but couldn't do anything about, and sleeping with Calvin's uncle in a desperate attempt to get to the truth. I can't help imagining how she must've felt. My skin crawls." She paused, thinking they would probably never find out what really happened that night when Dan came calling, and how he ended up dead, shot in the back. She knew now that Avery had sent him to get Julie; she'd heard the conversations between Avery and Mitchell, his eldest son; that part was clear. But why did Cheryl stay in town, after she'd killed Dan? Why give Victor the opportunity to come calling? Had she assumed, much like the detectives had, that there was only one killer taking girls, and she'd done away with him? And why not call the cops?

A bullet in the back might've required a lot of explaining, and the risk was considerable. They were lovers, Cheryl and Dan. The argument of self-defense invoking what seemed like nothing more than a strange tale at the time would've surely landed Cheryl in jail, and she would've lost custody of her daughters.

In favor of the Montgomerys.

Aah… That's why she hadn't called for help. But why stay?

Maybe there would be a way to find out, when Julie would feel better.

"Any news from Julie?" she asked Elliot, but Deshawn popped his head out from the ambulance.

"She's in intensive care. She was malnourished and severely dehydrated, but they're estimating she'll make a full recovery."

"Awesome!" On an impulse, she walked over to the EMT and hugged him. Her heart swelled, imagining the reunion between Julie and her sisters. "Thanks, Big D."

"Thought I heard your voice, loud and chipper," Sheriff Logan said, approaching quickly, paying little attention to the mud puddles he was stepping in with his military-issue boots. "Are you cleared by medical?"

"Yes," she replied decisively.

At the same time, Deshawn said, "No," just as decisively.

Logan raised his arms in the air then let them fall. "Great. I'm glad you guys agree about something." He took two steps closer to Kay. "You know what you have to do."

She sighed. "Yes." Her thoughts kept returning to Julie and her sisters. "What's going to happen to the girls?"

"Well, the DA says the only family member we're not charging is Lynn Montgomery. She appears to have been completely removed from all this mess. Do you know her?"

A wide smile had bloomed on Kay's face when she heard her name. "Yes, I do."

"I take it you're okay with her taking the girls?"

"I am, yes." If her relationship with Jacob continued, Kay could have the girls close to her. The thought of staying in touch with them—of helping them with their recovery—wouldn't let that smile wane from her lips.

"We still don't know where Victor is—"

"Wait, what?" she said, feeling a chill travel down her spine.

"Victor Montgomery, he's—"

"I downed the sick son of a bitch and left him lying in the mud right there by the office door," she interrupted Logan again. "You mean to say he's gone?"

Logan had already pulled his radio from his belt. "Yeah. Anywhere we should be looking?"

"Yeah," she groaned, checking the time. He had a good three hours lead time. "He's heading south, to Mexico."

"Did he tell you that?" Logan's radio drew closer to his lips a few more inches, then stopped in midair.

"I kind of suggested it." She smiled sheepishly.

Logan shook his head. "I'm not going to ask." Then he pressed the button on the radio. "I want roadblocks and the APB updated on Victor Montgomery. He's headed south."

"He was wearing a Vipers sweatshirt," Kay said to Elliot. "You were right. We still don't know how he got it, though, not that it matters anymore. He went to college here, in California."

"Well, turns out that when you ask the wrong question, you don't get good answers for a while," Elliot quipped. "I handled this one like I was raised in a barn." His cheeks colored a little. "I've been told the Vipers are not a college team; they're a high school one, and he was there for his senior year. I just got the text message an hour ago."

She laughed in the warm rays of the sun. "We would've caught him anyway."

"And caught him we have," Logan said, beaming, his chubby cheeks lifted by his grin so high his eyeglasses rested on them. "He got picked up for speeding, just north of San Fran, little over an hour ago, snake shirt and all, bleeding from his temple. I guess that's your handiwork?"

Kay raised her hand in the air. "Guilty as charged. I'm actually surprised he was able to run." She stared at her hands, her thin fingers, clenching and unclenching her fists. She felt weak, feeble. "I might need to go to the gym, build some strength. Can't have perps running off on me like that."

Logan chuckled. "You do that, Detective. For now, we're buried in work, thank you very much. We have hundreds of buildings to inspect with ground-penetrating radar and mobile X-ray, and we're still trying to figure out what will happen if we find bodies buried in the foundations of functional buildings. Do we demolish them to get to the bodies?" He scoffed, all the good humor gone from his face, replaced by a look of frustrated bitterness in his eyes. "Thankfully, that's for the DA to decide, in what could end up being a legal battle lasting who knows how many years."

"I can help somewhat," said Kay, looking at the site once more in the dimming twilight. A shiver traveled up her spine when she looked at where the concrete was poured over Julie's body. There was a space between that place and the edge of the form, and she suddenly realized why. That was where her body was supposed to be… Avery had saved her a spot by the crown of the landslide. Choked, she cleared her throat quietly. "They never buried girls in foundations unless the weather was bad. I can correlate the dates of the missing persons reports with buildings they were erecting at the time—specifically those that were impacted by storms—and we can start from there, with only forty-three buildings, not hundreds."

"You're sure about that?" Logan asked, scratching the roots of his buzz-cut hair.

"Positive," she replied without a trace of hesitation in her voice. "Avery had a thing for building on top of hills, like Ash Brook Hill, and believed the storms to be Mother Earth's anger, demanding human sacrifices." She remembered her conversation with the meteorologist. "Barren hills like this one are prone to landslides in heavy rain, but he thought it was supernatural."

Elliot whistled. "The man had his share of cobwebs in his attic."

Kay lowered her head for a moment. "In my original profile, I had him pegged as a mission-driven serial killer, although that didn't really fit, because the victimology was off. I was somewhat wrong." She looked at Logan apologetically. "He was what profilers call a visionary serial killer—mentally insane, hearing voices that guided him into what lives to take and how. At the same time, much like a mission-driven killer, he was able to function in society, establish relationships, be extremely successful, and coopt his children into following his path. He proved to be highly organized, and a cool-headed perfectionist when it came to his abductions and killings. That's what threw me off. That's why he wasn't caught for so long."

"Were his sons crazy too?" asked Logan.

She pressed her lips for a moment. "I'd have to say no, at least not to the extent Avery was. Even him—after speaking with him and seeing him interact with others—I hesitate to slap the label of clinical insanity on him, because he was so well-organized. I will have to study this further, and I'd love to invite my former Quantico mentor to take a look at this case." She paused for a moment. "I'll have the opportunity to interview Victor, and I'll use it to gain more understanding into their motivations and how they evolved over three generations." Logan nodded, while Elliot looked at her intensely. "I don't think Mitchell and Victor had the same urge to kill. No, I believe they were coopted and coerced to follow in Avery's footsteps." Going through the family members in her mind, she remembered the one that stood out like a sore thumb. "How about Marleen?"

"The DA will charge her, although he said that everything we have against her is circumstantial at best. He believes we should be digging into her whereabouts some more."

"I believe she was a key part of the cross-alibi game they were playing."

"What cross-alibi game?" asked Logan, his hands firmly propped on his hips.

"From what I heard them saying, whenever a girl was taken, they would plan it carefully, so that most family members would have rock-solid alibis, and the others would be vouched for by one of the cleared family members." She smiled with eager anticipation, remembering Marleen's deceitful arrogance. "It wouldn't be the first time we turn a perp against another, huh? She'll break like a twig."

"Ha," Logan reacted, "I bet she will, Detective." He looked at the scene swarming with cops and crime scene technicians, and she followed his gaze. Several LED lights had been installed and lit. The top of Ash Brook Hill shone like the stage of a morbid theater, but she was eager to leave. She already knew how the story ended, with years of continued investigations and mountains of reports to write. With closure for all those families who had spent decades wondering, hoping, grieving, unable to heal. With the unceremonious death of the firstborn-daughter myth.

As if reading her mind, Logan said, "Get yourself checked out, Kay. That's an order." Then he walked away.

She watched him leave, her gaze lingering on the scene, savoring the moment. It was over.

"How about some dinner?" Elliot asked. "I bet you'd appreciate a double cheeseburger right about now. I know I would."

Her face lit up. "You bet. Fries too, and some beer." Her mouth watered.

Elliot offered her his arm and she took it, glad for the support. Her legs seemed a little weak, a side effect of all the adrenaline that had flushed her muscles with energy, priming them for battle. A spell of dizziness hit her, but she clenched Elliot's arm tighter and kept up with his enthusiastic pace, eager to get out of there. "But first, I'd love a shower."

"You got it," he replied, warm laughter tinting his voice. "Although, even if you're the worst dressed, muddiest date I've ever had by far, I still think you look just fine."

"Date?" she asked, realizing how much she liked the thought of that.

"Uh, I meant, like a work date, right?"

"Right," she replied, dragging the vowel just a touch and dipping her voice in laughter.

She struggled to keep up the pace; it felt like she was hanging from his arm, being dragged away, leaning on him more and more. Where the hell was Elliot's SUV?

That's when everything went dark.

CHAPTER FIFTY-FOUR

Rain Check

When Kay woke up, Julie was standing by her bedside, staring at her with fearful eyes. She wore a loose hospital gown with a small, floral pattern that hung weirdly on her thin shoulders. She held on to an IV stand on wheels she'd dragged with her from the bed next to Kay's. An IV line ran from the bag to the needle taped to the back of her hand. Kay read the black letters on the transparent IV bag: five percent glucose.

She pushed herself up against the rustling pillows and smiled, but the fear in the girl's eyes didn't wane. She was pale, her skin almost translucent. Her dilated pupils didn't budge, fixed on Kay with an unspoken question.

Kay had questions of her own. She had no recollection of getting there, what hospital it was, or what day of the week. Through the partially open window blinds, she could see a perfectly blue sky filled with sunshine, not a trace of the storm that had passed.

"What is it, Julie? Do you need anything?" she asked, reaching out for the teenager's hand.

The girl pulled away, seemingly scared to touch her. "Are you here to watch me?" she asked.

Kay placed her hand at the back of her skull, where she felt something unusual. They'd dressed her wound, and probably stitched her scalp. It was less painful than she remembered it, maybe because it was closed now, but it still throbbed.

"No," she replied, smiling and putting humor in her voice. "Do you think I'd go through this just to watch you?" She pointed at the back of her head, continuing to smile.

Her pupils remained dilated, but shifted toward the hallway. "Then, is he?"

Through the closed glass door, Kay saw Elliot sleeping on a couch, his hat covering his face. His badge was in plain view, hanging from his belt.

"No," Kay replied. "I'm pretty sure he's here for me, not you." She couldn't help giving a light chuckle. "What's on your mind?"

A tear rolled down the girl's face. "Are you going to arrest me?"

Kay pulled herself a little higher against her pillow and patted the space next to her with her hand, inviting Julie to sit. Hesitating and fidgeting as if Kay's proximity was dangerous, she reluctantly sat on the edge of her bed.

"Why would I arrest you, sweetie?"

Julie lowered her eyes and squeezed them shut, releasing more teardrops from her lashes. "You know why," she whispered, "you're a cop, right?"

"Yes, I am a detective, but I can't think of a reason why I should arrest you."

She sniffled and looked around, panicked. "He was strangling Mom. I shot—"

Instantly, Kay's fingers touched the girl's lips and silenced her. The pieces of the puzzle were falling into place, leaving few questions unanswered. That's why Cheryl had gone to such lengths to hide the self-defense shooting of Dan Montgomery. That's why she never called the cops.

She was protecting her daughter.

Eyebrows raised and pupils dilated, Julie stared at Kay, a shade paler than before. Their eyes locked and held for a long moment, while Kay considered what she was about to do.

Julie would never be charged for Dan's shooting, considering the abundance of evidence uncovered about the many killings perpetrated by the Montgomerys. That aside, her name would forever be associated with that shooting, and she would be known to anyone who'd run an internet search as the girl who shot a man, albeit in self-defense. In the age when no one had the right to be forgotten or forgiven anymore, where everything that hit the internet was out there forever, destroying lives and ruining futures, Kay was better off keeping that secret. Otherwise, Julie would never be admitted to a decent college or land a good job. Her life would be wasted, forever destroyed by the same man who'd killed her mother and tortured her. Nothing was gained if this tiny piece of truth came out; absolutely nothing. It was the right thing to do.

Kay caressed Julie's long hair with gentle fingers. "Let me tell you what the police know about what happened, all right?" The girl nodded and swallowed with difficulty. "We know that your mother shot and killed Dan Montgomery to protect you. Then she loaded him in the truck by herself and dumped him by the side of the interstate. We know for sure—based on your sister's testimony—that you were upstairs with your sisters when it happened. The investigation into Dan Montgomery's death is officially closed." She smiled encouragingly, noticing how Julie's shoulders relaxed just a little. "So, you see, there's no reason whatsoever for me to arrest you. Clear?"

Julie nodded again, lowering her gaze and hiding a rebel tear. "Thank you," she whispered.

Kay opened her arms and the girl settled by her side, with her head on Kay's shoulder. "Now, can you tell me, what day is today?"

"Sunday, I think," she whimpered, not lifting her head.

"What?" said Kay in a humorous voice. "I've been out of commission for two days? No wonder I'm hungry."

Julie chuckled between silent tears.

"One thing I'd like to know, if it's not too painful for you to tell me." She paused, waiting for an answer, but there was none, just a long, pained breath. "Why didn't you all leave, after Dan died? Why wait?"

Julie's shoulders heaved as she broke down in sobs. She lifted her face from Kay's arm but avoided her glance. "It was my fault. Mom died because of me."

"Tell me how that happened." She didn't believe that to be true, but there were still a few unanswered questions. "Step by step. What happened after your mom went away in Dan's truck?"

She whimpered and sniffled. When she spoke, her voice trembled, brittle. "We waited and waited. She didn't come back until Sunday afternoon. I was scared someone caught her, but she just…" her voice trailed off as she sniveled and wiped her nose with the back of her hand, quickly. Kay reached for the box of tissues on her side table and placed it casually on the bed, within Julie's reach. She took one and crumpled it, then wiped her nose and held on to it, as if afraid to let it go. She took a deep, shuddering breath before continuing. "She walked across town, through the woods, so that no one would see her."

It made sense. From the new postal building, where they'd found Dan's truck, to Angel Creek Pointe, there were some twenty-five miles as the crow flies, maybe thirty or more on the road. Her heart sunk when she imagined Cheryl crossing through the woods alone in that storm, on foot in the dead of night, so that no one would be able to place her anywhere near where Dan's body or truck were found. As far as anyone knew, she'd spent Saturday night and Sunday morning with her daughters, in the house.

"I see. Why not leave on Sunday, when she returned?" Kay asked, knowing Cheryl might've been too tired to stand at that point. Driving hundreds of miles in a storm must've been out of the question.

Julie's eyes remained lowered, but her whimpers had eased somewhat. She looked at Kay briefly, apparently ashamed. "We didn't have any money. Mom didn't want to use her cards once we left, and the banks were closed. She didn't want to ask anyone."

"And Monday?" Victor had come to their house on Monday night, when their bags were packed, but they were still there.

A heart-wrenching sob left Julie's chest. "Because of me… and that's why she died, because I was stupid." Kay caressed her hair gently and waited. "I, uh, went out on a date and, uh, I didn't get back until it was really late, and the weather was bad." She paused for a while, whimpering. "It was the last time I was going to see Brent. I wanted to say goodbye. But he… doesn't care that much about me. I've been such an idiot."

"Oh, sweetie," Kay said, folding Julie into her arms. "It's not your fault your mother died." Somehow, her words fueled the girl's tears, but she allowed her the time to grieve, gently holding her, reminding her she wasn't alone. "You're safe now, and everything will be all right." She kept whispering soothing words, as her mind wandered, thinking of the tragedy that had struck their family.

Calvin might've died in an accident, or maybe he'd wanted to break free of his family's homicidal tradition and was executed for it. Avery might've considered he knew too much and was a liability. That part, they'd probably never know for sure, although Victor was still alive and if he knew, she'd pry it out of him. But Cheryl's suspicions of Avery supported that theory. It must've been something Calvin had told her before he died that had fueled her relentless quest for justice.

The door slid open with a muted whoosh and Lynn came in, smiling shyly, holding Heather and Erin by their hands. Behind her, Jacob, with a wide and proud grin as if the girls were his already and he'd been named father of the year.

She squeezed Julie's hand and said, "Look who's here, sweetie." Then she watched the reunion, fighting to hide her own tears. Jacob approached her bed tentatively, his gait on a spring as if he were getting ready to run out of there if she as much as sneezed, and placed a kiss on her forehead.

"When are you coming home?" he asked, cutting straight to the point, like always. "You might've heard, things got a little bit complicated for Lynn and me."

Kay chuckled. "Nah… you'll be fine. All of you."

Julie had kneeled on the floor, to bring her face closer to her sisters, and was holding them tight, sharing their tears and whispering to them.

"I knew you were okay," Heather told Julie, pointing her hand at Kay. "She's kind. I slept with her too." Kay bit her lip to fight back tears. It was the first time Heather had spoken an entire phrase since the day her mother died.

Kay's gaze wandered toward the hallway, searching for Elliot. He was standing in the doorway, hat in hand, his tousled blond hair a rare sight, his blue eyes sparkling with laughter as he heard Heather's words, and something else too, something she couldn't name, but would've loved to get lost in.

He approached her bed hesitantly, while she pulled her covers a little higher, to hide her horrible hospital gown.

"I guess we won't be going on our—"

"Dinner date?" she asked happily, smiling. She watched him veer his eyes for a moment, then meet hers.

"Yes." He looked at Jacob quickly, then at Lynn and the girls, huddled together and all talking at the same time. "We could take a raincheck, if you'd like."

Her smile vanished, leaving her lips pressed in an expression of feigned disapproval. "We could take a lot of things, Detective. We could take any type of calamity check you'd like. An earthquake check or even a snow check. But I never, ever want to hear the word rain again."

His eyes, worried for a moment or two, lit up. Leaning over the bed, he said, "Just so you know, you're still the worst-dressed dinner date I ever had."

A LETTER FROM LESLIE

A big, heartfelt **thank you** for choosing to read *The Angel Creek Girls*. If you enjoyed it and want to keep up to date with all my latest releases, just sign up at the following link. Your email address will never be shared, and you can unsubscribe at any time.

www.bookouture.com/leslie-wolfe

When I write a new book I think of you, the reader: what you'd like to read next, how you'd like to spend your leisure time, and what you most appreciate from the time spent in the company of the characters I create, vicariously experiencing the challenges I lay in front of them. That's why I'd love to hear from you! Did you enjoy *The Angel Creek Girls*? Would you like to see Detective Kay Sharp and her partner, Elliot Young, return in another story? Your feedback is incredibly valuable to me, and I appreciate hearing your thoughts. Please contact me directly through one of the channels listed below. Email works best: LW@WolfeNovels.com. I will never share your email with anyone, and I promise you'll receive an answer from me!

If you enjoyed my book, and if it's not too much to ask, please take a moment and leave me a review, and maybe recommend *The Angel Creek Girls* to other readers. Reviews and personal recommendations help readers discover new titles or new authors for the first time; it makes a huge difference, and it means the world to me.

Thank you for your support, and I hope to keep you entertained with my next story. See you soon!

Thank you,
Leslie

Connect with me!

LW@WolfeNovels.com

www.WolfeNovels.com

wolfenovels

Follow Leslie on Amazon: http://bit.ly/WolfeAuthor

Follow Leslie on BookBub: http://bit.ly/wolfebb

Visit Leslie's Amazon store: http://bit.ly/WolfeAll

FROM THE AUTHOR

The Enduring Myth of the Walled-Up Wife

The first time I heard this folksong, "The Walled-Up Wife," I was traveling through Europe with my parents, and I was about ten years old. It stuck with me; dark and compelling and gripping, the way a good story should be, although it lacked a happy ending. There was something deeply disturbing about it—about the thought of masons walling in their spouses to appease dark, evil spirits that would ruin their work during the night hours.

Who would do that, right? Who would sacrifice a loved one for their work? Figuratively, almost every successful professional does, these days; a sad mark of our modern times. As for literally, back then, I didn't know the answer. Now, I still don't know for sure, but I have a few theories of my own.

But first, about the myth itself. Per Professor Alan Dundes of the University of California, Berkeley, it transcends centuries, the oldest documented version of it going back more than a thousand years. It is said to have originated in India, and spread via the Balkans into Europe, reaching as far as Germany and England. There are many documented cases of immurement in old English churches.

Regardless of the local flavor, the folksong tells the same story, with small variations. The buildings can be wells, bridges, churches, or entire cities. Regardless of setting, the legend shows a group of masons tasked to build an edifice, whose work is demolished overnight by supernatural forces. Invariably, said forces demand a sacrifice, usually the chief mason's wife, although in some versions, the spirits demand the sacrificed woman be the first to arrive on site, and that happens to be the lead mason's wife, a symbolic example of what a good wife should be, the one who's first to bring nourishment and joy to her husband at work.

I loved this particular version of the folksong best, because it supports the theory that this myth is, in fact, a metaphor—illustrating in powerful imagery the many sacrifices a wife makes after marriage. She gives up her freedom, her mobility, her life, for the personal and professional success of her husband, ending up as the unseen force that supports the edifice he builds. Quoting from Professor Dundes's book, *The Walled-Up Wife: A Casebook,* "By entering marriage, the woman is 'figuratively immured.' Kept behind walls to protect her virtue, she is treated as a second-class citizen." In the same book, another scholar, Paul G. Brewster, wrote about women that were ritually killed as a form of foundation sacrifice.

With respect to these, the most surprising finding of our modern times is the forensic validation of the myths. In several such locations, where local folklore spoke of women being walled-in alive, demolished buildings have revealed corpses that supported the words of the old songs, adding an unexpected weight to the tales. Several English churches were found to hide skeletons of age-old sacrifices. According to Paul G. Brewster, the Bridge Gate at Bremen, Germany, revealed the body of a child; the castle of Niederburg in Manderscheid, Germany, revealed the body of a young woman when, in 1844, the wall was broken open at the point indicated by the legend.

I have a couple of theories myself, in stark contrast with the rather romantic mainstream that speaks of sacrifice and metaphor.

What if serial killers existed far longer ago than we are used to believe? In the United States, H.H. Holmes was the first documented serial killer; he died in 1896, after ending more than a hundred lives. But before him, throughout history, there have been several notable serial killers, going back as far as 331 CE, when an association of 170 matrons in ancient Rome, known as the Poison Ring, was found guilty of killing over ninety men. Let this sink in for a moment: the first serial killer documented in history was a woman; better even, a group of them!

Then, from nobleman Gilles de Rais, who killed over 140 children in fifteenth-century France, to Elizabeth Báthory, a countess credited with the torture and murder of hundreds of servant girls in Hungary in the late sixteenth century and early seventeenth century, history is not short on serial killers. Then—what if—during the times when one didn't have many options to hide their proclivities in small, tight-knit communities, and lacked modern-day means of transportation and body disposal, serial killers were able to deceive the masses by telling stories about sacrifices that were requested by supernatural forces, hence killing in plain sight? It's not that farfetched, is it? Not when knowing what we know now about the Dark Ages and the various forms of blood-lusting deviance we've learned to associate with names such as the French author Marquis de Sade or Spanish inquisitor Tomás de Torquemada.

Here's another theory. What if what brought the mythical buildings down at night wasn't some supernatural force, but… gravity? Rebar was invented in the 1800s and then largely used as structural reinforcement beginning in the early 1900s. Did you know that bone has an elasticity that is comparable to concrete, but it's ten times stronger in compression? As for steel (the component of rebar), bone has a similar compressive strength, but is three times lighter. Combining the two—human bone and concrete—maintains the compressive strength of concrete but lends the bone-reinforced material more elasticity, more tensile strength. Then, I'm asking, is it too farfetched to imagine that back in the olden days, when rebar wasn't invented yet and construction engineering was in its infancy, some poorly designed buildings fell apart, and only a maiden's bones would stabilize them? Just like Avery, who couldn't bring himself to stop building on top of hills, risking landslide after landslide, those masons must've known their foundations needed reinforcements. Some of them, thankfully only some, decided their work was worth the sacrifice of human lives, revealing their true nature as serial killers, while others probably found different, less challenging lines of work.